Fall from Grace

ryan phillips

DESTINY IMAGE₀ PUBLISHERS, INC.
P.O. Box 310, Shippensburg, PA 17257-0310

"Speaking to the Purposes of God for This Generation and for the Generations to Come"

This book and all other Destiny Image, Revival Press, MercyPlace, Fresh Bread,
Destiny Image Fiction, and Treasure House books are available at Christian bookstores and
distributors worldwide.

For a U.S. bookstore nearest you, call **1-800-722-6774.**

For more information on foreign distributors, call **717-532-3040.**

Or reach us on the Internet: **www.destinyimage.com**

ISBN 10: 0-7684-2360-0
ISBN 13: 978-0-7684-2360-0

For Worldwide Distribution, Printed in the U.S.A.
1 2 3 4 5 6 7 8 9 10 11 / 09 08 07 06

The consciousness of loving and being loved
brings a warmth and richness to life that nothing else can bring.
—Oscar Wilde

By this we know love, because He laid down His life for us.
—1 John 3:16

part one

Fireworks and Butterflies

1

Grace studies her reflection in the church's full-length mirror and smiles. A year of planning and organizing and compromising and arguing and stress has led up to this exact moment.

She smoothes the full satin skirt of her dress and fingers the intricate beading and ornate embroidering on its strapless bodice. Her heart flutters. *This is it.*

She turns slowly to her left, taking in her long, regal train, and runs her gloved hand along the trail of tiny buttons down her back. *This is it.*

She gazes over at the classic bouquet of roses and baby's breath lying on the chair beside her and then down at the three-stone ring resting snugly on her finger.

"This is it," she whispers.

"That's right." A familiar voice startles her from the doorway. "And there ain't no goin' back."

Grace turns to see Malikah standing behind her, a smile on her face.

Grace laughs. "God knows it wouldn't be a wedding without my favorite cousin."

"You ain't lyin'," Malikah says smugly.

"What about me?" Trina asks, entering the small dressing room. She and Malikah look like twins in their matching bridesmaids' dresses.

Grace spreads her arms for a hug. Trina slips into her embrace, careful not to get any makeup on her best friend's stunning Vera Wang.

"It wouldn't be the same without you either," Grace says.

Malikah grunts, her lips spread into a tight, censorious line. "Naw, it'd be better."

Trina's eyebrows furrow. "I'm going to take the high road," she says, her jaw set, "and let that slide."

Malikah rolls her eyes. "You couldn't find a high road if you had a map."

"Says the cousin with two kids by two different men," Trina sneers.

Grace tenses as Malikah takes a step closer to Trina, wagging her index finger just inches from Trina's face. "Watch it," Malikah warns.

"You're going to have a hard time carrying your flowers down the aisle with only nine fingers," Trina snaps, slapping Malikah's hand away.

"'Bout as hard a time as you gonna have gettin' down the aisle with my foot up yo—"

"Hey!" Grace says, her tone hushed, but firm. "That is enough."

Neither of them budges. They continue to glare at each other with clenched fists and heaving chests.

Grace hikes up her dress and steps between them. "I said, that's *enough!*"

Trina is the first to turn away. She can't stand Malikah and would love nothing more than to put her in her place, but one glance into Grace's beseeching eyes and the fight in her wanes. Grace has been so good to her, a better friend, in fact, than Trina can ever hope to be.

This time last year, their tight foursome was completely dismantled. Grace had fled to Detroit, Mike escaped to New York, Ron was too fed up to be bothered, and it was all Trina's fault. She had never meant to lie. The last thing she ever wanted to do was hurt the three people she loved the most, but she screwed up. She made brash assumptions, said things she had no business saying, and before she knew it, all of their lives were unraveling. Each of them had retired to their own corners, angry and hurt, trapped in webs of misunderstanding and deceit—webs that Trina, however unintentionally, had spun.

That was a year ago. Now they've all settled into an uneasy détente and no one ever mentions what happened—but no one's ever really forgiven her for it either. No one that is, except for Grace.

"I'll see you out there," Trina says, not bothering to look up.

Malikah's fiery stare burns holes into Trina's retreating back, and only after Trina's left the room does the tension in Malikah's shoulders ease.

"You said you were going to behave," Grace whines.

"I said I would *try* to behave."

"Don't do this to me," Grace pleads. "I'm supposed to be getting married, not refereeing."

Malikah tilts her head to the side. "Yeah, I know," she says softly.

"Good," Grace says with a definitive nod, "because weddings are traumatic enough without having to make sure your cousin and your best friend aren't choking each other every time you turn your back."

A shadow crosses Malikah's face. "She ain't your best friend."

Grace throws up her hands in exasperation.

"Ya know I'm right," Malikah says, hands on hips. "And I'mma keep sayin' it till you hear me. She's like cancer and you gotta cut her outta your life before she does any more damage."

Grace shakes her head vehemently. "I don't want to have this discussion again. Not today. All I want to do today is get married, and I want everyone to be a part of it. *Everyone!* I have the rest of my life to sort out the good from the bad, to decide where Trina does and doesn't fit, but for right now," Grace says, a deep sigh escaping her lips, "I just want to walk down that aisle and claim my sliver of happiness."

Malikah can't help but smile at the sight of Grace in her delicate tiara and long white gloves. Sporting an engagement ring that would turn any woman green with envy and a dress that takes up half the room, her cousin looks like a princess straight out of a fairy tale.

"What?" Grace whimpers.

Malikah takes Grace's hand and pulls her close. "You deserve more than a sliver," she says. "You've earned the whole pie."

There's a rap at the door. "My, my," a familiar voice sings, "look at you." Grace's face lights up at the sight of her dad, Grandma Doria, and Grandpa Mearl.

"You clean up good, Girl," her grandpa says, taking her in with one swift glance.

Grace's dad nods in agreement. "The most beautiful bride I've ever seen."

"A vision in white," Malikah adds.

"What do you think, Grandma?" Grace holds out her arms and spins, a bit awkwardly given the full skirt and heavy train, to give her the full effect.

Tears spill from Doria's eyes. "Your mother would be so proud," she says, choking back a sob. "So proud."

Grace fights the lump rising in her throat.

The weeks leading up to the wedding had been hectic and exciting and full of the rarest kind of hope. Last-minute decisions had to be made, details had to be finalized, and reservations had to be confirmed. Grace had handled it all in stride. But in the evenings, when the phone stopped ringing and the lights were turned out and everything was still, Grace stopped being a master negotiator. She was no longer an arbitrator, no longer a bride. The fittings and the flowers and the invitations stopped mattering; they stopped being real. The only truth Grace understood, the only truth that made a difference, was that her mother was gone.

She wasn't going to be there to help Grace into her wedding dress or to watch her walk down the aisle. She wouldn't make a toast or dance the night away. She wouldn't be in the photos. She wouldn't be part of the memories, and those realizations haunted Grace.

Each night, she was held captive by the same fierce agony and indescribable grief that sidled its way through her body when her mother first died. It consumed her bit by bit until she felt paralyzed, unable to think or pray, unable to breathe.

In those desperate moments, she would turn on her praise music or crack open her Bible, or she'd call Mike and sink into his voice or get lost in fantasies of their future together. In fact, that's how she'd made it *this* far, how she'd managed to press on when everything in her wanted to give up.

At first, it had felt more like surviving than living; but as one day gave way to the next and weeks turned to months, the pain became less intense, less debilitating. She could laugh at a joke or enjoy a sunset without feeling guilty, without feeling as though her mother was fading away.

That continues to be Grace's biggest fear, the thought that one day she'll wake up to discover that she can't recall her mother's scent or that she's lost the sound of her voice, that someday she'll have to rely on photos to remember what her mother looked like.

Right now, however, as she peers into her family's beaming faces, she's reassured that today isn't about losing memories; it's about making them.

Grace blinks back tears and nods. "Yeah, you're right, Grandma. Mom would be proud."

"Alright, that's enough," Grace's grandfather barks, swiping at his own tears. "You start cryin' now and you won't have anything left for the ceremony."

Malikah laughs. "He's right."

"Go on and get your seats," Grace says, giving each of her grandparents a hug before they leave.

"You ready?" Malikah asks, a knowing sparkle in her eyes.

"Of course she is," Grace's dad answers. "She was born for this."

The sound of crooning instruments wafts from the sanctuary as the string quartet begins to play "Pachelbel Canon in D."

"That's my cue," Malikah sings. She gives Grace's hand one last squeeze before she jets out of the room to take her position in the long procession of flower girls, ring bearers, groomsmen, and bridesmaids that make up the wedding party.

Grace grabs her bouquet and follows her dad into the church's lobby. Once there, Grace gently slips her hand into her father's proffered arm, and they take their place at the end of the line up.

Pair by pair the elegantly clad chain of carefully selected friends and family shortens. First to saunter past the rows of packed pews are the three sets of bridesmaids and groomsmen. (Thanks to Malikah's and Trina's constant bickering, Grace had made the executive decision not to have a Matron or Maid of Honor). They each take their time, stepping in unison, just as they'd rehearsed the night before.

Next, the ring bearers, Grace's two youngest cousins, ease carefully down the carpeted walkway. They're four and six and markedly handsome in their black tuxedos and matching cummerbunds. Threatened earlier with the consequences of what would happen if they didn't take their ring-carrying responsibilities seriously, they each hold their satin-and-lace pillow, which cradles a diamond-encrusted wedding band, as though it's a nuclear bomb that might explode if dropped.

Finally, the flower girls, in their lilac dresses and white Mary Janes, make their way down the aisle, dispersing liberal amounts of red and pink rose petals as they go.

Grace's heart skips a beat as she approaches the arched doorway on her father's arm. The "Pachelbel Canon in D" gives way to the "Wedding March," and all 300 guests rise to their feet.

Her stomach churns and for a second Grace thinks she's going to be sick. For a split second the sight of all those peering eyes makes her hands shake and her feet turn to ice. For just a second, anticipation morphs into anxiety.

But then her eyes lock with Mike's. He's standing in his tuxedo, his small, orderly dreadlocks falling neatly around his chiseled face. His eyes are just as tender, his lips just as soft, his shoulders just as broad, his heart just as golden, and his love just as pure as when they first met. He's waiting for her with an unmistakable expression of pride and adoration. Without saying a word, without moving a muscle, he beckons her—and just like that, everyone else disappears.

There's no music, no stained-glass windows, no flowers, no church or pews, no bishop, no guests. There's only Mike and Grace as she processes down the aisle, her smile mirroring his. Their love is all that exists.

This is it! This is it! This is it!

Until this very moment, Mike had always been under the impression that breathing was an involuntary action, but as he watches the resplendent vision that is his future wife float toward him, he has to remind himself to exhale.

They'd been over mountains and through valleys. They'd battled monsters, endured loss, swallowed pride, and redefined humility to get here. In the simplest of terms, they are partners, companions, allies. There's no one else with whom he'd rather share his life, no one he trusts in or relies on more than Gracie. How he ever survived his first 35 years without her, he doesn't know.

Mike waits for Grace's father, Anthony, to kiss Grace's cheek before he steps forward and takes her hand.

"Hey," she whispers, her excitement audible.

"Hey," he whispers back through a smile. "You ready?"

Her eyes mist and her chin begins to quiver. She nods. "I love you," she mouths.

It takes every ounce of self-control in his body not to lean forward and kiss her. "*I* love *you*," he mouths back.

"Dearly beloved, we are gathered here in the sight of God and these witnesses to unite Michael Cambridge and Grace Naybor in holy matrimony. As believers in Jesus Christ, they recognize that it is God who instituted marriage and who said, 'It is not good for man to be alone. I will make a helper suitable for him.'"

Someone's sniffling has grown into quiet crying. Mike glances to his left to see his mom, red-eyed, accept a handkerchief from Deonté, Malikah's husband, and blow her nose.

Despite her tears, Mike knows that his mom loves Grace and treats her like a daughter. She told Mike once that she'd taken an instant liking to Grace the day she popped up on her doorstep.

"I knew what she wanted before she ever opened her mouth," his mom had said. "And I respected her for it. She was a woman who wasn't afraid to sacrifice herself, to put everything on the line and fight for what she loves."

If it hadn't been for Mike's mom, Grace might never have found him in New York, might never have shown up at his hotel room with a humble plea and her heart on a platter. They're here, in great part, because of his mom, because she's also a woman who isn't afraid to sacrifice, who isn't afraid to put everything on the line and fight for what *she* loves.

"Michael and Grace, the vows you are about to take are not to be accepted without careful thought and prayer. For in them you are committing yourselves, one to the other, for as long as you both shall live."

Mike gazes at Grace half-expecting her to bolt out of the nearest exit, half-expecting to wake up and discover it's all been a dream. As if reading his thoughts, Grace gives his hand a reassuring squeeze.

"Do you, Michael, take Grace to be your wife? Do you promise to love, honor, cherish, and protect her, forsaking all others and holding only unto her?"

"I do," he says, his voice thick. He fights back his emotion as the bishop repeats the question for Grace.

"I do," she answers, a solitary tear sliding down her cheek.

The bishop turns back to Mike. "And now repeat after me...."

Though he had practiced saying his vows the night before, Mike is relieved that at this moment all he has to do is echo the words that have just been spoken. "I, Michael," he begins, his voice quaking. "Take thee, Grace, to be my lawfully wedded wife."

Grace caresses Mike's fingers as he takes a deep breath and tries to compose himself enough to continue.

"To have and to hold, for richer or for poorer, in sickness and in health, in good times and in bad. I promise my love to you as long as we both shall live."

With the bishop's guidance, Grace repeats the vows back to Mike, and the ceremony goes on as planned. By the time the rings have been exchanged, the Bible verses have been read, and the soloist has performed, nearly everyone has dissolved into puddles of tears.

"I now pronounce you 'Husband and Wife,' in the name of the Father, and the Son, and the Holy Spirit. Those whom God has joined together, let no man put asunder."

The bishop smiles, and Mike holds his breath, listening for the five words he's been longing to hear: "You may kiss the bride."

Grace smiles up at him, and Mike falls in love with her all over again. In her, he sees possibility and promise. He sees happiness and hope. In her, he sees forever. Gently, he cups her face in his hand and kisses her deeply, with an intensity he never would have dared to express before he had the right to call her his own.

"Ladies and gentlemen," the bishop exclaims over the thunderous applause of the congregation. "I present to you: Mr. and Mrs. Michael Cambridge."

2

Trina, along with the rest of the wedding party, files into the Peabody Hotel's Grand Ballroom. The space is truly magnificent with its high ceilings and imperial chandeliers. Quite a few of the guests have already arrived and are milling around, chatting and enjoying the gourmet hors d'oeuvres being served by the gracious, tuxedo-clad wait staff.

Trina makes her way to the dais and searches for her seat. She had expected to be placed next to Grace, so naturally she's a little disappointed to see that *that* seat has been reserved for Grace's father. However, she is stunned and absolutely appalled to see the seat next to Grace's father belongs to Malikah.

Incredulous, she continues down the long, elegantly set table. Seated next to Malikah are the two young ring bearers, and next to them is Stephanie, Grace's cousin and third bridesmaid, and then next to her are the two flower girls. Trina reaches the very last chair, and there, resting on the crisp linen tablecloth, is a place card bearing her name in gold calligraphy.

This can't be right, she thinks. *Someone must've rearranged the place cards.* Trina's eyes gravitate to Malikah, who smirks and pretends not to notice Trina's dumbfounded expression.

The blood runs hot through Trina's veins as she stomps over to Malikah. "You took my seat."

Malikah sighs. "Go away, little girl."

"I will not go away," Trina huffs. "You took my seat, and I want it back."

"If it was up to me, you wouldn't have a seat."

"Well, it's not up to you," Trina replies icily. "So I suggest you get out of that chair, before I remove you from it."

"Trina, Girl," Malikah says, her voice on edge, "I'm warning you."

"How old are you?" a male voice asks. Trina looks over Malikah's shoulder to see Ron, shaking his head in disgust. "Are you seriously about to start a fight over a stupid chair?"

Trina finds herself at a loss for words as she usually does on the rare occasions that Ron deigns to speak to her.

Over the past year, Ron has mastered the art of avoidance, dodging Trina at holiday parties, picnics, church gatherings, and Bible study. Just last night at rehearsal, he excused himself when she tried to join a conversation he was having with Grace. And later, at the rehearsal dinner, he asked to switch seats with Mike's mom under the guise that he needed more leg room, but Trina knew it was so he wouldn't have to sit at the same table with her.

Not so long ago, they were inseparable. A day didn't go by that Ron didn't tell her how much he loved her, how blessed he was to have her in his life, and how he could see them growing old together. He was a different guy then—charismatic, affectionate, and kind.

He had warned her that night after she caught Grace in what she thought was a compromising position with a married man. "Don't jump to conclusions," Ron had counseled. "If Grace said that it's not what it looked like, then there's probably more to the story than you know."

"Uh-huh," Trina had grumbled, half-listening.

"Promise me you'll leave it alone and let them work it out," pleaded Ron.

Trina had promised, but as hard as she tried, she couldn't let it go. She couldn't watch Grace continue to have her cake and eat it too. She'd seen Grace wrapped in another man's arms. She'd watched their lips press together, witnessed the horrified looks on both of their faces when they realized they'd been caught. At the time, the situation seemed painfully obvious. Grace was cheating on Mike and with a married man no less. Nothing and no one could have convinced Trina otherwise.

It just wasn't fair.

Ever since Trina could remember, Grace had gotten everything she wanted, Mike included, and the very idea that Grace was cheating on him, that she was unappreciative enough, conniving enough, to disregard his love so callously, had made Trina's skin crawl. Given the circumstances and her certainty, Trina felt that there was only one thing to do: Tell Mike.

Mike had refused to believe her at first. "There's got to be some misunderstanding," he kept saying.

"Look, no one is more shocked about this than me, but you're my friend too, and I think you have the right to know."

"But she's supposed to be working on her novel," he argued.

"What novel? She told me she was under deadline for another installment of *Simon and Eddie*."

Wrinkles spanned Mike's forehead. "Why would she lie?" he wondered aloud.

"The worst part is," Trina continued, "the guy's married with a kid."

"Gracie wouldn't do that. She's not that kind of person."

"Then why did she sleep with him on their first date?" Trina had cringed after she uttered those words, partly because she wasn't 100 percent sure they were true and partly because of the frosty glaze that had settled over Mike's eyes. She suspected that maybe she'd gone too far, that maybe she should have heeded Ron's advice altogether and minded her own business. But it was too late. The words had been said, the deed had been done, and she found herself powerless to stop the devastating ripple effect it caused.

Since then, she has apologized a dozen times, pleading with Ron for just one more chance, but his response is always the same: "I forgive you and I'm glad you learned your lesson, but what's done is done between us."

He swears there are no hard feelings, that they'll always be friends, but she sees the contempt in his eyes, hears the resentment in his voice. He can't stand to be near her and that pierces her to the core because she misses him so much—and because she hasn't been the same since he walked away.

"I'm not trying to start a fight," Trina says, her tone decidedly less hostile. "I just want my seat."

Ron groans. "What difference does it make where you sit? We're all going to get served the same thing at the same time."

That's easy for you to say, she thinks. As the best man, Ron's seat is right next to Mike's. Trina sighs. "I just wanted to be by Grace."

"Well," Malikah asserts with an arrogant grin, "she obviously don't wanna be by you."

"Obviously," Trina murmurs dejectedly and heads back to her seat.

Trina pulls out her chair and plops down, feeling exiled. A moment later she feels a tap on her arm. "Hi!" chirps Danielle, the younger of the two flower girls. "I need help, please," she says, handing Trina her Sponge Bob sippy cup. Trina watches as the little girl climbs into the empty chair next to her and settles in.

"Ladies and gentlemen," the DJ's voice rumbles through the ballroom. "Put your hands together for Mr. and Mrs. Michael Cambridge!"

Trina musters up enough enthusiasm to stand with the rest of the cheering guests and clap, if somewhat feebly, as Grace and Mike enter hand in hand.

By this point, Trina has had just about all she can take. She's sick of Grace's relatives and fed up with Mike's friends. She's beginning to wonder why she ever agreed to be in this miserable wedding. In fact, she's beginning to wonder what she's doing here at all.

Trina watches Grace bound toward her, Mike in tow. "Hey!" Grace squeals, her face glowing. "Isn't this great? I'm having such a good time."

Trina scoffs. "Yeah, nothing says a good time like rubbery chicken, flat soda, and stimulating conversation with a five-year-old about Sponge Bob Square Pants."

Grace's face falls as she blinks in stunned silence. Trina instantly regrets her sarcastic remark, which honestly came out a lot nastier than she intended.

Mike steps closer. "Would it kill you to have some fun?" he asks. There's a smile on his face, and his tone is calm and even, but his stare is flinty.

"If you don't mind,"Trina snaps, "I'm talking to my best friend."

"No," Mike says with a firmness to his voice that neither Trina nor Grace have ever heard before. "You're insulting my wife."

"Baby," Grace says, placing her hand on Mike's chest, "just give us a minute."

Trina sees his reluctance. Still he obliges, but not without casting her one last glare of warning.

"What's the matter?" Grace asks. Her expression is one of concern, not anger.

Trina pouts and folds her arms across her chest. "Nothing."

"If you're still hungry, I can try to get one of the chefs to whip you up something special to eat," Grace offers.

Trina, aware that Mike is hovering only a few feet away, shakes her head. "That's not it," she sulks.

Grace rubs Trina's arm. "Talk to me."

"How come... I mean, I just don't get..."

Grace waits patiently for her to find the words.

"Why did you put me at the end of the dais?"Trina finally manages.

"What?" Grace's eyebrows arch in surprise.

Trina blushes. As plaguing as it was all through dinner, now her complaint just sounds childish and petty. "I felt like I was out in No Man's Land," she mumbles, "like you didn't want to be near me."

"No," Grace soothes, her eyes sympathetic. "That wasn't it at all. I spread out the adults and placed the kids in the middle; so you guys could supervise for me."

If that was the case, Trina reasoned, Grace could've seated Stephanie on the end or put Malikah and the two ring bearers towards the middle. There was a myriad of possible seating combinations, countless ways to keep the kids supervised, so why did Grace choose the one that put the most distance between the two of them?

"I don't know," Trina mutters. "It just feels like things are changing."

"Of course they are. They have to," Grace explains kindly, her brows furrowed with compassion. "I'm married now."

"No, I mean it feels like this is it, you know? Like this is the end of the line for us."

"Don't be silly," Grace says, dismissing the notion with a smirk. "We'll always be Trina and Gracie."

"Stop pretending," Trina says, her eyes moist. "We haven't been Trina and Gracie in a long time. For a while I thought maybe we were getting back on track, but who am I kidding? Mike's your best friend now."

Trina waits for Grace to tell her that she's wrong, to reassure her that Mike can never replace her. But Grace just looks at her with those sad eyes, pity seeping from her pores.

"Don't think about any of that now," Grace coaxes. She grabs Trina's hand. "Come dance with me."

Irritated at how Grace is trying to handle her, Trina snatches her hand away. "I don't want to dance," she says loudly, grabbing the attention of several nearby guests.

Mike is by Grace's side in three long strides.

"You again," Trina says, her words dripping in disdain.

"What is the problem?" His tone is hushed yet curt.

"How many times do I have to tell you there's no problem?" Trina asks, her neck swaying from side to side. "We're having a discussion that doesn't involve you. It happens. She may be your wife, but she's still my best friend."

"Why don't you stop *saying* you're her best friend and start acting like it."

"What is that supposed to mean?"

"It means being happy for me," Grace answers sternly, her patience expended. "Even if you think the meal was revolting and the DJ is cheesy and you hate the bridesmaid's dress and you disagree with the seating arrangement. It means hugging me and wishing me the best even if it terrifies you to let go."

"Is that what you want?" Trina asks. "You want me to let go?"

"Well, not completely, but come on. We can't live our lives only belonging to each other. We have to open new doors, start new chapters."

Trina wipes away a tear with the back of her hand. She knows Grace is right, but that doesn't make her words sting any less. She needs Grace right now. She needs someone to anchor her. Pre-Mike, Grace would've sensed that. She wouldn't be shrugging Trina off; she would be counseling her, comforting her. But clearly things change, people change, and there's nothing she or anyone can do about it.

Trina smiles feebly. "Fine." She gives Grace a quick, stiff hug. "I wish you the best," she says coolly and then turns on her heels and pushes her way through the crowd.

"Trina," Grace calls after her. "Trina, wait...," but it's no use. Trina easily disappears into the sea of guests.

"She'll be alright," Mike says.

Grace's shoulders slump with worry. "Maybe I should go find her."

"And do what?" Mike asks. "Apologize for getting married? Ask her forgiveness for wanting your own life?"

Grace sighs. "I didn't think she'd have this much trouble adjusting."

"She'll get over it," Mike says, unsympathetic and more than just a little fed up.

"Put yourself in her shoes," Grace says. "What if your mom got remarried and you felt pushed out?"

"But you're not her mother, Baby. And even if you were, she's grown."

"I'm her family," Grace says. "No matter how old she gets."

Mike's resolve softens. As disenchanted as he is with Trina and her penchant for causing trouble, he respects Grace's uncompromising loyalty.

"I'll tell you what," he says, folding his arms around her. "You come dance with me, and in a little bit, we'll both go look for her and make sure she's okay."

Grace gazes up at Mike and she's reassured that everything will work itself out. She worries about Trina, about her attitude lately and the wayward direction in which her life is turning. But she also wants a day off, one day when she's allowed to put her happiness first, just one day when the only person's life she's saving is her own.

"Okay," Grace agrees, smiling as Mike leads her to the crowded dance floor. The heavy bass of the fast-paced music reverberates throughout the entire ballroom. Grace's spirits lift immediately as her body loosens and she finds her groove.

Mike steps stiffly from side to side trying desperately to look suave.

Grace laughs. "I forgot what a bad dancer you are."

"Get outta here," he says. "You wish you had this much rhythm."

Grace stops dancing and observes him as he jerks and bobs between the beats of the music. She shakes her head, barely able to contain her laughter. "You look like you're having a seizure."

"Yeah, well, what I lack in natural bootie-shaking ability, I make up for in artistic flare," he says, breaking into a horrendous move that closely resembles the Funky Chicken.

"Boy, what is wrong wit chu?" Malikah asks, walking up behind Mike, her forehead wrinkled in wonderment. Grace howls.

"I'm bustin' a move," he says, transitioning into a very stiff version of the Running Man.

"You keep that up and you *gonna* bust somethin'."

"Don't hate," he teases and tries his best to attempt the Tootsie Roll.

"God help us all," Malikah says, her eyes glued to Mike's convulsing body. Grace doubles over in laughter.

"Look," Malikah says. "I don't usually do this, but since you family now, I'mma help you out."

Mike snaps his fingers and spins. "No need," he says. "I got this."

Malikah shakes her head. "You ain't got nothin'. Now stand still and watch me." She takes four steps to the right and then four steps to the left. Mike follows suit. "Good, now four steps back," Malikah instructs.

"Oh no," Grace whines as she realizes where Malikah's impromptu dance lesson is headed. "Anything but that," she begs.

Malikah ignores her. "Now dip forward," she orders. Mike obeys.

"Uh-oh, y'all!" the DJ's voice booms through the speakers. "I think it's about that time."

Grace rolls her eyes and waits for the words she swore she would never allow at her wedding reception.

"Everybody Hustle!" In a matter of seconds, every last one of the 80 or so guests on the dance floor are lined up and stepping in perfect sync with one another. Despite herself, Grace smiles. *Trained army platoons take longer to fall into formation.*

"Come on, Cuz," Malikah says, grabbing for Grace's hand.

"There's no way," Grace laughs, stepping away. "I hate this dance."

"Aw," Mike goads. "You're just mad because you can't keep up with the big dogs."

Grace grins. "You're gonna have to do better than that."

In one swift movement Mike hooks his arm around Grace's waist and sweeps her off her feet into a tight embrace. Grace squeals with delight. "How's that?" he asks, their lips only inches apart.

Grace beams up at him, breathless. "That," she says, leaning in for a kiss, "was perfect."

Trina stands by the set of double doors, her arms folded across her chest and glares at Grace and Mike as they laugh and dance, periodically stopping to kiss.

She cannot believe that Grace didn't follow her when she stormed off. Trina had waited on the other side of the room for ten minutes, certain that eventually Grace would find her and apologize for being so harsh, for letting Mike get into their private business, and for pushing her to the periphery all day. She had stood there, her foot tapping, compiling her arguments along with a handful of snippy reprimands, but Grace never came.

Slowly Trina's anger had turned to worry. Had she pushed Grace too far? Was Grace distraught now? Off crying in a corner? Trina had then begun canvassing the area, checking bathroom stalls, the hotel lobbies and restaurants. Grace was nowhere to be found.

With mounting worry, Trina had rushed back to the ballroom, scanning any woman wearing a white dress who crossed her field of vision. That's when she had spotted Grace, snuggled up with Mike on the dance floor without a care in the world.

Now fuming, Trina's gaze moves to Malikah, who's dancing with her husband, her head thrown back in laughter. Next to them is Ron, who spins and dips a petite, short-haired brunette, whom Trina has never seen before.

Immense loneliness settles into the pit of Trina's stomach. None of them are the slightest bit aware or even bothered that she's missing.

"Don't I know you?" a smooth, baritone voice asks. The guy is so close that Trina can feel his warm breath on the back of her ear. She turns, ready to tell the loser to buzz off, and freezes.

"Hey, Beautiful," Darius says, flashing his million-dollar smile.

Trina blinks, her mouth agape.

"Nice to see you too," Darius says, his gaze dropping from her face to her cleavage.

"How did... Wh-what are you doing here?" she asks. She hasn't seen Darius in two years, since the day he came home and split open her lip for revealing his affair with his boss to his boss's husband. She'd heard through mutual friends and old acquaintances that he'd sold his house in Memphis and moved back to Detroit. *Good riddance*, she remembers thinking, perfectly content, at the time, in her relationship with Ron.

Darius shrugs. "I came with a friend."

"How nice for you," Trina says, turning to walk away.

"Wait," Darius pleads.

Trina halts, intrigued by the desperation in his voice.

"Can we talk?" he asks.

Trina tilts her head and examines Darius in his sharp black suit. He's not as tall as she remembers, not as attractive. "I think all our words have been said."

"I know at least two that haven't." His eyes are round with sincerity.

"And what are *they?*"

"I'm sorry."

Trina sneers. "You're two years too late."

"I can make it up to you," he says, running his finger down the length of her exposed arm. "Just give me a chance. Let me buy you a drink."

Trina glances back at the dance floor. They've all switched partners. Mike is dancing with his mother, Grace is dancing with Ron, and Malikah is proudly swaying to and fro with her oldest son.

It's a fuzzy Kodak moment with no place for Trina. *Might as well accept it*, she thinks with a sigh. It's time for her to stop making a fool of herself, to stop trying to salvage relationships that have long since fallen by the wayside. She decides right then and there that if Grace wants her to let go, that's exactly what she'll do. She doesn't need them. She doesn't need anybody.

"Why not?" Trina says, sidestepping her better judgment. "One drink couldn't hurt."

Grace positions herself in front of the group of clamoring, single women and turns around. "On the count of three," she yells over her shoulder.

"One!" everyone shouts. "Two! Three!"

Grace tosses her bouquet behind her and turns around in time to see it sail through the air and land in the hands of Mike's widowed aunt, Barbara. The room bursts into thunderous applause as Auntie Barb holds the flowers above her head in victory.

Grace smiles distractedly as the other ladies "boo" Barb in good fun. She wants to enjoy this moment, to share in everyone else's excitement, but she can't, not without Trina.

Earlier, Grace had searched for Trina for the better part of an hour, but to no avail. She had looked in the bathrooms and the main lobby, even the kitchen and the limos, but there was no trace of her anywhere. Grace didn't want to toss the bouquet without Trina, and she certainly didn't want to leave without telling Trina how much she loves her, how important she is, and how, even though their dynamic is changing, they will always be the best of friends; they'll always be sisters.

However, when her search proved to be futile, Grace realized that she wasn't going to get the chance to tell Trina anything. The uneasy feeling in the pit of her stomach deepened into intense sadness as the truth eventually took hold: *Trina had left without saying goodbye.*

"Why would she do that?" Mike had asked, as Grace cried into his chest.

Grace's only response was a muffled sob.

"What can I do?" he said, gently wiping the tears from Grace's cheeks and chin. "Do you want to go by the loft?"

"No," Grace had answered emphatically. "I won't play these games. We're not kids anymore. I can't keep letting her dictate my happiness."

But now, as Grace stands in front of the ballroom full of guests and waves good-bye, she knows that in some way her happiness is, in fact, tied to Trina's—if by no other reason than habit.

Maybe letting go is going to be harder than she thought. Clearly change, even when it's for the better, is painful.

Grace takes one last glance at all the smiling faces shouting their congratulations and best wishes. Then she and Mike rush out of the ballroom, through the foyer, and into their new life as husband and wife.

3

The presidential suite with its rich cherry oak furniture, hand-carved moldings, and refined decor can be described in two simple words: Southern opulence. The heavy blackout curtains are drawn, and resting on the desk adjacent to the oversized couch is a massive gift basket, stuffed to the hilt with various fruits, syrups, chocolates, and preserves. Vanilla-scented candles, strategically placed throughout the spacious sitting room, emit a romantic glow, and a trail of rose petals lead the way from the foyer to the master bedroom.

Mike effortlessly carries Grace over the threshold, down the marble foyer, through the double doors leading to their bedroom, and gently sets her down on the rose-petal-covered bed.

Grace's smile is broad, her eyes wide. "We did it!"

"And lived to tell the tale," Mike says, kneeling in front of her and resting his head in her lap.

"Awww," Grace coos and rubs his back. "It wasn't that bad."

"I will never do that again," he swears into her dress.

"Well, yeah," Grace grins. "That's sort of the point."

Mike lifts his head. "Have I told you today that I love you?"

"Hmmm." Grace raises her eyes to the ceiling in playful thought. "Only about a hundred times."

"Only a hundred?" Mike shakes his head. "I'm slipping."

Grace shrugs. "You're getting old."

"Was it everything you wanted?" he asks, his tone eager.

Grace strokes his cheek, touched by his genuine desire to please her. "Everything and more," she says.

"Good." He plants a soft kiss on the back of her hand. "Then it was worth it."

Grace leans forward and kisses him slowly, surely. She savors the feel of his dreadlocks between her fingers and the softness of his neck, his scent, the taste of his lips, the warmth of his tongue. She's kissed him hundreds of times, but never like this. Never with this much freedom.

There are no pretenses, no misapprehensions. She knows this man, and he knows her. They've taken the time not only to fall in love with each other, but to stay in love, and they did it while remaining pure.

Grace couldn't offer Mike her virginity, which saddened her. Yet she was glad that during their courtship they had honored the Lord and kept their vow to respect themselves, each other, and their relationship by abstaining from any form of premarital sex. It hadn't been easy. In fact, some days were nothing short of torturous. But they'd set boundaries and agreed early on that there were topics they wouldn't discuss, things they wouldn't watch, and places they wouldn't go in order to make it here, to this night, together and undefiled.

Mike's kisses move from her lips to her jaw and down to her neck. Grace gasps at his warm breath on her skin. Her body aches for him.

He takes her hand, gently tugs her off the bed, and turns her around. "May I?" he whispers, reaching for the buttons on her dress.

Grace nods, unable to speak.

Gingerly, he undoes each button. Grace's heart beats faster as the dress becomes progressively looser and then falls to the floor, revealing her carefully selected lingerie. She turns to see Mike gazing at her, taking in every curve of her body.

His fingers tremble as he reaches out and runs his hands tentatively across her exposed skin. His nervousness, his timidity, makes him that much more attractive to Grace. She will be the first and only woman he will ever make love to and she's so proud—proud and honored. He had fought temptation, steadfastly denied his flesh, and held true to his convictions. He had done what some men can't—and most men won't—and he did it for her. He did it so that he'd have more than just words to offer her on their wedding night.

"It's okay," she whispers, drawing close. She doesn't want him to feel inhibited. She wants him to fumble and learn, discover and enjoy in his own way. Kissing him deeply, she sinks into his firm touch and strong embrace. She easily unbuttons his shirt and slides it off of his shoulders. She grips his back, pressing herself into him. He shudders. His breathing quickens, and his kisses grow more intense. He pulls away only to slip his undershirt over his head.

Mike lies down on the bed and tenderly pulls Grace down on top of him. A moan escapes his lips as she plants a trail of kisses across his smooth chest. He relishes the feel of her skin, the weight of her body pressed so closely against his that he can feel her heartbeat.

He allows his hands to roam and caress Grace in ways and places that he never, until this evening, would have dared. And he draws pleasure from her pleasure. He memorizes her sounds and notes her reaction to every touch, every kiss. He takes time to familiarize himself with the curves of her legs and back, the way they hug and arch, the way she moves.

Grace is overcome with emotion at Mike's attentiveness. Each stroke is thoughtful, soft, and meaningful. He anticipates her desires, her needs, and he fulfills them lovingly and willingly.

He is her husband, her beloved, and she is his wife. Her body was meant for his and his for hers. Now finally, they can be united as one.

Mike pulls back the comforter, and Grace slips between the sheets and waits for him to remove his pants and rejoin her in bed. Her heart flutters.

He reaches for the light, and the last thing Grace sees before the room goes black is her wedding ring gleaming up at her.

4

"There's no place like home. There's no place like home," Grace chants breathlessly as she stumbles, saddled with luggage, into their loft. She drops her Tumi suitcases and falls prostrate on the cool marble floor of the front hallway.

Mike staggers in behind her, two duffel bags hanging from each shoulder. He takes one look at Grace kissing the ground and smiles. "A little dramatic, are we?"

Grace rolls over and crosses her arms behind her head. "You can't tell me you aren't happy to be back."

The four overstuffed bags hit the floor with loud thuds. Mike offers Grace his hand and pulls her back onto her feet. "Alone with my beautiful wife on an unspoiled island paradise in the Indian Ocean," he says, tenderly kissing her neck. "Hmm... I can think of worse ways to spend two weeks."

"Yeah, but what about the mosquitoes?" Grace asks.

"It was worth it."

"And the lizards?"

"Worth it."

"The strange food?"

"Worth it."

"And the lost luggage?"

"Still worth it."

"What about my snoring?"

Mike pauses, his eyes cast upward in contemplation. "Yeah, you've got a point."

"Wrong answer!" she says, socking him playfully.

"Ow!" He rubs his arm. "You asked."

"You're a married man now. You've got to learn the subtle art of Truth Manipulation."

"And what, pray tell, is that?"

"It's the only way a husband can truly keep his wife happy."

"Sounds crucial," he says with mock earnest. "Should I be taking notes?"

Grace shakes her head. "It's very simple. All you have to do is tweak the negatives until they become positives. For example, my snoring isn't *bothersome*; it's *melodious*. When you hear it, you know I'm lying next to you and you sigh with contented relief because all is right in the world."

Mike grins. "You want me to lie?"

"It's not lying. It's finding the silver lining."

He chuckles. "Gracie, I love you, but your snoring could level a house. I will single-handedly be able to keep the earplug industry afloat for the rest of my natural life. Where is the silver lining in that?"

Grace gazes up at him dotingly. "Looks like I've got my work cut out for me."

"Really?" he asks, pulling her close. "Because I always thought of myself as more of an 'As Is' model."

"Nope. You're a definite fixer-upper."

"Well," he says, kissing the top of her head, "you have an entire lifetime to get me the way you want me. So what do you say we leave the revamping for another day and go get some lunch?"

"It's a date."

"Good. Give me a few minutes," he says, rounding the corner to his office. "I just have to check my voice mail."

"What about the luggage?" Grace calls.

"Leave it. We'll get it later."

Grace stands in the middle of the long vestibule, which is lined with Mike's funky, one-of-a-kind art, unsure of what to do next. She's been in this loft hundreds of times. She's cooked meals here, entertained guests here, and hosted countless Bible studies here. She knows where Mike keeps the extra blankets and fresh towels. She knows where to find the phone book and how to change the water filter in the refrigerator. She knows where the floor creaks and the exact sound of the air conditioner when it kicks on.

Over the past couple of years, she'd grown accustomed to this breathtaking place, its grand magnificence having given way to comforting familiarity somewhere between botching their very first dinner party and opening wedding presents. But today, as Mrs. Grace Cambridge, the loft is just as magical as it was the first day she set foot into it.

She saunters into the tidy, sun-filled living room, sits down on the couch, and marvels at how different everything looks and feels.

The leather ottoman is just a little more chic than she remembered, the 25-foot ceilings just a smidge higher, the gleaming hardwood floors just a bit shinier. She smiles as she realizes why.

This is not just Mike's ottoman; these are not just his ceilings and floors. This is *their* ottoman now, their ceilings and their floors. This is *their* home.

With a sudden urge to check out the rest of Mrs. Mike Cambridge's new home, Grace hops up from the couch and makes her way down the long, carpeted hallway and into her new bedroom. Though Mike had offered, several times, to swap his dark oak bedroom set for something more unisex, Grace had opted not to change anything. After all, she likes his four-poster, king-size bed with its plush, beige comforter and huge, fluffy, down pillows. She loves the black-and-white art, the photographs of Mike's parents, Earl and Lani, the beautiful suede couch, and the muted cerulean walls. In fact, the only thing she had felt compelled to add was a framed photo of her mother.

The closet, however, was a different story. Mike, like most men, is a simple dresser. He has a few suits for work, several button-down shirts and slacks for church, a couple of sweat suits for lounging, and jeans, T-shirts, and sweaters for every other occasion. Simply put, his wardrobe is defined by necessity.

Grace's daily attire, on the other hand, is dictated solely by her mood. Some days she feels bright and airy, other days dark and introspective. Some days she's creatively daring, and on a few, select days, she's just plain bloated. Her varying moods, coupled with her fluctuating weight and pack-rat tendencies, had made for an extensive wardrobe, so extensive that there wasn't room for it all.

She had been forced to spend a weekend pruning down her outfits. It was agonizing, to say the least, but she had managed to cram most of it in—minus the clothes from her overweight days, several faded, tattered jeans, an assortment of outdated dresses, and a box of shoes.

The bathroom had proved to be a similar story. Apart from a couple of bars of soap and a few razors, the master bathroom, before Grace's invasion, had been a relatively uncluttered space. Now, however, there are scrubs, lotions, perfumes, powders, exfoliants, moisturizers, cleansers, wrinkle-reducers, astringents, clippers, trimmers, liners, brushes, curlers, shadows, blushes, foundations, glosses, polishes, tampons, shampoos, conditioners, bath beads, shower gels, and loofah sponges filling every drawer and covering every free inch of counter space.

"So what do you really look like?" Mike had joked upon seeing her extensive collection of beauty products.

Grace had caught her face growing warm with embarrassment. She suddenly realized that her morning rituals, her subconscious routines, her nonsensical habits—the little idiosyncrasies that are the essence of who she is—would no longer be private. That's when it hit her that living with someone, even the man of her dreams, was going to be a challenge. There would be no hiding from Mike, no pretending that she wakes up with perfectly coiffed hair, shiny lips, and minty fresh breath. No acting like she doesn't stink when she sweats or that she's not plagued with the occasional bout of gas or that she doesn't mumble in her sleep.

That's when it hit her, when it really set in: Marriage isn't bunnies frolicking in rolling emerald meadows. It isn't clear blue skies and soaring doves that fade to a syrupy pop ballad and scrolling credits. It's work...exposure...revelation. It's discovering your partner on a simple, yet profound, level and striving daily to love them regardless.

Grace had started to learn that from living with Trina. They'd been to hell and back together, several times, over the course of their 18-year friendship. They'd survived nutty boyfriends, an abortion, the loss of loved ones, financial strain, a cross-country move, and countless other challenges. But it wasn't until Trina left Darius and ended up rooming with Grace that their relationship changed in a fundamental way.

Living together they saw sides of each other—distasteful, vindictive traits—that shattered their rosy perceptions and forever changed their rapport. Even now, after an entire year of walking on eggshells, things aren't quite the same. They don't share like they used to; they don't laugh and joke with the same carefree ease.

An unshakable tension has settled between them and Grace hates it. She hates how distant Trina's become, how angry and resentful she is about the way things turned out with Ron and Mike. There's so much they'd both do differently, so many words they would say or wouldn't say, if they could only go back. But they can't, and as content as Grace is with Mike, as ecstatic as she is about her writing career and all the hopeful possibilities that loom on her horizon, she's saddened at the prospect of Trina not being part of her future.

A pang shoots through Grace's chest as she realizes that it's been two weeks since she's heard Trina's voice. Because Trina had skipped out of the wedding early, Grace never had the opportunity to talk to her before she and Mike left on their honeymoon. Grace had thought about calling Trina a couple of times while she was away, but in the end decided not to chance an expensive, cross-continent screaming match—which inevitably would have taken the focus off Mike and their special, private time together.

Grace grabs the phone and flops down on the neatly made bed. She figures they've all had enough time to calm down and get rational. Maybe there's still a chance to get things back on the right foot. There's no reason why her best friend and her husband can't get along—why they can't find a way to blend civilly into each other's lives.

It's a beautiful, sunny Saturday afternoon, Grace reasons. She'll invite Trina to lunch with her and Mike. They'll talk and eat and Mike can give Trina the carved mask and beaded purse they bought her. *It'll work itself out*, Grace thinks as she dials. *These things always work themselves out*.

"Hello?" a groggy, male voice answers. Grace looks at the receiver, her brows furrowed. "Hello?" the voice calls again.

"Sorry," Grace replies, slowly. "I must have the wrong number." She returns the phone to its cradle and wills herself not to jump to conclusions. Was it just her imagination, or did that voice sound vaguely familiar? She picks the phone back up and carefully, meticulously redials the number.

"Hello?" the same sleepy voice answers.

"Who is this?" Grace asks.

"Who is *this?*" the man replies.

"Darius?" she says incredulously.

There's silence on the other end, followed by muffled whispers and then a dial tone. Grace stares at the phone in furious disbelief.

"Let's go to Panchos," Mike says, entering the bedroom with a smile. "I'm in the mood for Mexican."

"There's no way," Grace fumes, her jaws clenched. "There's no possible way."

Mike's smile fades. "Or...we can do Italian."

"She is absolutely unbelievable," Grace exclaims, hopping off the bed. She brushes past Mike and stomps back to the living room where she retrieves her keys from her purse.

"You want to clue me in?" Mike asks, rushing to keep pace with Grace as she boards their penthouse elevator. Barely waiting for the doors to close, Grace stabs at the buttons with her index finger.

"I'm going to kill her," Grace mumbles, mostly to herself, her foot tapping anxiously as the elevator makes its way down to the third floor.

"Trina?" Mike asks.

"Who else?" Grace huffs out of the elevator and marches swiftly down the hall, straight to the loft she had previously shared with Trina. She slides the key into the lock and throws the door open. The air is stale, and the living room is cluttered with an assortment of take-out containers, half-empty beer bottles, and dirty clothes. Grace picks up a glass that has left a ring on the end of her coffee table and blinks at the cigarette butts bobbing up and down in its murky content.

"Trina!" Grace calls sternly, her blood boiling. There's no reply, only the faint sound of a television program playing from behind the closed bedroom door.

"Trina!" Grace calls again, this time louder and with more force.

"You don't have to shout," Trina says, emerging from the kitchen. She's wearing a robe and carrying two mugs and a carton of orange juice.

"What is going on here?" Grace demands, nostrils flaring. "Have you lost your mind?"

"Not since I last checked," Trina says, her tone glib. She sets down the juice and mugs and perches on the arm of the love seat.

Grace seethes. "Well, maybe you need to check again."

"Why are you so tense?" Trina asks, her arms folded complacently across her chest. The split in her robe slips open, revealing a generous amount of leg. Her gaze moves from Grace to Mike and back to Grace. "Trouble in paradise already?"

"Look at this place!" Grace shrieks, waving her arms around her sullied living room.

"It's not a big deal," Trina says, nonchalant. "I'll clean it up later."

Grace picks up a crushed beer can. "You're drinking now?"

"It's a free country."

"And what about this?" Grace points to the glass of floating cigarette butts.

"Well," Trina shrugs, "you don't have any ashtrays."

"You don't smoke!" Grace snaps, her pitch rising.

Trina meets Grace's demanding stare, her chin raised defiantly. "It's never too late to try new things."

Grace studies the scantily clad woman sitting amidst the filth in her living room and uneasiness settles in her gut like a two-ton weight. It's been a while, but Grace recognizes the daring demeanor. She knows the arrogant aloofness.

Somehow, in the midst of all of the festivities, all of the changes and shifts, the old Trina had crept back—the Trina pre-Memphis, pre-Ronald, pre-Christ. It's the woman who will justify unjustifiable selfishness, the woman who will reason self-accountability out of any equation, the woman who will sell her soul out of spite.

"Where is he?" Grace asks, her chest heaving. "Where is Darius?"

Trina nods in the direction of her bedroom. "Sleeping."

"You actually brought him here—to my house," Grace says, her voice teeming with disgust.

"*Your* house?" Trina asks, her forehead wrinkled with feigned puzzlement. "Ah! Yes, that's right," she says, sardonically. "It's only *our* house when I play by *your* rules."

Grace shakes her head. "Believe what you want."

"I'm not Mike," Trina says, her glare icy. "I'm not going to snivel behind you like a lost puppy and bow to your every command."

With steely determination, Mike ignores the jab.,.

Grace's stare is unyielding. "You can*not* have sex in this house," she says, her words clipped with anger.

"I hate to break it to you, Grace, but I'm grown. I can do what I want, with *whomever* I want, *whenever* I want."

"Then go be grown somewhere else."

Trina tilts her head to the side and raises a derisive brow. "So what, you're kicking me out now?"

"You've got two options," Grace says, her stance wide. "You can either start acting like you've got some sense or you can start packing."

Trina rolls her eyes. "So self-righteous," she utters with a sneer. "Just like your mother."

Grace's hands ball into tight fists as rage surges through her body. She bites her tongue to fight back the expletives straining to fly from her mouth.

Mike steps in. "That was uncalled for," he says, his jaw set.

"Right," Trina throws her head back, "I almost forgot. Where would the pretentious princess be without her knight in shining armor?"

"You need to calm down," Mike warns.

"You need to butt out!" Trina shouts.

"Hey!" Grace shouts back, ready to close the 20-foot gap between the two of them and slap Trina silly. "You don't talk to him like that."

Mike takes hold of Grace's wrist and gently tugs her back.

"Whatever," Trina sighs, bored. "Listen, Natasha, I think it's time for you to take Boris and run along." She stands, tightens the belt on her robe, and then picks up the two mugs and tucks the carton of juice underneath her arm. "I've got better things to do with my time."

"Where do you think you're going?" Grace asks as Trina turns toward her bedroom.

Trina raises the mugs above her head. "Breakfast," she says, not bothering to turn around.

"You think this is a game?" Grace asks.

Trina continues to saunter away with no response. Grace sees red.

In one swift motion, Grace snatches the glass of cigarette butts and launches it at Trina. The glass sails through the air, just over Trina's shoulder, and smashes against her bedroom door. "I'm not playing with you," Grace yells as Trina leaps back to avoid the spray of glass and ashy water.

"Grace," Mike cautions. "That's enough."

Darius rushes from the bedroom, sporting nothing but boxers and an expression of befuddled terror.

"You take your stuff and your little friend and you get out!" Grace screams. Her thunderous voice sounds foreign to her own ears.

"Gladly!" Trina screams, her volume matching Grace's. "I'd rather sleep on the street than spend one more second in this loft!"

"Then stop talking," Grace snaps, "and start stepping."

"You make me sick!" Trina screeches, turning on her heels toward her bedroom.

"Yeah, well," Grace says, already headed for the front hall, "the feeling's mutual." They both stomp off in opposite directions and give one last, exasperated, shriek before slamming their respective doors.

Mike and Darius are left speechless in the living room.

"Uh, don't worry," Darius says, glancing down at the shards of glass strewn across the wet hardwood floor. "I'll clean this up."

"Yeah, thanks." Mike forces a smile. "That'd be great." They stand for a few moments with an uncomfortable silence between them.

"Well," Darius says, awkwardly shifting his weight from one foot to the other. "I should probably...uh...you know?" He points in the direction where Trina exited.

"Yeah," Mike nods and tosses a thumb over his shoulder. "Me too." Shaking his head, he turns to leave.

"They'll work it out," Darius assures him with audible amusement. "They always do."

Mike doesn't respond, but as he lets himself out and heads down the hallway toward the elevator, he finds himself hoping that this time they don't.

5

Mike finds Grace pacing the length of their loft, muttering to herself with each furious stride.

"Can you believe her?" Grace seethes. "Where does she get off? I mean really, how dare she! And Darius!" she exclaims with a stomp. "Of all the stupid things she could have done, going back to him takes the cake. What? Is that supposed to punish me? Is her bedding down with that woman-beating, two-timing loser supposed to teach me some sort of lesson? Tell me, please, where is the logic in that?"

Mike doesn't attempt to answer Grace's string of questions. Instead, he takes a seat on the sofa and waits patiently for her irate ranting to give way to inevitable hurt.

She scoffs. "There I was on my honeymoon—*my honeymoon*—worrying about her and feeling guilty about how we left things, and what was she doing? Boozing it up, and getting it on with her ex-boyfriend, in *my* loft! Unbelievable! You would think she had more respect for herself. You would think she had more respect for *me*." Grace sighs and rakes her hands through her hair.

Mike watches her shoulders slump as the fight in her wanes. "And how could she say that about my mother? How could she…" Grace's voice cracks and her bottom lip trembles.

"C'mere," Mike beckons, his arms spread open.

Grace trudges over to the sofa and sinks into his lap.

"What happened?" Grace sniffles as the tears stream down her face. "I called to invite her to lunch and I ended up kicking her out. How did the situation get so out of hand?"

"Well, there were some unforeseen elements," Mike offers as he rubs her back. "Darius was there, and the place was a pit."

"She'd been drinking and smoking," Grace adds with a whimper.

"And let's not forget the glass-throwing," Mike pokes. "That's always a surefire way to spin an argument out of control."

Grace closes her eyes and groans. "What was I thinking?"

Mike chuckles. "You weren't."

"I'm just so frustrated," Grace confesses. "I've tried everything. It's never enough with her. I don't know what else to do."

"Can I ask you a question?"

Grace nods.

"Without you getting mad?"

She sits up and studies Mike's concerned face. "What is it?"

He opens his mouth and then pauses to carefully weigh his words. "Why do you try so hard?" he finally asks. "Why do you fight tooth and nail to hang onto a relationship that only causes you pain?"

"Every friendship has ups and downs."

"Baby," Mike says, shaking his head, "it's not just ups and downs with Trina. It's monumental betrayals and gross disrespect." He lets out a deep sigh. "I'm not trying to dictate your relationships. You know I wouldn't do that but, there *is* such a thing as people becoming too different—growing too far apart."

"I know," she says quietly. "I just… It's harder than it seems. She's been part of my life for as long as I can remember."

"But you bring out the worst in each other. Seriously, who *was* that back there throwing glasses and slamming doors? That's not you. That's not my Gracie."

Grace nods solemnly.

"And the thing is," Mike continues, "you're not the only one who keeps getting taken for a ride. I'm trying my best to be patient—to let you work it out in your own way—but I don't know how much longer I can sit back and watch her take advantage of you." He strokes her cheek.

Grace buries her face in Mike's chest and groans. "I hate this."

"I know," he soothes gently. "Me too."

"It all just got so complicated so quickly, you know? I mean, it wasn't that long ago when me, you, Trina, and Ron were like this," Grace says, snaking together her index and middle fingers. "And now… I don't know," she sighs heavily. "Everything's changed. We're all in pieces."

"Not all of us," Mike says, sitting her up and pulling her close. "I think that you and I make a pretty perfect whole."

Grace can't help but smile. "Yeah," she agrees. "Now if only I could get the rest of my life to be as perfect as my marriage."

"Hey," Mike hooks his index finger under her chin and slowly raises her face until their gazes are level and their eyes lock, "we're gonna figure this out."

"Together?" she asks, her voice small.

Mike nods, his smile bearing the warmth of a breezy summer afternoon. "Together."

The tension eases from Grace's neck and shoulders as she sinks into the certainty of his words. Impossibilities simply don't exist when he's by her side.

"No matter what," he says, tightening his grip and holding her even closer, "I love you."

"I know," Grace whispers through an adoring smile. "I love you too."

Trina slings her suitcase onto her bed and throws the flap open. The only thing she regrets is giving Grace the opportunity to throw her out. *I should've done this months ago*, she thinks, snatching her clothes from the closet and dresser drawers.

"I'm going to file a police report," she huffs. "You saw her throw that glass at me. That's a crime, isn't it? Domestic violence or something. I could have her arrested—see how smug she is after a night in jail."

Darius enters the bedroom, fully dressed and slurping the leftover milk from his bowl of Rice Krispies. "You're not gonna call the police," he says wryly. "You'll both cool down and in a couple of days go back to being best friends."

Trina snickers bitterly. "We haven't been best friends in a long time," she says, half-folding, half-rumpling her suits and cramming them into the case.

"You've got to get a grip," Darius says. He sets the bowl down and stretches across her bed. "Just because she's married doesn't mean you can't be friends."

"Did you hear the way she talked to me?" Trina fumes. She storms to the bathroom and returns a few seconds later with an armful of toiletries. "Why would I want to be friends with someone like her?"

"Did you hear the way you talked to *her*?" Darius asks. "You weren't exactly the embodiment of politeness yourself."

Trina glares. "Whose side are you on?" she snaps.

"No one's." Darius says, rolling over and propping himself up on one elbow. "This whole thing is stupid."

"Yeah, well, stupid or not, I'm not staying here another night."

"So, what're you going to do? Waste money on a hotel room until one of you swallows enough pride to apologize?"

"I'll just stay with you," she says, fishing under her bed for stray shoes. "When Grace is ready to talk, she can come find me." Trina looks up to see Darius standing over her, his eyebrows furrowed, his arms folded.

"What?" she asks, an edge to her voice.

"When had you planned on telling me this?"

She shrugs. "I'm telling you now."

Darius shakes his head. "I don't think it's a good idea."

"Well, it's not like I have much choice in the matter," Trina replies with a loud, annoyed sigh.

"You know half of Memphis. Call up one of your other girlfriends. Tell them you need a place to stay for a couple of days."

"I don't have girlfriends," Trina argues. "I have coworkers and acquaintances."

"Does it really matter? In twenty-four hours—forty-eight, tops—this'll be over and you'll be wishing you hadn't wasted so much energy lugging all of your stuff out of here."

"I'm not coming anywhere near this place *or* that brat until she checks herself and snaps out of Mike's trance."

"She's not entranced; she's in love." Darius smirks. "And you're jealous."

"Please," Trina jeers with a wave of her hand. "Who wants to be married to a cocky, overbearing, holier-than-thou jerk like Mike?"

Darius shrugs. "Apparently you do."

Trina casts him a steely glance. "Get real."

"You may not want Mike," Darius reasons. "But you want what Grace has with him."

"No, I don't," Trina argues, with downcast eyes, her voice puny. The conversation lulls as Darius watches Trina pitifully gather the last of her belongings into two black trash bags.

"Listen," he says, breaking the silence. "I'm not trying to make this any harder for you than it already is. I just…," he exhales loudly. "We tried the whole living together thing once, remember? It didn't work out."

"I get it," Trina says, stepping past him and rolling her bulging suitcase into the living room.

"Don't be like that," Darius pleads.

"Don't be like what?" Trina asks. "Hurt? Offended? I'm sorry, I forgot. What's the proper response to getting played?"

"I didn't play you," Darius says, his tone serious.

"No? You show up at Grace's wedding, uninvited, with a mouthful of apologies and empty promises. Then you sleep with me, practically live here for two weeks, and now, suddenly, when I need a place to stay, you don't want to be with me anymore. What do you call that?"

"I never said I didn't want to be with you. I *am* sorry for what happened and I *do* think we still have a future together. I just want to take it slow."

"Fine! I'm not asking you to marry me, Darius. I need a place to crash— that's it."

Darius kneads his temples. A roommate is more than he had bargained for, but he looks at Trina's belongings gathered by the door and can't bear the thought of her shacked up in a raggedy motel room or roaming aimlessly around Memphis in her old beat-up car. "Alright," he relents. "But only for a few days."

Trina nods. "A few days."

"This is a *temporary* arrangement," Darius stresses.

"Right, temporary. Got it."

He grabs her trash bags, ignoring the knots in his stomach, and plods out of the front door toward the elevators. Trina takes one more look at the loft that has grown to become home over the past couple of years. Her throat tightens with a sob as she blinks back tears. She doesn't want to live with Darius any more than he wants to live with her. But she can't go groveling back to Grace. She won't give her the satisfaction.

Her only hope is to ride it out and pray that Darius is right—pray that tempers will cool, pride will be swallowed, and apologies will be exchanged; pray that today's fiasco will fade into nothingness, sooner rather than later.

But something tells her, as she flips off the lights and shuts the door, that a line's been crossed and things will never quite be the same.

"Dinner of champions," Mike says, affectionately rubbing his belly.

Grace rolls her eyes. "You do realize that you ate your own body weight in pizza, right?"

Mike grins. "What's for dessert?"

"Oh, no," Grace says, shooing him out of the kitchen and switching the lights off behind them. "You keep this up and you're going to get fat."

"You'd still love me," he says, leading the way to their bedroom.

Grace snorts. "Don't be so sure."

Mike turns to face her, his eyes wide. "I am shocked," he says, trying his best to feign offense. "You vowed to stay with me for better or for worse."

Grace laughs. "And I will. As long as you don't get fat."

"I loved *you* when you were—"

"Watch it," she teases, giving his T-shirt a tug.

Mike moves closer and cups her face in his big hands. His wedding band is cool against her right cheek. Grace smiles. He smells like sausage and onion.

"I was going to say, 'when you were pleasantly plump.'"

Grace's eyes narrow. "Nice save."

Mike puckers for a kiss, and Grace happily obliges.

"Sleepy?" he asks, once they've pulled apart.

Grace nods. "Exhausted."

They'd skipped going out for lunch and instead had spent a leisurely afternoon joking and unpacking, sorting through souvenirs, sending emails, and making calls.

It's still early, but jet lag is setting in, and despite her sincerest efforts, Grace's eyelids are drooping to half-mast. With her stomach full and her mind hazy, her only desire is to curl up next to Mike and fall asleep to the rhythm of his quiet breathing.

They go through their bedtime routine, which is still strange and new, yet comfortable at the same time. Standing side by side at their slate Jack and Jill sinks, they brush their teeth together. Grace has spit and rinsed and moved on to her face cream by the time Mike returns his toothbrush to its holder and removes his floss from one of the bathroom drawers.

She wraps her hair, laying it flat with strategically placed bobby pins, and watches as he meticulously works the thin string between each of his teeth, then pulls his dreads back and sloshes a mouthful of Scope. Grace lotions her arms and legs and joins him in the large walk-in closet where they change out of their clothes and into their pajamas—loose-fitting cotton bottoms for Mike and a lace-trimmed baby doll nightie for Grace.

Mike kisses her shoulder before heading to the bedroom, and Grace returns to the bathroom where she rinses the overpriced, aromatic gunk from her face and dabs astringent on her forehead and nose.

She studies her reflection and is pleased with her round cheeks and rich, sepia skin. For perhaps the first time in her adult life, there's nothing she would change about herself. Having been overweight and underweight in just the span of a year, she's content with her size-ten waist and ample hips.

She turns to her side, sucks her stomach in, and raises her chin. Something's different. She looks healthier—happier. Her eyes are vibrant, her face is glowing, and she can't, for the life of her, stop grinning. *Must be love*, she concludes with a shrug.

She gazes down at her wedding ring. It's still there, beaming up at her in all its brilliance. The day after their wedding, on the first leg of their two-day journey to Mauritius, Grace couldn't stop flashing it every chance she got. She paid for her bottled water and magazines using her left hand, she handed over her tickets and passport using her left hand, she even ate and sipped her coffee using her left hand. Mike thought it was hilarious and teased her mercilessly.

"God forbid you ever lose that thing. You'd probably drop dead of a heart attack."

Grace had stretched her arm out, tilted her head, and admired the ring for the umpteenth time. "Probably," she said.

"You keep staring at it like that," he warned jokingly, "and it'll lose its luster."

She'd resolved from then on not to obsess over it anymore, a feat that's proven harder than she anticipated.

She wants to keep it fresh and new for as long as possible, but as she pries her eyes off of it and traipses the short distance to the bedroom, she's certain that the ring, like her marriage, isn't some passing phase. Some days it may shine more than others, but it'll always be precious. It'll always be hers.

"Your turn," Mike says, scooting the Bible toward Grace.

Grace props her pillow against the headboard and climbs into bed.

"Actually," she says, taking the Book and setting it on the nightstand, "I was hoping maybe we could just talk tonight. There's some stuff I need to get off my chest."

Mike sits up. "Sure."

"I've been thinking about what happened today with Trina and what you said afterward about growing too far apart and learning to let go."

"And?"

"Everything you said made perfect sense. It was logical and right and probably exactly what I should do."

"But?" Mike prompts.

Grace bites her bottom lip and sighs. "But sometimes friendships just aren't logical," she says with a shrug. "I know Trina's not your favorite person right now. She's not mine either, but that doesn't mean I don't love her. She's still my best friend, and I still want good things for her."

"Yeah," Mike reaches for Grace's hand and entwines their fingers, "but does she want the same for you?"

"Yes," Grace answers, her nod resolute. "I know her actions haven't shown it lately, but she's got a solid-gold heart."

Mike smirks and hikes a cynical brow.

"She *does*!" Grace insists, giving him a playful shove. "She's a good person. It's just all of this, you know?" she says, gesturing between the two of them and then around the room. "She doesn't take change very well."

"So what do you want to do?" Mike asks.

Grace searches his face as though she might find the answer in his big, caring eyes. "I have absolutely no idea," she admits. "All I know right now is that I can't just write her off, and I need you to be okay with that."

Mike quietly mulls over her request. "I'm okay with it," he says, his voice soft and genuine.

"Really?" Grace asks. She's as relieved as she is surprised.

Mike shrugs. "I can't say I fully understand it, but I trust you and I respect your intentions. After everything that's happened, you love her and you're trying to be a good friend. How can I be upset with you for that?"

"Yeah, I guess," Grace murmurs, secretly unsure of how to be a good friend to Trina, who seems to have booked a one-way ticket to Calamity-ville on the Self-Destruction Express.

"You do what you think is right," he says, giving her knee a supportive squeeze. "At the end of the day, my opinions don't count for much. You're the only person who can decide when enough's enough."

Grace considers his words, which per usual, make all the sense in the world. The only problem is, she's not really sure how to gauge when enough is enough. She suspects that "enough" has come and gone, several times, over the course of her 18-year friendship with Trina, but she's redrawn the line so many times that it's been blurred into nonexistence.

"You know what," she says, scooting closer and taking hold of Mike's other hand. "Let's pray about it and then leave it to God."

Mike smiles. "I like that plan," he says. "You start."

"Dear Heavenly Father," Grace begins, her head bowed, "I come to You tonight, humbled and ashamed, for the way I handled the situation with Trina today. I ask Your forgiveness for the hurtful words I spoke and my crass actions. I let my flesh and my emotions overtake me, and as a result, I failed to exhibit both Your mercy and Your love. I'm so sorry. Please continue to mold and fashion me into the woman You want me to be; a virtuous wife, a righteous mother, an obedient daughter, a gracious friend, and above all, a servant."

"Yes, Father," Mike whispers.

"My heart's desire is to be near to You. Align me with Your will for my life—our lives," she says, squeezing Mike's hands. "And show us where to go from here. Be in control of all of our actions, words, and thoughts and help us, no matter what, to continue to love Trina because You are love."

"And Father," Mike jumps in, "even more importantly than our relationship with Trina, is her relationship with You. She knows You, Father, even if her actions lately haven't shown it. She's wounded and struggling and has obviously lost her way, but no one is too wounded for You to heal, or too lost for You to find. The devil is a liar, Lord. He has her searching for contentment in the deceitful pleasures of the world. But we speak truth over Trina's life. Open her eyes; get her back on Your track, by any means necessary, and we'll be mindful to give You all of the honor, glory, and praise. In Your name we pray, amen."

"Amen," Grace echoes.

"Now," Mike says, tossing back the comforter and patting the empty spot beside him, "for my favorite part of the day."

Grace smiles and crawls over to his side of the massive bed. His warm breath tickles the top of her head as she snuggles close to him and closes her eyes.

"Mmm," he moans contentedly, cradling her tenderly against his chest. "Perfect fit."

6

"Can you make it out to Shantel?"

Grace smiles politely. "Sure," she says, scrawling one of her four routine phrases. "Thanks for your support," she says aloud as she writes. "Best wishes, Grace Naybor." Her signature is wide and loopy with an elegant slant.

She marvels at how foreign her maiden name sounds after only a few months of being married. When her dad had first suggested that she keep "Naybor" as her pen name, she had scoffed. She had no desire to be one of those new millennium women who were too liberated to take a man's name. She was excited to become a Cambridge and wanted the world to know about it. Yet as her novel's preproduction hoopla intermingled with her demanding wedding plans, she found herself grateful at the way the two names allowed her to switch hats so easily.

Grace Naybor is a writer, but at the end of the day when her feet are sore and her brain is scattered, Grace Cambridge is the wife who gets to curl up blissfully next to her husband.

"You're my favorite author," Shantel says, bouncing excitedly. "I drove all the way from Arkansas to see you tonight."

"That means so much," Grace says. "Thank you."

"Your story," she grips her chest, "it really spoke to me. Alexis and Joy's friendship, John's alcohol abuse—I could relate to everything. I'm telling you, your book changed my life."

"How wonderful," Grace says, her tone genuine.

"You're gonna write a sequel, right? You have to. How can you not? We need to know what happens with Wes and Callie, and if John ever gets his act together."

Grace nods distractedly. "It's a definite possibility," she says glancing down at her watch and then up at the long line of other eager readers waiting patiently to have their books signed.

"You have a real gift, you know. Keep using it to serve the Lord."

"I will," Grace says. "Thanks for coming." She hands Shantel her book, in a gentle attempt to hurry her along.

Shantel turns to leave, but then stops. Despite her best efforts, Grace's chest tightens with impatience.

"Can I..." Shantel peers down at Grace with her chin tucked, suddenly shy. "Can I have a hug?" she asks.

Grace's frustration deflates like a helium balloon. "Of course," she says, standing and leaning across the table. She gives Shantel a warm, tight squeeze. "You take care."

Twenty minutes and thirty signatures later, the line is no shorter. Grace finds herself glancing down at her watch in three- and four-minute intervals. Finally, at half past six, she's forced to come to terms with the fact that she's going to have to postpone—again.

She signals to the neophyte manager, a nervous young man, no older than 20, who has spent the past three hours pretending not to stare at her from behind his post at the information booth. He scurries past the registers and around the bargain books and is at her side in a matter of seconds.

"Yes, Mrs. Naybor."

"It's Cambridge," she corrects sweetly. "And I told you, there's no need to be so formal. Just call me Grace."

"Okay," he says, his head bobbing up and down.

"Listen," she says, her tone hushed, "I've got to make a phone call."

He glances nervously at the waiting patrons.

Grace senses his hesitation. "It'll only take a minute," she assures him.

Amidst a slew of irritated groans and curious whispers, she graciously excuses herself, slips into the employee break room, and grips her cell phone. Her stomach flutters as she tries to rehearse what she's going to say. Three months into their marriage and they're already spending more time apart than they are together, thanks to their hectic work schedules.

This'll be the third time this week that Grace has had to cancel her plans with Mike. Tuesday they were supposed to go to the movies, but at the eleventh hour her dad asked her to substitute for his evening Creative Writing workshop.

"Dad," she had said, turning away to avoid Mike's slumped shoulders and disappointed gape, "it's, uh, it's kind of short notice."

"I know, Honey. But I wouldn't ask if I didn't really need your help."

She had hesitated, caught between the two men she loved most in the world. Everything in her had wanted to escape reality for a couple of hours and nestle close to Mike in a dark theater with a tub of buttery popcorn just like they had planned, but there was desperation in her father's voice.

"Yeah, okay," she'd finally replied, cringing as Mike tossed his keys onto the hallway table, walked to his office, and shut the door.

Their second attempt at quality time was on Thursday. Grace was slated to speak at a women's convention in Arizona. She was supposed to fly there and back in the same day, which meant an early evening. "I'll be home around four," she'd promised. "And then we'll go to dinner—just the two of us."

But as fate would have it, a few technical difficulties and a couple of long-winded speakers ran the entire event off schedule. Grace missed her plane to Memphis, and the next two flights were full. She was put on standby and forced to wait in the airport terminal for five agonizing hours. By the time she'd made it home, just past midnight, Mike was fast asleep.

How is she going to explain herself this time? Mike was already upset that she'd agreed to a Saturday book signing. "I thought we decided not to work on the weekends."

"I know, Baby, but this is a real opportunity to market the novel and get some local exposure."

He'd shook his head, his full lips spread into a disapproving line. "Grace, you've got to start setting boundaries."

"I do," she said somewhat indignantly.

"Yeah, but what good are they if you don't stick to them?"

"It's only a couple hours out of the day," she argued. "Besides, I can't cancel now. They're expecting me."

"Well, what about tonight?"

"I'll be here."

His brow rose skeptically.

"I *will*. I promise," she said, turning to leave. "Rabid dogs couldn't keep me away."

Those parting words echo in her ears as she dials home, her finger punching each number in slow motion. With bated breath, she listens as the phone rings once, then twice.

"'Darling, please don't make me wait too long,'" Mike's voice croons off-key to Barry White's 1975 classic, which is playing at full volume in the background. "'I wanna love you, Baby. Can't you see it's only you I want and you I need?'"

Grace laughs heartily and waits for the end of his serenade. "What're you doing?" she asks, once he's turned down the music.

"Me and Barry are gettin' ready for you," he says merrily.

Her countenance changes as her entire body grows weary with regret. "I wish I was there," she says longingly.

"You should be getting your wish soon, shouldn't you? It's almost seven."

"Sweetie, listen," she sighs, "I—"

"Grace," Mike says, his voice stern, "this is becoming a habit."

"It's not my fault," she croaks. "I don't have a choice."

"You always have a choice," he says with an unsympathetic calm.

"Baby, it's out of my control," she insists. "There are thirty women waiting for me as we speak."

"What about me, Grace?" he asks, his words thick with a jarring mixture of hurt and insult. "I've been waiting for you all week."

"What do you want me to do, Mike? Slip out of the back door and leave them all standing there just so we can eat leftover takeout and fall asleep in front of the television?"

Mike looks down at the spread of finely diced vegetables, fresh, peeled shrimp, and gourmet pasta in front of him. After she'd left earlier, he had gotten on the Internet and hunted down a recipe similar to that of her favorite dish at her favorite restaurant.

Armed with a list of ingredients, half of which he couldn't even pronounce, he'd made a special run to the Fresh Market, where he spent the better part of an hour on a frustrating search for ginger root and allspice berries. But the vision of her arriving home to a surprise dinner sparked his excitement and made the effort worthwhile.

Wandering up and down the aisles on his way to checkout, he couldn't resist the urge to pick up a delicate bouquet of Star Gazer lilies, a romantic card, and a "Kiss the Cook" apron.

"Special night?" the cashier had asked with a sly wink.

Mike had grinned and swiped his credit card. "Special woman."

Little did he know that a mere two hours later he'd be struggling to control the irritation roiling in his chest. "You do what you have to do," he says frostily.

"Please try to understand," Grace begs.

Mike sets down the knife he's holding. "I am," he says, wiping his hands clean on the dishtowel next to the sink. "But you don't make it easy."

Grace waits for him to say something else—anything else—but all she hears on the other end is the sound of his soft breathing. "I'll be home as soon as I can." She opens her mouth to say "I promise," but the words stick in her throat like dry cotton. She's said them too many times over the past month and they're starting to lose their conviction.

"You should go," he says quietly.

"I'll see you later."

Mike doesn't respond, and for the first time since they've been married, they hang up the phone without saying, "I love you."

"How many?" the hostess asks.

"Four, but I'm sure they've already been seated," Trina says, scanning the chic restaurant swarming with ambitious hopefuls who only tolerate the under-seasoned food and exorbitant prices because, on a Saturday night, this is the place to see and be seen.

"Over here, Teeny," Joss calls.

Trina recoils at her new nickname and works to unwrench her face as she teeters past dozens of leering eyes to the back of the room.

"You're late!" Josselyn, Tai, and Kendra exclaim simultaneously, each of them looking sultry as they nurse their half-empty glasses of wine.

Trina gives a slight shrug and twirls. "It takes time to look this good," she says, glancing down at her dress, which could stand to be a few inches longer, and her heels, which could stand to be a few inches shorter.

The girls laugh. "Sit your conceited self down." Joss scoots over, making room for Trina to take the empty seat next to her.

"We ordered you the grilled eggplant," Kendra says.

Trina forces a smile. "Sounds good," she says, as the vision of the pepper-corn steak and creamed spinach she had planned to order floats into oblivion.

Her stomach growls ferociously. She takes the linen napkin from the place setting in front of her and lays it across her lap. With great restraint, she bypasses the basket of toasted rolls in the center of the table, grabs the salad tongs, and serves herself an unappetizing heap of lettuce.

"So what are we talking about?" she asks, as she takes her fork and transplants the croutons in her salad onto the small saucer where her dinner roll would be.

"Tai and Alan's latest fight," Joss offers, as she fills Trina's wine glass. "He left."

"Again," Kendra adds with overt disgust.

Tai's eyes brim with tears and she lowers her face.

"Kendra," Joss snips, her gaze is strong, her voice is low but firm, "cut her some slack."

"Or she could cut herself some slack and dump the guy already," Kendra suggests, taking a sip of her wine. "I mean, come on. He's a bum."

"I'm sure that's not true," Trina says, casting a sympathetic glance at Tai.

"How would you know," Kendra asks snottily. "You've never even met him."

Trina holds her tongue and concentrates on her soggy salad.

After two weeks of living with Darius and still no word from Grace, she'd decided that it was time to move on and start turning some of her acquaintances into friends. She had approached Joss, Tai, and Kendra at work on her lunch break. They were sitting at one of the tables in the cafeteria, each with a bottle of Voss in hand, having an animated discussion about knock-off Louis Vuitton bags. Granted it wasn't transcendentalist philosophy or even MTV news, but Trina just wanted to know what it felt like to belong again.

They had welcomed her easily into their small, mismatched clique, and Trina had set to work blending into their world of designer clothes and power lunches. But even now, after regular weekend dinners and hours of frivolous office gossip, she doesn't feel a connection with any of them.

Fair-skinned with scattered freckles and a head full of short, tight curls, Joss is the Plain Jane of the group. With an aversion to makeup and gaudy jewelry, she considers herself a natural beauty. She's comfortable with her size-14 waist and wide hips and doesn't feel the need to explain her strong personality. Articulate and educated with a master's degree in Economics and another in International Studies, she considers herself a free spirit and, for much of her life, has refused to be shackled down by a nine-to-five. Over the years, she's been a hairdresser, a DJ, a caterer, and an event promoter, and she claims to have loved every second of each job. "My happiness is defined through worthwhile memories and experiences," she's said on more than one occasion. "Not by the title on my business card or the emblem on my car."

Kendra was born and raised in Philadelphia. The oldest of three siblings, she was the first one in her family to go to college and graduate—a semester early with honors, no less. She's got a soft side, but it's often overshadowed by her need for control, which manifests itself in her rigid schedule and strict diet. If she's not working, she's exercising; and if she's not exercising, she's shopping. Her life revolves around those three things in that exact order, and she makes no apologies for it. Her svelte five-feet, nine-inch frame, along with her high cheekbones, full lips, deep-set dimples, and thick, lustrous hair, ensure that she's the center of attention wherever she goes, which explains her unshakable cockiness. While Trina appreciates Kendra's strength, she's appalled and downright shocked, at times, by her callous pragmatism.

The product of a Japanese father and a Cuban mother, Tai is a biracial masterpiece. Her wide, slanted eyes, and thick, auburn hair, combined with her golden hue and shapely five-feet, three-inch body gives her a sexy intrigue. But she's too obsessed with Alan—the wayward loaf who's been jerking her chain for three years—to even notice her rare beauty.

Convinced that Alan is only a problem because Tai allows him to be one, Kendra and Joss's take on the matter has been consistently insensitive. Trina, on the other hand, remains quiet on the subject; after all, she understands Tai's dilemma. Darius is Trina's Alan.

"I just wish he would call," Tai says, her eyes sad.

"He will," Trina says. She pats Tai's knee. "He'll be back. He always comes back."

"Only because you let him," Kendra mumbles.

Trina holds her breath for the next three words—the *only* three words that Tai ever seems to come up with.

"I love him," she whines.

"Yeah, well, there are a lot of things I love," Kendra says, unmoved. She glances around the table. "Like bread, for instance. I love bread. Just the smell of it makes my mouth water, but I don't eat it. You know why? Because it's not good for me."

"You can't compare a three-year relationship to your excessive fear of carbs," Trina argues.

"I think what she's saying," Joss cuts in, "is that everything and everyone we want isn't necessarily what we need."

"Exactly!" Kendra pounds the table and points her lipstick-stained fork at Tai. "This was old two years ago, now it's just sad. You could have anyone. Why Alan?"

"Why not Alan?" Trina counters.

"Because he's destroying her," Kendra says. "The old Tai used to be so vibrant—so in love with life. Now all she does is cry and eat."

Joss shakes her head solemnly and sighs. "You're too young to be so depressed. And you're really starting to get—"

"Don't," Trina pleads, her eyes wide.

"I'm getting what?" Tai asks, oblivious.

Joss and Kendra look at each other and nod. "Fat," they say simultaneously.

Tai's face scrunches up as big, salty tears escape from the corner of her eyes and trickle down her cheeks.

Trina's jaw drops. *How can these people possibly call themselves friends?* she wonders, tossing her napkin on the table. "Do you have to be so nasty?" she asks, her demanding stare shaming Kendra first and then Joss.

"No," Tai cries. "They're right. I'm huge."

"You're not huge," Trina says gently.

"I am," she sniffles. "I'm a full-grown cow."

"No, you're not," Trina assures her.

Kendra swallows a mouthful of tomato and smiles. "Well, not *full* grown anyway," she says.

Joss snorts and pretends to brush crumbs from the tablecloth to avoid Trina's murderous glower.

"Why would you say something like that?" Trina asks.

"What?" Kendra shrugs innocently. "It was a joke."

"What gives you the right to be so smug?"

"Her life's perfect, that's what," Tai says, swiping at her eyes.

Trina gives Tai's hand a reassuring squeeze. "That's not true," she says. "Nobody's life is perfect." She arches her brow and waits for Kendra and Joss to back her up.

"Yeah, I guess," Joss says weakly. "I, uh, I got passed up for that promotion last month, remember? And my car's older than I am."

Tai's tears slow to a drip as she soaks in Joss's words.

"Oh! And I have man hands," Joss adds, holding up her sizeable palms as evidence.

"See?" Trina nudges Tai.

The three of them turn their attention to Kendra. "What about you?" Trina prompts.

"What *about me*?"

"You're life's not perfect, right?"

Kendra scoffs. "If you say so."

"Come on," Joss coaxes.

Kendra shrugs. "I don't have any complaints. I love my life. Is that a crime? Besides," she downs the rest of her wine in one gulp, "perfection is a state of mind."

"What does that mean?" Joss asks.

Kendra shrugs. "I take each day one step at a time and live each moment to the best of my ability—no regrets and no doubt. Does that mean my days are problem-free? Of course not. Do I think there are things I can improve on? Maybe. But the bottom line is that happiness is more than a choice; it's a responsibility. And that's what your problem is," Kendra says to Tai. "You're hell-bent on making Alan responsible for your happiness, when it's not his job. It's yours."

"I disagree," Joss says as she slathers her third roll of the evening with a generous spread of butter. "Nothing is that black and white. Especially not matters of the heart. Take me and Eli for instance."

The table erupts in groans. When Joss is around, Trina has quickly learned, every conversation, every debate, every thought, and every example inevitably yields itself to yet another boring, drawn-out, told-for-the-tenth-time story about her and Eli.

Nobody likes Eli, not even Tai—who, with a couple of tequila shots and little bit of coaxing, could slur a convincing list of Judas's endearing qualities.

Eli calls himself an inventor, a term that Kendra and Trina have concluded is just lazy-guy code for broke and unemployed. When he's not napping, he's surfing the Internet or listening to techno music or formulating prototypes for inane ideas like organic chewing gum and edible erasers. His wardrobe consists of one pair of jeans, complete with a hole across each knee, a couple of flannel shirts, and a pair of sneakers that look like they've survived a pit bull mauling.

He smells like pepperoni, he spits when he talks, he cracks his knuckles nonstop, he belches at will, he chews with his mouth open, he bites his nails, and he winks when he says "Hello."

Even on a good day, he's annoying, and though Joss has been dating Eli for a while, Kendra, Tai, and now Trina can't understand her attraction to him.

"Spare us," Kendra pleads.

Joss glares at them, her lips pursed. "All I'm trying to say is that it's impossible to know true happiness when you're alone. If we weren't meant to love and be loved, then we wouldn't be equipped with such intricate, complex ranges of emotion."

"Please," Kendra sneers. "That same delicate range of emotion is also responsible for postal shootings and serial rapists. Love and happiness and anger and rage are illusions, at best."

Joss leans forward in her seat. "Then why do you feel so euphoric when you meet someone new?" she asks intently. "Where does all the hope and excitement come from?"

Kendra shrugs. "Hormones."

"Come on," Joss throws her head back in disbelief. "Not even you are that jaded."

"I'm not jaded," Kendra says, crossing her lithe legs. "I'm rational."

Trina tunes out their mindless babble and wills the food to come so she can go home. Every Saturday they meet at the newest club or the hottest bar or the trendiest restaurant, recycle the same futile argument, and contrive the same ridiculous answers to problems that have only one solution.

Love is not an illusion. God didn't send His Son to die on the cross because His hormones had run amuck. He doesn't forgive us because He's disillusioned by our natures. He cares for us; He grieves for us; He longs for us. *He* is love. As confused as she is about her life, Trina at least knows that much. But she doesn't argue her point. That would be like speaking Russian to ducks. Instead, she fills her glass to the brim and drowns out their absurdity with four swift chugs of wine.

"Love, whether real or imagined, and loneliness both produce their own versions of happiness and pain," Kendra concludes her ten-minute mono-logue. "In the end, it's up to the individual to pick her poison."

The three of them fall into a heavy silence, the official sign that the topic has been flogged to a depressing death. Trina sighs, thankful.

"Speaking of poison," Joss smirks, the way she always does when she's get-ting ready to lighten the mood, "did you guys watch it?"

Tai and Kendra both grip their stomachs and fake gagging as Joss reels into a vivid reenactment of her favorite reality TV show's latest shenanigans. Trina, who spends her weeknights either sleeping or reading, hasn't caught an episode yet. Watching couples scale buildings and eat roaches for cash prizes that aren't even enough to pay for the therapy they'll need when they get home, isn't exactly her cup of tea. But Kendra, Tai, and Joss were hooked the minute the show aired and have dissected each mindless, asinine stunt ever since.

The food eventually arrives, another bottle of wine is ordered, and the discussion jumps from reality TV to shoes to deodorant and back to shoes again. Between the laughter and teasing and the clanging of silverware on porcelain plates, no one notices that Trina has bowed out of the conversation. She picks at her eggplant and smiles and nods on cue, but her mind is somewhere else.

She misses Grace. She misses the loft. She misses her old life. Kendra, Joss, and Tai are not what she had in mind when she set out to develop meaningful relationships. Half of the time she's around them, she's yearning to be someplace else.

Be patient, she has kept telling herself. *Give it time. You're still in the "getting to know you" phase*. But that argument has long since gone stale. She swigs her fifth glass of wine to settle the persistent dread in her stomach. Nearly three months of their high school cattiness has taught Trina only one thing: People really don't appreciate what they have until it's gone.

7

Trina stumbles out of the elevator and down the hall. Her feet are heavy, and she stops to take off her painful pair of satin Jimmy Choo knockoffs before she plods the rest of the way to Darius's front door.

She rummages through her small, beaded clutch for her keys, but keeps pulling out the same tube of waterproof mascara.

The corridor is dimly lit with ultra-modern light fixtures that are bolted onto the cozy, burnt-orange walls. When she first came to stay, the sleek, contemporary look of the building was impressive. But tonight, more than just a little drunk with a pounding head and a twirling stomach, all she wants is to be back at the loft with its generic white walls and bright overhead lights. That way she could actually see what she was doing.

"Want some help?" a familiar voice asks.

Trina nods gratefully and smiles as Darius retrieves the set of keys he had made for her, unlocks the door, and flips on the living room lights.

"I'll take these," he says, relieving Trina of the heels still dangling from her limp fingers. "You look like you had fun tonight."

"What're you doing here?" she asks as Darius leads her down the hall to the bedroom.

"I live here, remember? This is my condo."

"No," she says, stopping to collect her thoughts. In her present state, thinking and walking simultaneously is not an option. "I mean, what were you doing in the hallway?"

"I just got in. My meeting ran late," he says, unable to look into her glazed eyes. "I left you a message."

Trina vaguely recalls checking her voice mail before she left for dinner. He'd said something about making final adjustments to an important presentation. The words are hazy, but she distinctly remembers not believing him.

"How'd it go?" she asks, trying to ignore the spinning room long enough to concentrate on his answer.

"Okay, considering I was thinking about you the whole time." He gives her provocative outfit the once-over. "And it looks like I had good cause."

She ignores his overture and steadies herself against the wall so she can remove her earrings.

He chuckles as he watches her struggle to unclasp her watch. "Dinner was good, I take it?"

She shrugs, wobbly. "I've had better."

"Well," he says, joining her next to the bed, his voice suddenly husky, "you feel like a little dessert?"

Trina groans. "The last thing I want to do is eat."

"That's not the kind of dessert I was talking about," he says, sliding one of her dress straps off of her shoulder and kissing her neck.

Trina smiles, but takes a step back. As much as she'd like to take Darius up on his inviting proposition, there are other, more pressing issues at hand. Like the fact that the cocktail (two parts lettuce, one part eggplant, seven parts Merlot) floating around in her stomach is about two coughs and a gag away from spewing all over his Berber carpet. Not to mention the topic of discussion over dinner.

"Do you love me?" Trina asks.

Darius slides off the other strap. "What kind of question is that?" He plants a trail of kisses down her arm.

Trina gently pushes him away. "A serious one," she says, sitting on the edge of the bed.

Darius searches her face. "What's with you tonight?"

"It's important to me," Trina says. "We hardly ever talk about our feelings or the future. We just kind of stumbled into this living arrangement, and I can't help but wonder sometimes what we're doing."

"We're taking our time," he reasons. "And having fun while we're at it."

"That's not an answer."

His jaw tenses. "You've been listening to your nosey girlfriends again, haven't you?"

"No," she answers, feebly.

Darius rolls his eyes. "Last week, Tai had you convinced that you should get Lasik surgery. And the week before that, Joss almost talked you into highlighting your hair. Oh! And let's not forget last month, when Kendra started the Atkin's diet and converted you into one of those anti-carb extremists."

Trina whimpers, "Am I really that pathetic?"

"Yeah," he says, drawing close for a kiss, "but it's cute."

This time Trina doesn't resist. She kisses him back, slowly at first. His lips are damp and firm; his hard, aggressive pecks are nothing like Ron's soft, affectionate ones had been. He kisses her cheek, then her jaw, deliberately taking his time to move down her neck. His breath is warm, his hands eager.

Trina closes her eyes as he leans her back, his torso pressed so firmly against hers that she can feel the poke of his ribcage.

"I don't think we should," she pants.

"Stop thinking," he whispers. He kicks off his shoes; they hit the floor with two thumps.

"It's late," she protests.

He unzips her dress, slides it down her legs, and tosses it over his shoulder. "So?" he asks, caressing her stomach.

"What about church?"

He chuckles and slips his shirt over his head. "God will forgive you."

"That's what you said last Saturday."

But his only response is a deep, arousing kiss that leaves her hands trembling and her body aching for more. Tomorrow will make the third Sunday in a row that she's missed church, and the second month that she's forgotten to tithe—well, not so much forgot as opted to buy a new pantsuit and a cashmere sweater set instead.

She doesn't like shirking her responsibilities. But in the moment, with Darius in her arms, wine in her system, and an inexplicable emptiness in her heart, all she wants to do is let go and forget.

Mechanically, she pushes the pillows onto the floor, pulls the comforter back, and slides under the sheets, where Darius joins her. He reaches for the lamp, and the last thing she sees before the room goes black is her Bible resting on the dresser.

Grace slips off her heels before tiptoeing out of the elevator. The foyer's marble floor is cold beneath her sheer stockings as she follows the soft glow of light coming from the kitchen. It's ten past nine, two hours later than when she promised to be back. Her mind races to remember the argument she'd pieced together on the drive home.

Mike had known that getting her book off the ground was going to require hard work and long hours. It was part of the business, just like weeklong board meetings and three-hour conference calls were part of running his company, *Life Sketch*. They'd discussed it in pre-marriage counseling; they'd prayed about it and agreed to make their schedules work, no matter what the compromise—no matter what the sacrifice.

There'd been many times, in the course of their relationship, when Mike cancelled or postponed their plans. Was it irritating to her? Yes. At times it was downright infuriating, but she understood how much his company meant to him, how much of himself he'd invested in it and all the reasons why. *Life Sketch* was his dream, and he had fought, against all odds, to turn it into a reality. Now she's trying to do the same thing with her writing, but it's going to take patience and support. That's all she's asking of him—to give her a little grace while she does what it takes to make *her* dreams come true.

She grins inwardly, pleased with her negotiating skills, and enters the kitchen, her airtight case resting on the tip of her tongue. But Mike is nowhere to be found.

She walks through the kitchen and into the adjoining dining room. Her cheeks grow warm at the sight of two beautiful place settings, complete with linen napkins and candles. Resting under a vase of beautiful pink and white lilies in the center of the table is a note:

Gone to bed. Dinner's in the oven.

Grace fingers the flowers' delicate petals and grows sick with guilt as the feisty spunk she's mustered evaporates. She sits down at the table where she was supposed to enjoy Mike's romantic dinner and takes in his thoughtfully prepared surprise. "I'm a terrible wife," she mutters, in absolute disgust. How could she let this happen? How could she have been so inattentive? So insensitive?

And to make matters worse, she had had the nerve to get testy with him—the audacity to be irritated and indignant. She hangs her head, frustrated by her lack of perspective, her lack of appreciation.

There are women who will marry and divorce and marry again, five times over, but will never experience the kind of passionate, focused love she receives from Mike. They won't ever know a gentle touch or hear a fervent prayer or experience a spur-of-the-moment romantic gesture. There are women who wake up every morning to the sad reality that their husbands are strangers, women who are permanently hardened by the belief that Prince Charming is a myth.

In a world in such short supply of good men, Mike is the rarest of gems. He could've had anyone, but he chose her. He wants her—loves her. Maybe *that's* the dream come true she needs to focus on.

Ashamed and humbled, Grace schleps down the dimly lit hall toward their bedroom. She turns the knob slowly and eases the door open. With the lights off and the thick, heavy curtains drawn, the room is black. She stands still, her eyes adjusting to discover Mike lying in bed. He's facing the wall, his bare back turned to her. "Mike," she whispers.

He doesn't move, but she can tell by his soft, synchronized breathing that he's not asleep. Slipping off her suit jacket and tossing it onto the couch, Grace crawls into bed with him and places her chin on his arm.

"You mad at me?" she asks, her voice small and pitiful.

"Depends," he says.

"On what?"

"How sorry you are."

"I feel awful," she says with a whimper. "You have no idea."

"I bet," he grunts, clearly unconvinced.

"Baby, why didn't you tell me you'd planned dinner?"

"I was trying to surprise you," he says. "Besides, it wouldn't have made a difference."

Grace swallows hard, her regret briny. He's right. Dinner or no dinner, she wouldn't have left the signing early. "I messed up," she says. "Big time. I'm sorry. I am. How can I make it up to you?"

"It's not a big deal, Grace." He shifts his weight and hugs his pillow to the side of his face. "Just forget about it."

"No," she says, tugging at his shoulder. "I don't want you to go to sleep angry with me."

"I'm not angry," he says, shrugging her away. "I'm disappointed."

Grace moans. "That's worse."

Mike doesn't respond.

"What can I say? Tell me what to say to make it better?"

"Nothing." He yawns. "Just let it go. It's over."

She hops off of the bed and flips on the bedroom lights. "We have to talk this out," she says, hands on hips. "I can't go to sleep with this tension between us, and if I don't sleep, you don't sleep."

Despite his most fervent efforts, Mike can't suppress a grin. He rolls onto his back and crosses his arms behind his head. "Is that so?"

"I'm your wife," she stomps, her bottom lip poked out, "and I'm asking you to tell me how to fix it."

"Grace, it's okay—really. These things happen. You don't have to say or do anything."

She sighs, still unsatisfied.

"We have church in the morning," he says, patting her pillow. "Why don't you go get ready for bed?"

She trudges gloomily to the closet and changes out of the rest of her pantsuit into her nightgown. Part of her wanted to be chastised—rebuked for her deplorable behavior. If he had raised his voice or uttered something harsh, she would know they were alright—she could be sure he'd gotten it out of his system. But all he would say was, "It's okay," when clearly it wasn't. And as backward as it seems, that only makes her feel worse.

Grace grabs her night scarf, bobby pins, and brush and turns to go into the bathroom, when her foot kicks something across the closet floor. She looks down to see one of Mike's Barry White CDs and smiles, remembering his sweet, albeit dissonant, serenade.

A thrill darts up her spine. She drops everything but the brush and sashays back into the bedroom with the dramatic flare of a veteran lounge performer. "'There's only, only one like you,'" she sings into the hairbrush, offering her best Barry White impression. "'There's no way they could have made two.'"

Mike laughs with gusto and sits up. "'You're all I'm living for,'" she continues, cavorting across the room before climbing onto the bed. "'Your love I'll keep forevermore.'"

"'You're the first,'" she sings, inching closer and planting a kiss on his forehead. "'You're the last.'" She kisses his jaw softly. "'My everything.'"

Mike shakes his head, amazed. "You win," he says.

She falls into his arms, relieved and grateful once again for his willingness to understand and forgive. His kiss is amorous—sincere and keen.

They settle on their sides, their legs entwined, their faces only inches apart. Grace relaxes against the weight of his hand on the small of her back and caresses his cheek with her thumb.

"That was a world-class rendition," he says, smiling.

"Hey," she admonishes. "Be nice."

"I'm serious," he says smirking, his voice hushed with fond amusement. "You should go on tour."

Grace laughs. "Just what the world needs."

"No," he says, his smile fading. "Just what I needed." His gaze is intense and penetrating.

"What?" she whispers, searching his face, curious as to what he sees.

He brushes a strand of hair from her forehead. "I miss you."

The glint of forlorn loneliness in Mike's eyes invades Grace, pillaging the last of her half-hearted excuses and mundane apologies until she's left with nothing but blistering remorse. Slipping her arm under Mike's, and hooking it around his waist, she buries her face into his warm chest and sighs.

"I miss you too."

"Maybe we need help," he says, running the tips of his finger through her hair. The words rumble and vibrate against Grace's ear.

Grace lifts her head, her brows furrowed. "What, like a marriage counselor?"

"No, no," he chuckles and lays her head back down. "Like an assistant. You know, someone who's good at logistics—someone who can coordinate your schedule."

"Hm," she hums, the idea corresponding perfectly with her need, like the last piece of an intricate puzzle. "Why didn't I think of that?"

"We can put out an ad on Monday," he says.

Grace's stomach responds with a decisive growl followed by several noisy gurgles.

Mike smirks. "What was that?"

"I'm hungry," she says, rubbing her belly. "Is it too late to have dinner?"

He kisses the top of her head. "Of course not."

They untangle themselves, and Grace follows Mike down the hall and into the kitchen.

"Go sit," he says with a playful pat.

She waits patiently in the dining room as he reheats and arranges the food. He emerges a few minutes later looking adorable in his flannel pajama bottoms and "Kiss the Cook" apron.

"Smells good," Grace says, eyeing the steaming plate of food in his oven-mitt-covered hands.

Mike sets her dinner down on the embroidered linen place mat in front of her and watches for her reaction. He's pleased as Grace squeals, a smile spread from ear to ear.

"Is that Caribbean pasta with shrimp?" she asks, excitedly.

"Well," he shrugs, "my version of it, anyway."

"You made this?" she asks, her head tilted to the side, her eyes brimming with glee.

"From scratch."

"I don't deserve you," she says adoringly.

Mike smiles. "Let's see if you still feel that way after you've tasted it."

She places the linen napkin in her lap and picks up the fork. Mike observes her expression as she takes her first tentative bite. "Mmm," she moans. "This is good."

He beams as she spears a shrimp and pops it into her mouth. "No, seriously," she says, chewing intently, "this is really, really good."

"What can I say?" He folds his arms smugly and leans back in his chair. "When you've got it, you've got it."

Grace eyes him suspiciously. "You sure you made this?" she teases.

He grins. "Pretty positive."

"Well then, you know what this means." She shovels a mound of pasta into her mouth.

Mike surveys her rapidly depleting portion of food. "You're not going to share?"

"*That*," she laughs, "and you're now officially in charge of all the cooking."

"But that's *your* job."

Grace looks at him, her loaded fork hovering midair. "Excuse me?"

"It's true. The virtuous woman in Proverbs 31 got up while it was still dark and provided food for her family."

"Yeah, well," Grace snorts, "her husband probably couldn't cook."

Mike laughs. "I'll tell you what," he says, glancing down at the last shrimp on her plate. "You let me have that and I'll cook you dinner every Saturday for the next month."

She sinks her fork into the lone morsel of seafood and waves it temptingly under his nose before yanking it away. "Dinner every Saturday for the next two months and a kiss every night," she barters.

He leans forward. "Dinner for the next *three* months," he says, taking hold of her wrist and guiding the shrimp toward his mouth, "a hundred kisses every day, and my heart for all of eternity."

"You drive a hard bargain," she says, smiling as his lips close around the fork. "But what woman in love could ever refuse a deal like that?"

He runs his hand down her thigh. "Leave the dishes," he says.

Knowingly, she gets up, and hand in hand, they return to their bedroom where they close the door and turn off the lights.

8

"Excuse me. Sorry. Excuse us. Thanks. Sorry. Excuse us," Grace and Mike mutter as they shuffle sideways down the row of seated churchgoers, careful not to step on anyone's tucked shoes or trip over the array of Bibles and purses obstructing their tight path.

"Well, well," Ron says, standing. His blue eyes twinkle gray in the sanctuary's soft lighting. "Look what the wind blew in."

"You look familiar," Grace teases and gives Ron a warm hug.

"Hey," he says, stepping back and gesturing toward the woman seated beside him, "you remember Tamara, right?"

"Of course," Mike says. He stretches out his arm and leans over Grace and Ron to shake Tamara's hand. "It's good to see you again, Tammy."

Grace smiles kindly as she tries to figure out: first, when, if ever, she's met this woman before; and second, how Mike knows her well enough to call her "Tammy."

Her name doesn't ring a bell, though her light, honey-hued skin, deep-set eyes, and elfin hands remind Grace a lot of Trina. Only in place of Trina's shoulder-length curls, Tamara sports shortly cropped hair with bangs that sweep dramatically across her forehead. *She's pretty*, Grace thinks, as she takes in Tamara's sharp facial features, regal neck, and ripe lips. She's more than pretty; she's stunning, and she's not the kind of woman Grace would forget meeting.

"Your wedding was lovely," Tamara says, her eyes pinched together sweetly. Her smile reveals two rows of perfectly white, perfectly straight teeth. "You made a beautiful bride."

"Thanks," Grace preens, uncertain of why she's so surprised by Tamara's kind words. "That's really nice of you." At least now she knows why she doesn't remember meeting her. The President of the United States could have come to the wedding and Grace wouldn't have noticed. She was too busy being the buffer between Trina and everyone else.

"We're glad you came," Mike adds.

"Oh! It was my pleasure," she gushes. "Any friends of Ronnie are friends of mine."

Grace watches Ron's cheeks flush as Tamara takes hold of his hand and strokes his knuckles. Uneasiness grips her stomach.

"So how's it going?" Ron asks.

Grace isn't sure to whom the question is directed. She can't seem to pry her eyes away from Ron and Tamara's tightly entwined fingers. She's seen Ron with other women. He's been in several relationships since Trina, but none of them have lasted. No other woman fit him the way Trina did. No one could produce the same chemistry, the same ease—until now.

"Things are going well. Really well," Mike answers. "How've *you* been?

Ron's shrug is served with a smirk. "Pretty good considering two of my favorite people have been neglecting me."

"Oh come on," Grace says. "Neglect is a strong word."

Ron laughs. "Neglect is the *only* word. I haven't seen you guys or even talked to you in almost a month."

"Really?" Mike tilts his wrinkled forehead. "Hasn't felt like that long."

"It's nice to know I've been missed," Ron says, his chin scrunched with mock indignation.

"Have a heart." Tamara leans into him. "You know how newlyweds are. They can't get enough of each other in the beginning."

"She's right," Mike chuckles. "Give it a couple more months, though. I'm sure we'll have made the transition from love-struck soul mates to bitter, estranged roommates by then."

"I've waited this long." Ron smiles. "I guess a couple more months can't hurt."

"That's the spirit," Grace says, her nod firm.

"In the meantime," Ron says, stealing a quick, shy peek at Tamara, "I'll just have to get to know some of my newer friends better."

There it is again, that roil in her gut. Grace crosses and uncrosses her legs in an attempt to get comfortable.

"Well, before we go back to ignoring each other," Mike says, "why don't you let us take you and Tammy to lunch after church?"

Ron bounces his brows expectantly at Tamara.

"Sure," she says. "Sounds like fun."

The first few chords of "I'm Glad to Be in the Service" are pounded out on the piano, signaling the beginning of service. Grace, Mike, Ron, and Tamara stand to their feet along with everyone else and clap in rhythm as the choir processes joyfully down the side aisles and onto the stage.

"'He didn't have to let me live,'" Grace sings distractedly. "'He didn't have to let me live. I'm glad to be in the service one more time.'"

She surveys the sea of rejoicing attendees with their upturned, beaming faces and wonders if Trina is somewhere in the crowd. Slowly, she peruses the packed rows within her line of vision, squinting, hoping to discover Trina safely tucked into the throng. Grace has played this game every Sunday since Trina moved out, but she's only spotted her once—three weeks ago.

Trina had come in late and alone, wearing wrinkled slacks that sagged at her waist and pooled over her heels, a fitted, low-cut blouse, and no makeup. Her hair was pulled back and slicked down, and her lobes were saddled with a pair of gaudy chandelier earrings.

She had looked tired and small, fragile even, her shoulders hunched, as she gripped her program and followed the usher down the aisle.

Grace had studied her mannerisms. She watched Trina sit and stand mechanically. She watched her stare absently into space as everyone else recited the responsive reading. She watched her check and re-check her watch, fish through her purse, apply two coats of lip balm, and pop mints through the entire sermon, never once cracking open her Bible.

She had seemed strangely removed and detached from everything going on around her, as if she was existing instead of living.

"I should've just talked to her," Grace had admitted that night as she watched Mike pack for his flight to New York the following morning.

"You could always call her," he said, disappearing into the closet and emerging seconds later with two ties and a pair of slacks.

She shook her head. "I can't. It wouldn't be right. She's the one who messed up. *She* should come to *me*."

Mike smirked. "How old are you again?"

"Why should I offer the olive branch when I didn't do anything wrong?"

"You're right," he said, zipping the bag closed and joining her on the couch. "It makes much more sense to just brood over it."

"I'm not brooding."

"Really?" He scanned her furrowed brows and folded arms. "What do you call it?"

Grace shrugged and sank sadly into the cushions. "I don't think I'm even angry anymore," she said. "I just want her to apologize. To stop acting like a victim and admit that she was wrong."

"I know." Mike ran his thumb down her jaw. "But it doesn't always work that way. Sometimes you have to swallow your pride and take solace in knowing that you're the bigger person."

Grace had awoken the next morning determined to do just that. Clad in her pajamas and slippers, she shuffled to the living room and retrieved her cell phone from her purse. She would teach Trina by example and that would be its own reward.

"Hey Trina, it's Grace," she'd practiced aloud, as she scrolled through her phone's address book in search of Trina's office number.

"Trina!" she tried again with more enthusiasm. "Hey it's me, Grace! I'm just calling to say hi," she said breezily. "How's life been treating you?" She shook her head. That sounded too casual—too rehearsed. Wiping her palms, which had suddenly grown clammy, against her soft flannel pants, she took a deep breath and regrouped.

"We need to talk," she said, abandoning her light, carefree approach for a calm, rational one. Only instead of cool and collected, she sounded icy and confrontational.

She shifted her weight from one foot to the other and cleared her throat. "Can we talk?" she tried again, this time her tone syrupy. Too artificial.

"I was hoping, if you had a sec, that maybe we could talk." She shook her head again and sighed. Too desperate.

Eighteen years of friendship reduced to this, she thought resentfully, as she flopped across the love seat, her legs dangling over the armrest. She could rehearse as many different versions of the same conversation for as long as she wanted. Nothing was going to sound right coming from her lips because the words that needed to be said belonged to Trina.

Grace had stared at Trina's number on the phone's miniature screen. "Be the bigger person," she murmured, her finger hovering over the green *Send* button.

Just then, a slight movement across the room had caught Grace's attention. She watched as a large dust bunny tumbled its way down the length of the baseboard and into the corner where several other balls of dust had accumulated. She took one more look at Trina's number and flipped the phone closed. She'd call after she vacuumed.

By the time Mike came home three days later, the kitchen was spotless, the hallway closets were organized, the library was dusted, the floors mopped, the windows washed, and the bathrooms disinfected. She'd also finished another chapter of her manuscript and replied to all of her readers' emails. But her cell phone remained in its cradle, untouched.

"Are you pregnant?" Mike had asked, stepping out of the pristine pantry that she'd organized alphabetically.

"What?" she tittered, incredulous and amused in equal measure.

He looked down at the buffed marble floors and then up at the gleaming appliances. "This is what pregnant women do, right? They nest."

Grace had laughed. "I'm not nesting," she said, plopping onto one of the stools lined against the center island. "And I'm not pregnant."

"Too bad." He ran his finger down the sanitized countertop, checking it for dust. "I could get used to this."

"Not helping," she bleated.

Mike's grin was cast with warm sympathy. "I can't help if you don't tell me what's wrong."

"It's Trina," she said, her eyes wide, her voice small and helpless. "I'm worried about her."

"But not enough to actually call her," he postulated.

"I know," she sighed. "It doesn't make any sense."

He leaned against the counter, one leg crossed over the other. "Who said it has to? When you're ready to talk to her, you will."

"But she needs me *now*," Grace had argued, still haunted by the sight of strewn beer cans and Darius in his boxers. She could only envisage the dysfunction taking place under their roof.

"Maybe that's the problem," he said, his soft gaze searching her face. "It's not enough anymore that she needs you. You have to *want* to be there for her."

Grace had lain awake in bed that night, the comforter pulled up to her chin, her eyes planted firmly on the shadow-streaked ceiling, thinking.

For as long as she'd known Trina, they'd operated by one set of rules: Trina made the messes, and Grace cleaned them up. Whether they were in junior high where Grace spent her weekends completing Trina's extra credit assignments so Trina wouldn't fail, or in college where Grace went to Trina's classes and took notes while Trina slept off a night of binge drinking, or as adults when Grace gave Trina a place to stay after Darius beat her up and kicked her out. Grace was always right there to break Trina's fall without question or grouse because the arrangement worked; because Trina needed help and Grace wanted to be needed.

But between finding her father, losing her mother, getting married, promoting her first novel and writing a second one, Grace's priorities had changed. Keeping track of Trina and her endless procession of dramas and traumas wasn't as crucial as it once was. Grace had other relationships to maintain, other trials to pass, other mishaps to endure.

Suddenly, paying Trina's parking tickets so her license wouldn't get suspended or filing her taxes online the day before the deadline because she forgot to do it herself didn't seem as important as greeting Mike when he got home from a business trip or having an impromptu lunch with her dad.

Grace no longer confused being loved with being needed. She guest spoke at her father's classes and picked up Mike's dry cleaning and hosted book signings because she wanted to, not because she felt obligated or required. But with Trina, everything was a necessity, an intrinsic need. If Grace didn't do it, it wouldn't get done, and they would both suffer in the long run.

She could forgive Trina for the wedding and for the cigarettes and for the beer and for Darius. She could even shelve her ego and offer the first apology, but then what? They'd hug and promise never to fight again, but in time, there would just be more of the same: more last minute errands and eleventh hour fixes, more loans, more refereeing, more crossed boundaries—more messes for Grace to clean up.

As much as she loved Trina, as much as she worried about her, Grace couldn't revert to their old roles, to their old rules. She'd changed.

Grace glances at Ron and Tamara huddled cozily over the open Bible resting in both their laps. Everything's changed. And the feeling is strangely bittersweet.

"What time is it?" Trina croaks, her voice raspy, her throat dry and sour. She tries to roll off of her stomach and onto her side, but her neck can't bear the heft of her head, which feels like a two-ton weight. The dull throbbing in her temples quickly graduates to a persistent rhythmic pounding. She groans and collapses back into her original position.

Thanks to her hypersensitive hearing, courtesy of her monstrous hangover, the spastic clatter of mid-morning traffic nine floors below sounds more like evening rush hour barreling through the bedroom. She winces at the ringing in her ears.

"Water," she pleads into her pillow. "Water and Tylenol." She breaths deeply and swallows back a wave of nausea. "Extra strength."

Darius doesn't stir.

"Hey," she mutters, reaching out her limp arm to shake him awake. "Did you hear me?" Her hand fumbles across the vacant space where he's supposed to be lying. She sits up gingerly and studies the dented pillow and thrown back comforter next to her in his place. Her forehead wrinkles.

It's starting all over again: the implausible Saturday night meetings and early morning disappearances. Twice last week, he got "roped" into "unavoidable business obligations," and both times just happened to "forget" his pager and "accidentally" turned off his cell phone. She knows this pattern—she knows what it means. How can she not? This is almost exactly where they'd left off two years ago.

He's in the beginning stages now, where he comes home late with glassy eyes and stale excuses, where he still tries to appease her with wet kisses and passionate trysts. But it's only a matter of time before she's bumped off his list of priorities altogether. It may take one month or four or six, but eventually, he'll swagger home five hours late with his tie dangling carelessly from his pocket and a chip resting squarely on his shoulder. He'll breeze past her with pursed lips and a set jaw and warn her to back off before she's even had the chance to say anything. That's when she'll know that she's lost him—how she'll know that they've come full circle.

Resting against the cool lacquer headboard, she closes her eyes and fights, once again, to disregard the fact that her life has turned into a pathetic version of *Where's Waldo?* Only instead of spotting a smiling cartoon character sporting Coke-bottle glasses and a red and white beanie, she wakes up every morning and is forced to acknowledge the invariable list of problems with her present situation.

I could call it, What's Wrong With This Picture?, she cogitates with bitter irony as she surveys Darius's sparsely furnished, unkempt bedroom and glances down at the rumpled sheet covering her naked body.

Disgust and disappointment churn in her gut like emotional indigestion. How did she regress back to this? Back to this papier-mâché existence with its shellacked shell and hollow inside. She's been here before; she's done this—the live-in relationship and vain girlfriends, the unfulfilling Saturday nights and Sunday morning hangovers. It all looks so chic, so reasonably modern and uninhibited, so *Sex and the City*.

Only in the daylight, exposed, with her matted hair, banging head, and missing boyfriend, reasonably uninhibited feels more smarmy than chic.

Before this detour, before she had unwittingly unraveled her own life to punish Grace, mornings had been her favorite time of day. She'd open her eyes, turn over, and glow with gratefulness for another fresh start—for another 24 hours nascent with opportunity and possibilities. She'd spring out of bed with praises on her tongue and marvel with rehabilitated vigor and hope at her surroundings.

But now, so deeply ensconced in a lifestyle that goes against her beliefs, she would rather hide away in a bedroom that's not hers and cling to the sheets of a man who's not her husband than get up and face herself and all of her deficiencies.

Like a broken VCR, her mind replays the tension-filled wedding reception and the heated scene between her and Grace at the loft. Regret grips her lungs each time she pictures Grace's face contorted with shocked hurt.

Would it have been so hard to say, "Congratulations, I wish you well?" Couldn't she have just thrown her arms around Mike and, however tearfully, told him to take care of Gracie—to love her enough for the both of them every day? It all seems simple now, clear and concise. She only had to put Grace first—to love her the way she'd always claimed to love her—to make Grace's happiness a priority, even if that meant stepping aside and watching someone else become her best friend.

In hindsight's wake, Trina would do everything differently. She would've never skipped out on Grace's wedding reception. She would've stayed to the very end, regardless of the seating arrangements, regardless of Ron and Malikah. She would've stayed for Gracie—no matter how excruciating it would've been to watch her move on, to move forward for the first time to a place where she couldn't follow. And she wouldn't have left with Darius. She would've turned and walked away like she should have—like she'd started to.

If she had, she'd be at church right now, sitting next to Grace and Mike, listening to an electrifying sermon or singing an inspired hymn instead of lying in the proverbial bed she made, miserably dreaming of what she could have or should have or would have done differently.

She sighs. *Shoulda, Coulda, Woulda*—that's been her swan song lately. Like a cocky prize fighter, Trina had bobbed when she should have weaved; she had spoken when she should have stayed silent, stomped her feet when she could have smiled, clung extra tightly when she should have let go, and as a result, she's been knocked flat on her back.

But how can she slink back to Grace after all these months—after all the hurtful words she's spewed, all of her cheap shots at Mike and selfish tantrums—and ask for forgiveness? Saying "I'm sorry" seems far too inadequate—like attempting to pay a million-dollar debt with a one-dollar bill.

Besides, Trina reasons, it's not like Grace has gone out of *her* way to forge any sort of reconciliation. It takes two people to maintain a friendship and it takes two to let one die. It's not like Grace doesn't know where Trina is or where she works. She could have left a message or just happened to be in the neighborhood. She could have come up with a dozen different excuses to get together. In fact, Trina had been banking on Grace's caving in. Grace always caves in.

But as the first few days at Darius's place stretched into anxiety-filled weeks and now into heart-wrenching months, Trina realizes that the ball is in her court—not Grace's. If she wants her best friend back, she's going to have to go get her—pride on platter, foot in mouth, and egg on face.

Queasy at the thought, Trina sluggishly climbs out of bed, the sheet wrapped tightly around her petite frame, and schleps to the kitchen to retrieve her own Tylenol and water.

The cool liquid is soothing as it glides down her parched throat. Greedily, she gulps the first glass and then fills it a second time and carries it with her back to the bedroom.

Setting the sweaty glass on the waist-high dresser, Trina runs a damp hand through her stiff hair and studies her reflection in the mirror hanging on the wall in front of her. Her fingertips graze the delicate wrinkles at the corner of her eyes and mouth. She frowns as she hikes up her sagging cheeks and tries to smooth away the oval bags under her eyes. It's been a long time since she's looked or felt this old. But then again, it's been a long time since she let her life veer this far off course.

What she needs is someone to talk to—someone to be her sounding board, to tell her where to go from here. Because the truth is, she can't bear the thought of spending one more week pretending she wouldn't give anything for Grace to be on the other end of the phone when it rings. She can't endure any more empty, drunken weekends or soul-stanching nights of pre-marital lust. She won't sit by and watch herself morph into a morally devoid cliché in the name of societal normalcy.

There has to be a way out—a healthier solution than stewing in a vat of her own never-ending mistakes. Someone has to have an answer—an answer better than the few she can provide herself.

But what do you do when you're too ashamed to face God and your previous source of succor is now the source of all your confusion and doubt? Trina wonders.

She stifles a sigh, picks up the phone, and dials, with chilling uncertainty, the closest person she has to a friend.

9

"So, Tammy," Grace says, leaning back against the restaurant booth's cushy upholstering, "tell me about yourself. How long have you and Ron been…," she pauses, unsure of their official status and reluctant to label it for them. "Friends," she finally concedes.

Tamara looks at Ron to collaborate an answer. "What would you say? Two—three months?"

"Sounds about right," Ron says behind a sip of iced tea.

"They met at a job fair," Mike offers.

Grace eyes Ron. "I didn't know you were in the market."

"I wasn't. My company sent me to recruit new blood."

"She asked for an application," Mike says.

"I asked her on a date," Ron continues.

"And the rest is history," Tamara finishes.

Grace's eyes move from Mike to Ron to Tamara and back. The three of them are like a well-oiled storytelling machine. Their rapport is unnerving. "How do you know all of this?" she asks Mike.

"The wedding," he answers, a tortilla chip with artichoke dip halfway to his mouth.

"Well, where was I?" Grace inquires.

"One guess," Ron bleats rather frostily.

The table quickly falls silent.

Since the wedding, Trina has become a conversational Bermuda Triangle; dialogue or discussion that ventures anywhere near her mysteriously disappears.

Anytime Grace tries to brave the topic of her execrated best friend, her father politely yet swiftly changes the subject, Ron sneers and mutters snide comments, and Malikah's latest reaction is to ask, "Trina who?" Aside from Mike, it's as if everyone is content to pretend like Trina no longer exists.

"It was a whirlwind day," Mike says in an attempt to resuscitate the conversation. "I'm surprised we could remember our own names when it was over."

"I know what you mean," Tamara says with an earnest nod. "I helped to plan my sister's wedding a few years back, and it completely consumed me. I mean, invitations and menus and reservations and fittings and rehearsals—it's a never-ending cyclone of detail."

"Yeah," Grace sighs, her smile small and wistful, "but it's worth it."

Tamara gives a cynical snort. "Let's hope," she says. Her lofty tone doesn't match her unassuming smile. "I read somewhere recently that fifty percent of all marriages fail in the first two years. It's just sad—a true testament of how far gone we are as a society."

Grace blinks, nonplussed and uncertain how to respond. There's something underhanded about what Tamara just said, but she can't quite put her finger on it.

"Well, if any couple can stand the test of time, it's Grace and Mike," declares Ron.

"Oh! Of course," Tamara says, wide-eyed, one hand pressed against her chest. "I wasn't trying to insinuate that your marriage would fail."

"Don't be silly," Mike says. "We know what you meant."

Grace doesn't respond. *If that's not what Tamara was insinuating, then why did she say it?*

"So, Mrs. Big-Time Novelist," Ron turns to Grace, "how's the book doing?"

"Really well, actually," she says, thankful for the change in subject.

Tamara claps her hands like a trained seal. "As soon as Ron told me you wrote a book, I ran out and bought a copy," she announces proudly.

"Really?" Grace asks, not so much flattered as suspicious. "What did you think?"

"I haven't gotten around to finishing it, but from what I've read so far, it's an admirable first effort."

Again, Grace finds herself at a loss, unable to provide a civil response to yet another one of Tamara's not-so-civil observations.

"Is the tour keeping you busy?" Ron asks.

Grace shrugs. "It can get hectic at times, but I'm hanging in there."

"Barely," Mike says. "We're taking out an ad on Monday for a personal assistant. She's liable to burn out at the rate she's going."

"You know," Tamara says, "I spent six years as an administrative assistant at the *Commercial Appeal*."

Mike nods. "I remember you mentioning that."

Grace's stomach knots as she mentally fast-forwards the discussion to its inevitable conclusion.

"Maybe I could interview?" Tamara asks, her voice sweet and smooth like caramel. She tosses her head to the side, demurely flicking her bangs from her eyes.

What a twit, Grace thinks, incredulous. *There's not a snowball's chance in—*

"Yeah, sure," Mike agrees, picking up his glass of water. "Couldn't hurt. Might save us the trouble of weeding through a bunch of potential wackos."

Tamara peers up at Mike from underneath her batting lashes and giggles. "You won't be disappointed," she trills.

Grace digs her heel into Mike's foot.

Water spews from his mouth and dribbles down his chin as he hacks fiercely and leans forward in an effort to catch his breath.

"You alright?" Ron asks.

"Yeah," he croaks, dabbing at the spots on his shirt and tie with his napkin. "Water went down the wrong pipe."

"So when should I come by?" Tamara asks.

Mike heeds the throbbing in his foot and waits for Grace to answer.

"We'll call you," she says coolly.

A moment later the entrées arrive. After they bless the food, Mike and Ron dig into their steaks while Tamara combs aimlessly through her salad with her fork.

"Did the waitress forget your dressing?" Mike asks.

"I don't eat dressing," Tamara informs them. "It's too high in fat."

"They have a lite vinaigrette," Grace says.

Tamara shakes her head. "Too much sodium." She spears a cucumber. "Fat, sugar, and sodium are going to bring this country to its knees," she says matter-of-factly. "Mark my words."

Grace resists the overwhelming urge to roll her eyes. Somehow potato chips and candy bars don't seem quite as lethal as AIDS, war, and drugs.

"Thirty percent of Americans are obese," Tamara continues. "And fifty-four percent are overweight," she says, cutting her eyes accusingly at Grace. "We've got to wake up. It's an embarrassing epidemic."

Grace washes down a forkful of her smothered chicken and gravy-covered mashed potatoes with a sip of cherry cola. "Personally," she says, "I think society places far too much emphasis on the physical."

"That's easy for you to say. You, at least, have a pretty face," Tamara counters, chewing slowly on a wisp of Romaine. "Not everyone has stunning eyes and a distinctive smile to fall back on."

Grace stares, outraged and dumbfounded. If she weren't the target of Tamara's verbal assaults, she might be impressed by them. It takes skill to insult someone multiple times in a group setting without making anyone else flinch.

In a last-ditch effort to keep herself from saying anything she'd have to ask the Lord to forgive her for later, Grace stuffs her mouth with another forkful of food and concentrates on getting through her meal and away from Tamara as quickly as possible.

"See?" Kendra pants, decelerating her treadmill with the push of a button. Her glistening shoulders and forearms flex as she dabs at the sweat sliding across her temples and down her neck. "Didn't I tell you a good, hard work-out would put everything into perspective?"

Trina grins through her scowl and nods. "Oh yeah," she sneers, her tone sardonic. "Nothing like a twenty-minute run to solve all of my problems."

"If you think this was cleansing," Kendra says, seemingly impervious to Trina's contempt, "just wait until our aerobics class."

"Can't wait," Trina grumbles.

Trina had called Tai hoping they could get together and talk—just the two of them. "I woke up this morning feeling lost," Trina had confided, her voice low and forlorn. "Like I don't know where I am or how I got here."

Tai had cooed sympathetically. "I know how that feels. It's like you just can't seem to figure out which way is up."

"Yes!" Trina exclaimed, relieved and excited to know that she wasn't alone—to know that her feelings weren't untraveled terrain. "I can't remember the last time I was this confused."

"I know exactly what you need. Get dressed," Tai ordered. "I'm coming to get you."

Trina had put down the phone and had drawn in a deep breath, the malaise already dissipating from around her. A ladies' day out was just what the doctor ordered. Maybe they'd go to a matinee or indulge in a little retail therapy at Wolfchase Mall like she and Grace used to do, she predicted, throwing her hair up into a haphazard twist and fastening it in place with a clip.

They could buy a couple of warm, Mrs. Field's chocolate chunk cookies and people-watch, she thought, forgoing her usual shield of makeup for a coat of lip gloss and a couple of strokes of mascara. Or they could swing by Smooth Moves and browse the outdoor antique shops on Union Avenue. She slipped into one of Darius's faded, crewneck sweaters and her worn Levis with the ripped back pocket and tattered hem.

It didn't matter if they strolled around the block or rocketed to the moon, Trina was just grateful to stretch her legs and her mind—to escape from her thoughts and from Darius and Grace, even if it was only for a little while. And Tai, with her sweet disposition and empathetic heart, was just the fairy godmother to whisk her away.

But 45 minutes later when Trina opened the door, she was dismayed to discover Cruella de Vil in black spandex and a Nike sweatband.

"You're not dressed," Kendra snipped, taking in Trina's getup, loafers to limp hair, in one swift glance.

"What're you doing here?" Trina asked, unable to hide her annoyed disappointment.

"We know you're depressed," she said, leaning forward, her voice hushed as if it was a shameful secret she didn't want the neighbors to overhear. "And we're here to help."

Trina looked past Kendra into the deserted hallway. "Who's we?"

"Tai and Joss are downstairs waiting for us in the car. Here," she said, flinging a wad of fuchsia Lycra at her. "Put this on."

Trina emerged five minutes later looking like an extra in a Barbie Buns of Steel workout video. "I'm not wearing this in public," she said, tugging at the skintight shorts.

"Don't be ridiculous," Kendra shrugged. "You're adorable, and by the time we get through with you, you're going to *feel* as good as you look."

⌣‿‿‿⌐

"And SQUAT! And squeeeeeeze!" Kat, the sprightly aerobics instructor, shouts over the pop music blaring from the boom box behind her. She's all of 20 with a taut, jiggle-free body that Trina would resent, if she weren't focusing all of her energy on not having a heart attack.

The roomful of breathless women, Trina, Kendra, Tai, and Joss included, crouch with their arms out and silently pray for the stamina to hold the position for eight more beats.

"And three...and two...and one," Kat croons serenely, a plastic smile fixed on her face. "Good, now walk it off," she says and starts marching in place. Her arms pump energetically and her steps are noticeably higher than Trina's, who would rather stuff her spandex gear with prime rib and scale an electric fence into a den of starving lions than hold one more squat, lift one more knee, or do one more biceps curl.

"You're doing GREAT ladies!" Kat exhorts with more enthusiasm than anyone's entitled to in the middle of a strenuous workout. "Sixteen more beats and then we're going to move into LUNGES!" Kat's eyes are wide with anticipation, like she's expecting them to jump and cheer at the prospect of more torture.

Trina glances at Kendra and Joss, who've achieved some sort of Zen-like state of mind and are facing forward, brows furrowed in concentration, as they tirelessly march to the beat of the music. Tai, on the other hand, looks like she's one more high kick away from toppling over. Trina is not sympathetic.

How did, "Don't move. I'll be right there," turn into a morning of group *Death by Aerobics?*

"And...LUNGE!" Kat orders. "Come on, ladies, hands on hips," she instructs, leaving her mat in the front of the room and traveling slowly up and down the rows of outstretched bodies, inspecting each person's form. "Remember, back straight," she says. "Three...two...one and SWITCH!"

Trina flinches at the pressure of two hands, one on either side of her hips. "You've got to really dig deep if you want results," Kat says, pulling Trina's bottom down until her front thigh burns and her back leg feels as though it might pop off. "Feel the difference?"

Trina gives her a thumbs-up and bites her bottom lip to keep from screaming. After lunges are bicycle crunches and after bicycle crunches, side kicks. By the time Kat counts them through two sets of leg lifts and three sets of push-ups, Trina is convinced that her time has come and that here, on a blue foam mat, in front of 20 women in a Memphis gym, is where she will take her last breath and die.

"Well done, ladies!" Kat says, hopping to her feet. "Time to stretch."

Trina clambers to a standing position.

"Arms out. Good. Roll the right shoulder."

Trina's eyes circulate the room of sweating, wheezing, shoulder-rotating women and wonders if they subject themselves to this masochistic routine on a regular basis. *How can this possibly be considered healthy?* she wonders, bending over with the rest of the class and reaching for her toes.

This is the first time ever—in 30 years of life—that she's experienced chest pain. God knew what He was doing when He blessed her with a fast metabolism and a small appetite because a lifetime of this nonsense, 90 minutes a day, 4 days a week, would surely have killed her by now.

"FANTASTIC!" Kat cheers. She bounds the few steps to the boom box behind her and stops the music.

Trina sighs with relief, grateful that she survived.

Joss takes a swig of bottled water. "How ya feelin'?" she asks, her skin flushed and clammy.

Trina considers the question. Her back is sore, her limbs are numb, and she's fairly certain that there's a blister the size of Montana on her left heel, but oddly, she feels invigorated by her sense of accomplishment. An hour ago, she was ready to draw the shades, climb into bed with a box of Cheerios, and sleep the day away. Yet now when Darius saunters home and asks, with that condescending little smile of his, if she did anything useful today, she can say, "Yes." Who knows? *She* just might be the one to come in late with no explanation.

The idea is warming. "Pretty good," she answers with a smile. Maybe Tai was right; maybe this is exactly what she needed.

"That was an AWESOME warm-up!" Kat says.

Trina freezes in horror as Kat retrieves another CD from her bag, pops it into the boom box, and pushes *play*. Instantaneously, fast-tempo techno music pours from the speakers and fills every corner of the room. "Now, let's see you all put that same ENERGY into your workout!"

Kat begins to jog in place, her ponytail flopping from side to side. Every-one else follows suit. Trina closes her eyes, swallows hard through gritted teeth, and hopes for a miracle.

⌒

"I don't like her," Grace says, tossing the collection of decorative pillows from their bed onto the couch.

"Who, Tammy?" Mike asks and pulls back the comforter. "How come?"

Grace thinks back to lunch, back to Tamara's sour smirks and clandestinely catty one-liners. "There's just something about her—she's got an evil vibe."

Mike laughs. "Give her a chance. Take the time to get to know her."

"I tried that already," Grace says. "You were there. Two hours sitting across from her and I don't even know her last name."

"That's because you didn't ask."

"I also didn't ask for a crash course in American rates and statistics, yet I now know that fifty percent of all marriages fail in their first two years, eighty-two percent of Americans are obese, ninety-eight percent are over-weight, and six out of ten people don't exercise enough."

"No, I think it was thirty percent obese," he tilts his head. "And fifty per-cent overweight."

"Whatever!" Grace says, snatching her hand cream from the nightstand beside her. "The point is, she's strange. I mean who does that? Who walks around reciting a bunch of useless facts?"

"Maybe she was nervous," Mike suggests.

"Oh yeah, she looked really nervous while she was chomping on her dry lettuce and calling me fat."

"She never called you fat."

"She told me I had a pretty face—same thing."

"Yeah," he chuckles, "nothing says, 'You're a porker,' like telling someone they have stunning eyes and a distinctive smile."

"Subtext," Grace says, slumping grimly against the headboard. "It's not what she says. It's how she says it."

"You know what I think?" Mike asks softly. "I think this is more about Trina than it is about Tammy."

Grace huffs. "What're you talking about?"

"I think you're afraid to give Tammy a real shot because if you do and you end up liking her, it's like you're betraying Trina—like you're replacing her."

It sounds like a rational diagnosis, but Grace knows it's not entirely correct. Yes, she misses Trina. Yes, it's awkward for her to see Ron with other women, but there's something more, something deeper. This is about Tamara's snobbery—however covert. It's about the way she managed to disguise her debasing comments with backhanded compliments and how she weaseled her way into an interview with a couple of strategically placed giggles and a sexy smile. But mostly it's about the way she was flirting with Mike. All of the coy eyelash batting and bang sweeping might have been lost on him, but Grace picked up Tamara's signals loud and clear.

"Just give her a chance," Mike pleads. "That's all I'm asking. Take a look at her résumé. Talk to her, one-on-one, and see if you can find some common ground."

Grace scrunches her nose. "And if I can't?"

"Then we'll keep looking." He shrugs. "But you might as well try to find something to like about her because she's not going anywhere. Ron's crazy about Tammy, and she's crazy about him."

"Or…maybe she's just crazy."

"Grace." Mike's tone is one of warning.

Grace groans. "Alright, fine! She can interview for the position, but I'm not making any promises."

Mike grins. "Fair enough," he says, clearly pleased with the results of their little parley. "You'll see." He rolls over and reaches for the lamp. "Tammy's got a heart of gold. She just made a bad first impression."

Grace grunts skeptically and prays, for Tamara's sake, that Mike is right.

part two

S. O. S.

10

"You look like death," Kendra says, her arched brow paired with a probing smirk. "Fun night with the boyfriend?"

Trina grunts and dumps a second packet of artificial sweetener into her cup of tepid coffee. "If your idea of fun is tossing and turning on a squeaky sofa bed, then yeah, I had a blast."

Kendra leans in the doorway of the employee break room, her arms folded, her mood suddenly solemn. "You want to talk about it?"

Trina shakes her head, and her shoulders stiffen. Her entire body is still experiencing the repercussions of Kendra's last attempt to cheer her up. "Everything's fine. I'm just a little tired."

"You sure?" asks Kendra, her head tilted, her eyes straddling the thin line between curiosity and concern.

Trina nods. "Coffee and a couple of aspirin are all I need."

Kendra shrugs, seemingly discomfited by her semi-genuine attempt to show compassion, and straightens her blazer. "Good, because I'm counting on you to look alive this afternoon. I need you at a hundred and ten percent for our meeting with Quinn."

"Two o'clock. I'll be ready." Trina's nod is emphatic. "You will have me at a hundred and ten percent." She offers Kendra what she hopes is a reassuring smile and brushes past her into the main hallway and through the maze of occupied cubicles that lead to her small office.

Of all the things Trina doesn't want to do, and all of the people she doesn't want to do them with, a meeting with Kendra and their boss, Quinn, is at the top of Trina's list. In the two years that Trina has worked at Home Sweet Home, she's only had the misfortune of encountering Quinn twice—once at her initial job interview and again a year later at the company's Christmas party. Neither experience was particularly pleasant, but the interview was, by far, the worst.

Quinn hadn't bothered returning the smile or the "Good morning" that Trina offered as she entered the office that fateful day. "You're late," Quinn had said without looking up from the stack of papers she was reading.

Trina had sneaked a peek at her watch and then at the clock hanging on the wall above Quinn's stacked bookcases. "Your secretary told me ten o'clock sharp," Trina said, working to control the slight quiver in her voice.

Quinn removed her glasses, placed them into their velvet-lined case, and snapped the case shut before turning her derisive stare to Trina. "So your tardiness is my secretary's fault, is it?"

"No, not at all." Trina felt a wave of heat flush her neck and cheeks. "I wasn't... I just..." She motioned toward the clock on the wall. "The interview was scheduled for ten and it's ten."

Quinn leaned back into her plush, leather throne of a chair. "This meeting was scheduled to *commence* at ten o'clock," she'd snipped, her jaw set, her folded hands resting on her concave stomach. "That means you're here at five till, so by ten o'clock you're seated in front of me and ready to begin instead of standing in my doorway wasting my time."

Trina had stood motionless, gutted and stunned by Quinn's callousness. "I apologize," Trina managed. "It won't happen again."

Quinn's sharp gaze had moved from Trina's face, down the length of her body to her feet, and slowly back up again. Trina willed herself not to fidget, not to breathe, as Quinn sized her up like a hungry predator. Suddenly, the gray, tailored suit, pearl studs, and black pumps she'd chosen felt flimsy and inadequate in more ways than one.

"Take a seat," Quinn had ordered.

Trina obeyed, quickly slipping into the chair opposite Quinn.

"Ms. Calloway, I've skimmed through your résumé, and for the most part your credentials are impressive." Quinn reached for something on her desk but grasped a handful of air instead. Her expression grew stone-cold.

She poked the orange button on her phone; it buzzed, and seconds later her secretary was standing in front of the desk next to Trina.

"Yes, Mrs. Dawson."

"Adrienne," Quinn began, her voice eerily calm, "something's not right here. Can you tell me what it is?"

Adrienne cast a nervous sideways glance at Trina. "I don't know," she said, her words were slow and cautious. "Did I forget something?"

"You tell me."

"I got here an hour early so I could redraft those memos like you asked. I rescheduled your one o'clock. I printed out your itinerary for next week." She paused and looked around Quinn's large corner office. "Shades are drawn," she murmured to herself. "Computer's on." Her eyes grew wide. "Your coffee! I'm sorry, Mrs. Dawson, it slipped my mind."

"Why isn't that surprising?" The question was dry and clearly rhetorical.

"Really, I don't know what I was thinking. It was an honest mistake," Adrienne said, wringing her hands. "I'm sorry."

"I'm sure you are, and yet for all of your apologizing, I still don't have a cup of decaf in front of me, now do I?"

"Right," Adrienne said, wagging her index finger. "Five minutes," she pleaded, backing slowly out of the office. "Five minutes. It won't happen again. I promise."

Quinn shook her head, disgruntled, and sighed. "Fourth personal assistant in two years," she informed Trina, her tone gritty.

Trina blinked. If ever there was a time to embrace the idea that silence is golden, it was then. Clearly the slightest misstep merited a scathing reaction from Quinn, and Trina didn't want to be the catalyst for her next tantrum.

"I don't get it." Quinn tossed her hands in the air. "How hard can it be? All they do is shuffle papers, answer the phone, take messages, and brew a couple pots of coffee. Simple enough, right?"

Trina's shrug was accompanied by a lost whimper.

"The most basic, gum-chewing, acrylic-nail-wearing nitwit should be able to play office effectively and efficiently for a mere eight hours a day. I mean, let's get real; it's not like they're splitting atoms."

The veins on either side of Quinn's neck protruded from beneath her skin, and her voice grew more insolent with each word. Trina gripped her purse and nodded blankly, all the while mapping out possible escape routes as Quinn continued to rant about the lack of competent, hirable help in Memphis.

Adrienne reentered a few minutes later carrying a steaming mug along with a blueberry muffin and a napkin. "Here we are," she said, gingerly arranging everything on Quinn's desk. Quinn eyed the pastry.

"I—I thought you might want a little breakfast," Adrienne said, following Quinn's angry gaze.

"I'm a fully grown woman, Adrienne. If I wanted breakfast, I would tell you that I wanted it or I would get it myself."

Trina's leg bounced nervously as she folded and unfolded her arms, uncomfortable with her front-row seat to Quinn's office rendition of *Les Misérables*.

"Of course," Adrienne said, quickly removing the muffin from Quinn's desk. "I didn't mean to imply that you couldn't…you know. It was just an afterthought. I didn't mean anything by it. I just——"

"I don't eat bread," Quinn said, taking a sip of her coffee.

"Right," Adrienne nodded, her shoulders slumped. "You told me that."

"Twice."

"He who does not listen has no advantage over he who cannot hear, right?" Adrienne asked in a pathetic attempt to glaze over her second fumble of the morning.

"Then I suggest that she who has not been listening figures out a way to unplug her ears. Otherwise she'll find herself downtown with he who cannot hear, filing for unemployment."

"Yes, Ma'am," Adrienne said quietly.

Only after Adrienne shuffled out of the door did Quinn turn her attention back to Trina. "Where were we?"

Trina's forehead was clammy, her hands twitchy. She shrugged. "Not sure."

"Let me cut to the chase," Quinn said, pushing her coffee to the side and leaning forward. "We're the only organization in Memphis that works hand-in-hand with its foster care system. That means that in order to fulfill our duties to the city and to the community, we must operate under a mind-set of diligence, efficiency, and systematization at all times.

"Family emergencies and baby/daddy drama don't constitute acceptable excuses here. No quarter-life crises, no interoffice feuds, no fraternizing—we can't afford it. Leave your personal troubles and your opinions at the door because I expect composure, professionalism, and the highest level of dedication from all of my employees, especially my directors. Now, does that sound like something you can handle?"

"Definitely," Trina said after a hard swallow. Her voice was small and not at all as certain as her answer.

"Good." Quinn stood and walked around her desk. "You're hired. I'll see you at eight o'clock on Monday."

Trina flinched. Hearing those words was not nearly as joyous an experience as she'd anticipated before walking through Quinn's door—before she'd discovered that her boss was evil incarnate.

The job itself, she'd quickly discovered, made up for the fact that Quinn was scary and garish. Aside from directing and managing the program budget, services, and personnel as well as the Community Management Team, Trina, as the company's director of child psychology, worked closely and personally with a select bunch of children in the city's foster care system. Many of them were forlorn teens and preteens who felt forgotten, destined to ride out their parentless state until they turned 18.

Trina would meet with them, assess their needs, and team them with mentors and advisors and dedicated social workers who offered them hope, if not through finding them a permanent home, then through working with them to map out and implement positive plans for their futures. The work was never-ending, robbing her of sleep and often forcing her to sacrifice what little of a personal life she had, but she loved every minute of it.

Unfortunately, less than a year after Trina was hired, Home Sweet Home underwent major restructuring. Her department, as well as several others, was eventually phased out, and she was left to oscillate between two equally undesirable choices. She could either accept a much lower position as a case manager or accept a paltry severance package and look for work elsewhere.

She chose the former and dolefully accepted her new title and mundane, tedious responsibilities as a glorified paper pusher.

Case managing is not nearly as fulfilling as her old job was, though it's just as demanding in its own way. That's because there are exponentially more cases than case managers to handle them. No matter how early she arrives and how late she leaves, Trina's desk remains stacked with files of children who are in desperate need of a loving family.

Quinn's dedication to diligence, systematization, and efficiency often means that siblings are split, special needs are overlooked, and serious, underlying problems are patched instead of healed. And Trina, as a mere manager, whose job is only to confirm court dates, to update files with new charts, records, and progress reports, and to ensure family compliance with CPS policies and standards is helpless to do anything about it.

Trina had graduated with a degree in child psychology because she wanted to make a difference—because she wanted to couple her love for children with an understanding of how they feel and reason and, in turn, lend a voice to those youth who wouldn't otherwise have one. But at Home Sweet Home, she's just gotten lost in the shuffle, aiding abandoned kids to the satisfaction of the system and not to the satisfaction of her heart.

Sullenly, Trina ogles the latest mound of manila folders on her desk and sighs. Her eyes shift to the framed photograph beside her open laptop. Darius stares back at her. His jaw is set, his brows even. He's handsome, but his expression is clouded, mysterious, or is it just coldly indifferent? She can't tell. She can't tell anything anymore. Like the night before last—shouldn't she have seen it coming? Shouldn't she have at least sensed that something was amiss?

She doesn't know what time he came home. She'd given up waiting at half past one and resigned herself to another night of snuggling alone, burrowed beneath the flannel covers. A loud bang in the living room was the first thing she had heard, as she was jarred from sleep, followed by the sound of his heavy footsteps. Before she could gather herself, the bedroom lights flipped on. "I'm feeling crowded," he mumbled, trudging to the bed and tucking the two unused pillows beside Trina under his arm.

"Get up," he half-ordered, half-pleaded. "Come on, get up."

Trina followed him out of the bedroom and down the hallway, unsettled by his tense swagger. The loud bang she'd heard was the sleeper sofa. She started at the sight of it, pulled out, its thin mattress, stained and uninviting.

"It's a queen," he said, tossing the pillows next to a couple of sheets and a musty quilt he'd produced from the hall closet. "You'll have more space," he said to the floor. "We'll both have more space."

She stood in the middle of the room, clad in nothing but an oversized T-shirt, and glanced at the pullout, then at Darius, then back at the pullout. "There's no way." She folded her arms and bit her bottom lip defiantly. "I'm not sleeping on that."

He shrugged. "Then sleep on the floor."

"You've got to be kidding," she shrieked, her bare foot stomping the hardwood beneath it.

His arms flew up and his head flew back in simultaneous exasperation. "Sleep in the bathtub for all I care."

"Gee, let me think about that," she snarled, her hip poked out. "No." She turned toward the bedroom, more than just a little annoyed that he'd dragged her out of bed for such nonsense.

He gripped her forearm and yanked her back. "You're not hearing me," he said, his tone menacingly flat, his breath seething with contempt. "This is not what I signed up for. 'A few days.' That's what we said. 'A few days.'"

Trina pried herself from his clenched fingers and rubbed her throbbing arm. "I know."

"Then why are you still here?" His voice vibrated angrily throughout the room.

"Why are you shouting?" she asked, taking a couple of cautious steps back. The memory of their last break-up fight, replete with her split lip and black eye, was still all too fresh in her mind.

"I don't want this," he said, meeting her gaze for the first time that night. "I don't want a wife. I don't want a roommate. I don't want..." He sighed, visibly worn and frayed like a coat that had seen its last winter. "I don't want *you*."

Trina felt fragile as she wrapped her arms around herself, feeling abandoned, and clung to the downy fabric of her shirt. She waited for the pain of it all, the rejection, to claw its way to the surface. She ducked her head expectantly, as if at that moment the ceiling would give in or the floor would give out and swallow her whole, but neither happened.

Instead she stood stoically and listened to Darius rattle off a slew of seemingly dispassionate and cogent reasons why she needed to move out and make it on her own. "I'm sorry," he murmured. "I am." He reached for her, not sexually, but compassionately, as though he pitied her—as though she'd turned to glass and he could, for the first time, see straight through her to her pathetic soul.

She recoiled from his touch, not wounded, yet not unscathed; not broken, but not quite whole. Deciding not to risk Darius's anger, she resigned herself to the couch.

The villainous ache she'd waited for finally began its siege as the sun rose over downtown Memphis and peeked through the living room's uncovered windows. Nearly four hours of tossing on the pullout's squeaky mattress and probing coils had taken its toll. With her shirt draped over her knees and her knees tucked under her chin, Trina cried. At first, just trickling tears of indignation. After all, she'd been abandoned by everyone she'd ever loved or blindly hoped would love her; everyone from her mother to Darius to Ron to Grace—probably even God. She was entitled to a little purge.

But as she rocked back and forth, she was plagued by one persistent notion: *Maybe people like me are genuinely unlovable.* The despair in that thought drew her to a chilling edge and turned her trickling tears into streaming sobs. She rocked and sobbed and rocked and sobbed until she was numb, anesthetized by the bleak truths of her orbit.

Drawing herself back to the present, Trina takes the photograph of Darius, frame and all, and tosses it into the trash can beneath her desk. Without thought, without hesitation, she picks up her phone, and with trembling fingers, dials Grace. If ever there was someone who has loved her or who could love her again, surely it's Grace. With bated breath and a desperate heart, she grips the phone and listens as it begins to ring on the other end of the line.

11

"Are you going to get that?"

Grace shakes her head. "If it's important, they'll leave a message," she says, her gaze fastened on the scene before her.

Perched primly on Grace's living room couch, decked in a tweed pantsuit, pearls, and suede slingbacks, Tamara is a stark contrast from the woman Grace encountered just a week earlier at church. Her bangs are swept off her face, tucked neatly behind her ears, and held in place by two understated clips. She's forgone her cerise lips and smoky eyes for a more sophisticated look of pale gloss and barely-there foundation.

"Can I get you anything?" Grace asks. "Coffee? Juice?"

Tamara's nervous swallow is audible. "No, thank you. I'm fine," she quietly murmurs. Her eyes dart from the ceiling to the art-lined walls to the floor to Grace and back to the floor.

Who is this demure flower with folded hands and pressed knees? Grace wonders. *What happened to the stealthy quipster with her matter-of-fact opinions and devious witticisms?*

"Relax," Grace says, easing into the love seat across from Tamara. "I don't bite."

Tamara offers a polite chortle, but her tightly clasped hands and pained expression betray her attempt to play it cool. "This job is really important to me," she admits, her smile as stiff as her posture.

"Really?" Grace asks, skeptical. "Why?"

Tamara shrugs. "How many people get the chance to get in on the ground floor of a brilliant, driven author? It's a once-in-a-lifetime opportunity."

"Brilliant and driven?" Grace echoes, her nod slow and contemplative. "That's a bit over the top for someone whose novel was merely 'an admirable first effort,' don't you think?"

"Not at all," says Tamara, her words noticeably slower—cautious. "I know your next novel is going to blow everyone out of the water. How can it not?" she asks, eyes wide. "Your first one showed such promising potential."

"Well, thank you," Grace says sweetly, her head tilted. "That's quite the compliment coming from someone who never got around to finishing it."

Tamara smoothes her slacks before re-clasping her hands and placing them back in her lap.

Grace waits patiently, secretly relishing the awkward silence, as Tamara scrambles for a viable response.

"You know, I think I *will* take that juice," she says, stroking her neck. "I'm a little parched."

A dose of your own medicine usually does that, Grace thinks. "I'll be right back." She leaves Tamara in the living room to re-strategize. Just as Grace had suspected, Tamara's expertise is subtext—and only subtext. Once the cloak is removed from her cloak-and-dagger routine, she's about as threatening as an obsequious puppy.

Grace drops several ice cubes into a glass and combs the refrigerator for the carton of orange juice.

Tamara's probably gone most of her life sparring with unsuspecting women, knocking them out in the first round with a couple of well-placed verbal jabs and undercuts, Grace thinks. *Well, not today.* "Today you've met your match," she quietly promises, filling the glass to its brim and returning to the living room.

"I was just admiring the art," Tamara says, motioning toward the piece over the fireplace. "It's magnificent."

Grace's smile is guarded. "Mike painted that," she says, glancing around the admittedly stunning space. "He painted most of the pieces in here, actually."

"So…where is Mike?" Tamara asks.

No doubt that was the first thing she wondered the instant she stepped foot from that elevator, Grace thinks disdainfully. "In New York on business."

"Oh," Tamara murmurs, clearly disappointed. "I just assumed he'd be here."

I bet you did.

Grace had purposely scheduled the interview for when she knew Mike would be gone—and for good reason, given Tamara's suddenly sullen expression.

"He's gone a lot then?" Tamara asks.

Grace shrugs. "Two—three weeks out of a month."

"That would put a strain on anyone's marriage," she notes.

Grace glowers, put off yet again by Tamara's audacity. "We manage," she snips.

But Tamara's attention has returned to the art above the fireplace. Grace studies her as she studies the art, her face turned upward, her eyes dancing over each stroke—taking in the shadows, depth, and textures. "He's pretty amazing, huh?"

"That's why I married him," Grace says, aware of the smugness in her voice.

Tamara's smile quickly withers to a grimace. She takes a sip of juice and places the glass on the coaster in front of her. "You're a lucky girl."

"We don't believe in luck, but if we did, I'm sure Mike would consider himself just as lucky."

Tamara's nod is curt. "I'm sure he would."

"May I speak plainly?" Grace asks, leaning forward.

"Of course," Tamara says, her eyes narrowed attentively.

"I appreciate your enthusiasm, but I don't think you're the right person for the job."

"Don't you think you should talk it over with Mike before you make a decision? Get his input?"

Wouldn't you love that? Grace thinks, flashing back to their lunch of rude jibes served with a side order of flirtatious giggles and a tall glass of underhanded manipulation. Grace knew that if she hadn't been there to intervene, Mike would have hired Tamara on the spot and brought her home wide-eyed and hopeful like a child who begs to keep a stray cat.

"My husband already has a personal assistant," she says, her jaw set. "The decision is mine and mine alone to make." Grace slides Tamara her résumé. "And I've made it."

"I'm a fast learner," Tamara pitches, a twinge of desperation in her eyes. "And I'm a hard worker. I'm organized and efficient and I don't sleep until *you* sleep—until *you're* happy."

"I'm sure all of that's true, but the answer is still no."

"Well," Tamara sighs and sinks dejectedly into the couch cushions, "could you at least sleep on it? Take the time to check my references?"

"Frankly," Grace says, her arms folded obdurately across her chest, "our last encounter was reference enough."

"I'm sorry?"

"I don't trust you," Grace says, laying all of her cards on the table.

"But you don't even know me."

"I know enough." Grace's tone is definitive. "I know that your insults weren't lost on me last week at lunch. And I'm fairly certain that your interest in my husband goes beyond flattering admiration." Her gaze is fiery. "That's what I know—and that's all I need to know."

Grace waits for Tamara's response. *Will she finally strip off this ridiculous Mary Poppins façade?*, she wonders. *Will she accept defeat? Come to terms with the fact that she'd been unmasked and beaten at her own game?*

Tamara sits motionless, looking small, humbled, like an ornery teenager cut down to size by a fed up parent. "I...," she begins. "I'm... Wow, you must think I'm horrible," she blubbers.

Grace watches, speechless, as Tamara fights back tears.

"I always do this," she continues, her voice thick and quivering. "I never say the right thing. No matter how hard I try, people end up hating me."

"I don't *hate* you," Grace says, hastily reaching for a nearby box of tissues.

Tamara scoffs between sniffles. "Of course you do! How could you not? You think I'm after your husband."

"You're not?"

"No." Tamara shifts so that her whole body is facing Grace. "Never." Her voice is low and certain. "He has you, and I have Ronnie. I wouldn't do anything to jeopardize either relationship."

"I don't understand," Grace says, her defenses flagging. "What was with all of the snide comments?"

"I didn't mean to be insulting," Tamara says. "I just…," she shakes her head and sighs. "I get nervous and the words don't come out right."

"All that stuff about my book, though…," Grace says, still trying to understand how anyone could be that mean by accident.

"I wanted to seem smart," Tamara admits with a sigh. "I wanted you to like me." She forgoes the tissues and brushes a tear from her cheek with her knuckles. "I read a few of your reviews and one critic gave it four stars and called it 'an admirable first effort.'" She laughs feebly and lowers her face, embarrassed. "I thought you would take it as a compliment."

Grace studies Tamara's trembling chin and glistening lashes. It still doesn't all add up, but she sympathizes with Tamara nonetheless. How many times has *she* blurted out the wrong thing because she was nervous? How many conversations does she wish she could have over or, better yet, erase entirely? Too many to count.

"Let me get you some more juice," Grace says, retreating to the kitchen.

It's *Grace's* turn to re-strategize—her turn to be humbled. She'd spent most of the night and half the morning sharpening her verbal lance, concocting imaginary jousts in which she trumps Tamara. Not once did she stop to ask the Lord to help her operate in a spirit of love, of sisterhood. Not once did she pray for Tamara or for wisdom or for understanding. "Lord, forgive me," she whispers as she heads back to the living room.

"Here you go," Grace says, setting the glass down. She takes a seat beside a still snuffling Tamara. "Listen. Maybe we got off on the wrong foot. Why don't we start over? Totally clean slates for both of us."

Tamara's laugh is throaty despite her limp smile. "You don't have to. I mean, you probably think I'm completely crazy." She sighs into her lap. "Maybe I am."

Grace shrugs. "A little bit of crazy keeps us honest."

Tamara snorts. "Yeah, I guess."

"The only thing I want from you," Grace says, "is for you to be yourself. That's how we get to know each other. That's how we become friends."

Tamara smiles. "Fair enough."

"Well then," Grace says, reaching across the table. "What do you say we have a second look at that résumé?"

12

Trina presses the phone to her ear, hopeful as the ringing gives way to a soft click, but just like the previous four times she called, the voice mail picks up. She slowly lowers the receiver from her ear and gently places it back in its cradle. *Months of avoiding Grace at any cost and the day I finally decide to make peace, she is nowhere to be found,* Trina thinks. The irony is bitter yet fitting.

Square things with Grace. Go by Darius's after work. Pack her belongings. Move back to the loft. Live happily ever after. That is the plan—simple and potentially effective if only she could track down Grace and get the train in motion.

She contemplates the grim alternative. Rush to Darius's after work. Take a shower, change clothes, and be out of the bedroom before he gets home. Tiptoe, like a stowaway, until he goes back out. Nosh on another gourmet meal of stale chips and fruit punch, the only two staples in Darius's kitchen. Then suffer another night of sleepless torture on the pullout sofa.

The mere possibility of the latter releases a nagging sense of urgency in Trina. Like a homesick child, she reaches for the phone again and dials Grace's number for the fifth time that day.

"What're you doing?" someone asks.

Trina looks up to see Kendra standing in her doorway, her makeup fresh, her hair neatly coiffed, a bulging accordion file tucked under her arm. Kendra gawks at her watch and then at Trina seated at her cluttered desk, a pen shoved unceremoniously behind her ear, the sleeves of her silk blouse rolled to her elbows.

Trina holds up her finger and motions for silence. *One sec,* she mouths while simultaneously willing Grace to answer the phone.

"We don't have a second," Kendra says, marching the few steps to Trina's desk and disconnecting the call with the push of a button. "Look at you,"

Kendra says, her expression critical, her tone accusatory. "This is your idea of a hundred and ten percent?"

Trina brushes the crumby remnants of her lunch from her skirt and shrugs. "It's a meeting, not a beauty pageant."

"Get up, come on," Kendra orders. She snatches Trina's suit jacket off the hanger on the back of her door and flings it at her. "We're going to be late."

"It's ten minutes to two," Trina says, mentally mapping out the 20-second walk to the elevator, the 1-minute ride up to Quinn's floor, and the 10-second jaunt to her office. "We're in great shape."

"You know Quinn's a stickler when it comes to punctuality," Kendra says.

"Ah, yes," Trina says, slipping into her jacket. "God forbid we show up any later than five minutes early for a meeting."

"I don't make the rules," Kendra says, hoofing down the hall at a noticeably faster pace than Trina.

"No," Trina mumbles, as Kendra stabs impatiently at the up arrow. "You're just a slave to them."

They step into the crowded elevator where Kendra takes a last-minute inventory of Trina's appearance. "You should button your jacket," she says in a hushed voice. Her eyes linger disapprovingly on the run in Trina's nylons. "And tuck in your blouse."

"Who do I look like?" Trina whispers, her gaze never leaving the climbing numbers on the reflective metal walls. "Your long-lost daughter?"

"Just do it," Kendra snaps.

The elevator stops, the doors swing open, and several riders disembark while everyone else takes the opportunity to steal a quick peek at Trina's attire.

"This blouse isn't made to be tucked in," Trina says, smoothing back several maverick strands of hair. "Besides, you can't see it underneath the jacket anyway."

"It looks sloppy, and Quinn's a stickler when it comes to a tidy appearance."

"Quinn's a stickler, period," Trina says, her tone caustic. "She's like one Wet Wipe and a Percocet away from a private room at Bellevue."

Several stifled snickers wave through the small elevator. "Nice," Kendra snaps, as the doors open on Quinn's floor.

The two of them make their way down the long, quiet corridor leading to her office. On most floors, there's a constant, low murmuring—a sign that the employees are alive and working. The sound of phones ringing, copy machines whirring, faxes beeping, and break-room chatter signals a busy, productive office. But Quinn's floor is nearly silent. The halls are deserted, the office doors closed, the occupied cubicles unadorned, stripped of every last baby picture, family photo, or amusing knickknack.

At any given moment, Trina half expects to see tumbleweed gust past. Or better yet, Quinn flying overhead, straddling a broom, shrieking, "Work, my pretties, work!"

"It's like going to see the Wizard," Trina whispers, her mouth souring with each step closer.

Kendra rolls her eyes, unamused, but clearly nervous. "Just let me do the talking," she says, and raps on Quinn's closed door.

They wait for Quinn's summon and then enter, their breaths held, their palms sweaty. Trina's eyes circulate the spacious corner office with its springy, plush carpet, built-in television, and walls made of windows.

The décor has changed radically since she last visited two years earlier. Quinn has abandoned the somber ambiance of her black, leather sectional, regal desk, and cherry oak bookcases for the lighter feel of blonde wood furniture and two sand-colored couches. The space now has a Scandinavian feel to it, with its clean lines and stainless steel, razor-edged accessories.

The better with which to kill us and call it an accident, Trina thinks, slinking past a peculiar-looking, spear-like pole, which she can only pray is a coat rack.

Beyond the seating area, in the farthest, sunniest section of the room is a makeshift nook with three oversized armchairs and a glass-top table spread with an eye-catching assortment of delicacies. Trina ogles the bright medley of sliced pineapples, strawberries, and grapes; the baskets of giant, soft-baked cookies and colorful, butter cream petits fours; the containers of hummus and pasta salad; the platters of fresh carrots, celery, and cauliflower; and the trays of fluffed finger sandwiches, which someone has cut into perfect triangles and organized neatly in an intricate spiral pattern.

"Good to see you as always," Quinn says, giving Kendra a less-than-warm embrace and an air kiss on either cheek. "And Trina, what a delight," she says. "It's been a long time."

Trina nods. *Not long enough*, she thinks, her smile just as wide and synthetic as Quinn's.

"Come in and make yourselves comfortable," Quinn insists, waving them over to the waiting buffet of food. "I thought we might talk over lunch. Hope you're hungry."

Trina isn't. In fact, the spicy black bean burrito she inhaled behind her desk, not a half an hour ago, is already whirling up a nasty fit of indigestion, but there's a moist peanut butter cookie calling her name, and she's never been one to snub a craving.

"This is quite the spread," Kendra notes, as she serves herself a modest helping of fruit and two finger sandwiches. Trina swipes her cookie and grabs another one to keep it company. "What's the occasion?" Kendra asks.

Quinn's grin is stretched uncharacteristically wide. "Big things are happening, and your hard work has not gone unnoticed," she says, turning away to serve herself a dollop of hummus.

On cue, Kendra's top lip curls distastefully at Trina who's quietly standing, cookies in hand, beside the petits fours trying to decide just how big of a pig she would be if she snagged a couple of those too.

Glaring, Kendra thrusts a porcelain plate at Trina and tosses her one of the precisely folded linen napkins stacked by the silverware.

"Home Sweet Home is making some changes," Quinn continues. "And I want you two to be a positive part of the transition."

"Sounds exciting," Kendra chirps, her sneer wiped clean by the time Quinn turns back around.

Trina only blinks, too stunned to respond to Kendra's voluntary schizophrenia, and stacks her plate with several of the miniature cakes, another peanut butter cookie, and a couple of strawberries for good measure.

The three women settle themselves on the couches, Kendra and Trina on one with Quinn facing them on the other, and eat in tentative silence, only pausing between polite nibbles to comment on how delicious the food is. Trina ignores the press of her skirt button against her distended belly and polishes off every last peanut buttery bite of her cookies before turning her attention to her miniature pyramid of petits fours.

"Home Sweet Home is broadening its reach," Quinn says, setting the remnants of her lunch aside. She sips her water and dabs both corners of her pursed lips before continuing. "We're opening two additional branches: one in Collierville and one in Germantown."

Kendra sets her plate down and smiles. "That's wonderful."

Quinn nods. "Hiring for both branches is mostly complete." She pauses. "But we still need directors. I've been asked to handpick those two positions, and between you and me," she cocks her head pensively and leans forward, "I'd prefer to promote from within."

Trina's chewing slows, the swirl of creamy vanilla quickly turning tasteless on her tongue. She's never been accused of being the sharpest knife in the drawer, but there are only so many places this conversation can lead. And all signs point up the corporate ladder.

"I've heard nothing but glowing reports about you two," Quinn says, her glossed eyes twinkling. "Your work is impeccable, your performance appraisals are stellar, and you don't hesitate to go that extra mile." She clasps her hands. "You're remarkable across the board—real assets."

Trina beams, grateful for Quinn's praise, but mostly intrigued by the possibility of being bumped back up to a director. She and Kendra teeter on the edge of their seats, their ears perked like eager pets, and glom on to every one of Quinn's words, all the while fighting to contain their excitement behind a mask of stoic professionalism.

"There's just one small problem," Quinn says, pinching together her thumb and index finger and scrunching one eye shut. "I have a situation that needs to be addressed quickly and discreetly. Now," she folds her arms across her chest and slowly sits back, "if you two handle it for me—and handle it well—those last two positions have your names on them."

"Consider it done," Kendra says.

Trina's head bobs in agreement. "Whatever you need."

"Rebecca Schmidt," Quinn says. "Are you familiar with her case?"

Trina grins. "She's a great kid."

"She's the daughter of William Schmidt," Quinn says. "Have you heard of him?"

Trina has and long before she read his name alongside a list of heinous abuses in the stack of hospital charts and police records that comprise most of Becky's file. Councilman Schmidt was Memphis's golden boy. In his four-year tenure as city council chairman, he made himself indispensable to his district by doing away with traffic light surveillance cameras and instituting strict noise ordinances. But his real claim to fame was his Education First program, a five-year plan to funnel millions of dollars to build several new, state-of-the-art high schools, one in the heart of the inner city. He looked like he had the world by the tail until the city abruptly shut down his chain of day care centers. The rumor swirling around the office was that he'd been using them as a front to embezzle municipal funds. Trina had never gotten the whole scoop. It seemed the scandal vanished just as quickly as it had appeared.

"Bill and I go way back," Quinn explains. "He's a good guy and he's been good to Home Sweet Home. Every year he donates generously to our operation. Now he needs us to return the favor." Quinn pauses to study their faces as though she's trying to read their thoughts—as though she's deciding whether or not they can be trusted with what she's about to say next.

"Bill's been through a lot these past couple of years," she continues after some time. "He lost his wife to breast cancer, lost his company and now his daughter. His reputation's been sullied, and more than anything he wants to pick up the pieces of his life and move forward."

"Mm. Mm. Mm," Kendra grunts, her head swaying from side to side, like those First Sunday Sistas who come to church once a month and sit in the front row, their big hats cocked to the side, and moan and groan and holler like it's the Second Coming.

"He's up for re-election," Quinn says, steadying her eyes on Trina. "And he can't afford any more negative publicity."

"Which he's sure to get by the truckload with his only daughter in foster care," Trina deduces, the puzzle gradually coming together one unethical piece at a time.

"Exactly." Quinn's nod is curt. "He won't have a chance at another term if he's under investigation for child abuse."

"And no Councilman Schmidt means no donation," Kendra says.

"It's a truly precarious situation," Quinn says, her eyes lowered. The room falls into reflective silence as the three of them sit quietly—Kendra and Trina pondering all they have to gain, or lose, and Quinn weighing all that's at stake if Kendra and Trina refuse to cooperate.

"What do you need us to do?" Kendra's voice is first to slice through the dense tension in the air.

Quinn's cheeks rise as the edges of her mouth curl up into a slight grin. She wastes no time delving into the precise measures that must be taken: what needs to disappear, who needs to be contacted, and how it can all get done as neatly, swiftly, and legally as possible.

It might be the unorthodox mix of peanut butter, frosting, and beans, but Trina's stomach begins to churn uneasily. How can Quinn ask them to do these things, to take part in such a blatantly iniquitous scheme? Trina sneaks several furtive glances at Kendra in search of aid—of some sort of acknowledgment that a grievous wrong is being plotted in this room amongst the three of them. But Kendra only stares ahead, like a programmed robot; all steel, no heart.

Trina had almost forgotten. For all of Kendra's big words and eloquent debates, her intimidating wryness and brazen self-assuredness, she's nothing more than an unctuous coward—a modern-day lemming.

"Everything clear?" Quinn asks, after pummeling them with nearly a half an hour of instructions.

"Crystal," Kendra says, her back erect, her tone determined.

Quinn's questioning brow turns to Trina.

Trina had thought that her days of facing peer pressure had ended with training bras and Easy-Bake Ovens, but Quinn's lingering stare conjures the same grimy lump she'd felt in the back of her throat the day Vivi Kampanelli and her gang of misfits had dared her to take a drag off a cigarette they'd procured from the teacher's parking lot behind the dumpster. She hadn't wanted to. The butt was soggy and brown with soot, but she did it nonetheless. She did it because an indelible line had been drawn between the brave and the cowardly, the risk takers and the crybabies, the women and the girls.

Twenty years and countless dares later, she would have thought she'd mastered this lesson. She thought she'd long since outgrown the fear of making the right decision. But to her dismay, she only glances up at Quinn and nods. "Clear," she says, cringing at the sound of her own voice.

⌒

"All life's lessons can be found right here," Trina's uncle had once slurred. He affectionately patted a tattered copy of *Grimm's Fairy Tales* before handing it to her and passing out on his dilapidated lounger. He was a pensive drunk, the kind of guy who stumbled home after downing a few too many gin and tonics with the boys, and stood in front of the refrigerator, opening and closing the door, determined to figure out whether or not the light stayed on. But Trina loved him regardless and, at nine, often took his inebriate ramblings for gospel truths.

She had read the book, cover to cover, only to discover a make-believe world of red-eyed witches and talking foxes. In college she used to joke that the only thing more bizarre than her uncle's words was the fact that she'd carried them with her for so long.

Yet, as she and Kendra leave Quinn's office and head for the elevators, she has a feeling that her uncle may have been making more sense than either of them had realized.

"So…you want to be Hansel or Gretel?" Trina asks, shifting her weight from one heel to the other. She drums her fingers against her thigh, itching to get back to the safety of her office.

"I'm afraid to ask," Kendra says, tugging at her sleeves and then patting away the creases with her perfectly manicured hands.

"Don't you get what just happened in there?" Trina asks. "It was classic *Hansel and Gretel*. She lured us in with all that talk of 'glowing reports' and 'positive transitions,' fattened us up on cake and hummus, and then demanded our souls."

"Our souls," Kendra echoes, her tone wry.

"Yes!" Trina hisses. "And we just sat there and served them up to her on a silver platter."

"Don't be ridiculous," Kendra says. "You should appreciate that she trusted us enough to address the situation with us directly."

"It isn't right," Trina says, stepping closer and lowering her voice as several colleagues join their queue for the elevator.

"We do what we're told," Kendra says with a cavalier shrug. "No one will fault us."

"That's not the point," Trina whispers. "We can't ju—"

"The *point*," Kendra glares, "is that I've been waiting a long time for this promotion. I've been here four years." She juts her index finger at Trina's chest. "You've only been here two. I'm overdue for some appreciation, and if I have to shred a couple of records to get it, I will."

Trina steps back, staggered by the depth of Kendra's heartlessness, the cutthroat coldness in her voice.

"This business requires politicking just like every place else," Kendra says. She boards the elevator, but Trina remains in the commons, unable to compel herself forward. "No one has time for your moral dilemmas," warns Kendra across the open threshold. "You either get on board or you get left behind." And with that the doors close between them and Trina is left standing alone.

13

"Hello, Hello," Mike bellows, his basso profundo resonating off the walls and skidding down the marble vestibule. "Anyone home?"

He's met by brief silence, and then Grace rounds the corner, her expression segueing from surprise to confusion to joy in a matter of seconds. "What're you doing here?" she asks, scanning the luggage on the floor beside his feet.

"Thanks, Baby. It's good to see you too," he says, playfully indignant.

"You know what I mean," Grace says, the words spilling from her mouth with laughter. "I wasn't expecting you back until the end of the week."

"What can I say?" Mike inches closer, his arms outstretched. "I was lost without my better half."

Grace tilts her head in a vain attempt to disguise her insuppressible grin. "That's never been enough to bring you back early before."

"This is different," he says, folding his arms around her and resting his chin on the crown of her head. "Things have changed."

"Mmmm," Grace sighs into his chest, her cheek pressed against his cotton shirt. For as long as she lives, she will never forget his scent, a delicate mix of soap and aftershave, which has grown irrevocably tantamount to safety and comfort—to home. "No complaints here," she murmurs blissfully.

"No, really," he gently pulls away and peers down at her, "something big happened in New York."

Grace searches his face for clues. "Good? Bad?"

Mike sways his head from side to side, his chin puckered, as if he hasn't had a chance to categorize it. "I wasn't sure at first," he admits. "But the more time I've had to get used to it, the more I'm convinced it's for the best."

"Well," she tugs excitedly at the lapels of his jacket, "tell me!" Her voice is strained with gleeful anticipation.

"Okay," he nods, suddenly serious. He takes a deep breath and runs his hands up and down her forearms. "But I need you to be open-minded."

"Baby," Grace hooks her index fingers through his belt loops and pulls him closer, "I am, if nothing else, open-minded," she says, her eyes wide, her lashes flitting.

He tilts his head, one brow hiked skeptically. "Since when?"

"Come on," she prods, her voice barely a whisper. "Try me."

His eyes trace her upturned face with methodic thoughtfulness. "I love you," he declares softly, snaking his arms around her waist and hooking his thumbs on the lips of her back pockets. "So much."

"You think you're slick," she taunts, leaning her head back. "You're trying to take advantage of my short attention span."

He chuckles. "Never."

"Well, good," she says with an obstinate flick of her hair. "Because it didn't work." She straightens her posture, taking care not to wriggle loose from his embrace.

"It didn't?" He brushes his lips across her forehead. "Well, what about that?"

"Nice try," she says, offering his chest a consolation pat, "but no."

"No?" He nods slowly, his mouth arched into a contemplative frown. "Then, how about this?" He pecks her softly along her neck, just under her ear.

Grace leans into him, both willingly and unconsciously. "Close," she whispers. "Very close."

"I think I got it," he says, guiding her face toward his. But just as their lips are about to meet, he pulls away, his gaze fixed on something behind them. "Tamara," he says with a smile. He untangles himself from Grace and slips her an apologetic wink. "I didn't know you were here."

"I didn't mean to…," she points timidly at Grace and Mike, "interrupt." She shrugs, more embarrassed than contrite.

Grace smiles and proudly stretches her arm toward Tamara. "You're looking at my new personal assistant," she announces grandly, as though she were presenting a debutante.

"Really?" Mike's brows hike in genuine surprise given how he'd had to prod and plead with Grace to grant Tamara a second chance.

"She starts next week," Grace says with a satisfied nod.

"Ron should be here in about ten minutes," Tamara says, her tone as sheepish as her demeanor. "I'll just…," she motions down the hall, "I'll just wait in the kitchen."

"No, stay," Grace implores, trotting several steps to Tamara and linking arms with her. "Mike was just about to announce some good news." She looks at him, her face beaming with expectancy.

"It can wait," Mike says with a shrug. "No big deal."

"Don't be shy," Grace encourages. "Tammy's practically family now."

"There's nothing really to tell," he says, his calm voice a stark contrast from the insistence in his gaze.

"Two seconds ago something huge happened in New York and now it's nothing?"

"Grace," Mike sighs and shakes his lowered head.

"It's me," Tamara says, unhooking her arm from Grace's and backing away. "You two need privacy."

"Since when does sharing good news require privacy?" Grace asks, her puzzled gaze locked on Mike.

He sighs and runs one hand down his wide jaw. "Everyone's going to find out sooner or later anyway, I guess."

"So tell us already," Grace demands excitedly.

"I quit my job."

Tamara's breath catches, as though with those four words Mike has sucked all of the air from the room.

Grace blinks, ignoring her instinct to panic, and frantically beats back the rapid accretion of questions collecting in the forefront of her mind. She can only stare, paralyzed by shock, and wait for Mike to expound—to explain how this could possibly be considered good news; how this will affect their future, their plans; how he could make such a life-altering, monumental decision without discussing it with her first, without offering her the courtesy of a phone call at least.

But Mike only stands there, suddenly captivated by the floor, his hands clasped behind his back, like a little boy waiting to be scolded.

"What do you mean, you quit?" Grace asks, unable to bear the silence any longer.

"I quit." Mike shrugs. "I resigned."

"How can you resign? It's your company. You created it! You own it! You run it!"

"I created it, yes. But I don't own it and I haven't run it for a long time."

"I can't believe what I'm hearing." Grace runs her hands through her hair, entwining her fingers at the base of her neck, and shakes her head at the ceiling. "I feel like I'm in the Twilight Zone."

"Everything's going to be fine, Baby," Mike's soft voice conciliates. "It was the right decision."

"For whom?" she asks, her tone decidedly less gentle than his.

Mike grimaces, stung by her question, by her lack of support, her lack of empathy. "For us," he says, his voice a soft whisper.

"No." Grace shakes her head, her stare flinty. "If this were for *us* then *we* would have made the decision together.

"It wasn't like that," he argues, his forehead waved with indignation. "A choice had to be made, so I made it."

Grace sneers. "How perfect for you."

"I'm sure he had good reason," Tamara says, in an ill-timed attempt to mediate. "Just hear him out."

Grace glares at her through narrowed eyes and grinds her back teeth to keep from spewing something snide.

"She's right. I had good reason," Mike says. "I wouldn't have done it if I didn't. You know that."

Grace manufactures a smile through her pursed lips, all the while blinking back her ire. "Excuse us," she says to Tamara and brushes past her toward the master suite.

She stands at the window with her arms folded across her chest and waits. Mike follows her into the bedroom, closing the door behind them.

"Maybe we should discuss this after Tammy leaves," he suggests calmly—too calmly, like a negotiator trying to reason with an irrational criminal.

"If I were you, Tamara would be the least of my concerns," Grace snips.

"What do you want me to say, Grace? You've already drawn your own conclusions. I want to tell you, but…" He motions at her hostile posture and set jaw.

"Tell me," she says, uncrossing her arms. "I'm listening." She perches on the arm of the sofa and holds up her hands with a shrug. "This is me listening."

Mike thinks over the events of the past two days. So much had happened in such a short amount of time. He didn't know where to begin, how to explain the when, where, why, and how of his decision. The entire experience had seemed surreal as it unfolded, as if he were watching it from the sidelines instead of experiencing it firsthand. Still, through it all, he'd felt guided, sure of every step, though uncertain of why he was taking them or where they would lead.

But how could he convey that to his wife? He doesn't know. How can he tell the person he loves most in the world that she just has to trust his gut, his instinct? How can he verbalize his feelings when he doesn't know what they are, what they mean? The words don't exist.

"This has been a long time coming," he finally says.

"You're gonna have to give me more than that, Mike."

He slips out of his jacket and tosses it on the bed with a sigh. "I don't know if I can."

"Then we have a problem."

"It's like...," he searches for the words. "I knew it was going to happen eventually. I just didn't know when or how." He pauses, his eyes earnest. "I didn't go to New York expecting to come back unemployed and company-less," he says with a shake of his head.

Grace leans forward. "Then what happened?"

Mike recalls his assistant, the jarred expression on her face as she entered his office to see him seated behind his desk. "Sir, what are you doing here?" she had asked.

He waved a handful of memos, his brow puckered. "Working," he said.

"No, I mean, why aren't you downstairs?"

He blinked, baffled. In the eight years Annie had assisted him, she'd never been more perplexing than then, standing, flustered, in his doorway. "Why would I be downstairs?" he asked slowly. "My office is up here."

"But the board, Sir. They've been waiting for you in the conference room for nearly...," she glanced at the watch clinging to her wrist, "twenty minutes."

He leapt to his feet, tossing papers into his briefcase while hurriedly scanning his calendar. "I called a board meeting?" he asked, tearing through page after page of his packed schedule.

"No, Sir, you didn't."

"Clearly, I did," he said, his tone doused in impatience. He snatched his PDA from its cradle and scrolled quickly through the month. Nothing.

Annie rushed to her desk, just outside of his office, and returned seconds later, her own organizer spread open. "I'm telling you," she said, laying the meticulously kept book before him. "There was no board meeting scheduled for this month."

"Then why is my board convened in the conference room?" he asked, more to himself than to Annie, who shrugged.

"I thought you'd know," she said, her vacant expression a mirror image of his own.

It was at that moment that an unsettling tension seized his stomach. Rumors of discord and split allegiances had been swirling for months. At the board's insistence, Mike had made several attempts to merge with two smaller firms. With their added manpower and clientele, *Life Sketch* would become the uncontested leader in its field, filling a very specialized niche that linked publishers with artists. But each time the deals fell through, Mike became more and more certain that he was swimming against the current of God's will. Yes, their numbers were projected to soar through the roof. Yes, they would be able to serve more publishers and more authors simultaneously. But would their quality of work stay the same? Would they still be able to demand and ensure the same moral standards?

After several days of prayer and fasting, "No," was the clear answer. In front of 12 angry board members, Mike had announced his decision to no longer pursue the mergers.

"That's suicide," one of the directors bleated.

"He's right," another said. "If you walk away from this deal, you're leaving the door wide open for the competition to swoop in and push us out."

Mike stood firm and gripped the truths that the Lord had revealed to him during his days of intense prayer. "Then so be it," he'd said.

The room rippled with incensed scoffs. "I'm sure your shareholders would love to hear that," someone huffed.

"You're not thinking straight, Mike. You're good, yes. But you're not invincible."

"My faith is in the Lord," was his only reply. It's the only reply he could offer. All of the data, all of the spreadsheets suggested he push forward, but the Lord had commanded him to be still.

Several of the members threw their heads back, their eyes rolling, their sighs heavy. Yet some, his fellow brothers and sisters in Christ, folded their hands, and silently resigned themselves to the fact that no amount of sulking and stomping would induce him to disobey the Lord. His decision was final, and their only course of action was to find a way to accept it.

The meeting had adjourned with tensions thick among the split board. "Are you sure you know what you're doing?" Janice Delano had asked. Janice was one of the newer board members, but a lifelong friend. She'd been there when *Life Sketch* was birthed and offered her wisdom and counsel when it was most needed. Eight years his senior, Janice didn't always agree with Mike's logic or vision, but she had always, without exception, exhibited unwavering faith in his faith in Christ.

"No," he admitted. "But I don't have to. The Lord understands and He'll reveal everything in His time."

The board had settled into a politically correct silence. The merger was not mentioned again, but the uneasy stalemate was precarious and bound to collapse, especially when *Life Sketch's* figures, after 12 years of steady growth, leveled at the beginning of last year and began a slow descent, eventually plummeting to an all-time low.

The short trip down to the conference room felt like a Dead Man's Walk. Mike knew what was waiting for him behind those double doors. He could just imagine what verdicts had been reached amongst the bottom-line board that had decided to convene behind his back.

They were silent as he entered and took his place at the head of the ostentatious round table. Not one of them looked him in the eyes, not even Janice. They each sunk, shamefacedly, into their high-back, leather chairs and waited for someone else to make the first move.

"I have to be honest," Mike began. "This is an unexpected disappointment, to say the least."

"It's business, Mike." Tom Einwitz was the first to speak up. "Some of us think you've forgotten that."

"All we ask is that you reconsider the mergers," said another member.

"It's not going to happen," Mike said with a resolute shake of his head.

"We have an obligation to our shareholders: to make sure the company grows and thrives, to make sure it outperforms its competitors. That's our responsibility as board members. We want *Life Sketch* to leave its mark for years to come," Tom said. "Let us do our jobs."

"Do you know how much business we've lost this past year?" Gill, another board member and golf buddy, asked. "Millions, Mike." His gaze was hard. *"Millions."*

"We send over thirty percent of our perspective clients to other firms," Debra McDugall, a founding member, added. She slid him the sheaf of charts and diagrams spread in front of her.

"And why?" Tom questioned, his eyes scanning the reticent members before settling on Mike. "Because they don't meet your…," he pauses, his upper lip turned up with disdain, "religious standards."

"We all operate under our own set of moral convictions, Mike," yet another board member chimed in. "But we don't bring them to work with us."

"*Life Sketch* can't afford to continue bending to your rigid values," claimed another.

"Look at the numbers," Gill said, pointing a spindly finger at the data. "You're single-handedly running this corporation into the ground."

"Our only hope of recovering from the past quarters' deficit is to restructure, commercialize, expand our clientele."

"And stop throwing away business."

"We've got to grab this bull by the horns before it gets away from us."

The once quiet room hummed with the board's insistent murmurs, each of them shaking their heads and grimly referring to the pages of figures in front of them.

Mike sat before them, wounded and betrayed, like an unjustly accused man before a hardened, biased jury, and silently implored the Lord for wisdom. "Is this how you all feel?" he finally asked above the clamor.

Their complaints lulled as a few of them nodded, and most of them averted their eyes.

"Concession is the only path to success—you really believe that?" Again, he was met by several meek nods.

"We believe in results," Tom answered for them. "We believe in the bottom line."

"There's the problem," Mike said, jutting an accusatory finger. "*Your* bottom lines are driven by green paper; mine are driven by living, breathing souls."

"Here we go," someone muttered. The board gave a collective sigh as several of them tossed down their pens and several more pushed their chairs from the table, grudgingly clasping their hands in their laps like little kids preparing themselves for an all-too-familiar lecture.

"When I started this company, my mission wasn't to rake in millions. I wanted to take quality artists and produce quality work that would glorify the Lord."

"Which was fine, *then*," Debra said. "But let's face it, this corporation has outgrown that mission. It's time to broaden our vision."

"And that's a *good* thing," Gill interjected. "You've got people beating down the door to sign on with *Life Sketch*."

Debra nodded. "All you have to do is answer."

Mike gazed into their determined eyes. They were prepared and well-rehearsed—ready to do business—and they weren't going to walk away until they got the answer they were looking for.

Of course he wanted *Life Sketch* to thrive. Like any entrepreneur, he hoped his business would live on long after he was gone, but he wasn't willing to thrust aside his beliefs to make it happen.

What business does light have with darkness? The question had pressed on his spirit hour to hour, from one day to the next, as he'd prayed and searched for God's guidance and will concerning the mergers. *What business does light have with darkness?* "None," he'd answered.

Then come out from among them and be separate! The reply had sent a chill up and down his kneeling body and raised the hairs on the back of his neck. He'd heard the Lord so clearly, but what did that mean? Come out from where, *Life Sketch?* How could he abandon the company he'd built, literally, from the ground up? Every chair under every desk in every office on every floor that housed every employee in his building had been put there through his blood, sweat, and tears; *his* visions, *his* prayers, *his* obedience, *his* sacrifice. He'd sooner dismantle the entire company, wipe the slate clean, and start again from scratch than hand over his life's work.

Come out, the voice had admonished again and again. But he'd refused to listen. Instead he'd espoused his own course of action. He put his foot down, told the board they would not merge under any circumstances, and assumed he'd been obedient enough. Only now, as he sat beneath the unwavering stares of his board, did he realize that "obedient enough" was not obedience.

His purpose at *Life Sketch* had been fulfilled. Of all the indeterminate emotions coursing through his veins, he was certain of that. The next thing he knew, before the doubt of his flesh could overcome him, he had asked to be bought out of his 49 percent interest.

"Is this your idea of a discussion?" Grace asks. "Me watching you stare into space?"

"I don't know what to say," he admits, his hands thrown up helplessly. "It was just time to go."

"That is unacceptable," Grace snaps, her tone cold and agitated.

"What would be acceptable?" Mike asks, chafed by her stern timbre and badgering gaze.

"Nothing!" Grace shouts. "Unless your explanation somehow involves someone putting a gun to your head and *forcing* you to leave—nothing!"

"I wasn't happy there anymore," he says, his words clipped with anger. "I asked to be bought out."

"Without talking to me? Without asking me how I felt about it?"

"I don't have to ask your permission to make decisions about my life," he fumes.

"*Our* life," Grace shouts, pounding her fist against the couch cushion. "Your decisions affect our life."

"If I had known in advance, I would've given you a heads-up," he said, his tone gentler.

"Given me a heads-up?" Grace stands, one hand on each hip, and paces the length of the bed. "Given me a heads-up?" she asks again, her glare venomous. "You are *un-be-lievable*," she snaps, her decibel level rising with each syllable. "You just don't get it."

"What don't I get, Grace? What don't I get!" Mike barks. His voice ricochets off the cobalt walls.

Grace flinches at his anger and the sheer volume of his words.

"I come home after one of the hardest and worst experiences of my life," he bellows, "and your first reaction is not compassion or support or even concern. The first thing you do is jump down my throat because you didn't have your say. Everything in this marriage can't be about you, Grace. As much as I love you, my entire world can't revolve around you all the time."

"I don't want your whole world," she says, her chin quivering. "Just a little bit of respect."

"Yeah?" he seethes, the muscles in his jaw tensing. "Same here."

Grace swipes at her damp eyes. "I may not be able to give you the respect you want," she says charging for the closet, "but I can certainly give you space."

She snatches an overnight bag from one of the closet's built-in cubbyholes and crams it with mismatched garments that she rips, by the fistful, from the dangling wooden hangers.

"What're you doing?" Mike asks. He watches her tear through the small space like a human tornado, stepping on his shoes and tossing his ties and jackets to the floor in her frenzy.

"What does it look like I'm doing?" she asks, stuffing a pair of sneakers into the bag and pushing past him into the bathroom. "I'm packing."

"Where are you going?"

She halts, her toothbrush and cold cream in hand, and hikes her brow resentfully. "None of your business," she snips. "If you don't have to discuss your decisions with me, then I don't have to discuss mine with you."

"Nice," he says, nostrils flaring. "Very mature."

"Hey," she shrugs and grabs a handful of cotton from the crystal dish on the vanity, "you made the rules. I'm just playing the game."

"You know what?" he asks with a languorous wave of his hand. "Go. I don't care what you do."

"Clearly!" Grace shouts, zipping the bag and stomping around him.

Mike lets out a coarse, aggravated grunt. "There are no right answers with you," he shouts and follows her back into the bedroom. "What do you want me to say?"

"Nothing," Grace answers, her chest heaving. "Just back off!" She flings the door open to find Trina and Tamara, both bug-eyed, standing next to each other.

"She said she was a friend." Tamara points limply at Trina. "You guys were...," she shrugs, "busy. So I buzzed her up."

"Are you okay?" Trina asks.

"She's fine," Mike says, leaning against the door frame. "We're fine. What're you doing here?"

Trina takes in Grace's streaked cheeks and packed bag. "You were yelling," she says, her eyes flooded with worry.

"It's nothing," Grace says. She finger combs her hair and tugs the wrinkles from her blouse. "Just a disagreement."

"Are you sure?"

"Yes, she's sure," Mike drones impatiently. "Can we help you with something?"

Trina ignores him, her eyes fixed on her disheveled friend, and waits for Grace's reply.

"What *are* you doing here?" Grace asks, her voice hushed—more curious than kind.

"I didn't know I needed a reason to stop by," Trina mumbles, her eyes lowered.

"It's been three months, Trina. No phone calls, no E-mails, nothing."

Trina shrugs and tilts her head guiltily. "I could say the same."

"I'm not the one who walked out," Grace says.

"I didn't walk out," Trina says, her eyes misty, her tone insulted. "You *threw* me out. You threw me out of the loft *and* your life."

"That's not true."

"Oh please," she slaps her hand against her thigh. "You got married, and I was the first thing to go. I didn't make the cut—wasn't good enough for your new, *perfect* life," she says, her words heavy and bitter.

The strident buzz of the intercom interrupts before Grace has a chance to respond. "I'll get it," Tamara says, quietly excusing herself.

"Who is she?" Trina asks, casting a contemptuous glance at Tamara's fleeting back. "Your new best friend?"

"She's my assistant," Grace says. "I hired her this morning."

"Oh." Trina nibbles at her bottom lip, slightly humbled and visibly relieved.

Grace's shoulders ease, and her expression softens. "I only have one best friend," she says. "We're not on the best terms right now," Grace grins, "and she's completely neurotic, but I still love her."

"Really?"

"You know I do."

Trina nods and looks away with glistening eyes. "I made a mistake," she says, the confession comes out as a whisper. "Me and Darius. It's not working out."

"There's a surprise," Mike mutters.

Trina glowers as a solitary tear glides down her cheek and slips under her chin. "What is your problem?" she asks.

Mike straightens his back and folds his arms across his chest. "You mean besides you?"

"Okay, okay." Grace holds up her hands and presses her eyes shut. "Let's not go down this road again."

"I need a place to stay," Trina says, hugging herself and shifting her weight from one foot to the other. "Can I move back to the loft? Just for a couple of weeks, until I find my own place."

"Of course," Grace nods. "Do you still have your key?"

"Wait a second." Mike steps forward, his stance wide. "I think we should discuss this."

"I don't really care what you think," Grace snaps, her tone frosty and matter-of-fact, her eyes daring. "I don't have to ask your permission to make decisions about my life," she says, regurgitating Mike's words. "Or my loft."

"Everything kosher?" Ron asks, emerging from the hall, his arm wrapped securely around Tamara's waist. He eases toward them, cutting his eyes suspiciously at Trina.

"Not exactly," Mike says, turning away from Grace's glare.

"Anything we can do to help?" Ron asks.

"We?" Trina grunts. She studies Ron and Tamara's closeness, their tactile familiarity. Her face hardens as the reality of their relationship begins to set in. "Are you serious?" she shouts, the anger and betrayal in her voice palpable.

"It's not what you think," Grace says, her head bowed apologetically.

Trina's gaze travels from Grace to Ron and Tamara and back to Grace. "You hired my ex-boyfriend's new girlfriend as your personal assistant?" she asks. It's an accusation, not a question.

"*That's* your ex-girlfriend?" Tamara asks, leaning farther into Ron's embrace, while sizing Trina up with a quick, smug glance.

"In the flesh," Trina says, haughtily, not to be outdone. "What can I say? I'm like a bad penny. He just can't seem to get rid of me."

Tamara snorts. "Not for lack of trying, from what I hear."

"Please don't," Grace says, pointing at Tamara, visibly irritated by her retort.

"It's between the three of them," Mike says to Grace. "It's none of your business."

"She wasn't talking to you," Trina says to Mike.

Mike glares at Trina. "And I wasn't talking to you."

"Trina *is* my business," Grace says.

Mike rolls his eyes. "Since when? Up until ten minutes ago you two had disowned each other."

"Ah," Ron heaves a sardonic sigh, "the good ol' days."

Tamara sneers.

"What're you laughing at?" Trina asks, jutting her chin at Tamara.

"Hey," Ron's voice is deep and threatening, "don't even think about it."

"Don't talk to her like that," Grace snaps.

"Why are you always butting in?" Mike asks.

Grace glowers. "Why don't you ever butt out?"

The five of them stand in the hallway, their loud, resentful voices echoing throughout the loft, a cacophony of snide comments and haughty accusations. Ron berates Trina, who jabs at Tamara, who pokes right back, which causes

Grace to jump to Trina's defense, which incites Mike to slate Grace, until they all eventually shift gears and turn their criticisms on someone else in the circle.

At the top of the sixth round, the argument shows no signs of ceasing. Grace is so heated at Trina for accusing her of lying about Tamara that she almost doesn't hear the phone ring.

She leaves the four of them hollering in the hallway and stomps to the cordless in the bedroom. "Hello?" she barks. The sounds of clanking glasses and muffled laughter sift through the receiver.

"Who is this?" Grace demands, eager to get back to the squabble.

"Grace?" a voice calls from among the distant chatter. It's small—hollow and eerily desperate, like the final plea of a dying man.

"Dad?"

"Gracie, I need you."

"What's wrong?" Grace asks, the angry voices of her friends and husband, mere feet away, seem to fade into silence.

"I'm sitting here, staring at a shot of bourbon." He laughs disgustedly. "My hands are trembling and all I have to do to make them stop is get up and walk away. But I can't." His confession is followed by several raspy, guttural sounds. It's not until he sniffles that Grace realizes he's crying. "Oh, God. Oh, God," he moans helplessly. "I'm about to swig away eleven years of sobriety and I'm terrified." His sob is throaty, as though he's choking on gravel. "I'm terrified," he says again, the words secondary to his shame.

Grace envisions her humiliated father amongst a roomful of strangers, his shoulders quaking with foreseeable regret as he slumps over a dank bar, trounced again by an addiction that has already robbed him of so much of his life. Her heart bleeds for him. "Where are you?" she asks.

He sputters the name of a midtown sports bar off Poplar Avenue. "I'm coming to get you, do you hear me? Stay right there. I'm on my way."

"Thank you," he manages between tearful gasps.

Grace hangs up the phone and breezes past the still-bickering foursome, stopping only to snag the overnight bag she packed.

"Hey, where are you going?" Trina asks, her nostrils still flaring.

"My dad has an emergency," Grace calls distractedly over her shoulder. She snatches a sweater from the front closet along with her purse.

Trina, Mike, Ron, and Tamara draw an ephemeral truce.

"What happened?" Mike asks, the anger in his eyes replaced by alarm. "Is he okay?"

"I don't know," Grace says, heading toward the private elevator, her keys in hand. "I gotta go."

"Hold on," Mike says. "I'll go with you." He dashes back to the bedroom to retrieve his wallet, which is tucked in his jacket pocket. But by the time he returns to the elevator, Grace is gone.

14

The bar is cavernous with its exposed brick walls and dim, recessed lighting. Grace stands just inside the doorway and squints, her eyes gradually adjusting to the gauzy milieu of stagnant smoke. The front room is cluttered with mostly empty chairs and tables. Bolted to the walls are random memorabilia and sports paraphernalia: framed jerseys, worn hockey sticks and baseball mitts, autographed photos of NBA, NFL, and NHL players who'd stopped by to pound back a few cold ones and try their hand at the infamous Monster Nachos.

She scans the flaccid patrons, scattered about, each nursing their ale of choice, looking glum and mired in misfortune. Her dad is not among them.

Mesmerized by the game playing on several of the televisions strategically anchored throughout the room, the bartender doesn't seem to notice her as she crosses the sticky hardwood floors toward the back area.

There she finds rows of pool tables and several outdated pinball machines. A couple of guys her age, maybe younger, pause their game of billiards to ogle her ample figure. The uglier of the two casts her a roguish smile, flashing a gold-capped tooth. Grace examines his dingy T-shirt, greasy forehead, and matted, unkempt 'fro before shuddering with repulsion and returning to her search for her father.

Finally, she spots him tucked in the corner of the very last booth, hidden beneath the shadows of a flickering neon sign. He's festooned in his perfunctory English professor's uniform of pressed khakis, a knit sweater vest, and a crisp polo shirt.

His bifocals dangle from a chain around his neck as he stares ahead, rapt by the murky shot of bourbon resting on the table in front of him.

He's oblivious to her as she approaches him. "Dad," Grace says and rests her hand on his wrist, gently and reassuringly drawing him from his trance.

He looks up at her, his eyes puffed with exhaustion, his cheeks and jowl sprouted with silvery stubble. "I didn't do it," he rasps, nodding at the brimming shot glass.

Grace remembers the stormy night she'd shown up on her father's doorstep, her broken heart in hand for him to mend—and 50 painkillers in her pocket in case he couldn't. He took her in without hesitation, gave her his ear and his shoulder, fed her, encouraged her, counseled her, and nursed her back to sanity. And he did it all graciously, without asking for anything in return. He did it even though they'd been estranged for most of her life, even though, mere months earlier, she'd callously rejected him in front of her mom, Mike, and Trina.

Now is her chance to return the favor—to reciprocate the same unquestionable love he'd offered her two years earlier.

Without a word, Grace removes the bourbon from in front of her father and tosses it in a nearby abandoned busboy bin. Then she slides into the booth across from him and waits, patiently lending him her silent support.

"I'm pathetic," he says, solemn and heavy-eyed.

"No, you're not." Grace tilts her head kindly. "You had a moment of weakness, that's all. It happens to everyone."

"I shouldn't have called," he says, parrying her sympathy.

"I'm your kid," Grace argues. "I *want* to be the person you call."

He shakes his head. "But that's just it. You're not a kid. You're all grown up now with a husband and a life of your own."

"And you're part of that life." Grace reaches her hand across the table.

Reluctantly he takes it in his own and squeezes.

"So what's going on?" Grace asks after a few moments of reflective silence. "This...," her eyes circulate the seedy, desolate bar, "this isn't you."

"How would you know?" he snaps, releasing her hand. "Maybe this is exactly who I am."

Grace sits back, stunned and wounded by his sudden abrasiveness. "Don't you want to be better than this?"

"It doesn't matter what I want," he sulks, his chin on his chest. "We are who we are and I'm too old to keep on pretending I'm something that I'm not."

Grace shakes her head, dizzied by her father's uncharacteristically defeatist attitude. "What aren't you?" she asks.

"Well for starters, I'm not this." He grips a handful of his signature sweater vest and twists it before letting it go with a bitter flick of his wrist. "I mean, come on," he snorts. "Who ever heard of a drunk turned college professor?"

"People change," she argues.

"No, they don't," he says quietly, his eyes glued to his lap. "They pretend."

"I don't think you're pretending, Dad."

He meets her compassionate gaze with a frustrated sigh. "You're still young," he says. "Give it time."

Grace shivers inwardly at the chill of his hopelessness. In the two years she's gotten to know and love him, her father has proven himself to be a diehard optimist, even, on occasion, crossing the line between sanguine and quixotic. He's jovial, a raconteur at heart, whose echoing words of insight were often her only succor at night when the world's burdens pressed on her spirits like an iron anvil.

But the man sitting across from her with his dead eyes and permanent frown is a stranger—a mere shell of the person who'd filled her life with so much joy, so much warmth.

"Where is all this coming from?"

"Don't you ever wonder what it's all for?" he asks, ignoring her question.

"What all of *what* is for?"

"Just life and all of the energy it takes to keep living—to keep pushing forward one day after the next, only to end up so close to where you began. It's like running in water, you know? Yards of effort for an inch of results."

"Dad, *please*," Grace begs, her mounting worry quickly turning to fear. "Tell me what's wrong."

"There are choices we make in life that we can never take back," he says, refusing to look at her. "All actions, *all* of them, have consequences." His chin wobbles with the passion of his conviction.

"But what about forgiveness?" Grace asks. "What about mercy?"

"We're born sinners and we die sinners," he answers dolefully.

"We all have the ability to become new creatures in Christ," Grace counters.

"One of the first things they tell you in AA is that alcoholism is a progressive disease." He straightens his back and bunches his lips sternly. "You can arrest it, but you can't cure it," he says in an exaggerated baritone voice, clearly mimicking the person who'd first spoken the words to him. "Imagine," he says, easing back into his own personality, "being told that there's no cure for the thing that's killing you—that no matter how diligent you are, no matter how faithful, your problem has no real solution. What do you do? What *can* you do?"

"Have faith," Grace says.

Her father shakes his head. "You can accept your fate or you can attempt to change it," he says. "I chose the latter." He stares blankly at the empty napkin dispenser. "It seemed noble at the time," he murmurs with a slight shrug.

"It is," Grace says.

"Yeah, well," he scoffs, his rancor audible, "look what it got me."

"What?" Grace asks, her voice pitched high with frustration and confusion. "Peace of mind. A job you love. Students who respect you. Colleagues who admire you. A daughter who adores you...," she ticks off each asset, "where's the tragedy in that?"

He grins tiredly as he examines her with somber eyes, his jowl heavy. "You're so much like your mother, you know that?"

Grace laughs and leans back into her seat, her mind involuntarily replaying a dizzying assortment of arguments and misunderstandings that had taken place between her and her mother over the years. "I don't know whether to be flattered or offended."

He chuckles, his eyes dancing with memories of their own. "She was a piece of work."

"And not always in a good way," Grace adds.

"Yeah." He sighs and tilts his head to one side. "But sometimes she knew just what to say to make things better."

Grace squints at him playfully. "Does that mean you feel better?"

"It means…," he pauses and runs a wrinkled hand over his stubble, "I'm ready to get out of here."

Without a moment's hesitation, Grace scoots out of the booth and offers him her arm. "Your wish is my command," she says, eager to get away from the smarmy haunt herself.

He takes it with a smile, struggling a bit to stand up, and together they make their way out of the bar and into the safety of the setting afternoon sun.

Traffic flows steadily as Grace follows behind her father, their mini, two-car caravan, snaking with ease down the tree-lined highway toward his modest, yet charming, neighborhood.

It's been quite some time since Grace has been inside his house. She swings by every now and then to pick him up for the occasional meal out— precious time alone with him that she's grown to treasure over the past few hectic months. But she hasn't taken the time to visit with him, to come inside, sit down and shoot the breeze over a cup of coffee.

The house is familiar as she sets her overnight bag in the front hallway and follows him the few, short paces into the living room. She takes in the bedraggled couch and faded recliner, the coffee table stacked with a week's worth of

Commercial Appeals, and the TV tray tucked neatly in the corner between the potted ficus and the heavy, oak bookcase. Nothing's changed. It's still comfortable and lived in; neat, but not orderly; decorous, but not stuffy.

Grace's dad eases into his faithful, worn recliner with a weary grunt. She sits opposite him on the afghan-covered love seat.

"You hungry?" she asks. "I can make you dinner."

He smiles off into the distance, his eyes closed. "You don't have to stay," he says. "I know you've got better things to do than baby-sit your old man."

Grace laughs despite the guilt that grips her. With no wife and no other children, he has no other family. If she doesn't carve out time to take care of him, who else will?

Maybe if she'd been more attentive, made herself more available, he wouldn't be grappling to hang on to his sobriety.

"There's no place I'd rather be," she says gently.

"What about Mike?" he asks. "Won't he be expecting you?"

She shakes her head, swallowing the instant wad of irritation that forms in the back of her throat at the very mention of her husband's name. "He's in New York on business," she lies. *Or at least he should to be.*

She kicks off her shoes and tucks her feet between the cool cushions. "It's just you and me tonight."

His glance is curious. "You're sleeping over?" he asks, his chin low, his tone suspicious.

Grace shrugs. "I'd rather be here with you than spend another night alone in that big, empty loft."

"Is everything okay?" he asks, sitting up, his eyes narrowed attentively.

"Fine," she mumbles, unable to meet his prying gaze.

"Grace," he intones knowingly. "What's going on?"

She hugs her knees to her chest and turns her face away. Even if she did want to talk about Mike and their fight, which she doesn't, how can she burden her father with the perils of her marriage when he's clearly battling inner conflicts of his own? "If you don't feel like company, just tell me," she says, her voice low and wounded.

He chuckles. "If I had my way, I'd lock you in this house with me and throw away the key. But," he adds, his expression serious, "I don't want you to hide out here if there's someplace else you should be."

"I miss spending time with you, that's all," she says, peering up at him earnestly.

He grins, his crow's-feet arching fondly. "Me too," he says softly.

Grace dotes over him for the rest of the evening, serving him dinner first and then tea with scones. She washes the dishes, wipes down the countertops, and lugs the bulging trash bag to the end of his gravel driveway. Then she curls up beside her dad, and they laugh at one sitcom after the next, until his lids droop with sleep and he dozes off.

She doesn't bother waking him. Instead she gingerly removes his glasses and props his head against the stacked pillows. Then she covers him with his beloved afghan, turns off the lights, and makes her way down the dark hall toward the room he'd dubbed, nearly two years earlier, her bedroom.

The bed is inviting, the sheets crisp as she slides beneath them and situates the pillows to her liking. But, there's something wrong. It's been months since she's gone to bed without Mike by her side, or at least, his scent embedded into the fabric of their comforter. Without his nearness—his breath against her forehead, his arm draped protectively across her waist, his breathing humming reassuringly in her ear—the bed seems extra empty and the night unbearably lonely.

She glances at the phone on the nightstand beside her. Maybe she should at least call to let him know where she is and that her father's alright. Better yet, maybe she should call and apologize for all of the rude comments she spewed in the midst of her anger—hurtful comments that should never be spoken between a wife and her husband. Or maybe she should call just to whisper, "I love you," and to let him know that even though she's still livid with him—even though she still feels disrespected and disregarded—she has every confidence they'll work it all out eventually.

She props herself on her elbow, picks up the phone, and with her heart beating inexplicably fast, slowly begins to dial home. Her thumb hovers stubbornly over the last number.

What if he's still upset too? What if instead of expressing relief, he chastises her for running out or for not showing him more compassion? What if she calls to make peace, but only gets more of the same?

She doesn't have the strength to continue where they left off. The best thing to do, she concludes, is to start fresh in the morning, when they've both had sleep and time to remove themselves from it.

Who knows? With time to think, Mike might realize what a colossal mistake he's made and everything that transpired today may be moot.

Plus, a night alone might be just what he needs to put his attitude in check. A little worrying might do him some good. Let him wake up next to an empty space and ache at what it's like not to have her there beside him. Maybe a night alone will keep him from taking her for granted again.

Hesitantly, she returns the phone to its cradle. *Call him*, persists a voice from within. *Call him now.*

Instead she switches off the lamp and, ignoring the nagging sensation in her gut, rolls over and tumbles into a fitful sleep.

15

"And after a string of beautiful, sunny days, it looks like we're headed toward some soggy weather. Let's go to meteorologist Jim Jaggers for more on our seven-day forecast. Jim?"

Grace absently abandons her overnight bag and purse by the front closet, all of her senses tuned in on the muted voices wafting from the end of the hall, and creeps slowly toward the closed door of their home gym.

"Thanks, Melissa. Well, if there's one thing we're going to get a lot of over the next few days, it's rain, rain, and more rain. We have two strong systems heading our way; one coming in from the north-northwest and the other from the northeast as shown here on the Doppler 3. Expect severe thunderstorms starting as early as this afternoon and continuing through Friday. We've got your full, in-depth coverage coming up in just a little bit. Melissa?"

"Thanks, Jim. Alright, you heard him, Folks. Strap on those galoshes. It's going to be a stormy week."

Grace gulps at the ominous forecast and presses her ear to the door. Along with the stifled voices of Channel 3's morning news anchors, she can also make out the treadmill's whirring motor accompanied by the steady rhythmic pounding of Mike's tennis shoes against its belt as he jogs.

She'd reached her hand out this morning to feel his warmth beneath it, but grasped a fistful of rumpled sheets instead. It took a few seconds for her to realize, as she blinked away her sleepy haze, that she wasn't in her room. And it took only a few seconds more after that for a sour mixture of regret and worry to form in the pit of her stomach.

Her father had already left for work by the time she staggered down the hall and into the living room to check on him. He'd left a note thanking her for everything and promising to call later that evening.

Coffee's on. Bagels are in the pantry. Stay as long as you like, was scrawled in his hasty, almost illegible professor's script. But a leisurely breakfast and a lazy morning were not options. She'd already stayed too long. What she needed to do was go home and talk things out with her husband like she should have done the day before.

Forgoing a shower, she splashed water on her face, threw her hair into a sloppy version of a ponytail, tossed on the mismatched change of clothes she'd packed, and weaved impatiently through morning rush hour traffic all the way back to the loft.

However, as she reaches for the brass knob of their home gym, something tells her that what waits on the other side of that door is not going to be pleasant.

She takes a deep, calming breath and pushes it open.

Mike's loping at a considerable speed, his eyes stern, his jaw clenched vituperatively, his glistening biceps flexing as he pumps his arms with each stride. He notices her as she slips into the room and stands sheepishly in the corner, but doesn't acknowledge her presence.

"Hey." Her greeting is meek and tentative. She offers a small wave.

He nods curtly without taking his eyes off the plasma screen anchored to the wall in front of him.

"My dad's doing better," Grace says, shuffling a few steps closer.

"Good to know," Mike huffs, his eyes still fixed ahead.

"I should have called," she says, her tone apologetic. "I just…" She sighs. "It was all kind of crazy, you know? By the time I got him back to his house, I didn't want to do anything but go to bed."

He doesn't respond, only wipes the beads of sweat from his forehead onto the bottom of his shirt, and continues to jog.

"So you're not talking to me now?"

"What…do you…want…me…to say?" he pants between labored breaths.

"I don't know." She shrugs and hugs herself tightly. "If you're upset with me then just say it."

"I'm past…upset." He decelerates the treadmill with the push of a button and snatches his water bottle from the holder beside the control panel. "I'm furious."

"Don't I even get the chance to explain myself?"

"No!" he barks, viciously wiping the perspiration from his neck and arms with a towel. "The chance for explanations has come and gone."

"You're not being fair."

"You storm out of here in the middle of a disagreement and don't bother coming back until the next morning and *I'm* not being fair?"

"It's not like you didn't know I wasn't coming back," she murmurs, her face cast downward. "I packed a bag."

"So what?" He chucks the towel against the metal stand of free weights. "You couldn't have at least called?"

"I said I was sorry."

"Sorry isn't good enough," he fumes. The words jut from his mouth slowly, coldly, each syllable frozen, midair, by his unrelenting anger.

Grace chafes at his tone and bold gaze. Less than 24 hours ago, he was the one in the hot seat. He was the one who'd schlepped home in need of a little bit of tolerance and a whole lot of understanding. Had she granted it to him? Maybe not as readily or abundantly as she should have, but if anything, that just evens out the playing field. He doesn't get to cast aspersions and hurl disdainful snarls her way just because he's suddenly experiencing what it feels like to be on the uninformed end of the stick. His absurdity is matched only by his hypocrisy, and she's ready to cauterize both.

"It's not like I abandoned you and treated myself to a wild night out on the town," she snaps, her index finger aimed dead between his eyes. "I spent half the evening in a seedy bar convincing my alcoholic father not to drown away his sorrows in a shot of bourbon, and the other half cooking his dinner and scrubbing down his kitchen. So excuse me if phoning home didn't top my list as an immediate priority."

"No!" he shouts and takes a step closer.

Despite herself, she flinches.

"I *won't* excuse you, Grace. You had me up half the night calling your relatives and local hospitals trying to figure out what was going on and if you and your dad were okay."

"If you were that worried, why didn't you just call me on my cell phone?"

"I did," he spits out, his eyes shooting daggers. "It rang and rang on the sofa table right where you left it."

"Well then, why didn't you call me at his house?"

"I did," Mike says again. "Repeatedly. No one ever picked up."

Grace's palms turn cold with guilt. She'd switched off the ringers on her father's three phones yesterday evening before they sat down to eat dinner. He'd been through enough for one day, and she hadn't wanted to chance any last-minute work emergencies or ill-timed phone calls from long-distance relatives. He needed to rest—to be served and taken care of with no interruptions.

She'd actually given herself a mental pat on the back as she watched him doze peacefully off to sleep on the couch, but now, twitching beneath her husband's interrogating stare, she realizes that cutting herself and her father off from the rest of the world was the furthest thing from a smart idea as she could get.

"I made a mistake, okay?" she shrieks, throwing her hands up in an odd combination of surrender and exasperation. "I'm sorry."

His pursed lips betray his disbelief. "What you don't seem to get," he says, turning away from her and pacing the length of the mirrored walls, "is that marriage is a team effort."

"Me?" she scoffs, incredulous. "You're the one who left for New York a CEO and came back unemployed—by *choice*, I might add."

He rolls his eyes and throws his head back in a manner that screams, *Here we go again!*

"Well, it's true," she argues.

"Yeah," he concedes with a nod. "And we've yet to have a civilized discussion about it because your solution to everything is to run away."

"What's to discuss?" she questions, her voice raised and insulted. "The fact of the matter is that I would never have made that kind of decision without consulting you first."

"Do me a favor." He glares down at her austerely, his nostrils flaring. "Don't tell me what you would never do in a situation until you've actually been faced with that situation, okay?"

"I don't need to be faced with a burning building to know I would never run into it," she snips, her neck swaying from side to side.

"Oh, it's that simple, is it?"

"If not simpler," she sniffs, her arms folded, her chin poked in the air.

"Fine, Grace. You win." He bows his head and steps away. "You want me to go back to *Life Sketch?* I'll go. Will that make you happy?"

She shrugs, caught off guard by his sudden white flag. "Yes?" she guesses, cautiously. "Well, I mean, I don't know—possibly."

"Even if you knew that God's undoubtedly closed that chapter in my life and that being there made me miserable?"

"Who isn't miserable at their job at some point or another?" she asks, with a questioning shrug. "That's why it's called 'work.'"

"That's your response?" he asks, his gaze as pained as his voice. "I tell you I'm miserable and your response is, 'Who isn't?'"

Well, when you put it that way... She bites her lip and cocks her head to the side. "That's not what I meant." She sighs. "I'm just saying that people—"

"Who did you marry, Grace?" he asks. "Who did you vow to spend the rest of your life with? Me or *Life Sketch?*"

"What kind of question is that?" she asks, annoyed.

"Judging from the way you're acting—a valid one."

She rolls her eyes. "Whatever."

"Answer the question," he demands. "Who do you love? Who did you marry?"

"You," she drones, bored.

"That's right!" His timbre is loud, forceful. "Me!" He slaps his chest. "I am your husband—your partner, your best friend, your lover, your confidante—and I'll continue to play all of those roles with or without *Life Sketch*. *I'm* still here. I'm still the same guy you married."

"I know," she says, surrendering her attitude.

"And we're still us," he says, motioning between the two of them, his gaze intense and penetrating.

She smiles weakly. "A strange, yet functional, balance of perfection...," she nods toward him, "and imperfection," she says, looking down at herself.

The corners of his mouth curve ever-so-slightly upward into the faintest semblance of a smile. It's the kindest expression he's offered her since she entered the room. "For the most part, anyway," he teases with a shrug.

She sighs. "I *am* sorry," she whispers.

He shakes his head. "That's still not enough."

"What will be enough?" she asks.

Wearily, he perches on the seat of the recumbent bike and massages his temples. "I'm in this," he says, after some time, "for forever, and I'm willing to do whatever it takes to make sure you're the one I grow old with." The anger in his voice gives way to an emotional quiver.

"I can't promise you perfection," he continues. "I can't guarantee we'll even come close. But I'm prepared to die trying, and no matter what, I'm going to love you for the rest of your life—and mine."

Grace blinks hard against the tears forming behind her eyelids.

"Forever's a long time, Grace," he says. "We're gonna get mad at each other a million times in the interim."

He looks up at her with his own tear-filled eyes. "And I'm okay with that." He nods his assurance. "Get mad. Scream at me, slam doors, roll your eyes, even hate me when it suits you, but always...," he clinches both fists, "*always* come home at the end of the day," he demands, his voice soft and pleading.

"My heart...," he grips his chest with both hands, one resting on top of the other, "it just...I can't take it when you don't. Always come back home," he says again. "That's what will be enough."

She nods fervently. She'd agree to dive in front of a speeding train if that's what would ease the utter despair in his eyes.

She wants to throw herself in his arms and plant kisses all over his face.

She wants to whisper promises in his ears.

She wants to squeeze him close until all of her thoughtless words and actions have been hugged away—but his furrowed brow and tense shoulders assure her that he doesn't want to be touched.

They remain mere feet away from each other, him sitting on the bike, her standing near the corner, both of them blanketed in silence and separated by unspeakable hurt and disappointment—both of them uncertain how to begin mending their own wounds, much less each other's.

"I'm gonna hop in the shower," he announces into the awkward stillness. He grabs his towel and empty water bottle and starts to shimmy past her toward the door.

"Hey," she says, tenderly tugging him to a halt. She rests her cheek against his chest and wraps her arms around him.

He hesitates before half-heartedly returning her embrace.

"I love you," she says, raising her puckered lips for a kiss.

He shrugs her off, his eyes closed. "Don't," he says, holding one hand up and shaking his head. "Please," he sighs, "I need time...and some space."

"Okay," she says, stung by his rejection, however gentle, and backs away.

"Call your grandparents," he advises without looking at her. "They're worried sick."

She nods and watches him as he turns toward the door and walks away.

16

The old loft is quiet and tidy. The remote controls rest on the coffee table between Grace's favorite set of jasmine candles and a framed photograph of her mother. The silverware is still organized in the drawer to the left of the dishwasher. The shades in the living room are drawn, and there's not a wrinkle or a crease in the pristinely made beds. Everything is just as Grace had left it months earlier after Trina had coasted out of her life, leaving a trail of ashes and beer cans in her wake.

A fine layer of dust blankets the mantle over the fireplace. Grace runs the tip of her index finger across it and sighs. She knew that Trina wouldn't be here—that despite the semi-kind words that had passed between them during their brief reunion the day before, Trina would not be able to erase the image of Ron and Tamara from her mind—that the betrayal Trina felt would be far too great an obstacle for her pride to hurdle.

Even so, there was a small piece of Grace that had hoped to find Trina's robe thrown across her unmade bed, her shoes in the front hall, and her breakfast dishes in the sink.

Despite all of her arguments, all of the valid reasons why she has kept her distance from Trina, Grace wants her best friend back. She *needs* her back.

She misses Trina's trademark spunk, her fearlessness, her unorthodox way of thinking. Trina would know just what to say about Grace's spat with Mike. She'd crack a couple of jokes to ease the mood, then offer intermittent words of comfort as Grace poured out her heart. She'd listen—really listen—and then dispense very practical advice. The best part is that if she thought Grace was wrong, she'd tell her, but gently, without rubbing it in her face or making her feel worse. At the end of their powwow, they'd hug, Trina would promise her that everything was going to be okay, and Grace, taking solace in Trina's confidence and company, would know it was true. That's the woman Grace so desperately misses—that's the Trina she loves and remembers.

If only they could go back. Grace yearns for the old days: for the time when their relationship made sense and life seemed so much simpler...back when she could just cross the living room, glide through Trina's open door, flop down on her bed, and gab for hours about nothing...when a walk to the mall with her best friend, two Mrs. Field's chocolate chunk cookies, and a handful of funny, old stories was the exact recipe for a perfect Saturday afternoon...when a cozy night in consisted of her, Trina, Mike, and Ron spread out on the living room floor with a stack of rented videos and a couple of pizzas.

Those were good times, Grace thinks to herself as thunder begins to roll in the distance. *Those were happy times.*

Even then, things weren't perfect, of course. Trina was as codependent as ever, constantly screwing up and constantly relying on Grace to bail her out. But they somehow managed to make it work. No matter what the offense or how traumatic the incident, they always somehow managed to forgive and come full circle. It's what made their bond—their sisterhood—so special.

Maybe that's why she hasn't sold her old loft, Grace thinks as she flops across the love seat. Why she still pays utilities for a home she no longer lives in. Maybe that's why she never changed the locks or gave away the furniture. She's been subconsciously waiting for everything to go back to normal—for the two of them to ease back into sync.

But it's become increasingly clear that if she wants things to go back to the way they were, she's going to have to take the initiative. And, for the first time since she and Trina went their separate ways, she's okay with that. It doesn't matter anymore who was wrong or who was right, who said what or who did what to whom. Her friendship with Trina is worth every ounce of energy it takes to maintain it.

Grace would rather that they brave the occasional fight as they grow together than submit to hating each other as they grow apart. Armed with that knowledge, she picks up the nearest phone and dials Trina at work.

"Home Sweet Home. This is Katrina," Trina recites like a trained parrot. The greeting's been so ingrained in her mind that she often has to check herself, after hours, when she answers her cell phone.

"It's me," Grace's voice trails through the receiver.

Silence.

"Can we talk?"

More silence.

"Yesterday was kind of a disaster." Grace pauses to see if Trina has anything to offer—a couple of words, even a grunt. Nothing.

"I wanted to explain about Tamara."

"No need," Trina says coolly. "I got your message loud and clear. Tamara's in and I'm out. Whatever. I hope the four of you are very happy together."

"We're hardly a foursome. I barely know her."

"What do you want, Grace?" Trina asks with a tired sigh.

"This has gone on long enough," Grace answers after a few moments. "Move back to the loft. I want things to go back to normal."

"What normal? There is no normal with us anymore." Trina taps her pen nervously against the yellow legal pad in front of her. "I don't even think there's an 'us' anymore."

"Please don't say that," Grace says, her voice a barely audible whisper. "You know that's not true."

"Oh yeah? Tell me one thing that's happened in my life in the past month."

"I can't," Grace says softly into the receiver. "But you don't know what's been going on with me either."

"That's my point," Trina says. "Real friends talk. And best friends don't wait months to call each other after a fight."

"We can work it out. Just come back," Grace pleads. "If not for me, then for you. It's better to stay at the loft than with Darius."

Trina glances at the comforter, pillow, and small overnight bag in the corner of her office. The rest of her things, two large trash bags of shoes, clothes, and toiletries, are tucked away in her car's rusty trunk.

She hadn't had the courage to go back to Darius's place last night after she'd left Grace's. It had taken all of her strength plus an extra dose of determination just to pack her things and leave. How could she crawl back to him, especially after how he'd treated her, and ask to spend another night on his rickety sleeper sofa? It was simply out of the question.

Kendra's place was out of the question too. After their meeting with Quinn, followed by their squabble in front of the elevators, Trina wouldn't have felt comfortable asking Kendra for a glass of water much less a place to crash.

Then there was Joss and Tai, who would have gladly lent her their spare bedrooms if she'd asked. But lately they'd both been joined at the hip with their significant others. To everyone's dismay, Eli had become a permanent fixture at Joss's cramped apartment, and Alan had schmoozed his way back into Tai's good graces, as well as her bed, with a bouquet of flowers and a sappy CD full of love songs he'd pirated off the Internet. Both Joss and Tai have been bitten by the love-bug, and Trina would've inevitably been a third wheel.

Aside from getting a hotel room she couldn't afford, her only other option was the loft. Yet every time Trina convinced herself to go back—just for the night—Tamara's smug grin and taunting eyes flashed in her mind.

Try as she might, she couldn't shake the image of Ron's arms wrapped protectively around Tamara's waist—the way they clung to each other possessively. Each time she thought of it, she felt sadness and loss, but more than anything, she felt betrayed by Grace.

Of all the terrible things that had transpired between the two of them, all of the hurtful words and thoughtless actions, Grace's hiring Ron's new girlfriend as her assistant felt like having the wind knocked out of her—repeatedly.

With no place to go and no one to turn to, Trina ended up camping out on her office floor, hidden behind her desk just in case anyone turned up in the building after hours and happened to pass by.

The floor, though carpeted, was hard, and the persistent hum of the vending machines and ice dispenser in the break room down the hall had kept her up most of the night. The experience was a dismal one to say the least.

But even now, with Grace waving her white flag and offering Trina the words she's waited months to hear, Trina can't sidestep her pride or shake the embarrassment she feels over yesterday's events.

"You and Darius aren't my only options," Trina sniffs. "I do have other friends, you know."

"Oh," Grace says, her disappointment plain. "Well, yeah, of course you do." She clears her throat in a vain attempt to sound calm and unfazed. "All I'm saying is that if you still want to stay at the loft, you can."

Trina leans back in her chair. "I don't know. I'm thinking maybe that's not the best idea."

"Because of Tamara?"

"And you and Mike," Trina adds. "It's all of you. It's everything. I just don't see a solution."

"So what're you saying? You don't want to be bothered with any of us anymore?" Grace asks.

"I'm saying that things change. People change. Including me."

"Fine, then we'll work on getting to know each other all over again," Grace suggests.

Trina grins, unexpectedly touched by Grace's persistence. "How do we do that?"

"We talk," Grace says. "We spend time together." She pauses. "I miss spending time with you."

"I know," Trina says, both her tone and her body relaxing. "Me too."

"Good," Grace says, her smile audible. "So what're we gonna do about it?"

Trina laughs. "Stop torturing ourselves and get together," she says, catching Kendra, just then, in the corner of her eye through her office's glass partition. She's plowing down the hall, past the cubicles, her "I'm on a Mission" scowl fastened firmly on her face.

"How about lunch?" Grace asks. "You want to meet at McCallister's?"

"Actually," Trina says, her stomach sinking as Kendra rounds the corner and appears in her doorway, "I'm kind of swamped at work right now. I'm probably not going to be able to take lunch today."

"Okay," Grace sighs. "Another time then."

Trina gazes up at Kendra, who taps the pointed toe of her heel against the floor and noisily shuffles through the folders cradled in the crook of her arm.

Kendra clears her throat obnoxiously. "Did you call County regarding files 2699876 and 2777040?" she asks, even though she can see, clear as day, that Trina is still on the phone.

Trina holds up her finger in a silent plea for more time. If this were an alternate universe and she had magical powers, she'd point her finger and, instead of shutting Kendra up, she'd zap her into nonexistence.

"I'll call you," Trina promises Grace. "As soon as things calm down here." Reluctantly, they say their good-byes. Trina hangs up and takes a long, cleansing breath. "Now," she says, grudgingly turning her focus to Kendra. "What did you need?"

Kendra repeats the question. Her tone is sterile and robotic; her pressed lips are framed in frown lines. This has pretty much been her M.O. since Trina balked at Quinn's dissolute request-slash-bribe the day before.

A line's been drawn and until Trina decides which side she wants to reside on, Kendra has brought a whole new meaning to the term, "business decorum." Aside from a laconic "Hello" in the break room this morning, their dealings with each other have been reduced to curt nods in the hallways and unpleasant exchanges that involve Kendra looming demandingly over Trina's desk, paperwork in hand, confirming statuses and prattling off questions.

On another day, when Trina hadn't spent a torturous night tossing and turning on her hard office floor, Kendra's attitude would seem less insulting and not nearly as irritating. But on the heels of two hours of sleep, the last thing Trina is equipped to do is withstand Kendra's passive-aggressive idiocy.

Trina blinks at the mountainous stack of untouched files on her desk and on the floor beside it. Her eyes then involuntarily move to the loaded, four-tier, metal file cabinet in the corner of her office. Expecting her to know a case solely by its number is equivalent to asking her to memorize all the cracks on every downtown sidewalk—impossible.

Files 2699876 and 2777040 might as well be resting at the bottom of the ocean.

"I'm not sure," Trina says, flipping insipidly through the folder closest to her in a pretend search. "What are the last names?"

Kendra juts out her hip and lets out an annoyed sigh. "Gonzalez and Morgan." She offers the names slowly, enunciating each syllable as though Trina is mentally challenged or hard of hearing, her tone teeming with impatience and the worst kind of inconvenience.

Unfortunately neither name rings a bell. "I'll look into it," Trina says, scrawling the information on the legal pad in front of her.

"You said that last week," Kendra quips. "These files needed to be submitted yesterday."

"So did twenty others," Trina says, her chin raised resentfully.

"It's not my responsibility to make sure your work gets submitted on time."

"I'm handling nearly a hundred and thirty cases right now," Trina argues. "There's only, realistically, so much I can do in an eight-hour workday."

"Is that what you'd like me to tell Gonzalez's and Morgan's social worker?" she asks, her gaze probing, her tone cynical. "We don't have their medical records because their case worker's workload is unrealistic?"

Trina tosses her pen onto her desk and folds her arms. "Why don't we talk about what's really going on," she says, challenging Kendra with a bold stare.

"And what exactly is that?"

"The fact that you're mad because I won't help you and Quinn sacrifice a six-year-old girl on the altar of her father's political career."

"Are you out of your mind?" Kendra snaps, her voice a frantic whisper. She dashes to the open door and pops her head out, scanning the hallway for any potential eavesdroppers, before closing it and settling her steely glare on

Trina. "That is not a matter to be discussed outside of Quinn's office," she says tersely, her words clipped with anger.

"Why? *We're* the ones doing all the dirty work."

"We haven't done anything," Kendra whispers. Her eyes dart suspiciously around the room as though she suspects that the whole place might be bugged and at any second federal agents might leap from behind the desk or suspend from the vents and drag her scandalous rear end, kicking and screaming, to the Big House.

"Not yet," Trina says.

"Not *ever*," Kendra snaps, "if you don't stop cowering behind your right-eous indignation and start acting like a woman with something to gain."

"What's worth more than peace of mind?"

"Oh, come off it!" Kendra exclaims, rolling her head to the side with disgust. "Save the 'church girl' act for someone else. If we don't do this, we're going to get fired," she says pointedly. "Tell me, where's the peace of mind in that?"

"We're not going to get fired," Trina mumbles unconvincingly.

"When a boss like Quinn calls you in and says, 'I need a file taken care of,' it's not a request; it's a demand. If we don't do it, she's going to get rid of us and find someone else who will. And trust me," Kendra says, her hands clasped tightly in front of her, "there are plenty of people foaming at the mouth for a break like this."

"Listen to yourself," Trina says, dismayed by Kendra's shameless oppor-tunism. "What we've been asked to do to Becky Schmidt is immoral and ille-gal, and you're acting like it's a once-in-a-lifetime opportunity."

"I'm not saying it's right; I'm saying it's going to happen either way." She perches on the corner of Trina's desk. "Why be victims of circumstances that are beyond our control when we have the option to benefit from them instead?"

Trina doesn't have an answer. The truth is, she doesn't want to benefit at the expense of someone else's happiness and security, especially not a defense-less six-year-old. But on the other hand, Kendra is right; Quinn's going to find a solution to the whole Councilman Schmidt conundrum with or without their help. In Quinn's eyes, she and Kendra come a dime a dozen; they're dispensable, merely two of hundreds of stockpiled employees, who can be replaced with a phone call.

Trina could take a stand and refuse Quinn's request, but what good would that do? Her words would most certainly fall on deaf ears, and Becky's fate would remain just as grim.

"Think about it," Kendra says, sensing Trina's wavering will. "In a matter of weeks, you could be a director again. You know what that means: thirty thousand more a year, a car allowance, an annual bonus, a huge office on the top floor of a brand-new building, a personal secretary, a reserved parking space, and most importantly, Quinn's undying gratitude and favor."

Trina nods. It is, indeed, a very tempting list of perks. The salary hike alone would put her in a position to provide for herself like she'd never been able to before.

She could finally afford her own place—really afford it. Not like all the other times when she'd managed to scrape up the first and last month's rent and the security deposit only to have to borrow money from her Aunt Arlene for groceries or from Grace for utilities.

She wouldn't have to pack up in the middle of the night and bail on her lease. She'd stay as long as it suited her and she'd decorate the place to her taste. No more of her aunt's secondhand Salvation Army scraps or Darius's tacky, lacquer headboards.

Then there's the car allowance, a perk that wasn't even offered to her as the director of child psychology. She'd be able to buy a new car—her very first *new* car—something shiny, with automatic everything, leather seats, and a sunroof; something dependable; something she'd be proud to be seen in.

And a secretary! Oh, she remembers when! How much easier life was with an assistant! She'd be able to delegate all of the monotonous busywork to someone else. She wouldn't have to waste hours filling out reports and requesting medical charts and jockeying for court dates. She'd be able to focus her attention on what matters: the kids, and making sure they get placed in homes that meet their needs.

In short, this promotion could provide for a multitude of needs. This is what she's been waiting for—praying for—for most of her adult life: the means with which to own her independence. She's watched all of her friends claim theirs, Grace and Darius included. They'd graduated from college, armed with degrees and dreams, and made their way in life. But Trina never quite took flight. All this time, she's been like a bird with a broken wing; for all of her effort, she can't get off the ground.

The closest she had ever come to being airborne was during her brief stint as director of child psychology for Home Sweet Home. The feeling was glorious, being able to pay bills on time, splurge on a few personal wants, and still have a little left over to put in her savings. She had plans and goals—big ones. But sadly, she hadn't held the position long enough to reap any real, long-term benefits. And while she'd love another shot at it, she has to ask herself, at what cost?

If she helps reunite Becky with her father and Becky lands back in the hospital, with the same familiar bruises and appalling stories, Trina will never forgive herself. And what if Becky's not as fortunate as she was the last time around? What if there's no attentive teacher? No one brave enough to call Child Protective Services on the revered Councilman Schmidt if things smelled fishy. The potential for tragedy is very real and very horrifying.

Still, Kendra has a valid argument. There's only so much they can do. If Quinn's determined to send Becky home, then home Becky will go. Why end up fired for refusing to do something that's going to happen anyway? And what's she's supposed to do without a job? Start temping again? Sponge off Grace? Grovel at Darius's doorstep? Move back to Detroit? *There's no way.*

A director's salary would quell all of those worries. Not to mention she'd have more rank. She could throw her weight around if need be, keep a close, personal eye on Becky, and if anything went awry, she could snatch her back and place her with a family who deserved her.

She could find a way to make it work—to make everyone, including herself, happy. Why should she be the only one who can't have her cake and eat it too?

"I'll think about it," she says, not quite swayed, but much closer to Kendra's side of the fence than she originally had been.

"Good." Kendra smirks, clearly pleased with her progress. "You'll see. A couple of months from now when you've got your feet kicked up in your corner office and a secretary running your errands and bringing you lattes, this'll all be forgotten and Becky Schmidt won't be anything more than a distant memory."

"Yeah, maybe," Trina says distractedly.

"So I'll see you at Heckles tonight?" Kendra asks, gathering the folders she came in with and detaching herself from Trina's desk.

Trina nods. "Eight o'clock. And, um, I might bring a friend, if that's okay."

"Whatever," Kendra says cheerily, her mood decidedly lighter than it was at the beginning of their conversation. "Just don't forget about Gonzalez and Morgan," she instructs, already halfway out of the door. "I still need their medical charts."

Trina nods mechanically, but Kendra's words don't register. Gonzalez and Morgan fall a far second to Becky Schmidt and all that's at stake if Trina agrees to take part in Quinn's underhanded scheme.

17

All hopeful anticipation of talking to Mike flies quickly out of the window when Grace returns from her old loft to find him holed away in his office, Billie Holiday blaring from behind the closed door.

Grace has become a pro at interpreting Mike's disposition through his music selections. Luther and Teddy mean he's in a great mood, and if he's singing along, that's even better. Miles and Duke mean he's got a lot on his mind—he's pensive, not necessarily angry, but he needs time by himself to think. But Billie Holiday means he's upset. Billie Holiday means he's painting to keep from hurting or yelling—or both. Her slow, bluesy voice and haunting brass accompaniments mean he's fighting to realign his heart with his mind.

At least it's not Bessie Smith, she thinks glumly as she turns in the opposite direction toward their library. Bessie means he's downright depressed. She prays that his funk doesn't regress to that. She doesn't know if she can take hours upon hours of "Worried Life Blues."

Her instincts tell her to knock on the door, turn off the stereo, and force him to talk to her. It doesn't have to be this way. If they could just apologize, agree that they both could've handled their respective situations with more care and consideration for the other person, then they could put this whole disaster behind them and move on.

But she doesn't follow her instincts. Instead, she opens her laptop and tries to focus on her second novel, which, over the months, has become more of a labor than a labor of love.

The first book practically wrote itself. The words came flooding to her faster than she could get them down on paper. She'd written the first two chapters in one sitting, after that horrible first meeting with her father. It's the closest to crazy she can ever remember feeling, apart from after her mother's death. The swelling emotions were more than her body could carry, and so, without hope or agenda, she purged her pain using a legal pad and a ballpoint pen. And from that cathartic passion, her first novel was born.

She had assumed early on, before the first novel had even been published, that the second novel would be more of a challenge to write. After all, the first one is simply her life story thinly veiled as fiction. The characters came already developed and the plots came authenticated from her own true-life experiences. But the latter would truly test her skills and work her imagination.

She had expected the frustrating blockages. She'd anticipated the agonizing rewrites. She'd even predicted the occasional bout of stifling doubt. She had not, however, expected to scrap entire chapters or fall in and out of love with one main character after the next. She hadn't anticipated the sheer panic that overtakes her each time she stacks her barely finished manuscript against her publisher's rapidly approaching deadline.

The blinking cursor taunts her—goads her to get on with it, to write something dazzling, something witty, something that will morph this work-in-progress into a masterpiece, something that will spark an eternal flame in anyone who picks it up and reads it. But her mind isn't on the cursor or the story; it's on Mike.

"Sometimes I wonder what's in store for me. Your love could open Heaven's door for me," Billie croons from down the hall. "But you don't care a straw for me. That's life, I guess."

Grace sighs as her chest tightens. *Is that what he thinks of our relationship?* she wonders glumly.

"The world was bright when you loved me. Sweet was the touch of your lips," Billie continues. "The world went dark when you left me, and then there came a total eclipse."

Grace shakes her head, her mood dampening. "These lyrics could push a dead person to suicide," she grumbles to no one in particular.

The song continues, "Nobody knows how cruel fate can be—how close together love and hate can be. Good-bye, just clean the slate for me. That's life, I guess."

They *have* to talk, Grace resolves. She'll wait for him to listen to the whole CD—a small, but cherished inheritance from his father—and when the music stops, she'll check in on him.

The plan is enough to settle her stomach, until an hour or so later, when the last of Billie's songs fades away and Etta James's raspy voice begins to resonate throughout the loft before Grace can even get out of her seat. She rests her face in her hands and groans inwardly. Etta is not a good sign.

"Oh, I can't go on, can't go on, can't go on," sings Etta. "Everything I have is gone. Stormy weather, stormy weather…keeps raining all of the time."

Not a good sign at all.

The phone rings, abruptly pulling Grace from her worried thoughts.

It's Trina. "You still want to get together?" are the first words out of her mouth.

"Of course," Grace says, her mood instantly lifting. "What'd you have in mind?"

"I'm meeting some girlfriends tonight at Heckles, and I want you to come."

"Heckles?" Grace asks, already leery.

"Yeah, it's a comedy club. I really think you'll like it."

"When I suggested we get together, I was thinking more along the lines of lunch or a cup of coffee," Grace says.

"Come on," Trina prods. "You said we were going to work on getting to know each other again. Well, this is a perfect way to start. It'll be fun—lots of laughs. Plus, you'll get a chance to meet my girlfriends."

Grace sighs. It's not that she doesn't want to spend time with Trina, even if it is with strangers at a comedy club. But how can she reward herself with an evening of lighthearted entertainment, given the certain turmoil brewing at home. What would it look like, her traipsing off to a comedy club as though she doesn't have a care in the world? How would she explain that to Mike? "I wish I could, I really do, but things aren't the best at home right now…," Grace says, her voice trailing off.

"You mean with Mike?" Trina asks.

"Yeah," Grace says, immediately delving into a detailed account of yesterday's events. "It's my fault," she relents with a sigh. "I should have called. But you know how I can be."

"Spoiled and stubborn," Trina says.

"I meant that more as a rhetorical question," Grace jokes.

"You know everything's going to be okay, right?" Trina asks, her tone serious. "Mike's a genius. He's like," she pauses, in search of an adequate analogy, "Donald Trump and Picasso rolled into one person. You two will sit down, hammer out a brilliant plan for the future, and be happier than you ever thought possible.

"And your dad, he's going to be fine. He had a moment—chalk it up to temporary insanity and let it go. At least you guys are at a point where you can depend on each other like you do. Three years ago, you didn't even know he lived in the same city as you."

"You're right," Grace says, soaking in Trina's encouraging words. They're soothing, like a cold compress on a throbbing bruise.

"So then come out with me tonight," she pleads again. "You need a break, and I know you. If I don't drag you somewhere, you'll be at home, crying over a pint of butter pecan ice cream feeling sorry for yourself."

Grace smiles. It's clear that the months she and Trina have spent apart, though awkward and painful, were necessary. "You really have changed," she says.

"Not as much as I'd like to believe," Trina confesses.

"No," Grace shakes her head. "You're different...I don't know. Happy. Stable."

Trina's not sure how to respond. She hadn't felt very stable all of those early mornings when Darius went missing or those sleepless nights after he kicked her out of his bedroom and onto his couch. And she definitely wouldn't describe herself as happy on those weekends she hangs out with Joss, Tai, and Kendra. Sure she laughs, she even has fun, but she's not *happy*—not in the way Grace means. She's not at peace. But she can't tell Grace that, not yet. "Did I tell you I'm up for a promotion?" Trina asks.

"What?" Grace squeals. "No! That's wonderful, congratulations!"

"It's not in the bag yet," Trina says. "I'm actually thinking of turning it down."

"What? Why?"

Because I'd have to sell my soul to get it, she thinks, but says instead, "I'd be directing all the case managers in Germantown and, I don't know, it's a big job—very demanding."

"So?" Grace says, dismissing Trina's doubts and replacing them with her own excitement. "If anyone can handle it, it's you."

Trina laughs. "What makes you so sure?"

"I've never seen anyone who loves kids like you do," Grace says. "You really have their best interests at heart. And you'll do whatever it takes to make sure the right thing gets done."

Trina strains to maintain a light tone as she swallows hard against the guilt stuck at the back of her throat. "You make me sound like a saint," she says.

"That's exactly what you are to those kids. You give them hope."

Trina titters nervously. The sound is forced and unnatural, but Grace doesn't seem to notice. *If only you knew!* Trina wants to shout. Hope is the last thing she'll be offering Becky Schmidt. "So are you in?" Trina asks, eagerly changing the subject. "The comedy club, I mean."

Grace dips her head from side to side as she considers. "Yeah, why not?"

Trina smiles. "You won't regret it," she promises.

They chat a while longer, catching each other up on some of the events and people they'd missed out on while they'd been apart.

Grace's outlook is brighter as she hangs up and turns her attention back to her ever-evolving novel—that is, until Mike's Etta James CD gets swapped out for Muddy Waters, who's followed by Ella Fitzgerald, who's followed still by B.B. King.

All afternoon he listens to an eclectic combination of the blues and jazz. He doesn't emerge once, not to use the bathroom or to fix something to eat, not to stretch his legs or to see if Grace is home. All through the afternoon and into the early evening, he remains in his office, with the door closed—just him, Billie, Etta, Muddy, Ella, and B.B.

Grace exercises every bit of unselfish restraint in her body and respects his space. But as the clock nears eight and her date with Trina draws closer, she knows she's got to speak to him, even if it's just to tell him she's leaving.

She changes into a fresh pair of jeans, slips into a lightweight, scoop-neck sweater, and brushes on a thin coat of lip gloss. Examining her handiwork in their bathroom's full-length mirror, she's pleased with the result. Her outfit says friendly, but taken.

She gives herself a couple spritzes of perfume and then makes her way, purse in hand, to Mike's office.

He doesn't respond to her first knock. She reaches for the knob, but to her dismay the door is locked. He never locks his office door, not even when he's on conference calls or conducting business with important clients. She instantly grows nervous and wipes her cold, damp hands against her jeans. "Mike," she calls, and knocks again, this time a little harder.

She hears his painting stool scrape the hardwood floors and then the sound of heavy footsteps.

He cracks the door and pokes his head out. "Yeah?"

Grace searches his face for any clues as to where his mood is, but he's neutral—a blank canvas. "You alright?" she asks.

"Fine," he nods curtly.

"Oh. Okay. I wasn't sure," she says, shrugging apologetically. "You've been in there all day."

"I'm working," he says, simply.

"Okay," Grace nods, unable, for some reason, to look him in the eye.

He examines her, his head tilted curiously. "*You* alright?" he asks.

"Yeah, sure." She forces a smile. "Actually, I'm on my way out with Trina." She pauses. "If that's okay."

"Yeah," he says, his tone blithe. "Have fun."

"Really? Because I don't mind staying here."

He opens the door a bit wider, his expression perplexed. "Do you *want* to stay here?"

"No…well, I mean…yes. If you want me to."

He shrugs and shakes his head simultaneously. "I'll be working the rest of the night. Might as well do your own thing. Enjoy yourself."

"Okay," she says slowly, unsure of what to make of his nonchalance. "Well, I won't be late and I have my cell phone if you need me."

He smiles. "K. See ya." And just as quickly as he emerged, he disappears back into his office.

See ya, Grace thinks and heads out to meet Trina for their estrogen-packed evening of carefree fun.

18

As planned, Trina is waiting by her car in Home Sweet Home's parking lot. She smiles warmly as Grace pulls up, but instead of the tight embrace Grace is expecting when she climbs out of her car, Trina's face falls and her brows furrow.

"That's what you're wearing?" she asks, scanning Grace from head to toe.

Trina herself is sporting a midriff-baring tube top and ultra (ultra-ultra) low-rise jeans—not exactly practical attire, given the chilly late-October wind swirling around them and the inevitability of an evening thunderstorm—but stylish and sexy nonetheless. It's the kind of outfit Grace could never (and would never) wear, no matter what the season. Even with her weight loss, Grace has a fundamentally different build than Trina. Trina is naturally slim with sinewy legs, narrow shoulders, and size-six feet. But reedy thighs and a concave stomach have never been in the cards for Grace. She's "big boned" and solid. "Built like a fire hydrant," Grandma Doria used to say.

"What's wrong with this?" Grace asks, smoothing out her sweater as if removing the wrinkles might render it less offensive.

Trina smiles politely. "Nothing." She scratches her head and eyes Grace's leather flats. "It's just that, we're going to Heckles."

"I didn't know comedy clubs had dress codes."

"It's not a code, per se…," Trina says, casting another derisive glance at Grace's sensible outfit. "It's just—you might be uncomfortable in that."

"You want me to go back home and change?" Grace asks, her tone a blend of irritation and affront.

"No." Trina holds up her hands and shakes her head. "If you're fine with it, then I'm fine with it."

"Good." Grace nods.

"Good," Trina echoes, seemingly satisfied, though beneath it all, she's anything but. *Maybe this really wasn't such a good idea.*

Earlier that day, after Trina had gone to the break room for a caffeine fix and had a second nerve-wracking run-in with Kendra, she'd begun to have second thoughts about inviting Grace to hang out with her tonight. She sincerely wanted to mend their friendship, and she'd meant what she said earlier about cheering Grace up and getting her out of the house.

But different situations and people call for different etiquette, and Trina knows that she's a different person around Tai, Kendra, and Joss than she is when she's around Grace. She has to be. Grace is a good girl, replete with the golden halo and fluffy, white wings. She doesn't drink or smoke. She obeys the speed limit, pays her bills on time, reads her Bible, and brushes her teeth every night before she goes to bed.

But Kendra, Tai, and Joss enjoy the edgier side of life. They aren't heathens, but they're also not afraid to cut loose. On occasion, they're more than willing to pay the consequences for an evening of unfettered fun. They work hard and they play hard—that's the only balance they know.

For the rest of the afternoon, Trina had worked to convince herself that they'd find a middle ground—an area that all five of them could inhabit for the evening, an open-minded place where Grace would loosen up and the girls would tone down and everyone would mesh instinctively. But one look at Grace's outfit tells Trina that the odds of such a place existing are very, very slim.

"Should we go?" Grace asks, still standing behind her driver's door.

"Sure," Trina says, patting herself down for keys. She snatches her purse from among her trunkful of belongings and joins Grace in her car.

"I'm excited," Grace says, pulling out of the parking lot and steering them downtown. "I think this is just what the doctor ordered."

"Yeah," Trina nods, her smile wide. "I hope so." And she does, even though the nagging worry roiling in her stomach suggests that this particular hope is nothing more than a futile dream.

19

Grace doesn't need to enter Heckles to understand why Trina questioned her outfit. She only has to look at the line of skimpily clad women shivering behind the velvet rope in front of the club's entrance. There are enough see-through mesh tops, hiked spandex skirts, bottom-bearing cutoff shorts, and "pleather" stilettos to shoot a full spread for *Playboy*.

"How could they come out of the house dressed like that?" Grace wonders out loud as she pulls into a parking space.

Trina gives her makeup one last check in the visor mirror before flipping it back into place. "Is this what you're going to do all night? Sit around and criticize strangers?"

"I'm not criticizing. I made a comment," Grace says, arching her brow. "Not dissimilar from the one you made about *my* outfit."

"We're here to have a good time," Trina says, punctuating every other word with a nod of her head as though she's trying to give herself a pep talk.

"And we will," Grace says slowly. "But look at that." She points back to the line of veritable porn stars in the making. "That's just plain tacky."

"Just try to loosen up," Trina instructs as they make their way down the aisle of parked cars and toward the entrance of the club. "This is a different crowd than you're used to, but they're a lot of fun."

"I'm fun," Grace argues.

"Yeah, but in a 'Let's eat Chex mix and play Scrabble' kind of way."

"What's that supposed to mean?"

"I invite you to a club and you wear loafers and a sweater," Trina says, tossing up her hands as if that's explanation enough.

"Maybe this wasn't such a good idea," Grace says, slowing her pace. "I don't want to, you know," she shrugs and casts Trina a hurt look, "embarrass you."

"Stop," Trina says, gripping Grace's wrist. "You know you could never embarrass me."

Grace nods, and they continue toward the club. But as they take their place at the end of the line, the uncomfortable silence that settles between them tells them both that Trina's words aren't entirely true.

Heckles, with its concrete floors, cedar rafters, exposed piping, and brick walls, is merely a warehouse that's been furnished with plastic tables and chairs. Twenty minutes until the opening act and the place is packed with people, some seated in front of the stage, most milling and mingling by the bar.

Trina snakes her way through the crowd with confidence. Grace follows behind, self-consciously tugging at her sweater and parrying questioning stares and snide smirks. They wind up right in front of the stage at a table occupied by, arguably, three of the most attractive women Grace has ever encountered in person.

"Teeny!" the three of them squawk simultaneously at the sight of Trina.

Grace raises a brow at the moniker, but Trina pretends not to see.

"Look at you," Joss coos. "Just as gorgeous and fashionably late as ever."

"You know me," Trina says with a smug grin. "I never disappoint. This is Grace," she says, stepping aside.

Grace nods and offers a quick, nervous smile. Kendra, Joss, and Tai, all sporting similar versions of Trina's outfit, take in Grace's dowdy attire and stiff posture, but say nothing.

"She needed to blow off some steam," Trina explains. "So I invited her to join in on our girls' night out."

"Sure." Kendra is the first to speak. "Welcome. The more the merrier, right?" She points to the chair across the table from her and motions for Grace to sit down. Joss and Tai introduce themselves.

"You picked a good night to come," Joss says, handing Grace a folded program. "The comics lined up for tonight are hilarious."

"You guys come here often?" Grace asks.

Trina shrugs. "Two, three times a month."

"So Grace," Tai chimes in, "how do you know Trina?"

"Oh, we go way back," Grace says with a smile. "We're really more like sisters. We grew up together."

"Hm." Kendra gives a curious grunt and takes a sip of the lime-green liquid sloshing around in her martini glass. "That's funny, Teeny never mentioned you."

"Oh," Grace says, more troubled by Kendra's antagonizing demeanor than the fact that Trina chose to omit their friendship. "Well, we haven't been able to spend a lot of time together lately."

"Yeah," Trina jumps in. "Grace just got married. So, you know how that is. She's been holed up with her husband for the past few months."

"I thought I wanted to get married," Joss says. "But I'm not so sure anymore. Eli is a complete slob."

"You're just now figuring that out?" Kendra asks.

"Eli is Joss's boyfriend," Trina explains.

"Soon to be ex-boyfriend," Joss says, grabbing a handful of nuts from the basket in the center of the table. "We used to connect on so many levels." The corners of her mouth turn down in a sour frown. "These days, the only place we seem to connect is in bed."

"And that's a bad thing?" Kendra asks.

"Well, yeah. You can't have a relationship purely based on sex."

"You can if it's good sex," Kendra says.

"But let's face it," Tai interjects. "How often does that come along?"

"At least three times a week, if I can help it," Kendra says with a self-assured smirk.

"Guys." Trina clears her throat and shifts uncomfortably. "I'm sure that's a little more information than Grace needs to know."

"Oh, come on," Joss groans, dismissing Trina's plea for decorum with a torpid wave of her hand. "We're all adults here."

Grace nods. "It's fine," she assures Trina. "It's nothing I haven't heard before."

"See?" Joss grins.

Trina shrugs, embarrassed. "Grace is a Christian," she explains apologetically to the others.

Grace leans away in surprise, her eyes narrowed angrily. "And you're not?"

Kendra's uproarious laughter turns heads at several nearby tables. "That girl curses like a sailor, drinks like a fish, and humps like a rabbit. I don't think she quite meets the criteria for Christendom."

"I totally plan on taking up a religion someday," Tai says.

"Me too," Joss agrees. "When I'm older—after I've had all my fun."

Grace stares at the four of them in disbelief.

"You know what?" Trina says, standing abruptly. "I need a drink. Refill?" she asks, pointing at Joss's empty bottle of beer.

Joss nods, and in an instant, Trina vanishes into the dense crowd.

Kendra leans forward. "So, Grace," she says, grinning curiously, "what do you do?"

"I'm an author."

"Oh," Joss perks up, "what do you write?"

"Initially children's books," Grace says, itching to leave. "But I just made the transition to novels last year."

"Cool," Tai says, nodding and interested. "So you're one of those brooding, starving artist types."

Grace laughs. "I don't know about brooding."

"Well, you're definitely not starving," Kendra murmurs, eyeing Grace's bulging mid-section.

"I'm also not deaf," Grace says, her voice cold.

"Don't take it personally," Tai says, her head tilted sympathetically. "Kendra has something to say about everyone."

"We usually just ignore her," Joss jokes in a mock whisper.

"Well, no offense," Grace says, her gaze firmly planted on Kendra, "but you don't know me well enough to say anything about me."

"Sorry," Kendra snips insolently, flicking her hair. "Clearly some people don't have a sense of humor."

"Or manners," Grace retorts.

Kendra scoffs, piqued, her mouth open, her eyes flaring, but before she has a chance to respond, Trina reemerges with two beers in one hand and a bottle of Perrier in the other.

Trina slides Joss her beer and sets the Perrier along with a napkin in front of Grace. "I hope that's okay," she says, refusing to look Grace in the eye. "It's the only non-alcoholic drink they had."

"It's fine, thanks," Grace says gruffly and pushes the bottle aside.

Trina, Kendra, Joss, and Tai continue with their idle chatter—making noise, but saying nothing. They laugh affectedly at Kendra's crude stories, sip their drinks, and babble on and on about the newest diets and latest fashion trends. Trina tries to referee, occasionally bidding Joss not to curse so much or begging Tai not to share another one of her risqué escapades. But Grace is still appalled. Even on their best behavior, these women, Trina included, are shallow and mean.

"Ladies and gentlemen," a male voice booms throughout the room. "Put your hands together and make some noise for the talented—the hilarious—the unforgettable…Danny Gleason!"

The club grows dark, as blue and green strobe lights streak across the stage and throughout the audience. Fast-paced music begins to blare from every corner of the room. Its heavy bass makes the air pulse as the crowd bursts into applause. Trina, along with the rest of her cronies, whoops and screams as the announcer continues to pump up the suddenly restless horde.

Finally the spotlight settles center stage, and the curtains draw back to reveal a gangly black man with a neatly trimmed Afro and an equally neat goatee. He's decked out in a bright blue, doubled-breasted suit with matching blue alligator shoes.

"How y'all doin' tonight?" he asks, pacing back and forth like a caged lion, microphone in hand.

The crowd responds with more clapping and screaming.

"Y'all lookin' good tonight," he says, stopping to examine his rowdy fans. "Mm-hmm," he hums, honing in on one of the half-naked women in the audience. He licks his lips and studies her more intensely, cocking his head to the side to get a better look. "Real, real good," he says.

Everyone laughs. The woman smiles, but tries to hide her face behind her date's shoulder.

"That's your man?" Danny asks, pointing at the burly guy seated next to her.

She nods shyly and hooks her arm through his.

"Brotha," Danny says, shaking his head, "now you know you one lucky son-of-a—," he stops short and shakes his head in lieu of finishing the profane phrase.

Grace coughs and takes a sip of her water. Trina casts her an apologetic glance, but promptly returns to laughing with the rest of the audience.

"I'm happy for you, though," Danny says, a devious grin on his face. "I really am. Because if an ugly gorilla like you can get a woman that fine," he throws up his hands, "there's hope for us all!"

The crowd hollers and cackles. Trina doubles over in laughter, her eyes dancing with delight.

The burly guy is clearly uncomfortable, but tries his best to laugh it off like a good sport.

Danny continues to roast random audience members. Grace chafes at his vulgar words and spiteful jibes, but no one else seems to mind. Eventually his insults move from the audience to the President and his Cabinet. He spends several unbearable minutes bashing everyone from the First Lady to the White House janitor. From there, he segues into how much better off the country would be if America would finally elect a black man as President. And then he spends several more minutes listing all the reasons why drugs should be legalized. His routine is irreverent and animated and peppered with coarse sexual innuendos and the worst kind of profanity.

Grace's knee bobs impatiently beneath the table as she silently wills the comic off stage so she can make an early exit and end this insufferable night.

"I grew up in church," Danny says. "How many of y'all grew up in church?"

The majority of the audience raises its hands. "You ever notice how Jesus changes colors?" he asks.

The crowd laughs. Grace's muscles instantly stiffen.

"Naw, I'm serious," Danny says. "In the church I grew up at, there was a mural on the wall behind the pulpit of Jesus feedin' some sheep. And dude was black. I don't mean high yellow, neither. The Jesus in my church was blue-black—nappy hair and er'thang. Lookted just like my Uncle Chester."

The room is filled with amused chuckles and stifled sniggers.

"So of course," Danny continues, "I grew up thinkin' Jesus was black. But then I got older, started traveling a lil' bit, and somehow or another, I ended up at this white church. I was, maybe, sixteen." He shakes his head and holds his hand up in earnest. "First time I ever seent Jesus with long blond hair and pasty skin. Man! You wanna talk about an identity crisis?"

He takes a second to laugh with the audience before continuing. "Was Jesus a Brotha or was he a white boy? I had to know. So, I did a lil' research of my own," he says, strutting across the stage, his chest poked out. "And guess what y'all? Jesus ain't black or white." He pauses for dramatic effect. "He's Puerto Rican."

The audience erupts into laughter. "Hold up! Hold up!" Danny says, beckoning them to quiet down. "I'mma tell you why I know that. The first and most obvious reason…," he shrugs, "His name is Jesus." He pronounces the name with a provocative Spanish accent. "Second, He was always in trouble with the law. And third," he puts his hands on his hip and sweeps the crowd with a menacing gaze, "His mamma ain't know who His daddy was."

The audience applauds and cheers uproariously, including Trina, who grabs a napkin from the table to dab the tears from her eyes.

Grace snatches her purse. "I gotta go," she says to Trina. "It was nice meeting you," she says to Joss and Tai, deliberately ignoring Kendra.

They exchange puzzled glances, but wish her a good evening all the same.

"Where are you going?" Trina whispers.

"Home," Grace says, not bothering to lower her voice. "I can't take any more of this garbage." Without bothering to wait for a response, she gets up and navigates her way through the sea of seated guests and out of the nearest exit.

The wind is blowing hard, and the air is heavy with the scent of brewing rain as she searches for her car in the poorly lit, overcrowded parking lot. Grace's only regret is that she didn't leave sooner. She kept hoping to uncover a little bit of substance in Trina and her friends—in their lifestyle—but there was nothing. Just blind superficiality.

"What was that all about?" an angry voice asks.

Grace turns around to see Trina plowing toward her. "You tell me," Grace says, her arms folded.

"I told you that you had to keep an open mind," Trina argues. Thunder rumbles above them in the distance.

"Yeah, well," Grace rummages through her purse for her keys, "I didn't know you meant at the expense of my morals."

"I thought we were having fun."

"That's your idea of fun?" Grace asks, incredulous. "Listening to some guy blaspheme Christ? You should've been offended. But, oh, yeah," she says, throwing her head back in mock earnest, "I forgot. I was the only Christian at the table tonight."

"That's not fair," Trina says, her chest heaving angrily.

"Is this the new you I'm supposed to get to know?" Grace asks sadly. "This is what makes you happy now, parading your body for strangers and surrounding yourself with vapid people?"

"No. Of course not. I'd rather be like you," Trina says, her glare venomous. "I just don't know where to find a pedestal that high."

"What's that supposed to mean?"

"Oh, come on!" Trina shouts. "Look at you: the quintessential business woman and happy housewife and perfect daughter all rolled into one unblemished package. Don't tell me you don't get off on it—being better than everyone else, being better than me."

"I'm not better than you," Grace says with a slow shake of her head. "*You're* better than *this*." She motions around them. "You're better than that seedy club and that vulgar comic and those silly women you call friends. You're better than all of it. You just refuse to see it."

"My friends may be silly, but at least they don't judge me. At least they're willing to accept me the way I am."

"That's because they don't know you," Grace says. "If they did, they'd demand more from you. And the very fact that they don't tells me they're not really your friends to begin with."

"This is who I am now," Trina says, her words slow and forceful, her tone indignant. "And I'm not going to apologize for it. If *my* life doesn't meet *your* standards, that's your problem."

"My only standard for your life is that you live it for Christ," Grace says. "And until you do, I suggest you concentrate less on the problems in your relationship with me and more on the problems in your relationship with Him."

"You just have it all figured out, don't you?" Trina shouts to Grace's retreating back. "Everything's just so simple for you! Must be nice!"

Grace doesn't bother to respond. Instead, she crosses the lot, hops in her car, and pulls away, just as the rain begins to fall.

Trina stares at Grace's tail lights until they round the corner and disappear. At which point, she whirls around and stomps back toward the club. Kendra is waiting for her at the entrance.

"You alright?" she asks.

"I'm fine," Trina huffs, as she huddles beneath the club's awning and wipes the rain from her bare shoulders. "Best-friend-less, but fine."

"Forget about her," Kendra says, tugging Trina toward the door. "You've got us."

Trina nods. "You're right. Who needs the drama?"

"Exactly. So let's go back in, get you dried off, order some more drinks, and have some fun."

"Sounds like a plan." Trina smiles and follows Kendra back into the club. "Oh, and that thing with Becky Schmidt," she says, her jaw set.

Kendra arches her brow. "Yeah?"

"Count me in."

Grace drives home, slowly, her windshield wipers swiping rapidly against the torrential downpour. She prays that Mike is in a better mood as she pulls up to the loft. She doesn't think she has the strength to endure any more upsets today.

She parks in her assigned spot and makes a mad dash for the door. But she's no match for the rain, which is coming down in heavy sheets. By the time she gets inside and to the elevators, her hair is dripping wet and her soaked clothes are clinging to her shivering body.

The loft is dark except for the strip of light peeping from beneath Mike's office door. He's abandoned Etta and Muddy for CNN, but when she leans in, she can make out the distinct sound of a paintbrush swiping against canvas.

She starts to knock, but stops herself. What's there to say? If this is how he needs to work things out, then the only thing she can do is leave him to it.

She slogs to the laundry room, abandons her wet clothes, changes into one of Mike's oversized T-shirts, and climbs into bed, alone, where she cries herself to sleep.

20

Grace flushes the toilet and closes the lid before slinking to the floor and pressing her cheek to the cold marble. It's the second time she's thrown up in the span of ten minutes.

She'd woken up this morning to the sound of Mike brushing his teeth.

"Hey," he'd mumbled as he passed by the bed, toothbrush protruding from his white-foam-covered mouth.

"Hey," Grace had mumbled back, her voice raspy. She tried to sit up, but was slammed with an overwhelming wave of nausea. Slowly, she eased herself back into a lying position.

Mike slipped on his gym shoes and returned to the bathroom to spit and rinse. He emerged a few minutes later, dressed in a velour sweat suit. "I've got some stuff I need to get done," he said, sweeping his dreads back into a pony-tail. "I thought I'd get an early start."

"Okay," is all Grace could manage.

Mike stepped closer. "You alright? You don't look so good."

"I got caught in the rain last night," she explained, swallowing hard against the rapid accretion of saliva in her mouth. "I think I may be coming down with something."

Mike cupped her face in his hands. "You don't have a fever," he said.

Grace didn't respond, only closed her eyes and relished his nearness—his touch.

"Try to take it easy today," he instructed, pulling away. "Stay in bed and take some Vitamin C. If you need me, I'll be in my office."

Grace nodded, her limbs heavy, and watched as he sauntered out of the room. She rolled onto her side and concentrated on taking slow, deep breaths.

Gradually, the nausea waned. She could hear Mike in the kitchen, opening the fridge, banging skillets, and grabbing silverware from the drawer. He was humming, a sure sign that he was in a better mood. Still, she couldn't help but note how he didn't give her his customary morning kiss on the forehead or offer to bring her some tea. Things weren't back to normal as she'd prayed they would be last night before she drifted off to sleep. He was still hurt—still angry—and though he was making small efforts to steer their relationship back to its usual ease, the silent strain between them was agonizing.

The smell of frying egg had wafted its way down the hall and into bed with Grace, snatching her from her thoughts. She'd instantly covered her mouth and dashed to the bathroom where she fell to her knees and hurled.

She groaned as she struggled to her feet and moved to the sink to rinse out her mouth. Then she trudged the short distance back to bed, but got a whiff of Mike's coffee and turned right back on her heels and hurled again.

She wishes she could take Mike's advice and nap the day away. Or better yet, she wishes she could stay right where she is, sprawled against the cold marble of her bathroom floor. But she's got to be across town in just a couple of hours for a book club reading she'd committed to months ago.

Slowly, and with much effort, Grace tugs off Mike's T-shirt and steps into the shower. The water has an instant cleansing effect as it pelts her skin. She stands under the spray long after her body is clean and enjoys the feel of it massaging her sore back and shoulders.

Only after the hot water runs out does she wrap herself in a towel and head to the closet to find something to wear. She's instantly struck by the commingling scents of the small room: her perfume embedded into the fabric of her dresses and shirts, Mike's cologne clinging to the collar of his coat, shoe polish, fabric softener, and soiled laundry. They all bombard her nostrils with unsettling force.

"What is with you today?" she asks herself, snatching her favorite pantsuit from its hanger, along with a comfortable pair of heels, and heading to the bedroom to change.

She doesn't bother drying her hair or fussing with makeup. She's too tired to be bothered with aesthetics. In the interest of time and simplicity, she bobby-pins her wet hair into a tidy chignon and sweeps a sparing amount of blush on each cheek, her forehead, and her chin.

By the time she makes it to the kitchen, Mike's dishes are in the sink and he's tucked away in his office, door closed and music blaring just like yesterday. He's abandoned the blues and progressed to gospel, which is very promising, but Grace doesn't have the strength or the energy to analyze what this shift means.

She manages to choke down a cup of black coffee as she scuttles around the loft, grabbing the materials she'll need and stuffing them unceremoniously into her already bulging briefcase.

The nausea still clings dangerously to the back of her throat, but she feels slightly better as she deposits her mug in the sink and heads for the elevators, out of the building, and into the pouring rain.

"Pull the file."

"Shred the file."

"Dump the file."

"Call when it's done."

Pull, shred, dump, call. Trina repeats the "four simple steps" to Kendra's plan as she does her best to saunter casually to the elevators. How she got roped into doing all of the actual dirty work, she's not sure. It's probably because she was incredibly drunk last night when Kendra unveiled her master strategy.

Not as drunk as Kendra, though, who'd started the tequila shots that got all four of them wasted. One round of shots turned into a second and then a third. The comics became a blur, as did the rest of the night. Somehow, they all ended up at Kendra's place, huddled in the living room around several, rather large, blue bottles of Skyy Vanilla Vodka. By the time the last drop had been poured, Trina could barely hold her head up. She had to prop her chin in her hand just to be able to look at Joss, who could not stop slurring on and on and on about her father and how it was his fault that she was so unlucky in love.

Tai was the first to get sick. She was babbling something incoherent, when suddenly her eyes bulged, her hand clapped over her mouth, and she darted for the bathroom, slamming the door behind her. Just the sound of her gagging pushed Joss over the edge, and she retreated hastily to the kitchen sink. That's when Kendra crawled to Trina, clumsily climbing over the pillows and blankets strewn across the floor.

"I got it all worked out," she said, breath wreaking, her eyelids stuck at half-mast.

First thing tomorrow morning, they would go down to the Records Room; it's where the master files are kept on all the kids at Home Sweet Home. If a child had passed through the Home Sweet Home system in the past ten years, his name would be found among those files. Technically, no one but management and human resources personnel was allowed down there. In fact, the room is fairly heavily guarded with someone posted at the front desk at all times.

But Quinn could arrange a brief window when the room would just happen to be unsupervised—front desk vacant, door mysteriously unlocked.

Because altering a master file would be both risky and time-consuming, Quinn had explained, Trina and Kendra would have to find Becky's master file and destroy it. Afterward, they'd need to clean up her case file, which was in Trina's possession, and tweak her computer file to reflect all of their changes.

It would be a cinch, Kendra had promised. If they stuck together, they'd be in and out in under five minutes. The trick was not to panic, to stay focused and alert. Trina nodded in agreement—anything to make Kendra shut up.

She had woken up this morning on Kendra's couch. The blankets had been folded and put away, the bottles of alcohol disposed of. Everything had been returned to its rightful place. No one would have guessed what they'd been up to. In fact, the only sign of their night of debauchery was Trina's splitting headache.

"You're gonna be late," Kendra said. She set two Tylenol and a glass of water, along with a tall glass of a brownish-red concoction, on the coffee table in front of her.

"What's that?" Trina asked, her voice as rough as sandpaper.

"Olive oil, ketchup, egg yolk, a little bit of salt and pepper, a smidge of Tabasco, Worcestershire sauce, lemon juice, and a dash of gold tequila for good measure."

"I'm not drinking that," Trina said, turning her face away.

Kendra smirked. "You will if you want any hope of getting off that couch."

Trina groaned. "I'll call in sick."

"No," Kendra snipped, her tone suddenly sharp. "You know what we have to do today. Quinn's getting restless. No more stalling."

The plan came dribbling back to Trina in bits and pieces. She sighed and sat up. "Where are Joss and Tai?"

"Gone," Kendra said, clasping her watch. "Alan came to get Tai a couple of hours ago, and Joss called a cab."

"Okay," she said, resting her elbows on her knees and massaging her temples. "Give me twenty minutes."

"You've got ten," Kendra said, disappearing into her bedroom.

Trina gulped down the Tylenol with the water, tossed Kendra's "Hangover Brew" down the sink where it belonged, and headed to the bathroom for a quick shower. Outfitted with only the jeans and tube top she'd worn to the comedy club, Trina was forced to borrow one of Kendra's suits. It was ill-fitting and too traditional for her taste, but she held her tongue in the interest of time, and was ready to go just as Kendra took her last sip of coffee.

On the way to work they rehearsed the plan, clarifying every last detail and playing devil's advocates just to be sure there weren't any holes. Each time Kendra repeated a step, she used the word "we." *We'll* go down to Records. *We'll* nab the file. *We'll* call Quinn.

But at noon, when most of the employees had dispersed for lunch and Quinn had arranged for their easy entrée to the master records, Kendra went AWOL. Trina assumed the plan was a bust until she discovered a cryptic voice mail, in which "we" had all of a sudden changed to "you."

"Hey, it's me," Kendra whispered, her words muffled as though she was trying to disguise her voice. "Everything's taken care of. I know you can do it. Once you're all settled, give me a ring. I'll be back in the office around two."

For a few stunned moments, Trina seriously considered not doing it. If anything were to go wrong, hers would be the only dirty hands among the three of them. If she was caught, she could lose her job, or worse, be charged with a crime. She wasn't so naïve to think that Kendra or Quinn would 'fess up to their involvement. They'd cry innocent to their graves.

But then she considered the alternative. After last night, staying at the loft or depending on Grace in any way was no longer an option. She needed this promotion. With all of her bridges burned and most of her resources milked dry, Quinn's offer wasn't merely an opportunity; it was Trina's only hope— her only way forward.

Trina takes a deep breath and shakes the jitters from her hands as the elevator reaches the basement and the doors spread open. *Pull, shred, dump, call,* she silently repeats to herself.

She tiptoes along the polished concrete floor until she reaches the end of the hall. "Hello?" Trina calls with audible nervousness. There's no reply. Just as she'd been assured, the door is open and the chair behind the front desk is empty.

Quickly, Trina slips past the *Restricted Area* sign and into the forbidden room of master files. Officially past the point of no return, she wastes no time mining through the rows upon rows of neatly kept records. She has a difficult time figuring out the filing system. She had assumed they would be alphabetized by last name, but as she wanders up and down the deep aisles, she realizes that they're labeled by case number.

Beads of sweat form on her forehead as her nervousness morphs into decisive terror. She doesn't know Becky's case number off the top of her head. She eyes the wall of manila files in front of her and the identical wall behind it and the identical walls behind it. She's supposed to be in and out in five minutes, but without the case number it'll take hours to locate Becky's record. Unless...

Trina flicks through several of the files in front of her. Her fingers move swiftly across the tops of the folders as she reads the date on each. An involuntary smile creeps up on her lips. The dates are in chronological order, and she knows exactly when Becky was admitted to Home Sweet Home.

She scurries down one aisle, around the corner, and into the next, periodically stopping to reference her location and to make sure she's still headed in the right direction. Her pace slows as she nears her destination. The file is there, right where it should be.

Trina snatches it, tucks it under her arm, and heads straight for the door, but just as she reaches the front desk, she hears the elevator ding and two voices echoing down the hall. Her chest tightens as she retreats back into the Records Room.

"Thanks for coming down to get it," the smaller of the two women says.

Trina crouches and peeks through the small Plexiglas window in the door. "No problem," says the other, taking a sip from the drink in her Styrofoam cup. "Dex has been badgering me about it all week. The sooner I get it to him, the sooner he'll get off my back."

The first woman nods and turns in Trina's direction. She stops abruptly. "What the...?" she murmurs, slowly moving closer.

Trina's entire body tingles with fear. How could she have been so stupid? She knew this was going to happen. So did Kendra and Quinn, she thinks, as her mind swirls with conspiracy theories.

"What's wrong?" the second woman asks.

"This door was not open when I left," the first woman answers. "I locked it myself."

Trina slips out of her shoes and hightails it, as quietly as she can, behind one of the walls of files in the back of the room. She hears the hinges creak as the door opens wider and the click of two sets of heels as both women enter the room.

"You're just being paranoid."

"No," the answer is firm. "This room was locked when I left."

"You want to call security?"

Trina gulps and holds her breath as their shadows move closer. She couldn't imagine a worse scenario: caught by the building's security, hiding in the back of a restricted area with a stolen master file under her arm. Images of being escorted out of the building in handcuffs and placed into a squad car, in front of all of her coworkers, makes her woozy.

The two women circle the large room several times, looking up and down each aisle. Trina ducks and dodges from one end to the other until she finds the perfect hiding place in a corner behind two rusted file cabinets. She remains absolutely still, silently begging God for an undeserved miracle.

"I must be losing my mind," the first woman says.

The other one chuckles. "Don't feel bad. I lose mine at least once a day."

"Well, while I'm in here, let me get you that file for Dex."

Moments later, they're gone. Trina's knees wobble and then buckle. She slides to the floor as she fights back tears. She knows she needs to get out of here, but she's too petrified to move—afraid of what will happen if she gets caught. She sits behind the rusted file cabinets for quite some time gathering her wits and listening for any more movement.

Finally, certain that no one besides her is lurking around, she inches toward the door and peers through the glass. The coast is clear. She slips her shoes back on, hides the file in the back of her waistband beneath her blazer, takes another quick sweep of the front desk area, and turns the knob.

Only the knob won't turn. She jiggles it, yanking hard. It's locked. "Oh no," she squeaks, breathless. "Please, please," she begs, pulling at the knob with all her might. "This can't be happening." But it's no use. The walls seem to cave in as Trina gives way to a panic attack.

She paces as she tries to come up with ways out. Natural instinct tells her to bang on the door and cry for help until someone with a key hears her. But she's not even supposed to be down here.

Will Kendra know where to check when I don't turn up? Trina wonders. *Would she even bother to look?* Because if not, she might as well have dropped off the face of the planet. No one else will know she's even missing. It's not as though

Darius or Grace will be expecting her. She could be stuck here overnight! The thought alone makes Trina's hand shake. Her thoughts grow increasingly irrational as fear sets in.

"Get a grip," she orders aloud. "Think."

She snaps her fingers excitedly and retrieves her cell phone from her blazer pocket. Work, she silently pleads as she dials Kendra. The phone rings on the other end once, and then disconnects. *No Signal* blinks up at her.

She moves to another spot in the room and tries again. This time Kendra picks up. "It's Trina, can you hear me?"

Her response is pure static.

"I'm locked in the Records Room," Trina says. "I need help."

More static follows before her phone disconnects her again.

"Please, God," Trina begs, "cut me some slack." But as she tries to dial out for the third time, she gets the distinct impression that her connection to Heaven is just as weak as her cell phone signal and that this time she'll have to find a way out of the basement all on her own.

21

"It's really coming down out there, huh?" Sue asks, setting a basket of pens and highlighters on the coffee table. She fluffs the couch cushions for the hundredth time and then disappears behind the swinging door made of stained glass that leads to the kitchen.

Sue is a slim, energetic woman. She looks like an exemplary suburban housewife and mother, with her checkered apron fastened neatly around her small waist and her soccer-mom bob. But her do-gooder ways reach far beyond the members of her household. She's an active part of the community, as well as the co-founder and president of the Women of Substance Book Club.

Grace had decided to stop making book club appearances after she got married. The meetings, which included readings, discussion, and Q&A sessions, tended to be even more time-consuming than public book signings, and they generated very little publicity. But upon learning that the Women of Substance had voted her novel the "Best Summer Read" for the year, Grace made an exception and accepted their invitation.

"I just can't tell you how excited we are that you're here," Sue says, emerging from the kitchen with a plate of freshly baked brownies.

Grace holds her breath in an attempt to circumvent her queasiness. "The pleasure's all mine—really," she says, once the brownies are a safe distance away.

"I was hoping we'd have a chance to sit and talk before the others came," Sue says, tossing the television remote control into the side table drawer while simultaneously dusting off the lampshade. "But you know how it is; mornings can be unpredictably hectic."

"Let me help you with something," Grace offers.

"No, no." Sue won't have it. She shakes her head vehemently. "It doesn't look like it, but I've got everything under control." She smiles. "I just need to take something for these cramps," she pats her belly, "and I should be okay."

Grace nods understandingly, but freezes suddenly, alarm incrementally clenching her gut. Her palms chill with dread. She can't remember the last time she had cramps. In fact, she can't remember the last time she had her period.

Her heart races as, desperately, she scavenges her memory. It's been six weeks, maybe seven. The nausea, the heightened sense of smell—it's now adding up to an answer she most definitely does not want to hear. "Can I use your restroom?" she asks.

"Of course." Sue points down the hall. "Around the corner, second door to your left."

"Thanks." Grace steps quickly, working to keep her breathing slow and even. She locks the door behind her and leans against it, enveloped by the dark. This can't be happening to me, she thinks, fumbling for the light switch.

Pregnant.

Crying.

Diapers.

Strollers.

Breast-feeding.

The words bombard her mind almost faster than she can process them. She presses her eyes shut. Of all the uncertainties looming in Grace's life, the one thing she's sure of is that she doesn't want to be a mother. She's not ready. The *implications* of motherhood, alone, wear her out.

She's never been the kind of person who fawns over babies. She doesn't melt when she passes through the newborn clothing section in a department store or coo when she watches young kids toddle down the street. And the prospect of motherhood has never once left her warm and fuzzy on the inside. To the contrary, it leaves her dizzy and unspeakably grateful for her child-free state.

In junior high, when all the girls, Trina included, would gather at lunch to fantasize about marrying famous actors like Todd Bridges—discussing what they'd name their future kids and how they'd furnish each of their mansions room by room—Grace would take her Jell-O to the playground and read *Mad Magazine* beneath the huge oak tree until the bell rang.

Mapping out a plan to obtain the perfect life and to create the perfect family didn't appeal to her. Probably because she knew, from experience, that perfect families didn't exist, no matter how manicured they looked from the outside.

When Grace was young, she lived in a three-story house on a cul-de-sac in one of Detroit's premiere neighborhoods. She went to a prestigious brick and ivy school filled with trust fund babies who drove luxury cars and bragged about their summer homes. She had money, the most up-to-date clothes, the hottest accessories, and a caretaker who was more interested in being her friend than in keeping order. She looked like she was living every teenage girl's dream.

Very few people knew that her father had skipped out on her when she was just a baby or that her mother, who was rarely around in body or spirit, was seemingly incapable and uninterested in showing her affection.

At times, the days were unbearably lonely, and the nights seemed even lonelier. She'd weep herself to sleep, tortured by a list of possible things she'd done wrong—all of the reasons her parents didn't love her like they were supposed to, the way she'd seen countless other parents love their kids.

Eventually, when she ran out of ways to hate herself, she became callous to the whole idea of marriage and family. She couldn't risk failing anyone the way she'd been failed. She couldn't risk passing along the same devastation she'd barely managed to survive. And her disastrous relationship with Stanley, her college boyfriend, only further affirmed her conviction.

But then she met Mike. Being with him was like tumbling into ecstasy for the first time—every day. He's the only man she's wanted to pledge her life to, and the only person, ever, who's loved her with the sure consistency she's always desired.

But a kid. Are we ready for that? Grace wonders. She takes a deep breath and studies her reflection in the mirror. It's not that Mike wouldn't make a terrific dad. He's the kind of guy who'd lasso the moon for his kid. And he'd jump at the opportunity to turn their duo into a trio even though it's not something they had planned or have even talked about except once, in passing, during their pre-marriage counseling.

But they haven't even been married a year. They've barely gotten the chance to settle into their roles as husband and wife. A child would only complicate things, and things are already complicated enough now that Mike doesn't have a job.

And what about *her* job? Grace tries to imagine herself touring with a protruding belly. What would it mean for her budding career if she couldn't travel the country to promote her books? What would it mean for her weight? Everything she'd gone through to lose it. All of that work—gone—just like that?

Her breathing quickens as dread sets in. She turns on the faucet, runs her hand under the stream of cool water, and dabs the back of her neck. Her hand moves involuntarily to her waist. She lifts her camisole and peers down at her stomach.

To think, there might actually be something growing in there—the very beginnings of a living, breathing person.

The doorbell rings, and Grace hears Sue's clicking heels followed by several delighted voices.

Grace snatches her hand away and straightens her blazer. There's no point in panicking—no point in even thinking about it any more until she knows for sure.

"Everything okay in there?" Sue asks, rapping lightly on the door.

"Fine," Grace chirps. "Just finishing up." She flushes the toilet for illusion's sake, spreads her lips into an engaging smile, and heads to the living room to greet the waiting Women of Substance.

22

Five hours locked in a basement with no means of outside communication and no foreseeable way of escape does something to a person. For Trina, it has opened her eyes to just how depraved a plan she's become embroiled in.

Becky Schmidt has been admitted to four different hospitals a total of seven times in her tumultuous six years of life. Trina knows this because she's read Becky's entire master file—several times—all 109 pages of it.

The first of Becky's unexplained injuries was diagnosed only three days before her first birthday. The following six injuries—a progressive series of scratches, bruises, contusions, and fractures—have left her with what multiple psychologists have labeled "potentially permanent emotional scarring."

Becky should have been removed from her father's care even before most of those injuries had a chance to take place. One of her trips to the hospital, at age three, revealed a fractured wrist and distinct bruises lining her back. The examining doctor described the bruises as "resembling a belt buckle" and determined the fracture to be "the result of physical abuse."

"*Detain child and alert CPS*" is written in red and underlined twice in the corner of her report. Yet Becky was discharged the very next morning, and the signature that had approved her release belonged to none other than Quinn.

Any other child would have been swiftly removed from her parents' custody and placed into foster care. Even if, after extensive prying, no definitive evidence of foul play could be determined, the state would still have required both parents to take a series of parenting classes before reuniting them with their child. And even then, they'd be required to undergo a year of random home inspections and follow-up counseling sessions.

Yet Councilman Schmidt wasn't asked to do anything until Becky's sixth hospital visit. She'd been rushed in unconscious and immediately diagnosed with a severe concussion. The examining doctor also noted that Becky was dehydrated, underweight, and physically dirty, with dark smudges covering her emaciated body.

Unlike all of the other emergency room physicians who had seen Becky, that examining doctor ignored protocol and did not contact CPS or wait for a Home Sweet Home representative. Instead, she called the police.

By the time the news had gotten to Quinn, Becky had already been placed in temporary foster care. But Trina suspects that Quinn still managed to pull a few strings because, according to Becky's file, Councilman Schmidt was only ordered to attend one therapy session. Two weeks later, Becky was returned to his custody.

However, Trina notices that all of the paperwork required to discharge a child from foster care is missing. There is no judgment or court order, no summary or recommendation from either Becky's or Councilman Schmidt's therapists, and no subsequent court dates or mandatory, state-approved, follow-up schedule.

Becky had just mysteriously been plucked from her foster home and given back to her father. The brief loss of his daughter must have sobered the Councilman to the seriousness of his abuse. Either that or it caused him to be more inconspicuous, since Becky was not admitted to another emergency room for over a year.

It wasn't until several weeks after Councilman Schmidt had been caught in an embezzlement scandal and all of his day care centers had been abruptly shut down that Becky turned up, in the middle of the morning, at the children's hospital in Little Rock, Arkansas—a city two hours away from where she lived. But it wasn't Councilman Schmidt by her side with all of his usual excuses and explanations. It was Georgia Kenny, Becky's pre-K teacher.

Georgia explained, in detail, who Becky was and why she had taken her from school, without permission, and across state lines.

Plain and simply, she feared for Becky's life.

She described Becky's deteriorating health and progressively disheveled appearance; how her father often dropped her off at school a half an hour early with no lunch, no backpack, and no school supplies. Becky, according to

Georgia's report, was a shy, yet vibrant, little girl when she started pre-K. But by the middle of the semester, she'd morphed into a shell of her former self. Skittish and reclusive, she would not talk to or play with her classmates. She had a hard time sharing and would not hesitate to fight if she felt cornered. She also refused to take off her shoes and sweater for naptime, which Georgia couldn't understand until she removed the sweater once when Becky was sleeping and discovered large bruises on her upper arms where someone had clearly gripped and yanked her with excessive force.

In the report, Georgia claims to have alerted school officials right away. She says they were just as appalled by the discovery as she was, but days passed and then weeks and nothing happened.

Georgia was convinced that Becky would die if she continued to live with her father; and because the powers that be in Memphis appeared helpless to rectify the situation, she'd fled to Arkansas.

"It's a shame," Georgia wrote, "that a child—a precious life, a gift to be cherished and nourished—has been disregarded as nothing more than a tool through which to beat out an adult's frustrations. Rebecca Schmidt has been left to die within herself. And there are certain days I watch her huddled in my classroom, and I fear she's ruined. A lesser person just might have succumbed to such a grim fate, but Rebecca is a fighter. She possesses a stamina and a will to live that I will never know. Her parents have failed her, the city of Memphis has failed her, the system has failed her, but I will not. I cannot. I will fight this battle with her, and on the days when she doesn't have the strength, I will fight it for her. I will do whatever it takes to make sure she survives. Rebecca doesn't need a miracle; she only needs the courage and determination of a few people who aren't too afraid or too selfish to do the right thing for the sake of being right, of being decent and moral—of being human. That's the saddest truth of this entire dilemma."

Becky Schmidt has not been back home since. Georgia Kenny's signed statement went several heads above Quinn's and even grabbed the attention of the governor, who was not pleased, to say the least, that Arkansas's officials had to be petitioned to do what Tennessee's officials should have done in the first place. Becky's things were immediately packed, and she was placed in a foster home.

Councilman Schmidt was ordered to attend anger management therapy and parenting classes, while the state underwent, what dragged on to be, a year-long investigation. In that time, the councilman has not been to a single anger management session, and he has only showed up to 1 of the 24 mandatory parenting classes. He's also only bothered coming to 4 of his 12 supervised visits with Becky.

Councilman William Schmidt is a man who, clearly, only cares about himself and his career. Though Trina has never met him, she can tell just from his statements in Becky's file and his documented actions (or lack thereof) that he's the worst kind of narcissist. The world only exists to serve him, to cater to his desires and ambitions. His life is a one-man show. Everyone else is in the way—including his own daughter.

Trina's conscience is hit hard by Georgia Kenny's letter. She wants to be one of those brave people Georgia wrote of, the proud few who aren't too afraid or too selfish to do the right thing simply because it's right.

As Trina sits on the cold, concrete floor, her legs stretched out, her back propped against the wall, she wonders what became of Becky's angel, Georgia Kenny. Did she get in trouble? Was she fired? Suspended? Reprimanded? Applauded? Becky's master file doesn't say. Maybe if it had, if there was proof that Georgia's good deed did, in fact, go unpunished, Trina could've mustered up the mettle to reveal Quinn's scheme. But, even now, in light of all the circumstances that surround Becky's situation, Trina knows she's too paralyzed by fear to put her job and her reputation on the line.

A loud click shakes Trina from her thoughts. Someone's unlocked the dead bolt. Trina jumps to her stocking-clad feet, secures the file in her waistband, and dashes to her trusty hiding space in the corner behind the two rusted file cabinets. The heavy door moans as someone pulls it open.

"Hello?" the person calls with a harsh whisper. "Trina, are you in here?"

It's Kendra.

Trina stands slowly, relieved, and yet inexplicably disappointed.

"Poor thing," Kendra coos sympathetically, though her smirk betrays her amusement. She shakes her head at Trina's wrinkled, untucked blouse and flat hair. "How long have you been stuck down here?"

"Since you bailed on me and I had to come find the file on my own,"Trina huffs. "And what took you so long?" she asks. "I thought I was going to have to spend the night here."

"It took me a while to figure out where you were," Kendra says. "Then I had to find a away to get in."

"How *did* you get in?"

Kendra shrugs. "Quinn arranged it." She dangles a set of keys from her index finger. "I've got to get these back to her ASAP."

"Fine. Whatever,"Trina says, dusting the soot from her skirt. "Let's just get out of here. This place gives me the creeps."

"Did you get the file?" Kendra asks.

Trina nods. "Yeah," she says, her eyes lowered. "I got it."

"And you know what to do?"

Trina sighs and heads for the door. "Back off, Kendra."

"I'm serious." Kendra grabs her wrist. "You need to stick with the plan."

"Like you did?"Trina snips, yanking her arm away.

"Both of us didn't need to go," Kendra says, defensively. "I thought one person would seem less suspicious. Besides, look what happened. What would we have done if we'd both gotten locked down here?"

"That's easy for you to say," Trina says, glaring. "You weren't the one skulking around in this dank hole like a scared rat."

"I'm sorry, okay?" Kendra asks, her tone the furthest thing from apologetic. "I'm sorry that you feel like I bailed on you and that you got locked down here for most of the day. But the job's not done yet. So pull it together and finish what you started."

"And if I don't?" Trina asks, moving closer, her eyes narrowed daringly. "Are you going to make me?"

Kendra takes a few steps back. Her smile is stiff, her laugh nervous. "I think you're forgetting that we're on the same team."

"You'll have to forgive me," Trina says, her words dripping with sarcasm. "I'm not used to being on a team where I do all of the work."

Kendra rolls her eyes. "Okay, I get it! You want me to get my hands dirty too? Fine, give me the file. I'll shred it."

"What?" Trina asks, alarmed. She's suddenly very aware of the folder pressing against her back. And for reasons she can't explain, she doesn't want to part with it.

"Give me the master file," Kendra says, holding out her left hand. "I'll get rid of it, and all you have to do is make the changes to the case and computer files. That way you can't say I didn't help."

"I've already come this far," Trina says, trying her best to sound nonchalant. "I can do it."

"No." Kendra shakes her head and holds her left arm out farther. "You'll just whine about it later," she says. "This way we'll have equal share in the responsibility."

"I don't want to do it that way," Trina says, her voice loud and a bit too insistent.

Kendra's eyes narrow suspiciously as she drops her arm. "Why not?"

Trina's heart races as she scrambles for a viable excuse. "I like to finish what I start," she says, hoping her response sounds convincing. "I need to. That way I can be sure it's done right—no mistakes."

"It's not brain surgery," Kendra says, her brows furrowed. "Five minutes with a paper shredder and it's done."

"Exactly," Trina says, nodding toward the exit. "So let's go. The sooner we get out of here, the sooner this'll all be over."

Kendra doesn't question Trina further, and they both board the elevator and head to their respective destinations: Kendra back to Quinn to return her keys and Trina back to her office to figure out exactly what she's going to do with Becky Schmidt's master file.

23

One blue line, two pink lines, a purple dot, and a red cross—four versions of the same answer: "Yes, you're pregnant."

Grace stares at the pregnancy sticks in front of her on the bathroom floor and blinks back tears. Four tests can't all be wrong. She picks up the instruction pamphlet to the EPT kit to make sure she'd done everything exactly right.

Earlier today, after barely managing to hold herself together at the book club meeting, she had made a beeline to the nearest pharmacy, bought an assortment of pregnancy tests, and sped home where she headed straight into the bathroom and locked the door....

Now facing the evidence lying around her, Grace is bombarded with questions. How far along is she? Is it healthy? When should her prenatal care have started? Should she be exercising? Eating or drinking certain things? Her knowledge of babies and pregnancy can be summed up in what she'd learned over a decade ago in her tenth grade health class. But she can't imagine that her morning caffeine hit—two, sometimes three cups of very strong coffee—has been a healthy influence on her growing fetus; nor the Extra Strength Tylenol she pops daily for her stress headaches.

A mother for two months and she's already got her kid strung out on pain pills and caffeine, Grace thinks to herself and groans. She's officially living her worst nightmare.

The reality of her condition hits her with unnerving force. She doesn't want this. She's unprepared and unfit, but more than anything, she's unwilling. There aren't too many avenues for women in her position, though. She could keep it and be miserable for a minimum of 18 years, abort it and live the rest of her days with the unbearable guilt of terminating a life, or put it up for adoption and always know that somewhere out there she has a child that she abandoned. None of those scenarios offers her much hope.

The next logical step is to make an appointment with an obstetrician to get all of the facts. She can't make an informed decision without all of the facts, she reminds herself.

A lone tear glides down her cheek. What if, even after she learns everything there is to know about her pregnancy, she still doesn't want the baby? As sweet and accommodating a husband as Mike is, he won't understand it—he will never agree with it.

She's instantly pained at the thought of losing Mike's respect. She chokes back a welling sob. If the choice came down to a baby or her marriage, which would she choose? She honestly doesn't know. Before she got pregnant, she would have said her marriage—no questions asked. But then again, before she got pregnant, she'd also tell anyone who'd listen all of the reasons why abortion was wrong and sinful—why it was murder and a direct affront to God's sovereign plan.

Turns out Mike was right after all. It's impossible to know what you'd do in a situation until you've actually been faced with that situation.

What am I supposed to do? Grace questions silently, her tear-streaked face turned up to the ceiling. *What do You expect me to do?*

There's no reply, but she knows the answer. She just can't accept it.

"Babe?" Mike calls. He knocks on the door. "You in there?"

"Yeah," Grace says, frantically gathering up the pregnancy sticks and kits and shoving them into the brown paper bag she'd brought them home in.

"Phone for you," he says. "You want me to have them call back?"

"No, I'll be there in a sec," Grace says. She rolls down the top of the bag and stuffs it in the back of the cabinet under the sink.

"Is everything okay?" he asks. "You sound like you're crying."

Grace splashes water on her face, quickly pats it dry with the hand towel hanging on the wall next to the sink, and then opens the door. "I'm fine," she says, smiling widely. "Must be the congestion from this cold."

"Then why are your eyes puffy?" he asks, sweeping a strand of hair off her forehead and tucking it behind her ear.

She shrugs and looks away. "I'm just tired. I haven't been sleeping much lately."

"Gracie," Mike says, his eyes kind, his tone soft.

But Grace won't let him continue—she can't. Because until she figures out what she's going to do, until she summons the courage to tell Mike what's going on, every word that passes between them will feel like a lie. "I should get the phone."

"Okay." He nods and backs away so she can get by.

Grace holds her breath as she crosses their bedroom to the door. She fully expects him to stop her, to ask more questions to which she'll have to concoct untruthful answers. But he doesn't say a word.

Relieved, Grace makes her way down the hall to the living room where she picks up the cordless.

"Mrs. Cambridge?" a cheerful female's voice floods the receiver. "This is Lola—the manager at The Shelf." The Shelf is one of Memphis's few super bookstores. It rivals the likes of Barnes & Noble and Borders, both in size and popularity. It has also played host to two of Grace's most successful book signings, and Lola, with her warm Southern charm, was the mastermind behind both functions. "I'm sorry to bother you at home."

"It's not a bother," Grace says. "What can I do for you?"

"Well, we had this whole event planned for tonight." She prattles off the names of five local authors. "They were all set to give readings, sign books...you know, answer a few questions, mingle with the public...but at the very last minute one of them canceled."

"And you want me to fill in?" Grace asks.

"I know it's incredibly last minute and I completely understand if you can't make it, but I just figured I'd throw it out there and see what you thought."

"What time does it start?" Grace asks.

"Seven o'clock, but there's already a strong showing. We're expecting in the neighborhood of a hundred, maybe a hundred and fifty, people."

"That only gives me a half hour," Grace thinks aloud.

"I've got plenty of your novels in stock," Lola says. "I could have your display table set up by the time you get here."

Might as well, Grace thinks. Anything would be better than sitting at home, dodging Mike's quizzical glances. This way, she'll have some space and time to think—to analyze her next move. "Okay," she agrees. "I'll be there."

She hangs up and goes back to her bedroom to change. Mike's waiting for her on the couch. "Who was that?" he asks.

"Lola," Grace says, strolling past him and into the closet. "She asked me to fill in for another author tonight at this thing at The Shelf."

"Are you going?" Mike asks.

"Yeah." Grace is careful to keep her voice light. "Should be fun. If nothing else, it'll be good exposure for the book." She waits for his response, but is met by silence. "Why? You don't mind, do you?" she asks.

"Course not," Mike replies, after a long pause. "I just—I thought we might talk."

Grace pairs her Seven jeans with a fitted tweed blazer and slips into a comfortable pair of ballerina flats. She emerges from the closet. "I kind of have to be there now," she says apologetically. Deep down, she's relieved beyond words. "Can we talk later?"

Mike nods. "You look great by the way."

"Thanks." She smiles. "I'll see you."

"Hey." He stands and reaches out his hand, pressing it firmly against her stomach to stop her from breezing by. Grace's heart leaps. For a split second, she wonders if he knows—if he can tell just by looking at her that their child is growing beneath his palm in her belly. "Don't I get a kiss?" he asks.

"Yeah, sure." Grace grins and lifts her puckered lips to his. But when he tries to pull her in for a hug, she wriggles loose. "I gotta go," she says, patting his chest affectionately. "Don't wait up."

24

"I haven't heard from you in a while. I don't know—I guess I'm worried about you. I hate the way you left here. It wasn't right. *I* wasn't right and...," Trina listens intently through the long pause, "and I miss you. I know you're mad, but give me a call. Please. We don't even have to talk. I just need to be sure you're okay. Okay? Call me. I love you. Bye."

Trina presses the pound key and replays the message from Darius again. The voice mail has been sitting in her cell phone since early this afternoon— around the same time she found herself trapped in the Records Room.

She didn't expect him to call. He rarely ever deigned to chase her in their relationship, not in high school and certainly not in college. It didn't matter if he was wrong, which he almost always was, if there was a rift between them, Trina was the one who did the mending.

He didn't exactly apologize, Trina notes. But he sounded contrite and he *did* make the first move. She flips her phone shut and smiles to herself, not entirely sure why his call has made her so happy. He was horrible to her and long before he threw her onto his sleeper sofa and then out of his condo altogether.

Their on-again, off-again, 12-year relationship has been volatile, by any-one's standards. They've fought, at times physically; cursed each other out; cheated, in his case multiple times; and broken up on more occasions than she can remember. But they always seem to be drawn back to each other. Some days, when she's feeling whimsical, she attributes their magnetic pull to a deep, soul-mate-like connection. Most days, though, she's lucid enough to realize that it's mutual stupidity that keeps them coming back for more.

Home Sweet Home's halls are silent as Trina makes a spread behind her desk like she'd done a couple of nights ago. She lies down and stares up at the ceiling. She could just call to say "Hi," she reasons. They've known each other most of their lives. It wouldn't hurt to be civil. Besides, she's not sleepy and she has a lot on her mind. She can either drown in her own thoughts or float on the familiar sound of Darius's voice.

Almost without thinking, she grabs her phone and dials his number. It rings and rings until his answering machine picks up. Trina disconnects the call without leaving a message. *He's probably out on one of his "business meetings,"* she thinks, as she envisions him in a quaint, dimly lit restaurant sitting across from a leggy woman with come-to-bed eyes and a cute giggle.

Her cell phone buzzes loudly beside her. She looks down to see Darius's home number pop across the Caller ID. For a nanosecond, she entertains the idea of not answering, but curiosity and loneliness easily get the better of her.

"Hi," she says, her voice a soft whisper.

"I'm sorry I didn't pick up a second ago," he says. "You caught me in the shower."

"I was just returning your call," Trina says.

"I'm glad," Darius admits shyly. "I've been waiting."

"How've you been?"

"Kicking myself ever since you left. I was a jerk...," he lets out a deep sigh, "and I'm sorry."

Trina grins, involuntarily warmed by his words. "It's okay. Maybe it was for the best, you know? We don't exactly have a stellar track record when it comes to living together."

"Are you back at Grace's?" he asks.

"Not exactly." The confession is slow and secretive as she searches for the right explanation. "I guess you could say that I'm between residences right now."

"If you need a place to stay..." He lets his sentence trail off.

"Your pullout's eagerly awaiting my return?" Trina jokes.

"No," his tone is serious, somber, and sincere, "but I am."

Trina closes her eyes, suddenly overtaken by the day's happenings. She doesn't know how to respond to Darius, and she doesn't want to say something out of exhaustion that might cancel out the kind words that have passed between them. "I should probably go."

"You have to?" he asks, his disappointment plain.

"Yeah. I'm tired."

"Can I call you tomorrow?"

Trina smiles. "You better."

They hang up, and she rolls onto her side. Her briefcase is in front of her at eye level, leaning against the wall. She reaches for it and pulls out Becky's master file. All evening she had tried to coerce herself into shredding it, but she just couldn't. When Kendra called to make sure it had been done, she'd lied and told her it had—said she'd tied up the confetti in a garbage bag and tossed it down the main trash chute.

Trina thumbs through the pages of medical charts, court orders, progress reports, psychological assessments, and signed affidavits. As if on cue, the file opens to Georgia Kenny's statement. Trina flips it shut. She doesn't need to read it again. She has it memorized.

The million-dollar question still looms persistently in the back of her mind: Will she be the one to do what's right simply because it's right?

She tosses aside her blanket, pulls her keys out of her purse, and walks over to the four-tier file cabinet in the corner of her office. She places the file in the small compartment above the first drawer and locks it.

Tonight, the answer is yes.

As for tomorrow, she'll wait to see what it brings.

25

Mike is waiting for Grace on the living room love seat when she arrives home just after one in the morning. She doesn't notice him at first when she flips on the hallway light.

"How'd it go?" he asks.

She jolts and presses her hand against her chest. "You scared me," she pants. "What're you doing up?"

He shrugs as if the answer is apparent. "Waiting for you."

"You didn't have to do that," she says, slipping off her blazer. "I know it's way past your bedtime."

"Did you have fun?"

She sighs. "Yeah, I guess. As much fun as you can have at those sort of things."

Mike tosses aside the decorative pillow next to him to make room for Grace on the love seat.

She still isn't ready to talk. In truth, she'd hoped that Mike would be fast asleep by now. It's why she'd lingered at The Shelf when the event ended; chatting with fellow authors, long after the last fan had left; and helping Lola and her employees clean up. She was trying to avoid this exact kind of run-in, where everything is said except the one thing that matters.

Grace gets ready to protest—to whine about how exhausted she is, how all she wants to do is change her clothes and hop into bed—but one look into Mike's pleading eyes sends her, grudgingly, schlepping over to the love seat. She sinks into the small, snug spot and cuddles underneath his warm arm.

"It's been a while since we've done this," he says softly, his words tickling the top of her head.

"What?" Grace asks, her eyes closed, her cheek resting against his chest.

"Held each other," he says, tugging her even closer.

"Mmmm," she agrees, apprehension giving way to a contented moan. "Too long."

"I owe you an apology," Mike whispers.

Grace gazes up at him. "For what?" she asks, struggling to ignore the immense guilt fermenting in her stomach. If anyone needs to apologize, she thinks, it's her.

"You were right. I should've talked to you about *Life Sketch*." He softly caresses her arm with the tips of his fingers. "I honestly don't think the outcome would've been any different. It was time for me to go. But I should've at least included you in the process."

"We both messed up," she says, shifting her angle so that he can lean his body into hers. "I shouldn't have reacted the way I did."

"We're gonna be okay. You know that, right? We've got plenty of disposable income, solid investments, and enough saved up to tide us over until we figure out what we want to do next."

Grace sighs. "Which is what, though?" she asks. "It's not like CEO positions are just lying around for the taking. I mean, yeah, we're set for now, but 'now' will be gone before we know it." *Possibly in nine months*, she thinks drearily.

"I have something to show you," he says, standing abruptly. "But you have to promise not to get mad."

Grace narrows her eyes. "I don't like where this is going."

"Come on," Mike holds out his hand, "just trust me."

Grace takes it and stands. He leads her down the hall, past the gym, and to his office. "Wait here," he instructs, disappearing behind the door before she has a chance to protest. She can hear him rushing from one end of the room to the other, slamming drawers and scooting around furniture. After a few moments, the commotion stops and the room falls silent. Grace leans closer, her ear only inches from the door, but hears nothing. She bites her lip, debating whether or not she should enter. Slowly, she reaches for the knob.

"Don't even think about it," Mike's muffled voice threatens from the other side.

Grace laughs. "Well, hurry up. I'm dying to know what you're up to."

Several unbearable minutes later, Mike pops his head out. "Okay," he says, visibly excited, his smile wide. "Close your eyes."

Grace groans. "You know I hate surprises."

"Close 'em!" he orders.

Grace complies, unable to suppress her grin.

"Good, now keep them closed," Mike instructs. Grace feels the heat from his chest as it presses against her back and his big hands cup over her already shut lids. Slowly, he leads her over the threshold and into the room. "Couple more steps," he coaxes, every so often. "Almost there."

"Any farther and we're gonna hit the wall," Grace says.

Mike sways her back and forth playfully, as they continue to inch forward, their steps synchronized. "Patience," he whispers, his lip grazing her ear.

Grace soaks in his scent and marvels quietly at the way his presence—his voice, the sure guidance of his body against hers—makes her feel safe.

"Okay," he says, stepping away. "Take a look."

Grace peers hesitantly through one eye, unsure of what to expect. Her mouth falls open at the sight before her. "Oh my…," she whispers.

"Is that a good or bad, 'Oh my…'?"

Grace shakes her head, nearly speechless. "These are amazing," she finally gushes.

They're surrounded by dozens of canvas paintings. Most of them are abstracts, some muted, but many in bold and vibrant colors. The strokes are wide and passionate, the textures nontraditional, but fitting. It's the type of art she's seen for sale in swanky New York galleries and proudly displayed on the walls of wealthy execs who fancy themselves art connoisseurs. Grace turns slowly, perusing one painting and then the next. It's like candy for the eyes. She can't get enough. "How could you possibly think I'd be mad at this?" she asks.

"Not at the art," Mike says. "At the plan behind the art."

Grace turns to face him, her head cocked curiously. "What plan?"

Mike opens his mouth to speak but then presses his eyes shut and bows his head like an actor who's forgotten his lines in front of a live audience. Grace can sense that whatever he has to say is big and has been weighing on him for some time. She quietly waits for him to gather his thoughts.

"This is what I want to do," Mike says, looking at her and then around the room at all of his inspired pieces.

"Paint," Grace says.

Mike nods. "I'm an artist, Grace. Painting, it's not just a creative outlet. It's my passion." He sighs and shakes his head, frustrated by his inability to articulate the depth of his conviction. "I can't explain it. All I know is that when I have a brush in my hand, I have a sense of purpose."

"And you didn't have that sense of purpose when you were at *Life Sketch*," Grace says. It's a realization, not a question.

He shakes his head. "Don't get me wrong. I don't regret starting the company. That was the Lord's call on my life then. This is a new season, though, and it's time to move forward. But I can't. Not if I don't have you in my corner."

Grace smiles, her chin tucked, her head tilted adoringly. "Of course I'm in your corner."

He chews on his bottom lip. "You haven't heard the plan yet."

"Okay." Grace laughs. "Then I'm all ears."

Mike exhales loudly and smiles. "I want to open my own gallery." He doesn't wait for Grace to respond, but delves into a lively, intricate description of his vision. He's already come up with a name, dreamed up an ambiance, scouted several available spaces downtown, calculated the gallery's start-up costs, as well as its projected first year's revenue, and, as is evidenced all around them, he's already started creating the merchandise. The more he talks, the more excited he becomes. His voice is hopeful and his eyes animated as he reveals his secret, burgeoning desire. "So?" he leans forward, cautious, but still eager to hear Grace's thoughts.

"So...," Grace croons playfully, as she circles the room, stopping for a few seconds in front of each canvas to admire her husband's work up close. "I think we should do it."

The wrinkles spanning Mike's forehead disappear as his apprehension gives way to relief and then to delight. "Thank you," he says, closing the space between them with two long strides and enveloping Grace in a loving, grateful hug. "This is all I've ever wanted," he says, squeezing her close. "And you're the only person I've ever wanted it with."

Grace leans into his embrace, and for the first time since she discovered that she's pregnant, the world doesn't seem like it's crumbling around her. For the first time, she starts to believe that they can do this. They can have this baby.

Her attitude about kids and motherhood hasn't changed, but maybe it will over time—if Mike supports her every step of the way like she plans to support his gallery. It's not like she's forging new territory. Thousands of babies are born every day. People manage. They grow into their roles as parents. Technically, she's already ahead in the game. She's got a nurturing husband who's devoted to her and who, she knows without a doubt, will be devoted to their child.

"Baby," she says, pulling away, ready, finally, to break the big news. "I have to tell you something."

But before she can continue, Mike kisses her. It's tender and unanticipated—affection that's long overdue. Grace has not yet ceased to be amazed at how Mike's touch after any period of absence is unbelievably refreshing, like the taste of cool water after a dry and dusty drought.

Standing on the tips of her toes, her arms thrown around his neck, she kisses him back. The memory of what she needs to tell him quickly fades to the recesses of her mind as she loses herself in his presence—in this moment.

Tomorrow, she tells herself. Tomorrow she'll let him know he's going to be a daddy.

Tonight, she just wants to be with him.

Their kisses grow more passionate as Grace slips her hand under Mike's shirt, relishing the feel of his smooth skin. Mike's breathing quickens as they stumble back down the hall, undressing each other every step of the way.

The phone rings just as they reach their room. Mike lays Grace across the bed and plants a trail of kisses from her shoulder to her wrist.

"We should answer it," Grace whispers.

"No," Mike says, softly kissing Grace's jaw and then her neck. "*This* is what we should be doing."

Grace laughs. "It could be important."

Mike groans and bangs his head against the mattress. "At two in the morning, it better be," he says, rolling onto his side as she reaches for the phone.

"Hello," Grace snips into the receiver, her tone terse, her irritation at being interrupted obvious. Mike drapes his arm over her stomach and nuzzles the tip of his nose against her earlobe.

"Are you Grace?" a woman snips back, her tone just as terse and equally irritated.

"Who's asking?"

"You know a guy named Anthony Harris?"

Grace sits up, her skin prickling, her senses dulled by fear, and reaches for the pole lamp beside the bed. "He's my father," she says, trying her best to fight back a sudden and vivid flashback of the call she'd received when her mother's plane crashed. "Is something wrong?"

"I'm the manager at McDougal's—we're a small pub off Union and Third. Your dad's here, passed out on my bar. I got your number out of his wallet."

"Passed out," Grace repeats slowly, her eyes stinging with tears. "You mean drunk?"

Mike sits up, his brows rutted worriedly at Grace's pained expression.

"That's exactly what I mean," the woman says. "My bartender tried to put him in a cab hours ago, but he started getting loud. We cut him off and gave him some coffee, tried to get him to sober up a bit, but he's out cold and I gotta close up."

Her tone softens. "Look, he seems like a good guy. That's why I gave this number a shot first instead of calling the police."

"No," Grace says, wiping at her tears with the back of her hand. "Thank you." She brushes Mike's arm away and slings her legs over the side of the bed. "I understand. We'll be right there."

26

The ride to McDougal's is quiet. Downtown Memphis is asleep; most of the stoplights flash yellow as Mike navigates the deserted roads. Grace stares out of the passenger's side window and tries to think of one reason—any reason—why her father would abandon 11 years of sobriety. After all he'd been through, after everything his addiction had cost him—and had cost everyone who loved him—how could he go back? Why?

She's confused and hurt; curious and miffed; heartbroken, scared, and worried. There just doesn't seem to be any satisfying answers to her mounting questions. The gamut of conflicting emotions leaves her breathless. She sighs heavily.

"We're almost there," Mike says, reaching for Grace's hand and entwining their fingers.

Grace only nods.

"Don't assume the worst," he counsels. "It may be a misunderstanding."

Grace snorts. "It's kind of hard to misunderstand, 'Come get your father. He's passed out on my bar.'"

"How could he have fallen off the wagon after so long?" Mike wonders out loud. "When you stayed the night at his house last week, did he mention anything that might have hinted at this? Financial troubles? Problems at work? Anything?"

"In other words, why didn't I see it coming," Grace says, snatching away her hand and folding her arms across her chest.

"That's not what I said." Mike's tone is calm. "Don't put words in my mouth. I'm only trying to figure out what's going on."

"Well, your guess is as good as mine," Grace huffs.

"Something had to set him off," Mike murmurs quietly to himself.

"Can we just—," Grace massages the bridge of her nose. "Let's just not talk about it."

Though he's irritated by Grace's unmerited harshness, Mike doesn't say another word. He drives them down a few unfamiliar streets and through an alley that leads them straight to the bar's parking lot, which is barren except for two pickup trucks parked by the side door next to a huge green dumpster.

Unlike the rambling sport's bar Grace had rescued her dad from just a few days earlier, McDougal's is compact with low, wood ceilings and dangling, stained-glass light fixtures. The small space, though virtually empty, has a friendly, cozy cabin feel to it. In place of sports paraphernalia, the walls are decorated with thousands of random messages and signatures from visiting patrons as well as obscure movie posters and old photographs encased in weathered frames.

The chairs have been turned upside down and placed on the tables. One of the waitresses is humming softly along to a song playing on the jukebox as she mops the floor.

Grace spots her dad immediately. The manager wasn't kidding. He is, literally, passed out on the bar. The sight of him propped on a stool, his limp body hunched forward, his cheek resting on his overlapping hands, fills Grace with pity and unexpected compassion.

She makes her way over to him, Mike trailing closely behind her, and pats his back. "Dad," she calls, shaking him gently. "Come on, get up. We're going to take you home."

He groans and shrugs Grace's hand away.

"You've got to get up now," Grace says, banging her palm against the top of the bar to rouse him. "They're closing."

"I'm not going anywhere," he slurs, "until I get another drink."

Grace recoils at his rancid breath, which is saturated with liquor.

"You've had plenty," Mike says, stepping on the other side of him and tugging at his arm. "It's time to go now."

"Go where?" he asks. His head bobs left and right as he tries to lift it off the bar and look at the two of them.

"Home," Grace explains, her tone patient but resolute.

He throws his arms up, disgustedly, narrowly missing Grace's nose. "I am home," he says, his eyelids drooping shut.

"No," Mike says firmly. "You're in a bar and you've got to get up now. Come on, I'll help you." He wraps his arm around Anthony's waist, drapes Anthony's arm over his shoulders, and lifts him, with much effort, off of the stool.

"I said, no!" Anthony shouts. He shoves Mike with such force that they both stumble backward.

"Stop it!" Grace cries, stepping between the two of them. "You can't stay here," she says, laying it out plainly for her father. "So you either come with us now or the manager's going to call the police and have you thrown in the drunk tank."

"It doesn't matter," he gurgles sadly.

"It does to me," Grace says.

Her dad rests his head back on the bar. His shoulders heave. "It's all over," he moans. "I tried. I tried so hard, but it doesn't matter now. It's all over."

"What's all over?" Mike asks.

"I need a drink," Anthony says between sniffles. "Get me a drink."

"Dad, you don't drink anymore," Grace reminds him.

"I don't?" he asks, lifting his head and gazing up at her through glassy eyes.

"No," she says, squeezing his hand. "You've been sober for eleven years."

"Right," he nods, his mouth turned down into a frown as his fogged mind strains to process this information.

"Don't you want to go home?" Mike asks. "Lay down in your own bed?"

He nods, the fight in him clearly waning. "Yeah," he murmurs. "Home sounds good."

"Can I help you up?" Mike asks.

Again, he nods. This time when Mike lifts Anthony off the stool, he cooperates. His limbs are heavy and his steps uncoordinated, but Mike manages to get him across the bar and out into the parking lot.

Grace rushes to unlock the truck and open the back passenger's side door. Heaving her father into Mike's SUV proves to be no small feat. She and Mike struggle to lay him across the backseat. Grace employs all of her strength to hold her father's legs while Mike darts around to the other side of the truck and pulls him, by his arms, the rest of the way in.

Disoriented and emotional, Anthony snores, mumbles, and cries the entire ride home. Grace stares out of the window, lost in thought. Every so often, she casts worried glances at her father, but she says nothing.

Mike doesn't speak either; he only holds Grace's hand, caressing her knuckles with his thumb, and silently prays.

Getting Anthony out of the truck is considerably easier than it was to put him in it. Grace unlocks the door to her father's house and flips on the lights in the hallway and the living room as she hurriedly makes her way to his bedroom to pull back his comforter and sheets.

Mike stumbles in a few minutes later, half-carrying, half-dragging Grace's father beside him. They lay him down gently, propping his head on two stacked pillows.

"I guess I should get him out of these clothes," Grace says.

Mike nods. "I'm gonna go lock the front door."

Grace tugs off her dad's shoes, then his sweater vest and his shirt. His stomach rises and falls in a steady rhythm. "What were you thinking?" she whispers, stroking his beard. She can hear Mike in the kitchen as she searches her father's drawer for his pajamas.

"Are you mad at me?" a voice asks.

Grace looks down to see her father peering up at her. "I don't think so," she answers honestly. "I'm just really disappointed. All those years of sobriety," she shakes her head, "wasted."

He looks away. "It doesn't matter anymore anyway."

"You keep saying that," Grace says, her voice quaking. "Of course it matters. Why wouldn't it matter?"

"Because I'm dying."

Those three simple words slam into Grace like the knockout punch of a prize fighter. "What?" she whispers, tears gathering in her eyes.

"I have cirrhosis," her father says, choking back his own sob. "Advanced cirrhosis of the liver."

Grace's trembling hand covers her mouth.

"That's why it doesn't matter anymore," he murmurs, drifting back to sleep. "It was all too little too late."

Mike enters with a steaming mug, a tea bag string dangling over the side of it. "Grace?" he asks, setting the mug down. "Gracie, what's wrong? Talk to me," he pleads, pulling her into his protective embrace.

But she can't—she can't find the words. She can only cry, her tears soaking Mike's shirt, and slowly succumb to the devastating realization that she will soon lose the only parent she has left.

27

"Please tell me there's a perfectly reasonable explanation for this."

Trina pries open one uncooperative eye to discover Kendra standing over her, her brow hiked, a smirk of utter bewilderment gracing her face. Groggy, Trina blinks several times, her eyelids heavy, and tries to grasp her bearings.

She's on the floor in her office, where she'd finally managed, after hours of trying, to tumble into a fitful sleep just as the sun was coming up. "What time is it?" she asks, combing her fingers through her stiff mane in a futile attempt to tame it. Her voice is hoarse with exhaustion.

Kendra glances at her watch. "A quarter past ten."

"Great," Trina groans, sitting up. "Can you, uh...," she points at the door, gesturing for Kendra to close it.

"You know, you're lucky security hasn't caught you," Kendra says, shutting the door and lowering the cheap, aluminum blinds.

"You make it sound like I sleep here on a regular basis," Trina says, standing and stretching her arms over her head.

Kendra eyes Trina's pajamas, her neat pallet on the floor, and her bulging overnight bag in the corner. "I wonder where I could've gotten an idea like that?" she asks wryly, tapping her index finger against her chin.

"I knew I'd be up all night finishing Becky's files," Trina lies. "I brought this stuff in case I was too tired to go home," she shrugs, "and I was."

"Darius lives five minutes away," Kendra says, clearly unconvinced. "You were too tired to drive five minutes?"

"What is this? An interrogation?" Trina asks haughtily, turning her back on Kendra's dubious stare to fold her blanket. "You should be thanking me for finishing your dirty work."

"Hey, I offered to do it myself. You declined, remember?"

"What difference does it make? The point is, it's done." Trina pulls a wrinkled change of clothes from her bag.

"Listen," Kendra says, taking a few steps closer, her voice soft. "Why don't you just stay with me for a while?"

"What're you talking about?" Trina scoffs, too embarrassed to meet Kendra's sincere gaze. "I'm not homeless." She snatches a face cloth from her bag's side pocket. "I'm overworked."

"Teeny," Kendra says, her head tilted sympathetically.

"Darius and I had a fight, okay? It's not a big deal. We just needed some space from each other. That's all," she says, punctuating her words with a resolute nod. "I didn't feel like wasting money on a hotel room."

"Do you want to stay with me until you guys work it out?"

"We already did," Trina says. "Last night. He called and apologized—asked me to come back." She shrugs. "I don't know. We'll see."

"Well, you can't keep sleeping here."

"Look." Trina sighs and flops tiredly into the chair behind her desk. "I know you're only trying to help, but there's no need—really. I'm a big girl. I can take care of myself."

Kendra shrugs, her best efforts at offering Trina help, shunned. "Fine," she says, backing away. "I'll get out of your hair. I just need Becky's new case file."

"Now?" Trina asks, trying to play off her alarm as curiosity.

Kendra's eyes squint suspiciously. "Yeah," she nods slowly, "I told Quinn I'd have it for her first thing this morning."

Trina hasn't started the modifications to Becky's case file or her computer file. Last night, when she should have been changing and deleting information, her thoughts kept bouncing back and forth between Georgia Kenny's letter and Darius's apology. She'd planned to rise early this morning, get washed up and changed before her coworkers arrived, and have Becky's new files finished before lunch. That plan, of course, has gone awry since she over-slept, but with a little ingenuity, may still be salvageable.

"It's not ready yet," Trina says.

"I thought you stayed up all night finishing it."

"I did. I just..." Trina scurries for a believable excuse. "I need to double-check everything."

"Quinn can do that," Kendra says.

"I want it to be perfect," Trina says, her eyes desperate. "This is my chance to make an impression. I don't want it to be the wrong one. Give me until lunch," she pleads. "I want to read through it one more time—make any little, last-minute adjustments."

"But she's expecting it now," Kendra argues. "What am I supposed to tell her?"

"I don't know. Anything. Stall for me." She offers a pout and her most pathetic puppy eyes. "Please?" Trina begs. "Just this once."

Kendra sighs. "It's got to be done by noon," she concedes reluctantly, wag-ging her index finger at Trina. "No excuses."

"No excuses," Trina assures her.

Kendra leaves, and Trina changes out of her long-sleeved T-shirt and plaid pajama bottoms into a pair of wool slacks and a button-down shirt.

She spritzes herself with a liberal amount of perfume to make up for the fact that she hasn't showered in over 48 hours and heads to the women's rest-room to brush her teeth, wash her face, subdue her wiry, unruly hair, and paint on a deceptively perky coat of makeup.

Fifteen minutes later she's back behind her desk, looking like a million bucks, smelling like a hundred, and feeling like ten. With her door locked, she pulls out the case file, along with a stack of blank information sheets, and sets to work concocting a new history for Becky Schmidt.

"We're not trying to turn him into a saint," Quinn had said of Councilman Schmidt. "So don't make the file squeaky clean," she'd instructed. "That might raise some brows. All we need to do is establish that he's been rehabilitated and that he's ready to take back custody of his daughter."

Trina transfers only the favorable information from Becky's original case file to the blank sheets, taking care to switch ink pens and to alter her handwriting every few pages so as to add to the fake file's authenticity.

She feverishly forges signatures, rewrites progress reports, and erases the bulk of Becky's hospitals stays. She spends a considerable amount of time downgrading Becky's long list of injuries. Suspicious hairline fractures change to less obvious sprains. Worrisome welts become innocuous bruises. Deliberate dehydration turns into a nasty stomach flu. On and on she scribbles, making one change after the next, until Becky's file looks almost normal—until seven suspicious emergency room visits turn into four understandable ones; until therapists are more hopeful than concerned; until Becky comes off as bubbly and energetic instead of reclusive and anxious.

She concentrates a fair amount of her effort on reconstructing Councilman Schmidt's attitude toward his daughter. She fabricates bogus letters of character by cutting and pasting statements from assorted friends, family members, and business associates. Now, thanks to her handiwork, they all believe Becky should be returned home to the councilman—who is, for all intents and purposes, a changed man.

Though she hadn't planned on doing so, she also adjusts Councilman Schmidt's attendance sheets. The new file wouldn't be believable with his current record of participation. She places him at every single anger management session, parenting class, and supervised visit he was ordered and expected to attend. With a few flicks of her red pen, he morphs from an uninvolved, fairweather father to an attentive, doting daddy.

Trina's shoulders ease as she reaches the end of the case file and glances at the clock. Twenty minutes until deadline and the only thing she has left to do is apply her changes to Becky's electronic file.

As she waits for her computer to boot up and log into the company's system, she gathers up the forms messily strewn across her desk and arranges them into a neat pile so she can stuff them back into their manila folder. That's when she notices the thin stack of construction paper clipped beneath a pad of blank behavioral performance forms.

She unclips the pad and slides it aside. Staring up at her is a child's drawing. In it are two people. One is a towering figure, made of two circles and stick limbs. He's wearing a tie and Becky's best recreation of a suit. He has short, spiked hair; hard, sharply slanting brows; red eyes, and jagged teeth. He's bigger than everything, taller than the sun and the birds and the apple trees that comprise the landscape. The other figure, standing beside him, is small, barely taller than the grass blades (a row of green lines that stretches from one end of the paper to the other) covering her feet. She stares ahead, eclipsed by the angry monster beside her, devoid of expression or emotion.

Trina flips to the picture underneath it and then to the one underneath that. They're all pretty much the same thing—one larger-than-life man, and one insignificantly small young girl.

Oddly, no assessments adjoin the drawings. But it doesn't take a psychoanalyst to figure out what Becky's portraits are hinting at. Trina doesn't have the heart to dispose of them. In her own way, without being able to read or write, Becky has communicated, through her art, the exact nature of her relationship with her father. Her drawings speak more than a sheaf of medical charts, affidavits, progress reports, attendance sheets, or psychological analyses ever could.

Before she has a chance to talk herself out of it, Trina gets up, unlocks the small compartment in her file cabinet, and places the drawings inside with the master file she'd hidden the night before.

Then she gets busy making all of the necessary revisions to Becky's electronic file. She types quickly, racing against the clock. By five minutes past noon, she's finished and saving her changes just as Kendra knocks on the door.

Trina rushes to unlock it and lets her in.

"Time's up," she chirps, holding out her hand expectantly.

"All done," Trina says, picking it up from her desk and giving it to Kendra. "I think it's perfect."

"Let's hope so," Kendra says, flipping through the pages, pausing to skim over random reports.

"What should I do with this?" Trina asks, waving Becky's old case file.

Kendra shrugs cavalierly. "Shred it," she says, turning to leave.

Trina nods, deciding at that moment to add it to the secret stash in her file cabinet.

But, as if reading her mind, Kendra abruptly turns back around. "On second thought, I'll take it."

"Oh, okay, sure," Trina says, reluctantly relinquishing the file. "Any reason in particular?"

"I just think Quinn might want to have something to compare the new report to. Can't hurt to make sure everything's to her liking, right?"

"Right," Trina says, forcing a smile.

"Are you okay?" Kendra asks, her gaze probing.

"I'm fine," Trina says, straightening her collar. "Just a little tired."

"A little?" Kendra scoffs. "I could pack the clothes for my next trip in the bags under your eyes."

Trina laughs despite herself. "Gee thanks, that makes me feel a whole lot better!"

"Say the word and my living room is yours," Kendra offers.

"No, I'm good, but thanks."

"You sure?" Kendra asks. "Comfy couch…hard office floor. Comfy couch…hard office floor," she chants, her hands out, palms up as if she's actually weighing the two options.

Trina smiles. "I'm sure," she says.

"Have it your way," Kendra shrugs. "But at least take the rest of the day off. Seriously, just looking at you makes me want to take a nap."

Trina nods. "Yeah," she says, considering Kendra's suggestion. "Maybe I will."

Satisfied, Kendra leaves to deliver the goods to Quinn, and Trina returns to her desk where, on a whim, she dials Darius at work to see if he might be in the mood to play a little hooky.

28

Grace discreetly studies the guests in the obstetrician's clamorous waiting room from over the top of her magazine.

The woman closest to the receptionist's desk looks like she's about to pop. Her cheeks are flushed with heat, despite the chilly temperature of the doctor's office, and the bun fashioned sloppily on the top of her head is being held in place by a pencil. She's got stains on her cardigan, and her ankles, which peek out from beneath her dowdy maternity dress, are swollen to the size of cans.

Sitting to her right is a rambunctious little girl. She looks to be about four. The chair next to her is occupied with coloring books, crayons, stickers, a half-naked Barbie doll, a sippy cup, and a small baggie of Cheerios—seemingly everything needed to keep a small child occupied. However, the little girl is more interested in kicking her dangling legs wildly back and forth while humming, "Twinkle, Twinkle, Little Star" as loudly as she can. Every now and then, her mother pleads with her to settle down, which she does for all of 60 seconds before seeking out an even louder, more obnoxious activity.

The same situation holds true for the woman seated just a few chairs over from Grace. She's got the same, overexerted, bursting-at-the-seams look, only instead of a hyper toddler wiggling at her side, she's got a fussy baby in a stroller.

The rosy-cheeked little guy is admittedly cute, decked out in a blue cap, a miniature blue track suit, and blue booties. But despite his mother's most fervent efforts, nothing is able to subdue his piercing cries. She tries everything to soothe him: bottles of milk and juice, a pacifier, several rattles. She tries picking him up, setting him down, walking him, rocking him, cradling him, tickling him, talking to him, and singing to him. His plump, little face remains scrunched, his eyes squeezed tightly shut and his mouth thrown open, revealing a tiny, pink tongue. For one hopeful moment, a teething ring dipped in applesauce seems to satisfy him, but no sooner do Grace's shoulders relax, than he tosses the teething ring out of the stroller and goes back to screaming at the top of his lungs.

His mother shrugs apologetically, gathers him up, and takes him into the hall for another calming stroll.

Grace notices that all of the pregnant women sitting around her look exhausted, even the ones without kids. They're not poised and radiant like the mothers on the cover of the *Baby and Me* magazines supplied on every table in the waiting room. They're not sporting the newest in chic maternity fashions or beaming with pride as they rub their budding bellies and stare off into the distance, hopeful and excited.

They all look wiped out—haggard—as though motherhood has already taken its toll. *Is that going to be me?* Grace wonders. Four, five, six, seven months from now, is she going to be one of these women, waddling in for her regular prenatal appointment, wearing a tent and a tired frown?

Last night, when she was in Mike's arms, she had almost wanted the baby. She could almost see the three of them as one big happy family. Almost.

The thing is, if ever there was a time when a baby didn't fit into the big picture, it's now. Now that she knows about her father's condition. She can't afford to be down with morning sickness or sidetracked by time-consuming doctor's appointments or incapacitated by unforeseen complications.

Taking care of her dad, attending to his needs, making sure he's not daunted by everyday tasks and necessities, and helping him stay as healthy as possible for as long as possible are her only chief concerns. She doesn't want to lose him the way she lost her mother: suddenly, in the middle of the night, without ever taking advantage of the many opportunities she had to express her love.

Grace's eyes continue to circulate the room. Her gaze falls on an African-American woman hunched over a clipboard. She's slight, with a mahogany complexion, manicured nails, and freshly pressed hair. Aside from the receptionist, she and Grace are the only other people in the room wearing lipstick and high heels.

She looks up and catches Grace staring. Grace offers a quick, embarrassed smile and goes back to reading her article on pregnancy and hemorrhoids (as if there aren't already enough reasons why she doesn't want to have this baby).

The woman finishes filling out the forms, hands them, along with the clipboard, back to the gaggle of medical assistants behind the glass partition, and promptly takes the seat next to Grace.

"First time?" she whispers, leaning close, her purse resting in her lap.

"Sorry?" Grace asks, flipping the magazine closed.

She nods at Grace's stomach. "First pregnancy?" she clarifies.

"Oh, um, yeah," Grace admits, somewhat reluctantly, though she's not entirely sure why.

"Me too," the woman says, smiling brightly. Her teeth seem too large for her small, oval face—big and boxy like two perfectly lined rows of Chiclets. "How far along are you?"

"I'm not sure," Grace says. "This is my first visit."

"I'm eight weeks," she says, gingerly patting her flat stomach.

Grace smiles and offers her congratulations.

"You want a tip I learned from watching my sister go through this?" she asks. Then, without waiting for an answer, she says, "Don't listen to what any-body tells you. Morning sickness does not go away by the end of the first trimester."

Grace laughs. "Good to know," she says. "Depressing, but good."

"My name's Beth, by the way."

"Grace," Grace says, introducing herself with a handshake.

"I'd ask if you were going it alone, but the blinding glare off that ring of yours answers the question."

"Yes, I have a husband—just married," Grace says, twirling her wedding ring around her finger with her thumb. "He's not coming, though." She shakes her head and smiles weakly. "He doesn't even know I'm here."

Beth nods, her eyes sympathetic. "Well, I hate to break it to you," she says softly, "but a pregnancy isn't something you can hide for very long."

"No, I know," Grace says. "I just need to get all of the facts together first and then figure out what I'm going to do. This—a baby—wasn't part of the plan, you know? I've got a career that I love, and my husband just revealed that he wants to start a new business. Not to mention, my father's health is failing." She sighs. "Where would a kid fit into all of that? How?"

Beth shrugs. "I don't know."

"I'm sorry," Grace says, embarrassed. "We met five minutes ago and I've got you playing my shrink. I'm not usually like this," she says with a sigh. "It's just that I hate keeping secrets; and for the past few days, that's all I've been doing."

Beth nods slowly, but doesn't say anything.

Grace cringes in the awkwardness of the silence, instantly regretting that she had blabbed so freely to a complete stranger.

"I told my husband I was pregnant, and he told me he wanted a divorce," Beth blurts out.

"What?" Grace asks, her voice hushed, her expression horrified.

Beth nods. "And the thing is, we planned this baby," she says. "My husband, Mark, he's always been a planner. There always has to be a clear objective—a goal and a time frame. Before we even walked down the aisle, he made us sit down and map out a blueprint for our marriage. First two years, we'd pay off debts. Third year, we'd buy our first house. And fifth year, we'd start a family." She shrugs. "As fate would have it, three months after our fifth anniversary, I wound up pregnant."

"So what went wrong?" Grace asks.

"I don't think it was any *one* thing," Beth says. "Just lots of little things that added up over the years. We stopped talking, stopped relating to each other, stopped trying. We kept making room for this growing gap between us, and the next thing we knew, it had swallowed us whole."

Grace studies Beth's face. Her features are as strong and bright as her attitude. But her story is still a sad one. "I'm sorry," Grace says.

"Don't be." Beth waves her hand dismissively. "The lesson here is that there's no perfect time to have a kid. We've been around long enough to know that even the best-laid plans can go awry. You just gotta learn to roll with the punches."

Grace considers her words. *Roll with the punches.* If only she could adopt the same outlook. It sounds so simple when Beth says it—so basic and right. All she has to do is make a few changes, sacrifice a few things, shift a couple of paradigms, and an unplanned pregnancy takes on a new light. Yet as soon as she considers exactly what changes, sacrifices, and paradigm shifts she'd have to make, and the consequences of making them, her doubt returns.

"I can't get enough of these things," Beth says, snapping Grace from her thoughts. She pulls out a half-empty, yellow bag of Swedish fish from her purse. "I'm like an addict," she says, popping one in her mouth and closing her eyes as she chews. "I can't make it one day without my afternoon candy fix." She tilts the open bag toward Grace.

"Cravings are normal, right?" Grace asks, taking a few.

"Yeah, but my sister craved healthy stuff like tangerines and cauliflower when she was pregnant with each of her three children. Finally my turn comes and I'm sucking down enough sugar to rot my kid's teeth out before he even has any."

"So it's a boy?" Grace asks between chewy bites.

"Dunno yet," Beth says. "It's too soon to tell; but I've got a hunch that it is. They say mothers just know."

"Cambridge. Grace Cambridge," a sprightly woman in a nurse's uniform calls from the office door.

"That's me," Grace says, standing.

"Hey, listen," Beth says, rummaging around in her purse. "If you ever want to hang out or talk or…," she shrugs, "or you just have a hankering for some Swedish fish, give me a call." She hands Grace her card.

"Thanks, I might take you up on that."

Beth smiles. "Good luck."

"Yeah, you too."

Grace makes her way to the waiting assistant, who introduces herself as Kim, and follows her down a long hall lined with closed doors. "You'll be in here," Kim says, ushering Grace into an empty examining room. "If you'll take your shoes off and follow me, we'll go across the hall and get your height and weight."

Grace obliges and follows Kim to a scale that looks wide enough to weigh cattle. She steps on, gripping the metal handle bars on either side, and balks as the blinking red numbers on the display register a seven-pound weight gain.

Kim records the number without comment, measures Grace's height, and then sends her off to the bathroom with a plastic cup for a urine sample.

As soon as Grace returns, Kim closes the door and takes Grace's temperature, blood pressure, and pulse. Then she launches into an exhaustive list of detailed questions about Grace's health: her menstrual cycle, her lifestyle, her habits, her nutrition, and her family's medical history. She also presses for the same type of information on Mike. Grace answers the questions as best she can, but her knowledge of his family's medical history is patchy considering that he's adopted.

No sooner does Kim finish jotting down information in Grace's chart, than Eliza enters, wearing rubber gloves and carrying big syringes and a handful of vials. Grace's palms instantly turn clammy, and her mind swims as Eliza explains that she'll be drawing blood to test for Grace's blood type, the HIV virus, hepatitis, anemia, and a positive or negative RH factor, among other things.

Grace gets through it all like a champ.

Eliza waits for the last vial to fill, then slides the needle from beneath Grace's skin, and with her one free hand, covers the puncture point with a Band-Aid. "You're all set," she chirps.

As if on cue, Kim enters, carrying a neatly folded paper gown. "Put this on for me," she says, handing it to Grace. "And Dr. Noguez will be in to see you in just a bit."

Several minutes later, there's a knock on the door and Dr. Noguez appears. He's tall with long, lanky limbs and erect posture. His skin looks olive beneath his white lab coat, and his hair, as well as his goatee, is streaked with gray. His slanted nose and pointy chin make him look stern and severe. But the instant he enters, he offers Grace a confident smile and a firm hand-shake that leaves her comfortable and at ease, despite the flimsy paper dress shielding her naked body.

He takes a minute to read over Kim's carefully taken notes. "Not very much family medical history on your husband," he comments.

Grace explains, again, that Mike is adopted.

"Is there any reason why he's not here with you today?" Dr. Noguez asks.

"He's out of town on business," Grace lies.

Dr. Noguez nods and scribbles something onto his pad.

"Why?" Grace asks, stretching her neck in an effort to make out what he's writing. "Is that a problem?"

"Not at all," Dr. Noguez says, his smile warm and reassuring. "It's just been my experience that the smoothest pregnancies are the ones where both parents are informed and involved. So the more appointments he can make it to, the better."

"Okay." Grace nods, forcing a grin. "I'll let him know."

"Good," Dr. Noguez says, setting the chart aside. He flips up the stirrups at the end of the examining table and locks them into place. "Now, let's have a look."

Grace lies still as Dr. Noguez pokes around with gloved hands and cold instruments. Now, more than ever, she wishes she'd tried harder to find a female obstetrician. It has always been her contention that Pap smears and other such exams should be done *by* women *for* women, but female obstetricians are few and far between in Memphis. The handful she was able to locate in the Yellow Pages were booked up months in advance, and she needed answers yesterday.

"Everything looks good," Dr. Noguez says, rolling away from the table and depositing his soiled rubber gloves in the trash. He lowers the stirrups so Grace can sit up and then washes his hands. "I'll give you a few minutes to get dressed, and then I'll come back and we can talk."

Gladly, Grace changes back into her clothes and waits, her foot tapping anxiously, for the doctor to return. Minutes later, he does.

"You're six weeks pregnant," he begins. "So far everything looks normal—healthy." He hands her a pink folder. The words, *Baby on Board*, stare back at her in white print. "That's a starter packet of sorts, if you will," Dr. Noguez says, pointing with his pen at the folder in Grace's hands. "It's full of helpful information that you and your husband should sit down and read together."

Grace flips it open. Inside is a suggested schedule of prenatal visits, a list of over-the-counter medicines she should stay away from, suggested reading, locations of Lamaze classes, emergency contact numbers, and pamphlets on breast-feeding and water retention and every other imaginable topic that pertains to surviving pregnancy and giving birth.

Stapled in the upper right-hand corner of the folder itself is a card with her baby's estimated due date on it: June 29th.

Dr. Noguez gives Grace a brief overview of what she can expect in the ensuing weeks, including weight gain, mood swings, loss of energy, food cravings, and chronic urination. He tells her the best natural ways to alleviate a sore back, indigestion, and headaches. He also orders her to start taking prenatal vitamins immediately and assures her that her morning sickness will likely disappear toward the end of her first trimester.

Grace can't help but think of Beth's "tip" and smile.

He goes over a rundown of screening tests that they'll be administering during each visit to detect potential problems in light of her family's history of high blood pressure and diabetes, and suggests that Grace begin a daily exercise regimen.

"Do you have any questions for me?" he asks.

"A few," she admits shyly.

"Shoot."

"Why didn't you give me an ultrasound?" she asks. "I thought I was supposed to get a picture or at least hear the baby's heartbeat."

Dr. Noguez smiles knowingly, as though he hears that a thousand times a day. "It's a little too early for ultrasounds and heartbeats," he says. "We'll reach that point at around the twenty-week mark. But," he opens one of the cabinets and pulls out a small pamphlet, "this is what your baby looks like now, at six weeks."

Grace examines the picture. It looks like a lima bean floating in a clear sack of water. She nods and tucks the pamphlet in her folder.

"What if," she pauses, "hypothetically, I didn't want the baby? Is it too late to…you know?" She looks away, shamed.

"Abortion is absolutely still an option," he says.

Grace nods, her eyes filling with tears. "And what does that involve, exactly?" she whispers.

Dr. Noguez hands her several tissues from the box by the sink. "It's relatively quick and painless," he says. "The hardest part, I've been told, is coping with the decision afterward."

He hands her even more literature in the form of pamphlets. These illustrate the procedure step by step. Grace listens closely as he narrates the entire process, from check-in to after-care and follow-up visits. He makes it sound no worse than a visit to the gynecologist.

"Abortions are safest the earlier they're done," he explains. "But you have all the way up until your fourteenth week to decide. My suggestion is," he says, patting her knee, "talk it over with your husband. Make the decision together."

She sniffles and shakes her head. "That's just not an option. He won't understand."

"Are you sure?" he asks, his tone as soft as cotton.

She nods and dabs at the tears dripping from her chin.

"Here's what I suggest to patients in your situation."

Grace looks up, hoping that, as a doctor, he knows of an option she hasn't yet thought of.

"Make the appointment," he says. "Set it as far in advance as you want. If you show up, that's fine. And if you don't, there's no harm done. Sometimes just having a 'D-Date' is enough to help you realize what you want."

It's not the advice she's looking for, but Grace takes it anyway. When she gets to the front desk, she makes two appointments: one for her next prenatal checkup and the other to terminate her pregnancy. She schedules it for the end of her fourteenth week—the farthest possible date away—secretly hoping that something will happen between then and now to free her from the burden of making a choice.

She sticks the appointment cards in her pink folder and heads home, where she has another good cry, hides everything in the brown paper bag under the bathroom sink, and then calls to check in on her dad.

29

Wolfchase Mall is surprisingly crowded for a Thursday afternoon. *Probably because of the rain*, Trina thinks, as she trots hurriedly through and around groups of slow, perusing shoppers.

Darius is waiting for her outside of the food court as planned. He looks sexy, casually dressed in a crisp, white, button-down shirt and loose-fitting, faded jeans. He smiles brightly as she approaches.

"I'm sorry I'm late," she says, breathless. "It took longer to get here than I thought it would."

"Don't worry about it. I'm just glad you called. You look great," he says, giving her a tentative kiss on the cheek.

Trina smiles. "Is that for me?" she asks, pointing at the Mrs. Field's bag in his hand.

"Yeah," he shrugs. "You're always saying how a trip to the mall isn't official until you get your chocolate chip cookie."

Trina laughs. "I can't believe you remember that." She retrieves one of the warm, gooey cookies from the bag and takes a bite.

"So what do you want to do?" he asks as they stroll past several shops.

Trina chews slowly as she considers his question. "Something fun," she says, "that requires very little effort and even less thought."

He laughs. "Work's got you *that* beat down?"

Trina groans and shakes her head. "Don't even ask."

"I think I know exactly what you need," he says with a sly grin. He turns her around and takes her hand.

"Where are we going?" she asks.

He smiles. "Just eat your cookie and leave it to me."

They walk at a leisurely pace, stopping every few feet to check out the splashy displays in the store windows. Darius leads her down two sets of escalators and past even more shops until they reach Sophia's, a cozy boutique she'd fallen in love with when she first moved to Memphis.

"Aww," Trina coos, her eyes already coveting a purse dangling from the arm of one of the stylishly dressed mannequins. "I haven't been here in ages."

When Grace was too busy or unwilling, she used to drag Darius all the way out to Sophia's to go shopping with her. She'd make him sit, sometimes for hours, as she modeled one outfit after another and then fawned over the bags and the jewelry and the shoes. He'd humor her, tell her how great she looked, how lucky he was to be with such a beautiful woman. Sometimes, he'd even buy her something, which was no small token of his love, considering Sophia's exorbitant prices.

But that was a long time ago—before he started sleeping with his boss, before his attitude toward Trina hardened and his behavior grew suspicious.

That was when he came home on time, when he gushed over her dinners and insisted that she rest while he washed the dishes. That was back when they used to dim the lights, snuggle together on the couch under a blanket, and predict just how happy a future they had in store for them.

They were both different people then—a little less wise, a little less tainted by reality.

"Don't you want to go in?" Darius asks. "Poke around?"

Trina shakes her head, all the while eyeing that purse. "I shouldn't," she says. "I'll wind up walking out with a bunch of stuff I can't afford."

"That's never stopped you before," Darius says.

"Well…" Trina nibbles on her bottom lip, her resolve already teetering. "Maybe just for a minute."

An hour later, she heads to the register with her gold-finds: a pair of strappy heels, a beaded grommet belt, two pairs of jeans, a bold pair of hoop earrings, and, of course, the purse in the display window.

She had really wanted to get the backless, moss-green dress hanging on the "New Arrivals" rack. It was the only one left and it fit Trina's petite frame perfectly, hugging and flowing in all of the right places. Darius's jaw had dropped when she stepped out of the dressing room and gave a playful twirl. He told her to buy it. "That dress was meant for you," he said. But the price tag told her otherwise.

She went back and forth on it a few times, mentally shifting her finances around, desperate to find a way to fit it into her paltry budget. Eventually, she had to resign herself to the sad fact that it was just too expensive, and as she watches the numbers on the cash register climb into the triple digits, she's glad she did.

Her tally comes to a whopping 600 dollars. It's money that a responsible person in her position would scrimp and put toward a few nights' stay in a motel room. But Trina's in need of a little boost and there's no therapy like retail therapy. She'll pay it off in the near future thanks to her impending promotion. In the meantime, she reasons, that's what credit is for.

She pulls out her wallet, quickly reviewing in her mind which cards are safe to try and which ones are maxed out. But before she can hand one to the waiting sales associate, Darius slides his across the counter.

"From me," he says.

"Are you crazy?" Trina asks, her eyes wide. "I can't let you pay for this."

"I want to do something special for you."

She shakes her head. "It's too much."

"You're worth it," he says, handing over his driver's license.

Trina beams. "I don't know what to say. Thank you!" she gushes.

He leans forward and gives her a soft, innocently sweet kiss on the lips. "You're welcome."

The sales associate smiles. "We can switch boyfriends any time," she says, bagging Trina's gifts and handing Darius the receipt to sign.

They head back out into the mall, hand in hand, Darius carrying Trina's shopping bag full of goodies. "So what's next," he asks.

Trina shrugs. "Lunch? A movie?"

Darius arches a brow and narrows his eyes. "We can do better than that," he says with a slow, sure nod.

Darius's idea of better turns out to be more shopping—for Trina, that is. He leads her out of one store and into another, waiting patiently as she tries on clothes, or samples perfumes, or rummages through CDs, or skims through books. The more she begs him not to pay, the more he insists on doing it.

They make their way through both levels of the mall, laughing and teasing and enjoying each other's company. Darius doesn't have to make any private phone calls or answer any mysterious pages. He doesn't snap and complain or prod Trina to hurry up. He doesn't ogle other women as they pass by or flirt with other shoppers under the guise of being friendly. His attention is consistent and earnest and completely focused on Trina.

"Who are you?" she jokes at one point, when Darius offers to take her bags to her car while she gets an impromptu pedicure.

"A man in love," is his response.

By the time they head out to the parking lot, the rain has cleared, the sun is going down, and the clouds are glowing a brilliant shade of pink and orange. Trina isn't ready for the day to end, but she doesn't know how to express that without sounding greedy or seeming ungrateful.

Wordlessly, Darius walks her to her car. "I had fun today," she says, breaking the silence.

He smiles and squeezes her hand. "Good, that was the goal."

Trina gazes intently into his eyes. "You think I'd have you figured out by now," she says, her voice soft, her tone sated with wonder. "But you're still full of surprises."

"Can I take you to dinner?" he asks, his face only inches from hers.

"Tonight?"

He nods and tugs Trina even closer. "Chez Philippe," he whispers. "Eight o'clock."

"But we don't have a reservation."

"It's been taken care of," he says. "Just say yes."

"Yes," Trina says, just as their lips fit together and his arm finds its way around her waist. His breath is warm against her skin.

"I'll see you in a bit," he says, reluctantly pulling away.

Trina nods and tilts her chin upward for one last kiss.

He obliges and then watches as she gets into her car and drives off into the sunset.

"I need to use your shower," Trina says, blowing through Kendra's front door, her arms loaded with everything necessary to transform herself into a ravishing dinner date.

"Hello. Good to see you," Kendra says, to Trina's retreating back. "My day was wonderful. Thanks for asking. How was yours?"

"A fairy tale," Trina calls over her shoulder. She unloads her things on Kendra's bed and makes a beeline for the bathroom.

Kendra follows her and sits on the edge of the tub. "I'm guessing Darius played the role of prince."

"You should have seen him," Trina says, rummaging through the linen closet for a washcloth and towel. "He was funny and chivalrous and charming and..." She shakes her head, at a loss for adequate words. "The whole day was just enchanting."

"Well, what'd you guys do?"

"We went to the mall."

Kendra blinks. "That's it?"

Trina nods. "He kind of treated me to a shopping spree," she says, her smile giddy.

"So that's why you're glowing like a light bulb," Kendra says with a laugh.

"Believe it or not—no. It's not the stuff; it's *him*. We were high school sweethearts. I know everything there is to know about that man, and today he blew me away. He was a completely different person."

"Sounds sorta dangerous," Kendra says.

Trina spies the shampoo on the shelf above the towels, but stops mid-reach and turns around. "What do you mean?"

"Like you said, you've known the guy most of your life. It's a little late in the game for him to turn over a new leaf, don't you think?"

Trina shrugs. "You know what they say, 'People change.'"

"They also say, 'If it seems too good to be true, it probably is.'"

"What's your problem?" Trina asks, piqued by Kendra's persistent negativity.

"I just think you're being a little naïve, that's all. Guys like Darius love the chase, not the woman."

"You barely know him." Trina fumes.

"So? I've met his type a hundred times."

"Maybe that's what this is really about," Trina says, challenging Kendra with a hard gaze. "You've dated half the men in Memphis and you still haven't found Mr. Right."

"Mr. Right is a myth," Kendra says. "But two-timing boyfriends are very real. Trust me. I've played the jilted girlfriend *and* been the other woman. I can smell a rat when he's near and Darius is as foul as they come."

Trina's cell phone chimes loudly from the bedroom. She goes to answer it, but not before casting Kendra a frosty glare. *How dare she*, Trina thinks, tossing clothes onto the floor as she forages through her pile of belongings. Kendra, the self-proclaimed queen of male conquests, is accusing Darius of harboring ulterior motives? It's laughable, but at the same time, infuriating.

She locates her phone under her lace slip and flips it open with a flick of her wrist. "Hello?"

"Are you busy making yourself beautiful?" Darius asks.

Trina feels every remnant of irritation drain from her body. "Just getting started."

"I got you something that might help—not that you need it," he adds smoothly.

"What're you talking about?" Trina asks, her smile audible.

"Check your trunk," he says. "I'll see you at eight."

Trina swaps her phone for her keys and rushes out to her car. Her breaths come in excited puffs as she slides the key into the lock, her fingers trembling with anticipation, and pops the trunk to discover a beautifully wrapped rectangular box. She tears through the paper like an expectant child on Christmas morning and lifts the lid.

Lying in a bed of delicate tissue paper is the moss-green dress she'd wanted so desperately from Sophia's. Her body swells with indescribable joy as she gingerly fingers its silky fabric. Her mind races to figure out how Darius could have possibly pulled something like this off. She thinks back to his sweet offer to run her shopping bags to her car. He must have bought it while she was getting her pedicure.

She squeals with glee and bounds back up to Kendra's apartment, her gift in tow.

Kendra takes one look at the dress and rolls her eyes. "He's good," she says. "I'll give him that."

"Could you just be happy for me? Please?" Trina asks, twirling playfully around the bedroom. "This has been one of the best days of my life, and you're standing over there like the Grim Reaper."

Kendra shakes her head. "Leopards can't change their spots," she warns with a shrug. "That's all I've got to say."

"Good." Trina skips to the bathroom. "Because I have to get ready." And on that note, she closes the door and hops into the shower.

30

"Mademoiselle," greets the maitre d' as he offers Trina his arm and gallantly escorts her across the dimly lit restaurant. She can feel the admiring stares of several male patrons against her exposed back as she saunters confidently between the marble columns, down the steps, past the mirrored walls and candelabras to the elegantly set table where her date is waiting.

Darius stands when he sees her approaching, his eyes sparkling amorously. "You look stunning."

Trina bows her head bashfully and smiles. "Stop," she says, feigning modesty, even though she knows he's right.

She'd blown her hair out and pressed it straight with a flat iron to achieve a shiny, sleek look, and then, to seal the deal, she'd given herself a sultry side part. She also spent twice as much time as usual applying her makeup, painting on smoky evening eyes and irresistibly glossy lips.

All of that painstaking work combined with her new dress, sexy slingbacks, and a beaded clutch make for a mesmerizing result.

Darius pulls out her chair.

"You look good too," she says, eyeing his sharp black suit as she sits. "Very GQ, but then again, you've always cleaned up nicely."

"It's been a while since we've done this, huh?" he asks, resting his napkin across his lap.

Trina does the same and picks up her menu. "Yeah," she agrees with a nod. "I wish we could have more days like today."

"We will," he promises.

Darius orders a bottle of Chateau Lafitte, and they toast to themselves and to a new start. The conversation is upbeat and flows easily. They reminisce and flirt, holding hands across the table and gazing into each other's eyes.

The meal is delicious. They both have the lobster bisque with vichyssoise martini and shaved truffles. And for the main course, Trina orders the spicy Ahi tuna with orzo pilaf and braised endive, while Darius savors every bite of his roasted lamb and sautéed foie gras, drizzled with sweet vermouth sauce. They clean their plates, one delicious forkful at a time.

Even though they're both stuffed by the time the waiter clears the table, they waste no time ordering dessert. Darius decides to try his hand at the soufflé, and after several indecisive minutes, Trina settles on the poached pears with caramel and mascarpone cream.

As soon as the waiter collects their dessert menus and disappears among the other tables buzzing with guests, Darius reaches for Trina's hand. "Come back home," he says. "I miss you."

Trina shakes her head, her expression apologetic. "I don't think that's such a great idea."

"Of course it is. Look at us; we're good together."

"When we work at it," she says.

"And we will—every day. I promise, just come back."

Trina considers Kendra's words of warning earlier. *Has this whole dinner— this whole day—been about "the chase" for Darius?* she wonders. *Or is he genuinely ready to devote himself to their relationship?* After 12 years of mostly bad history, she has a hard time getting herself to believe that this could be the start of something new for them as a couple.

"I see those wheels turning," he says, leaning forward. "What're you thinking?"

Trina smiles and takes a minute to weigh her words. "You're a wonderful man," she says. "And today, especially, has been unforgettable."

"But?" he prods, his jaw flinching in anticipation of the bad news.

"I think we should take it slow this time."

"You don't believe that I love you?"

"It's not that," she says, her head tilted kindly, her eyes wide and pleading.

"You don't love me?"

"Of course I do. More than anything." She tightens her grip on his hand. "It's just...," she sighs. "We have a history of jumping into these situations with our eyes wide shut and then we wonder what went wrong two months later when we're at each other's throat. I don't want to move back in tonight only to get thrown back out next week."

"That's not going to happen," he says solemnly, his words teeming with conviction.

"You don't know that."

"Yes, I do," he says, reaching into his jacket pocket.

Trina's breath catches as he pulls out a small, black velvet box. "What is that?" she whispers, tears already filling her eyes.

Darius slides the box across the table. "You tell me."

This is the moment she's hoped for and dreamed about ever since her senior year in high school when Darius announced that he'd changed his college plans and had given up a substantial scholarship to follow her and Grace to Michigan State University. That's when she'd realized that their relationship was more than just puppy love. It was the real thing—*they* were the real thing—and nothing could ever come between them.

A long and happy life together was the inevitable end to their story. For years, Trina would lose herself in elaborate daydreams of her perfect wedding, replete with chiffon and white doves, ice sculptures, and celebrity guests. She thought of every detail, the embroidery of her gown, the cut of her engagement ring. She even went to the library between classes and researched exotic honeymoon spots, where she and Darius could romp on white sand beaches during the day and, at night, make love beneath the moonlight.

But he had never popped the question. Instead, in their junior year in college, he took her to a bar the Friday before midterms and confessed that he'd been seeing someone he'd met the previous summer. He was confused, he'd said. Trina was his heart, but his freedom was really important to him. They were in college, after all. It might be good to date around—to see what else was out there and experience life without each other for a while.

She, of course, cried and pleaded with him not to throw away the past four years—everything they'd poured into each other and their relationship. But he only insisted that he had to let go for both of them and that, in time, she would see he was right.

"God Only Knows," by the Beach Boys, was playing on the dilapidated jukebox behind them. The melodic, sincere voices only seemed to drive home Darius's monologue, serenading his farewell when he finally got up and left her crying quietly, alone in the booth.

To this day, Trina hates that song.

Grace had let her mope for the better part of a month and then started sending her on blind dates. They were torturous in the beginning—uncomfortable and forced. But eventually her heart began to mend itself. It went from shattered to cracked to merely chipped, and the pain waned, as did her desire to be with Darius. She stopped calling him, stopped passing by his classes, stopped popping up at his dorm room, and started making new friends and finding new hangouts.

Just as things began getting serious with a guy from her Cognitive Psych class, Darius reappeared. He'd made a mistake, he said, his eyes misty. He didn't know what he was thinking. He couldn't live without her—didn't want to. What would it take, he'd asked, for him to make it up to her, to prove that she was the only woman for him.

She didn't know, she'd told him. So he promised to pursue her until she figured it out. And he did.

In no time at all, they were back together. Little did Trina know, that was to be the first of many trips around the breakup carousel. She stuck with him through the rest of college and into the real world, but her happy fantasies of a wedding and a house and kids faded over time.

Marriage dooms perfectly healthy relationships to fail, Darius argued on more than one occasion. They'd been together longer than most married couples he knew. They didn't need a little piece of paper to legitimize their union. He loved her and she loved him and that's what really made a couple husband and wife.

So Grace ended up getting the dream husband, dream wedding, dream honeymoon, and dream house, while Trina had to resign herself to the sad reality that Darius would never commit to her the way she wanted him to—that he just wasn't capable of it. Or so she'd thought...

"I can't believe this," she says, staring down at the box, dizzy, too shocked to move.

Darius smiles. "Aren't you going to look inside?"

She nods and lifts it off the table, her heart racing at the sudden realization that the next moment might be the beginning of the rest of her life. The feeling is euphoric. "Here goes nothing," she says, gasping as she cracks open the case.

She peers down at the contents, frozen by surprise and speechless with disappointment.

"Do you know what that is?" he asks.

She swallows hard against the lump in her throat. "It's a locket," she whispers, forcing a smile.

"Not just any locket," Darius says. "It's the locket I gave you at graduation, remember? It's the one my grandmother gave to my mother and my mother gave to you."

Trina nods. "Because I'm like the daughter she never had," she says, repeating Darius's mother's words.

"Right, and you lost it in the snow that New Year's Eve outside of her house. Remember? The chain broke."

"I remember," she says softly.

"You were so upset, and we searched the front yard with flashlights for hours, but we never found it."

"You bought me a replacement locket," she says.

"But you refused to wear it—said it wasn't the same, didn't hold nearly as much sentimental value. Well," he flashes a proud, toothy grin and points at the open jewelry case in her unsteady hand, "*that's* the original locket. My mom came across it a couple of years ago in one of her flower beds, but we'd broken up by then, so I've been hanging on to it all this time."

"Wow," she says, straining to make herself sound appreciative and upbeat. "I don't know what to say. That's amazing. Thank you."

"Tonight seemed like the perfect time to give it to you, as a token of my love—a reminder," he says, caressing her fingers, "that I'm just as committed to you now as I was back then."

Trina's moist eyes sting. The truth of his statement is unbearably painful.

"Are those tears of joy?" he asks.

"Yes," she lies, choking back a sob. She covers her mouth with her hand as the tears stream down her cheeks.

"I knew you'd love it," he says, removing the gold locket and delicate chain from the velvet box. He stands, walks around to Trina's side of the table, brushes her hair over her shoulder, and clasps it around her neck. "Beautiful," he says and kisses her cheek before returning to his seat.

Shortly after, the waiter arrives with their desserts. Trina's appetite has long since vanished, but she nibbles politely on her poached pears and smiles distractedly as Darius speaks animatedly about his job, catching her up on all that's happened since she moved out.

Dessert is followed by coffee and more one-sided conversation. Trina is too numb to be engaging, but Darius doesn't seem to notice or care that she's tuned out of the evening all together.

He pays the check, and they leave arm in arm.

"Thank you for dinner and the dress." She hugs herself to ward off the chilly air and smiles. "And the locket. Feels like Christmas in November."

He takes off his jacket and drapes it over her shoulders. "Come home," he says. "We shouldn't be saying good-bye standing in front of each other in a parking lot. We should be saying good night lying next to each other in bed."

"It's not like either one of us is going anywhere," she says with a shrug. "We don't have to figure it all out tonight."

"I love you." He cups her face in his hands. "And I don't want to spend another second apart from you."

Trina searches his eyes. They're intense and hopeful. How can she say no to him after all he's done for her today? She'd gushed and giggled all while he was spending his money on her. A new dress, new shoes, an expensive dinner, she'd accepted them all without question.

Before the locket, before she duped herself into thinking he was going to propose, she'd bragged to Kendra that he was a changed man. Has he really given her cause to go back on that statement?

He's still sweet, still earnest. She just got her hopes up.

This whole day has been one giant gesture—a good-faith offering of his devotion. He loves her very much in his own way. *Shouldn't that be enough?* she wonders. Besides, where else is she going to go? To Kendra's to hear "I told you so"? Back to her hard, cold office floor?

The closest she's going to come to Happily Ever After is standing right in front of her. It's not the fairy-tale ending she wanted, but it's better than what she's got right now, which is nothing and no one.

"Okay," she says. "I'll come back."

"Really?" his eyes spring wide in surprise.

She nods. "I'm all yours."

Darius kisses her excitedly. It's wet and hard and sloppy. "Thank you," he says, pulling her into a tight bear hug. "You won't regret it."

"I know," she whispers, even though deep down she already does.

31

Grace holds her finger up. "Just one more second," she promises, scurrying from the kitchen, through the living room, and into her bedroom.

Tamara sips her coffee. "Take your time," she calls.

Grace strips off her skirt, snarling down at the jelly stain, courtesy of her breakfast, before tossing it into the laundry basket and hurriedly rummaging through the closet for something else to wear.

It's barely noon, and the day has been one disaster after the next. While she was wrapped around the toilet with her usual bout of morning sickness, Mike knocked and informed her through the door that the Realtor had just phoned about a hot property listing downtown. It was large, as downtown studios go—perfect for an upscale art gallery—in a well-established area with plenty of pedestrian traffic. In short, the space was a rare opportunity at some prime Memphis real estate, and it wasn't going to be on the market for long. "I'm gonna head over now and take a look," he'd said, his excitement audible. "I'll call you as soon as I know something."

Grace croaked her consent right before expelling last night's dinner into the waiting porcelain bowl. It wasn't until she'd rinsed out her mouth and climbed back into bed that she remembered that Tamara was starting as her personal assistant today. Mike was supposed to hang around the house this morning, get Tamara settled, and explain the list of tasks Grace had comprised while Grace took her father to his doctor's appointment.

Grace tried calling Mike, but his cell phone was off. She left a message, hoping that he'd call right back as he often does. But he didn't, and a half an hour later she was on the phone with the receptionist at her father's doctor's office, trying to reschedule his appointment for later in the day. His doctor was booked solid through the week, she was told. But in light of her father's serious condition, they would squeeze him in between patients at two o'clock.

Grace thanked the receptionist profusely, her panic subsiding. But the relief was brief. Her dad phoned minutes later and explained that he didn't have the strength to teach his afternoon class and that he'd searched all morning but couldn't find a substitute on such short notice. Grace agreed to fill in for him and promptly called the doctor's office back to undo the new appointment and redo the old appointment.

The receptionist was not nearly as patient as she had been ten minutes earlier. If Grace called to change the appointment again, they'd charge her father a 50-dollar cancellation fee, she'd warned testily.

No sooner did Grace hang up with the miffed receptionist, than Jean Murphy from New Deliverance Temple called. She was the church's director of women's ministries and she just wanted to thank Grace in advance for agreeing to be the closing speaker at their seminar this evening. Everyone at the sold-out event, Jean included, was a huge fan, and they were all looking forward to her anointed message. "Is there anything you'd like us to do before you get here? Any special needs," Jean had asked.

Yeah, more time! And lots of it! Grace had wanted to shout. She'd completely forgotten that she was booked for a speaking engagement tonight. She doesn't know where New Deliverance Temple is located, she hasn't prepared a speech, and she doesn't even know what topics she's supposed to cover.

A distant voice in the back of her mind beseeched her to be still and pray, but she couldn't. Her spirit was too restless. There were too many calls to make, too many things to do, too many problems to solve, and not nearly enough time in which to do it all.

She mentally rearranged her schedule as she brushed her teeth, simultaneously making the bed and switching over the towels from the washing machine to the dryer. If she further postponed some badly needed housework, delegated a couple more tasks to Tamara, and ran a few nearby errands while her dad was at his appointment, she could get back in time to, at least, start working on her speech.

Then she'd head over to the university, quickly run through her father's material, collect his students' assignments, assign more work, dismiss them early, and rush back home to put the finishing touches on her homily before changing clothes and heading out to New Deliverance.

It could work, she tried to reassure herself, even though she hadn't factored in traffic or time to eat or breath. *Or time to spill jelly on my freshly dry-cleaned skirt*, she thinks, snatching her new wool gauchos from one of the dangling hangers.

She pairs them with a black turtleneck, a fitted jean jacket, and knee-high leather boots. Then, she grants herself one quick look in the mirror before rushing back to Tamara, who's been waiting patiently for over a half an hour for Grace to get her act together.

"I'm so sorry," Grace says for what feels like the hundredth time that morning. "I ask you to get here early and all I've done so far is run around like a dazed maniac. You must think I'm a complete nut job."

"I think you're overwhelmed," Tamara says. She smiles kindly. "And a little frazzled."

Grace snorts and shakes her head. "That's one way to put it."

"Well," Tamara stands, "I'm here and I'm ready to work. What do you need me to do?"

Grace produces the page-long list of tasks and instructions she'd put together. There are flights to book, appointments to confirm, a stack of invitations and requests for public appearances to accept and an even larger stack to regretfully decline, emails to answer, checks to deposit, contracts to fax, and itineraries to finalize. It's everything Grace either hasn't had the time or the energy to get done in the past several weeks.

"No problem," Tamara says, an all-work, no-play look of determination on her face. "What else?"

Grace sighs. "That's it for now. I might have you research maid services in a couple of days if things don't die down."

"What needs cleaning?" she asks.

"Are you kidding me?" Grace flails her arms around the dusty living room. "This whole place could use a good scrubbing. Speaking of which," she checks her watch and nods to her left, "there are dishes calling my name. Would you mind migrating to the kitchen?"

"I'll take care of the dishes," Tamara says, following behind Grace. "Really, it's not a problem."

"Are you sure?" Grace asks, clearly reluctant. "Housework wasn't in the original job description."

"That doesn't matter," Tamara insists. She heads to the sink overflowing with dirty dishes, removes her blazer, and rolls up the sleeves to her blouse. "You hired me to assist you with your day-to-day needs. And today, the dishes are a need," she says, unlatching the dishwasher.

Grace smiles. "I don't know what to say, other than, you're a lifesaver!" She watches Tamara get to work scrubbing, rinsing, and neatly loading the dishes.

Grace likes this Tamara: hardworking, professional, efficient, friendly. Those are hardly words she would've used to describe her at their first encounter. Even after their heart-to-heart during Tamara's interview, Grace had been a little skeptical about hiring her. She'd given Tamara the benefit of the doubt, in large part, because she'd felt so guilty about making her cry.

But so far, Grace's judgment has proven to be on par. Tamara hasn't uttered one snide comment or offered any derisive looks. She hasn't even mentioned Mike or asked about his whereabouts. She's been calm and accommodating, her attention focused solely on the job.

With a few unexpected spare minutes on her hands, Grace tosses her half-eaten, now stale, piece of toast in the trash and pours herself a glass of juice.

She plops down on one of the stools lined against the island and flips open the front page of the newspaper when Tamara gasps. Grace turns, just in time to see a bowl crash to the floor. Tamara grips her right hand and hunches over the sink.

"What happened?" Grace asks, standing.

Tamara sucks air through her clinched teeth as she runs her bleeding palm under the faucet. "I cut myself," she says.

"Is it bad?" Grace asks, tiptoeing her way around the shattered chunks of bowl to the sink.

Tamara raises her hand, revealing a sizeable slash.

"Oooo." Grace's forehead wrinkles and her brows furrow. "Here," she hands Tamara a clean dishtowel. "Wrap this around it. We've got peroxide and Band-Aids around here somewhere," she says, searching the cabinet next to the pantry where they keep the Tylenol, Milk of Magnesia, and other assorted medicines.

The phone rings. Grace grabs the cordless off the counter and goes back to her search. "Hello?" she answers distractedly. It's Mike.

"Did you get my message?" she asks. "You were supposed to stay here with Tammy, remember? My dad's doctor appointment."

He apologizes, but Grace can tell by his glum demeanor and sober tone that the meeting with the Realtor didn't go the way he'd hoped. "What's wrong?" she asks.

The space needs a lot of work. It's too small, doesn't have enough natural light, and it's way overpriced, he explains. He's disappointed because he had a good feeling about this property. He really thought it would be the one.

"Uh huh," Grace says, only half hearing what he's saying. She shrugs and shakes her head at Tamara who's still bleeding in front of the sink. *I can't find them*, she mouths.

"What about your bathroom?" Tamara whispers.

Grace nods and starts out of the kitchen.

"I can get it," Tamara says. "Finish your phone call."

Grace casts her an apologetic, yet appreciative, glance. "Master bath— cabinet under the sink," she calls after her.

"Are you listening?" Mike asks.

"Yeah, Babe," Grace says into the receiver. "I heard everything you said. I guess we'll just have to keep looking."

"Yeah," he says with a disappointed sigh.

"Don't factor without God," Grace reminds him like he often does her. "He's already got the perfect space picked out for the gallery. Obviously that one wasn't it. When it's time, He'll lead us where we're supposed to go."

"You're right," Mike says. The conversation lulls for a few seconds. "So…am I in the doghouse for leaving you hanging this morning?"

Grace laughs. "You should be, but no."

She gives Mike the abridged version of the hectic day ahead of her from her slew of errands to substituting for her father to writing and giving a message at a seminar she forgot about in a church she's never heard of.

"I can take your dad to his appointment," Mike offers.

"Really?" Grace asks. The idea is basic and yet brilliant, given her jam-packed schedule. She doesn't know why she didn't think of it.

"Sure," he says. "And I'll run the errands, just leave me a list."

"Thank you, Baby," she says, her voice sugary. "Between your help and Tammy's help, I might actually live through today."

"How's she working out so far?"

"Much better than expected," Grace admits. "I should go check on her though. She cut her hand just a few minutes ago when you called."

"Okay," Mike says. "Call me if you need anything."

They hang up, and Grace makes her way down the hall to her bedroom. "Did you find it?" she asks, rounding the doorway into the bathroom. She stops abruptly, her stomach instantly knotting at the scene before her.

"I wasn't snooping," Tamara says hastily, her eyes wide with a potent dose of shock and panic. "I thought maybe the peroxide was in here," she says. "That's the only reason why I opened it."

Grace blinks down at the bathroom counter. It's littered with her positive pregnancy sticks, her pink "Baby on Board" folder, as well as the extra pamphlets Dr. Noguez had given her—all the secret contents of her brown paper bag.

"It's fine," Grace says, rushing to conceal the booklet on abortion. She opens the medicine cabinet, producing a bottle of peroxide, and rummages through one of the bathroom drawers until she finds the Band-Aids. "Here." She hands them both to Tamara without looking at her. "This is what you want."

"Thanks," Tamara says. Silently, she cleans her cut, while Grace collects her pregnancy paraphernalia from the counter and places it back in the paper bag.

The tension is thick and suffocating. Tamara is the first to speak as she unwraps her Band-Aid. "So you're gonna be a mom," she chirps, her blitheness forced and tentative.

"Looks that way," Grace nods.

"Mike must be excited."

Grace perches on the side of the tub and sighs. "Mike doesn't know," she says. "And I don't want him to—not yet," she quickly adds. "I'm still figuring it all out."

Tamara nods slowly, her eyes pinched with sympathy. "I understand."

"I'm gonna tell him," Grace says, unsure of who she's trying to convince more.

"Of course you are," Tamara says, her head still nodding, her eyes still pinched.

"I just need a little more time."

"It's a big decision," Tamara says. "You should take as much time as you need to figure out what's best for you."

"Right now, what's best for me is for this to stay between us," Grace says with pleading eyes. "It's really important that no one else finds out."

"I won't tell a soul," Tamara says, pressing one hand to her chest and raising her injured hand, bandaged palm facing out, pledge-of-allegiance style. "As far as I'm concerned, this conversation never took place."

Tamara's words siphon Grace's worry, slowly relieving the stiffness in her neck and shoulders. "Thank you."

"I should get back to work," Tamara says, returning the peroxide and Band-Aids to their proper places.

Without another word, she heads out of the bathroom, but just as she reaches the door, abruptly turns around. "Just for the record, if you ever want to talk or you just need a sounding board, I'm here. I know 'friend' wasn't in the original job description either, but you seem like you could use one, and the truth is, so could I."

Grace smiles, but only responds with a nod.

She waits until she hears Tamara in the kitchen before stuffing the brown paper bag back under the sink. Then she gathers her wits, as well as her purse and keys, and sets out to conquer her hectic day head-on.

32

The next several weeks eek by miserably for Grace. With all that's on her plate, she thought the days would fly by. Instead, she's found herself tangled in the tedium of her work and everyone else's needs.

Each morning starts out the same: beastly bout of morning sickness, followed by breakfast, more morning sickness, and a cup of black decaf coffee. Then begins the paperwork—letters and memos composed by Tamara, the previous day—that need Grace's approval and signature before they can be mailed out.

Paperwork is usually followed by a visit to her dad's, which lately has evolved to include housecleaning and errand-running.

She gets back home from picking up her dad's prescriptions or folding his laundry just in time to take her afternoon nap. She didn't used to nap, but as her pregnancy progresses, she's noticed that her energy level has taken a nosedive. Try as she might, she can't fight the urge to rest mid-afternoon. No matter where she is or what she's doing, at around one o'clock her mind shuts down and her body soon follows. Feeling drugged, she'll make her way to the nearest couch or bed and doze for an hour or so.

Then it's off to teach her father's evening Imaginative Writing class—the last of her dad's three classes for which the university has yet to find a replacement professor. She unenthusiastically covers the material on his syllabus, often yawning through poorly written, uninspired stories penned by slacker students who are only taking the course to fulfill a credit requirement.

By seven o'clock, she's ready to call it a night and crawl into bed, but in a bid to be a dutiful wife, she forces herself to stay up and listen to Mike vent his frustrations about his fledgling dream.

Real estate is proving hard to come by; it's either non-existent or overpriced. And as he visits possible location after possible location, he's starting to think that downtown Memphis may not be the right place, after all, to start his business.

It doesn't possess the right atmosphere—doesn't attract the right clientele, people who he thinks will be able to appreciate an exclusive art gallery, much less buy its progressive art. He knows his desire is of the Lord and he can sense the Spirit's leading, but he's still not sure what to do. "Pray with me," is his perpetual, unchanging request.

They hold hands while Mike dedicates the dilemma to the Lord, and Grace counts the seconds until she can go to bed, which she does immediately afterward. Only to wake up, mere hours later, and do it all over again.

And that's on a good day, when she doesn't have to attend a book signing; or give an interview over lunch that she really doesn't have time to enjoy; or fly out of town after proctoring her father's evening class to speak at a seminar, just to catch a red-eye flight back so as not to miss one of the many appointments she has scheduled for the next day.

The only steady constant in Grace's whirlwind of affairs has been Tamara. To Grace, she's been worth her weight in gold. Tamara is truly a jack-of-all-trades, switching hats daily with pleasure and ease. No task is too large or too menial.

When flights need to be booked and hotel arrangements need to be made, Tamara slips into secretary mode. When the OJ is on "E," the coffee filters have all been used, and the pantry pickings are sparse, she morphs into a grocery shopper. When Grace is knee-high in rewrites, Tamara rolls up her sleeves, grabs a red felt pen, and becomes a keen-eyed editor. When the dirty clothes in the laundry room have piled up, and the floors need vacuuming, she turns into a housekeeper. There's very little that Grace needs to point out or explain.

It's not surprising. From the moment Tamara started as her personal assistant, they fell into automatic sync. Grace sometimes catches herself wondering if their easy rapport has anything to do with the secret they both share.

True to her word, Tamara has not mentioned Grace's delicate state or even hinted at it, but she does little things—kind things—that are meant to show her silent support. Like in the morning, when Grace is distractedly forcing down a slice of dry toast, Tamara will quietly slip her a vitamin with her juice.

And without being asked, she keeps the refrigerator door stocked with chocolate milk (Grace's first official pregnancy craving). She also takes extra pains not to schedule anything during Grace's "naptime." And hell has a greater chance of freezing over before Tamara will let Grace lift anything even remotely heavy.

Sometimes, Tamara's covert camaraderie is comforting, but most days it leaves Grace feeling unsettled. As well-intentioned as her actions might be, they're nothing more than a constant reminder that someone else knows what Grace has worked so desperately to keep hidden—especially from Mike.

Strangely, lying has become easier with the passage of time. Grace had assumed that her deceit would eat at her painfully from the inside out, like a raging parasite. But the guilt she once swallowed when she looked into Mike's eyes, or while cuddled up against his chest at night, has all but vanished.

She no longer feels like a liar every time he whispers, "I love you," and she whispers it back. She no longer cries over thoughts of what the future might hold or frets over the life-changing decision looming constantly over her head.

Somewhere between picking up the slack for her ailing father and juggling the many responsibilities of her demanding career with Mike's time-consuming ambitions, her pregnancy stopped being a monstrous lie and became a simple fact—an innocuous omission; just one more dilemma she hasn't yet found the time to solve.

Grace sighs and transfers the soup bubbling on the stove, from the pot to a bowl, and takes it, along with an array of colorful pills, to her dad who's dozing off in his recliner.

"I made you a little lunch," she says, stirring him from his nap. His eyes, which have turned yellow—seemingly overnight—from jaundice, pop open.

"Not hungry," he grumbles miserably.

"Come on, Dad. Won't you just try?" She offers her most pathetic pout. "For me?"

He bunches his chin, deciding whether or not he'll appease her today. To Grace's relief, he pulls the lever on the side of his chair and sits up. She rests the tray on his lap and replaces the empty bottle of water on the table beside him with a fresh one, still cold from the fridge.

He takes a few tentative slurps and sets his spoon down.

"You can do better than that," Grace says, easing into the couch adjacent to him. "You want some saltine crackers? That might make it go down easier."

Her dad only shakes his head and grudgingly picks his spoon back up like a little child being forced to eat his veggies.

Grace's heart goes out to him. His jaundice has been accompanied by excruciating abdominal pain that has whittled his once hearty appetite down to a feeble desire for food. He's lost a staggering amount of weight over the weeks, and every time Grace catches a glimpse of his sharp features and sagging skin, she finds herself doing a double-take. Most of his meals he ends up vomiting back up into a bucket beside his chair, but Grace continues to push him to eat for his strength.

They sit in comfortable silence for a while. The only noises floating between them are the faint cheers of a riled up audience on the game show on TV and the soft clinking of her father's spoon against his bowl.

"You wanna talk about it?" her dad asks out of the blue.

Grace opens her eyes and lifts her head. "Talk about what?"

"Whatever's bugging you," he says, taking a loud slurp from his spoon.

"Nothing's bugging me." The lie falls from her lips smoothly—convincingly. "I'm just tired."

"Well, you look beautiful," he says.

Grace laughs. "Flattery will not get you out of finishing your soup."

He chuckles. "I'm telling the truth. Lately you've had a glow about you." He studies her, his gaze probing. "And you've gained a little weight, haven't you?"

"Gee, thanks, Dad," Grace smirks. "Kick me while I'm down, why don't you?"

"There's nothing wrong with a little padding," he says. "Real women have meat on their bones. And real men like it that way—just ask your husband, he'll tell you."

"Mike's got more important things on his mind these days," Grace says.

"Still can't find the right spot for his gallery?"

"Not yet." Grace shakes her head. "But he hasn't given up hope. He's determined."

Grace's dad swallows another spoonful of soup. "He's a good guy."

"Yeah," Grace smiles. "That's why I fell in love with him."

"There's not much more a dying man can ask for," he says, his eyes sad. "To know his one and only daughter is married to someone who'll take care of her the way she deserves to be taken care of…means I can go in peace."

Grace tilts her head, her face long, her expression forlorn. "Please don't talk like that." The request comes out as a small whisper. "I'm not ready to hear you talk like that."

He lowers his eyes and clears his throat. "Look," he says, tilting his empty bowl toward her. "All done."

"Now *that's* what I'm talking about," Grace says, standing, a happy grin spread from ear to ear. She removes the tray from his lap. "Is there anything else I can get you?" she asks. "Tea? Hot chocolate?"

"No," he shakes his head. "The soup was plenty."

Grace turns for the kitchen.

"Actually," her dad reaches out his hand, "there is something you can do for me. It's something I've been wanting for a while now, but I see how busy you are and I know that the time you spend with me is a real sacrifice."

"Dad," Grace says, setting the tray down on the coffee table, "the time I spend with everyone else is a sacrifice. The time I spend with you is an honor and a pleasure."

He smiles, his glistening eyes dancing from her words of love.

"Now what is it? What have you been wanting?"

"A big Thanksgiving dinner," he confesses with a sure nod. "I want turkey and ham and mashed potatoes and stuffing and greens and pumpkin pie—the works. Even if I can't eat it, I just want to smell it. And I want everyone to be there," he says, his stare convicting. "Everyone. No more fighting, no more 'he said, she said,' just family and good friends gathered to give thanks for each other and for all of the Lord's blessings."

Grace doesn't know how to respond. Her father's request is a tall order. "Everyone" means Trina, which means Darius; and Ron, which means Tamara. God only knows how the four of them will get through a meal civilly. Then there's her cantankerous grandparents Doria and Mearl, not to mention her outspoken, ghetto-fabulous cousin, Malikah and her two "BeBe's."

And that's just Grace's side of the family. She can't, even for an instant, imagine Lani, her sweet, white, soft-spoken mother-in-law mingling with her loud, rambunctious, sometimes thoughtless, relatives.

"Please," her dad says, his eyes round and hopeful.

"Maybe we could all get together another time," she suggests. "When you're feeling more like yourself and your medication doesn't have you so weak and tired."

"Gracie, Honey, this is it for me. I don't think I'm going to get another chance," he says.

"Dad, please—"

He holds up his hand and silences her. "I know you don't want to talk about what's really happening because it hurts and you're scared. I get that. So am I. But whether or not you're willing to face it, the fact of the matter is, my time left here on earth is limited. And I don't want to waste it away lying in this old chair. I want to spend it with the people I love—even if, right now, they can't see how much they love each other.

"Now," he pulls the lever on the side of his worn lounger, reclining himself, and rests his clasped hands on his stomach. "You asked me if there was anything you could get me, and I'm telling you there is. I want a big Thanksgiving dinner and I want to share it with everyone I love." He sighs as his eyelids droop, the fatigue from his illness already beginning to overtake him. "Grant an old man his dying request," he pleads.

Grace retrieves her dad's afghan and drapes it lovingly over his frail body.

"Will you?" he asks, taking hold of her wrist.

She bends down and plants a light kiss on his forehead. "For you, I'll do anything," she says.

And with those words of assurance, her dad gives a slight nod and drifts off to sleep.

33

"You're all set," the delivery guy says, holding out his clipboard. "Just sign here."

Trina scribbles her signature, ignoring his flirtatious glances, tips him, and walks him out. Then, she flops down in her new leather chair behind her new oak desk and spins like a giddy kid, her arms spread wide.

She'd hired Memphis Business Interiors, one of the city's premiere interior decorating firms to design and install custom furniture for her new, spacious corner office.

Trina sighs contentedly as she surveys the grand space. It's easily triple the size of her old office, with floor-to-ceiling windows and a breathtaking panorama of Germantown.

Things seemed shaky for a while there, but Kendra turned out to be right; they had nothing to worry about. Becky's been back with her dad for two weeks without incident and Quinn followed through on her part of the deal: Trina and Kendra got their promotions.

With perks! Trina thinks, kicking off her shoes and squishing her stocking-covered toes between the plush fibers of her carpet. *Lots and lots of perks.* Including, so far, a generous bonus in addition to a generous raise; a top-floor, corner office; a personal secretary; and—as of five minutes ago, Trina pats her desk—new furniture.

It's the first time in her professional career that she feels like somebody— more than a gofer, more than just a number on an employee badge.

She'd always told herself that the good she accomplished through her job was payment enough. She didn't need a thank-you, didn't need to see any extra zeros added on to her paycheck. Every day, she was making a differ- ence—changing the world for the better, one child at a time. Very few people can say that about their careers, she'd remind herself. And the fact that she could, made her blessed beyond reason.

Some days, those sorts of pep talks were all that kept her from giving up—from handing in her resignation, packing up her desk, and going back to temping, where she'd make just as much money and endure half the stress.

Of course, that martyr mind-set changed once she realized just how sweetly a job well done could be rewarded. Aside from the obvious pecuniary advantages, her workload's lighter and her days feel like they've been cut in half.

That's because instead of managing a hundred and some odd case files, she now oversees 50 case managers. They're mostly new employees: young, fresh out of college and eager to please. They were the best and the brightest, coming to her straight from Quinn's comprehensive two-week training session—a newly implemented, mandatory, boot-camp-style prep course that Trina, thankfully, never had to attend.

While she doesn't envy her overworked subordinates, Trina respects them. They've been thoroughly versed in Home Sweet Home's policies, guidelines, and statutes. They can navigate the system as though it's second nature, fill out each and every one of the company's numerous forms in their sleep, and recite the page-long mission statement from memory at the drop of a dime.

Their focused efficiency coupled with their robot-like stamina and their tunnel-vision determination to meet any objective placed in front of them means they ask very few questions and make even fewer mistakes. And that means that Trina's free to have a little well-deserved fun and to enjoy the spoils of her labor.

The very first thing she and Kendra did, after their bonus checks cleared, was take the day off to shop for their new cars. Like unsupervised kids let loose in a toy store, they oooohed and ahhhhed and pointed and squealed through one dealership after another, test driving a variety of vehicles, some even out of their price range, in search of the perfect ride.

Kendra finally settled on a small Mercedes. The sporty two-seater, a bare base-model, devoid of any fancy gadgets or showy wood grain, was a stretch for her maxed-out budget, even with financing. Trina tried to talk her into going with something more sensible—something without a luxury emblem that she could load with all the bells and whistles her heart desired. But Kendra wouldn't hear of it. She'd wasted enough of her life being practical, she'd argued. She wanted her car to represent her new status and she was willing to go into major debt to make it happen.

Less caught up in appearances, Trina went with a pearl-white Audi. It doesn't turn heads the way Kendra's car does, but it's got everything from Corinthian leather seats to a navigational system to an automatic moon roof, and the best part is, she won't have to sell an organ or peddle off her firstborn to pay the monthly note.

Her favorite parts of the day involve climbing into her baby and inhaling a deep whiff of its new-car smell. The sensation is a gratifying mix of exhilaration and glee. In fact, the only feeling that can compare is the fluttering of delight in her stomach each time she thinks about her new and improved relationship with Darius.

When Trina first agreed to move back in, a large part of her thought the decision was a big mistake. Over the years, Darius has established a tried and true pattern of pushing her away only to beg for her back as soon as she starts to take flight without him. Darius is incapable of being happy in tranquil settings. Trina learned that early on. He thrives on chaos, on being the knight in shining armor, even when he's rescuing her from perils that *he* created.

After Kendra's aggravating, yet perceptive, warnings and the "proposal that wasn't" at Chez Philippe, Trina began to doubt that Darius had really changed. Maybe his lavish displays of affection—the gifts, the dinner, the unabated attention—were just fresh spins on an old game. And if so, she reasoned, it would only be a matter of days before his charming chivalry would be replaced by chilling cavalierness.

Trina braced herself for the worst, walking on eggshells, eating sparingly from the contents in his refrigerator and refusing to fully unpack or unload all of the belongings stowed in her trunk. But as one day gave way to the next, Darius's doting attitude remained the same.

She awakes each morning to his soft kisses and warm nuzzles. And lately, while she's in the bathroom, putting the finishing touches on her makeup, he'll head to the kitchen to toast her a bagel or to fix her a bowl of cereal. After breakfast, they head down to their cars together, hand in hand, and take off in separate directions for work, where Darius calls her several times a day just because he misses the sound of her voice.

Their cozy evenings of snuggling in front of the news with leftover take-out and a bottle of wine are just as intimate and relaxed as the rest of the time they spend together.

And the gifts haven't stopped coming either. When Trina broke the news about her promotion, Darius surprised her with a beautifully appointed Movado watch inscribed with her initials. And when she pulled up to his building for the first time in her brand-new Audi, he was right there, carrying a gift-wrapped box—what he'd later call a "Car-Warming Gift"—stuffed with every conceivable tool and widget a new car owner could ever want or need.

There *has* been the occasional mysterious late night phone call. They usually come in the evening while she and Darius are trying to enjoy a peaceful dinner or in the wee hours of the morning when they're both fast asleep.

When Trina answers, the caller promptly hangs up. When Darius answers, his strained voice drops to a low secretive whisper and he scampers off to the nearest room and closes the door. But instead of emerging ten minutes later, fully dressed with his keys in hand and a barely believable excuse about who was on the phone and where he's going, he only crawls back into bed, pulling Trina tightly to his chest and apologizes for waking her up.

Most of the time, their relationship feels normal—not necessarily healthy, but functional. That's how she'd categorize most of her relationships these days, she thinks; not ideal, but better than any of the other alternatives looming on her present horizon.

She transfers her wallet and checkbook from her briefcase to her purse and makes her way out of her office to meet Kendra, Tai, and Joss. "I'm off to lunch," she says, breezing by her secretary. "I should be back in about an hour. Make sure those records I gave you this morning are sealed and sent to County by two."

Her secretary murmurs her compliance, too engrossed by the spread-sheet in front of her to look up.

Trina sashays down the long corridor, past the cubicles and coffin-sized offices (identical to the one she'd called home just a few weeks earlier) to the elevator, which she rides down to her assigned parking space.

Her baby's there, waiting for her just a few steps away from the door where she'd reluctantly left it this morning. She disarms the alarm with a push of a button, hops in, relishing the overpowering new-car scent, and zips out of the garage with an ease and speed that her old, rusted jalopy could've never managed.

She weaves in and out of traffic with her windows cracked and her music blaring, feeling special and enviable.

Kendra's Mercedes is already parked outside of the restaurant by the time Trina arrives. She pulls into the space next to her and trots up the brick walkway to the crowded entrance.

Tai and Joss flag her down before the hostess even notices she's there. Trina squeezes through the waiting cluster of hungry lunch-goers and greets the three of them with air kisses before taking the last empty seat.

It's funny, when Trina first started hanging out with Kendra, Tai, and Joss, she found them, at times, unbearably fake. The way they dressed and spoke and laughed—it was all so affected, all so forced, like something she might expect to watch on an overacted soap opera. But here she is, after only a few months, guffawing and hair-flipping and air-kissing like a veteran.

"Have you ordered yet?" Trina asks, slipping out of her car coat.

Joss snorts. "We haven't even gotten menus yet."

"The service in this place gets worse with every visit," Kendra says, her voice louder than necessary. "I honestly don't know why we keep coming back here."

The hostess, who's commandeered a damp dishtowel and a plastic tub and taken up double duty as a busboy, nods as she wipes down the booth a few feet away from their table. "Someone should be with you ladies in just a few minutes," she assures them, breathless from the hectic pace of the lunch rush.

"Let's hope so," Kendra says.

"It's not like we need menus," Trina says, sipping her ice water. "We order the same thing every time."

"Not me," Tai says. "I'm starting this new diet I found online—all fish, veggies, and whole grains. You're supposed to be able to lose, like, ten pounds in the first week."

"But you hate fish," Joss argues.

Tai shrugs. "I hate being fat more."

"There's nothing wrong with your size," Trina says.

Kendra nods. "I agree."

Trina, Joss, and Tai freeze. The table falls instantly silent.

"What?" Kendra asks, her innocent eyes questioning all three of their dubious stares.

"You said something nice," Joss says.

"About someone else's weight," Trina clarifies.

Kendra folds her arms and leans back into her chair. "Yeah, so?"

"So you know what this means, don't you?" Joss asks.

"Our little ice princess is finally starting to thaw," Tai coos, a wide, teasing grin spread across her face.

"Awww," Trina and Joss sing in unison.

Kendra rolls her eyes. "Now I remember why I never say anything nice to you heifers."

They all laugh heartily, poking more fun at Kendra until the waiter finally arrives with their menus. Kendra, Tai, and Joss glance at the specials and then proceed to order exactly what they always get.

Trina orders the regular too: a chicken Caesar salad and a basket of honey croissants for the table.

Just as she hands back her menu, her purse begins to ring. After a few seconds of feeling, blindly, through her leather clutch, she pulls out her cell phone and checks the Caller ID. Her mood instantly darkens. She flips the miniature phone open with a flick of her wrist. "I'm busy, Grace," she says icily, her words chopped with irritation.

"I know," Grace says. "I'm sorry to bother you in the middle of a workday. But it's important."

Trina rolls her eyes, her lips pursed, but remains silent.

"So…how've you been?" Grace asks.

Trina sighs impatiently. "What do you want?"

"To invite you to Thanksgiving dinner," Grace answers tiredly.

"I'll pass," Trina says without missing a beat.

"It's really important to me that you be there."

Trina snorts. "I'll bet."

Grace sighs, all of her attempts at sweetness and small talk spent. "Would you please just come?"

"Why?"

"Give me a break," Grace exclaims, her exasperation plain. "Why does everything have to be a fight with you these days?"

"*You* called me," Trina snaps. She turns away from Kendra, Joss, and Tai who've all stopped pretending to have polite conversation amongst themselves and are hanging on to Trina's every word. "I've been just fine pretending like you don't exist."

"I'm sure you have," Grace says, her words pierced with hurt.

"Then you can understand why I'd rather not ruin a perfectly good holiday hanging around you and your holier-than-thou husband," Trina says, not a soupçon of emotion.

"I get it, okay? You hate me and my husband and if you never see either one of us again it'll be too soon. Point taken."

"And yet," Trina sings, her tone wry, "you're still on my phone."

"There are bigger things going on right now than what's happening between you and me."

"What're you talking about?"

"The dinner's not for us," Grace says, pausing as she struggles to maintain her composure. "It's for my dad."

Trina waits a few seconds for Grace to go on, but she doesn't offer any more details. "I don't know what that means," Trina says, her annoyance mounting. "And, truthfully, I don't have the energy to keep going around in circles with you. Just do us both a favor and spell it out in plain English so I can get on with my day already."

"My dad's dying," Grace blurts, her voice pitched high with insult and agony. "Is that plain enough for you?"

"What?" Trina gasps, her hand gripping her chest, her mind racing to wrap itself around the news. "What do you mean dying?"

"Who's dying?" Joss whispers, leaning in with Kendra and Tai.

Trina ignores them. "How? Of what? Are you sure?" she asks, the questions spilling out uncontrollably in rapid succession.

"I'm sure," Grace says, crying freely. "He's got advanced cirrhosis."

"When did you find out?" Trina asks, shock coursing through her body.

"A few weeks ago, but he's known for some time now. All those years of drinking were just too much for his liver to handle."

"There's nothing anyone can do? No sort of treatment or drug?"

"His doctors have him on a slew of medications, but at this stage, they're only prolonging the inevitable." She sniffs, her labored breaths filtering through the receiver in staggered puffs. "It's not a matter of 'if' he's going to die. It's a matter of 'when.'"

"Gracie," Trina says, every iota of her antagonistic attitude replaced by deep compassion and extreme regret. "I'm so sorry. I just—" She sighs and rests her forehead in her hand. "I didn't know."

Her chest tightens at the sound of Grace's sorrowful sobs.

"It's going to be okay," Trina says, tears filling her own eyes.

Kendra hands her a napkin. She, Joss, and Tai sit stoically around the table, worried, but unsure of what's going on or how they can help.

"Everybody keeps saying that," Grace hiccups into the phone. "But when is it ever really okay? I've been waiting. I've been waiting for months for things to be okay and they aren't. They just keep getting worse, and there's nothing I can do to make them better. So don't tell me it's going to be okay," she shrieks angrily. "I'm so sick of hearing that lie."

"I don't know what to say," Trina whispers.

But they both know there's nothing she can say. They both know from experience that words mean very little in instances like this and that comfort is nothing more than an unattainable illusion.

Grace sniffles loudly. "You don't have to say anything. Just come to dinner."

"Of course I will."

"He wants everyone there, Trina." Grace pauses for a few seconds so that her words can sink in. "Do you understand?"

"Ron," Trina answers softly.

"And his girlfriend," Grace adds. "And Malikah and my grandparents. I don't know how, but we're all going to have to pull it together and let bygones be bygones, if just for one night."

"Don't worry," Trina says. "We will. It'll work out; you just have to have a little faith."

"I'm all spent out on faith," Grace says, her voice hardening. "What I need is your word."

"You have it," Trina says. "I promise. I'll be on my best behavior."

"And Darius?"

"Him too. I'll make sure of it."

"Okay. Good," Grace says, her satisfaction audible. "Next Thursday. Five o'clock. I'll see you then."

"See ya...hey," Trina calls, raising the phone back to her ear. "You know I'm always here for you if you need me—for anything."

Grace scoffs, indignant. "Since when?"

Trina's eyes sting with tears, but by the time she musters the strength to answer, it's too late. Grace is gone.

34

"Some white lady just walked in," Malikah says, staggering past Grace, a large, heavy pot in hand. "She brought this." Malikah nods down at the covered pot and carefully heaves it onto the already cluttered island. She removes the aluminum foil and takes a tentative peak inside.

"What is it?" Grace asks, rinsing her hands.

"I could tell you what it looks like," Malikah says, her lip furled. "But I ain't 'bout to be blamed for makin' everybody lose they appetites."

"Whatever it is, just put it over there," Grandma Doria says, pointing her chopping knife at a bare spot on the granite counter by the sink. "I don't want it anywhere near my stuffing," she says and goes back to humming and hacking at the celery stalks in front of her.

Grace smiles as the familiar smell wafts its way over to her. She knows exactly what it is. The scent of Lani's apple cider is unmistakable. "It's good; you should try it," she says, drying her damp hands on a nearby dishtowel.

She unties her apron and heads out to greet her mother-in-law. "Oh," she spins around just as she reaches the kitchen's archway. "And no more of that 'white lady' stuff," she orders with a stern squint of her eyes and a wag of her finger.

"Her name is Lani. She's Mike's mother—adoptive mother," she adds quickly, in a bid to erase the am-I-missing-something look on Malikah's face. "Which means she's family. So be nice."

"I'm always nice," Malikah calls to Grace's retreating back. "But I don't care if she is family," Grace hears Malikah mumble, "I ain't drinkin' this mess."

"Baby, look who's here," Mike says as soon as Grace rounds the corner into the living room.

"There she is," Lani says, her arms spread as wide as her smile.

Grace slips into her warm embrace, squeezing her tight. "We've missed you," she says, her breath fanning Lani's thin, white hair. "It hasn't been the same here since you moved to Nashville."

"I've missed you both too," she says, pulling away. "But I just love it up there."

Grace looks down at the bundle of fur wagging by her feet. "Hello, Chewy," she says, her playful baby voice causing him to jump, spin, and bark all at once.

"I still can't believe you brought that thing all the way out here," Mike says.

"You know I couldn't kennel him. Besides," she smiles down at the floppy-eared dog, "he makes great company."

"How was the drive?" Grace asks.

Lani shakes her head and lets out a loud, exaggerated breath. "Long!"

Grace smiles. "Well, the change of scenery must agree with you because you look great."

"And marriage is agreeing with you," she says, holding Grace out at an arm's length. "You look beautiful."

"She's got a glow, doesn't she?" Grace's dad calls from the couch where he's sitting next to Grandpa Mearl, who nods his agreement.

Lani tilts her head and examines Grace, her probing gaze traveling slowly up and down her body, lingering just bit longer on her stomach. "Yes," she says, her nod slow, her brow arched. "She certainly does."

Grace had carefully selected her outfit—a loose-fitting sweater and an ankle-length skirt (with an elastic waistband to comfortably fit her ever-growing belly)—to disguise her nine-week pregnancy. And she had thought the plan was working.

She smiles at Lani, who's still surveying her with an intense, curious gaze. But now, she's not so sure.

A loud crash resounds from the guest bedroom—followed by a frantic "I didn't do it!" from Malikah's oldest son.

"If I have to come in there…," Malikah barks the open-ended threat from the kitchen. Momentary silence is followed by the unmistakable scuffling of guilty feet, followed by more silence.

"Let me go see what those knuckleheads are up to," Grandpa Mearl says.

"No, let me," Grace says, grateful for the interruption and a chance to get away from Lani's persistent stare. "You stay with Dad. Keep him company."

By the time Grace reaches the room, the boys are sitting quietly, one on the edge of the bed, the other Indian-style on the floor. They glance up at her, nervous, their shirts twisted and their shoes untied and quickly go back to pretending they're watching the music video on TV.

The bedcovers are ruffled, a sure sign that there's been some wrestling going on, and one of the table lamps is lying on its side, the once-whole base, now cracked into several large chunks.

"What happened in here?" Grace asks, hands on hips.

"It was an accident," they both murmur, prying their eyes away from the television only long enough to cast each other nervous glances.

Grace eyes them sternly. "I loved that lamp," she says. "And now it's ruined. That's gonna cost you."

The boys peek up at her, wincing in anticipation of a lengthy lecture, or worse, a spanking, which Grace thinks they've long since outgrown, but Malikah says she'll continue to do as long as they've got rear ends and she's got strength enough to raise a belt.

Grace raises a brow. "Two kisses each," she says, tapping her cheek.

They rise reluctantly, the looks on their faces assuring Grace that they consider themselves too old and too cool to dispense hugs and kisses. Still they all know, when it comes to punishment, a couple of pecks a piece is a lenient sentence for a broken lamp. "No more wrestling," she orders after they've each paid their penance.

They agree and promptly slip out of the room before Grace has the chance to reconsider her sentence.

Mike is standing in the doorway, grinning adoringly, his arms folded.

"Look at this," Grace says with an incredulous laugh. She motions at the chunks of clay and dented shade. "I'll be surprised if the place is still standing after tonight."

"Your dad's right, you know," Mike says, inching closer. "You do have a glow about you."

Grace rolls her eyes. "It's called sweat. You try running after my crazy relatives for an hour. You'll be glowing too."

Mike takes her hand and gently tugs her to him. "Have I told you how beautiful you look today?"

"Not yet," she says, her voice low. "But I've been waiting."

"You're gorgeous." He kisses the soft spot on her jaw, right beneath her ear. "And I love you," he whispers before pulling away.

"I love *you*," Grace says, tilting her face upward for a real kiss. Mike willingly indulges her and for a few precious moments, everything around them disappears as it always does when they're caught up in each other's touch—each other's nearness.

"Get a room!"

Grace and Mike pull apart to see Montez watching them from the hall, his head shaking, his lips turned up into an amused smirk.

"Don't hate the player," Mike says, with a teasing bounce of his brow. "Hate the game."

Montez laughs. "I would, if you had any," he says.

"You don't know anything about this, right here, Little Man," Mike says, wrapping his arm around Grace's waist. "I *invented* game."

Just then, Malik appears beside his brother, munching on a slice of ham he most likely pilfered from the kitchen when no one was looking. "Grandpa Mearl needs you to help him with something," he says to Mike.

"He can't right now," Montez shouts down the hall.

"Why not?" Mearl's gruff voice calls back.

Montez flashes a devious grin as he turns to leave. "Because he's back here gettin' busy with Grace."

Mike guffaws along with everyone else within earshot. Grace shakes her head and leans her cheek against his chest. "How are we going to survive this dinner?" she wonders aloud.

"Together," Mike says, giving her one last kiss. "I'm gonna go see what your grandpa needs."

Grace nods. "I'll be there in a sec. I just want to clean up this mess."

She straightens the disheveled bedcovers, tosses the destroyed lamp into the nearest trash can and makes her way down the hall. The elevator doors ding and swing open just as she walks by.

Trina and Darius are leaning against the left side and Tamara and Ron are leaning against the right. There's enough space between the two couples to fit a small car and enough tension to snap it clean in half.

Grace forces a smile and throws her hands up. "You made it!" she exclaims. "Come on in. Make yourselves at home. Here," she holds out her arms, "let me hang your coats."

"No, let me," Tamara says. "You should be doing as little as possible."

Ron and Trina cast her baffled glances.

"I mean since you've gone through so much trouble to host this wonderful dinner," Tamara blubbers, clearly desperate to cover up her slip.

It seems to work. "I'll take care of it," Ron says, collecting all four coats and taking them to the front closet.

"We brought peach cobbler," Tamara says, holding out a plastic-wrapped baking dish.

"You didn't have to," Grace says, smiling. "But thanks. It smells delicious."

"We brought the bubbly," Darius says, holding up two massive bottles of champagne, a cheap, red bow stuck on each. "Where do you want them?"

"Kitchen," Grace says, glaring at Trina. Only after Darius has made his way down the hall and around the corner does she yank Trina aside. "You brought liquor to my recovering alcoholic father's dinner?" she fumes.

"Okay, wait," Trina pleads, her words slow, her tone calm. "Darius insisted, and I didn't know how much I was privy to tell him about your dad's condition. So instead of betraying your trust, I thought it would be better to just let him bring them and then put them away."

"For the last time," Grace says, "this dinner isn't about you or me. It's not about betraying trusts or keeping secrets or sparing your boyfriend's feelings. It is about my dad."

"Everything okay?" Ron asks. "I'm sensing a noticeable lack of holiday cheer in this corner."

Grace ignores his attempt at lightheartedness. "Get rid of it," she snaps, her flinty stare stayed on Trina.

"Okay," Trina murmurs. She wrings her hands as she watches Grace stomp off to the kitchen.

"Just keep breathing," Ron says, offering a sympathetic smile and a reassuring pat on the back. It is, hands down, the nicest he's been to her since they broke up almost two years ago. For reasons she can't explain, his warmth brings tears to her eyes.

"Ronnie," Tamara calls. "Honey, could you come help us set the table?"

Ron shrugs and nods toward the dining room. "Duty calls. Chin up," he says, backing away. "It'll be alright."

Trina nods and hurries to the kitchen where she promptly pours out the champagne and hides the empty bottles at the bottom of the trash can. Then, she joins Darius in the living room where he, Mike, Grandpa Mearl, and Anthony are surfing television stations in search of the football game.

"What're you doin' out here with the menfolk?" Mearl barks.

"They seem to have everything covered in the kitchen," Trina says with a polite shrug. The truth is, between Grace's angry glares, Malikah's nasty sneers, and Tamara's catty comments, she'd rather take her chances roughing it with the guys.

For the next hour, the loft is filled with a symphony of lively chatter and boisterous laughter.

Malikah's boys abandoned real-life wrestling for the electronic variety, courtesy of their Playstation, which they brought from home.

Lani and Doria, who have already become fast friends, have made themselves at home in Grace's kitchen, chopping, slicing, baking, and basting while they swap favorite recipes and whisper secret cooking tips.

Malikah and Grace relieve Ron of his table-setting duties so he can join the rest of the boys, hollering and clapping at the football game on TV.

It's Tamara's idea to fashion some makeshift place cards out of a colorful array of post-its. They take great pains to arrange the mismatched bunch in a way that won't set off an impromptu episode of WWE Smackdown.

Every now and then Tamara ventures into the living room with a pitcher to refill glasses of iced tea. Grace appreciates her attentiveness and willingness to serve, but she can't help thinking that Tamara's more interested in making her presence known to Trina and Ron, who somehow ended up side by side on the love seat. They stop talking, pretending to be too engrossed in the game to notice her disapproving looks, each time she saunters into the room. In fact, no one pays Tamara much mind at all, except for Darius, who treats himself to a hard gaze at her long legs and ample backside (which is packed neatly into a pair of skintight stretch khakis) every time she bends over to pour some tea.

By quarter to seven the table is adorned with an aromatic, eye-catching display of food: honey-braised ham, mashed potatoes, stuffing, macaroni and cheese, cornbread, greens—everything Grace's father had requested and then some.

"I hate to break this up," Lani says. "But dinner is served."

"It's about time," Grandpa Mearl says, hopping up before anyone else and hobbling toward the dining room. "Y'all better come get you some before I finish it off," he calls over his shoulder.

They all laugh.

"You don't have to tell me twice," Grace's dad says, struggling to his feet. Mike takes him by the arm and leads him, slowly, to his seat at the head of the table. Everyone else follows closely behind, perusing the ornate place settings, once they reach the dining room, to find the plate bearing their name.

Sorry about the way she'd reacted over the champagne and mindful of Trina's hurt reaction to the seating arrangement at her wedding reception, Grace had made sure to put Trina directly to her right. She watches, pleased, at Trina's delighted expression when she finally locates her place card.

"Who wants to bless the meal?" Lani asks.

No one says anything, but all eyes gravitate to Mike.

He smiles. "I'd love to."

They join hands around the table, bow their heads, and close their eyes.

"Dear Heavenly Father," Mike begins. "We come to You this evening, blessed and happy to be in the good company of family and friends. We have so much to be thankful for. Our cups are beyond full; they are pressed down, shaken together, and running over. For that, we praise You. Bless the beautiful women who prepared this wonderful meal. May they always be served and loved in the same way that they serve and love others.

"As we sit down and break bread together, we ask You to preside over our conversations, and to reside in our relationships. May we exude Your love in all of our thoughts, all of our words, and all of our actions. We love You, Lord, because You loved us first, because You provide richly, because You are infinitely patient, but mostly, we love You because You are You. In Your precious and holy name, we pray. Amen."

Grace looks up just in time to catch Tamara and Darius making eyes at each other across the ham.

Both of their coy grins are wiped clean by the time everyone else raises their heads. "Amen," she choruses along with the rest of the table before sitting down.

Grace glances over at Trina. As usual, she seems oblivious to Darius's roaming eye.

"This looks fantastic," Grace's dad says. He shakes his head and smiles, but the bravado in his voice betrays his deluge of emotion.

"I think we're missing something," Lani says with a not-so-sly wink.

Grace nods, a knowing grin on her face, and motions for everyone's patience as she runs back into the kitchen. "Voila!" she exclaims when she returns moments later, carrying the beautifully garnished turkey on a silver serving tray. "La pièce de résistance," she says, gingerly setting it down amidst a diapason of plaudits and delighted gasps, in the empty spot in front of her father.

"Look at that bird," he says, leaning back to get a better look. "You guys really went all out."

Grace wraps her arms around her dad's shoulders and lands a kiss on his cheek. "You're worth it," she says.

"Hear, hear," Mike says, raising his glass. "To Anthony, cherished father and devoted friend!"

"To Anthony," everyone cheers, clinking their glasses.

They all dig in, passing the dishes of steaming food from one end of the table to the other and lavishing compliments on the cooks as they moan their approval.

Mike carves the turkey and Ron slices the ham, while Malikah's boys pile their plates high and then sneak out of the room and back to their video game.

Grace fixes her dad a plate, spooning him a small dab of everything. "It's a lot," she says, placing it in front of him. "You don't have to finish it all."

"I know." He picks up his fork and stuffs his linen napkin down the front of his shirt. "But you better believe I'm gonna give it the old college try."

Grace takes her seat and joins in the festivities, eating jovially and carrying on lively conversations with her neighbors. She notices that Trina remains relatively quiet. "I love your earrings," she says, a lame but earnest attempt at a peace offering. "They're perfect for you. Very Bohemian."

Trina smiles. "Thanks," she says, fingering the dangling beads strung together with braided gold. "I can get you a pair if you want."

Grace shakes her head. "They're too big. I could never pull them off."

"Yeah," Tamara nods, munching on an asparagus stalk. "They're not really Grace's style. She goes for more classic jewelry."

"Three weeks as her personal assistant and you're already an expert on her style," Trina says with strained politeness. "You must be a fast learner."

Tamara shrugs. "Just perceptive," she says. "You'd be amazed at how close two people can become in such a short amount of time. It's like we've been friends our whole lives." She returns Trina's plastic smile with one of her own.

"I know what you mean," Trina says, swirling her mashed potatoes around in her gravy. "There's nothing Gracie and I don't know about each other. Of course, that's probably because we actually *have* been friends our whole lives."

Those seated at the opposite end of the table are engrossed in their own conversations, but Ron, Mike, Grace, and her father eat silently, discomfited by the furtive feud unfolding right before them, clueless as to how to stop it without causing someone embarrassment.

Impervious to the catty banter taking place right under his nose, Darius, dense as ever, asks Malikah to pass the rolls.

"Come on now," Tamara says, her tone sweet as syrup and just as artificial. "It's impossible to know *everything* about someone. I mean, I can think of several things going on with Grace that you know nothing about."

"Wow," Trina says, her eyes wide with mock surprise. "That's impressive. I didn't know you *could* think."

"Well, there's a lot you don't know about me," Tamara says, her tone decidedly less kind.

Trina shrugs. "Thank God for small favors."

Ron smirks, but quickly shovels a forkful of turkey into his mouth when Tamara turns her shooting daggers from Trina to him.

"Hey, did you try the stuffing?" Grace asks, scooping a dollop onto Trina's plate. "Have some. It's my favorite. Grandma's secret recipe."

"Secret's out," Tamara announces smugly. "Nana Doria taught me how to make it this afternoon. I'd be happy to whip some up for you anytime you'd like," she says to Grace.

Ron clears his throat. "Would you stop?" He murmurs the stern request under his breath.

"What?" Tamara shrugs, the picture of unassuming innocence. "I'm just making conversation."

"So, Darius," Mike says, purposefully veering the discussion in a completely different direction, "how's work been?"

"Hectic," Darius says, his answer muffled by the glob of food crammed in his mouth. "I think Grace has got the right idea," he says after he chews and swallows. "I might need to go and get myself an assistant—someone with the right assets, you know, aggressive, ready to handle a large workload, maybe even willing to pull a few all-nighters."

This time, his libidinous glance at Tamara is not lost on Trina (or anyone else at their end of the table for that matter), nor is his overture.

An awkward, stifling silence settles between them. They sit quietly for several minutes, tossing worried glances back and forth between tentative bites and pretending to listen to the much friendlier conversation taking place down at the other end of the table.

Grace is the first to break the lull. "How is it, Dad?" she asks.

Though he's barely touched his food, he winks and pats his stomach. "Delicious. I couldn't have asked for anything more."

Grace smiles. "Good."

"Hey," Ron points his fork at Trina, "didn't you just get a promotion?"

"Yeah," Trina nods slowly, a faint smile on her lips. "How do you know that?"

"How *do* you know that?" Tamara asks.

Ron shrugs coolly, seemingly unfazed by Tamara's shrill, demanding tone and fierce glower. "Heard it through the grapevine," he says.

"So you took the job," Grace says. "Last time we talked about it, you were thinking about turning it down."

"I know. It was sort of a spur of the moment decision," Trina explains. "I guess, in the end, I just couldn't let that kind of an opportunity pass me by."

"Good for you," Mike says.

"How do you like it so far?" Grace asks.

"Um, well, I'm still getting acclimated," she says. "But so far so good."

"Please!" Darius scoffs. "She *loves* it. I've never seen her happier. She comes home every night beaming. But I guess a salary hike and a new car would have that effect on just about anyone, huh?"

Tamara's brow arches, a menacing smirk creeping on her lips. "So, you two live together then?" she asks.

Darius nods.

Trina lowers her eyes and shrugs. "It's an arrangement we fell into. We're not really in a rush to give it a label."

"That's funny," Tamara murmurs, sampling the cranberry sauce.

Trina cocks her head to the side. "Why is that funny?" she asks, her tone as challenging as her stare.

"Guys," Grace says, "not now." But her plea falls on deaf ears.

Tamara shrugs. "I just thought you were a Christian, that's all."

"I *am*," Trina snips. She folds her arms across her chest and purses her lips. "But then again, we've already established that thinking isn't exactly your forte."

"And reading must not be yours," Tamara says. "Or do you just skip over the parts in the Bible that condemn fornication as a sin?"

"That was unnecessary," Mike says.

Ron wipes his mouth and sets his napkin on the table. "I agree."

"Doesn't surprise me," Tamara says, her jaw clenched. "Considering you've made an art out of fawning over her all afternoon."

"Him?" Trina's laugh is both bitter and incredulous. "If anyone's been caught fawning tonight, it's the two of you," she says, pointing back and forth between Tamara and Darius.

"Here we go," Grace groans, slouching in her seat and shaking her head.

"Me?" Darius asks. "What did I do?"

"Oh, come off of it," Trina snaps, her angry voice a scratchy whisper. "I'm not an idiot."

"That's debatable," Tamara quips quietly.

Unfortunately, it's not quiet enough. "I'm gonna go," Trina says, pushing her chair away from the table. Its legs scrape loudly against the hardwood floors, drawing the attention of the rest of the Thanksgiving dinner guests, who up until that point had not caught wind of Tamara and Trina's brewing storm.

"Please don't," Grace says, taking hold of Trina's forearm.

"I tried," Trina says softly. "I did. But I can't do this. I'm sorry, it's too much."

"What's goin' on over there?" Malikah asks, stretching out her neck, her chin tilted upward. "Trina stirrin' up more trouble?"

"Give it a rest," Grace says, her gaze hard. "Nothing's going on. She's enjoying the meal like everyone else."

"Well, when you get a chance," Grandpa Mearl says, tapping an empty serving bowl, "we need some more string beans down on this end."

"I'll get them," Grace says. She aims her index finger at Trina. "You stay."

"I left them simmering on the stove," Grandma Doria says. "Might as well bring the whole pot."

"You should let me do it," Tamara says, standing.

Grace smiles. "It's fine. I got it."

"The pot's probably heavy. You don't want to strain yourself," Tamara insists, her wide eyes adding to her conspiratorial expression.

"Really," Grace says, her tone one of frustration. "I can handle it. It's not a problem."

Tamara dismisses the notion with a roll of her eyes and a wave of her hand. "Don't be silly. Sit, eat, stay with your guests."

"She said she's got it," Ron says. "So let her get it."

"I'm just trying to be helpful," Tamara says.

"There's helpful and then there's obnoxious," Grace says, her patience completely spent. "And right now, you're pushing the latter."

The entire table falls silent and all eating slows to a halt.

"Baby, the beans," Mike prompts.

Grace nods and turns toward the kitchen.

"I don't understand what I've done wrong," Tamara says. "I'm only trying to do my job."

"You're not on the clock right now," Grace says. "So just relax and let me handle things on my own, okay?"

"Sure," Tamara says, straightening her already erect posture. She glimpses anxiously around the table of near strangers blinking up at her, the humiliation of being called out in front of everyone clearly setting in. "I only offered because, under the circumstances, I thought it was in your best interest."

"What circumstances?" Trina asks, throwing her arms up. "The way you follow her around is ridiculous. Who strains themselves picking up a pot of string beans or hanging up coats in a closet for that matter? I mean, I could see if she was crippled or retarded or even pregnant, but she's not."

Tamara's cheeks instantly flush, her nervousness as transparent as glass. She shoots Grace an alarmed glance then quickly sits down.

"Oh my gosh," Trina utters, easily fitting together the pieces. She stares up at Grace. "Oh my gosh," she says again. "You're pregnant."

Mike drops his knife. Malikah's fork stops midair as does Lani's. The hush that falls over the room is deafening—utter silence, quiet enough to hear a cotton ball drop.

Grace closes her eyes and lowers her head, her racing heartbeat giving way to the painful dread amassing in the pit of her stomach. "Yes," she says, the confession reluctant. "I'm pregnant."

"Well, Sweetheart, that's wonderful," Lani says. "Congratulations!" She giggles excitedly, clasping her hands. "I'm going to be a grandma." The mood slowly lightens as the room buzzes animatedly with talk of a new addition to the family.

Grace doesn't have the courage to look at Mike, though she can feel the heat of his gaze on the side of her face.

"How far along are you?" Malikah asks.

"Nine weeks," Grace says.

The room bursts into more celebratory applause and happy chatter.

Trina shakes her head. "How could you keep this a secret?"

"I was going to tell you," Grace says.

"When?" Mike asks, his strong, angry voice slicing through the jovial atmosphere like a hot knife through butter. "When were you going to tell us?"

The tension in the room returns as the guests, once again, fall silent.

"You mean you didn't know?" Grace's dad asks.

"I just wasn't ready to break the news," Grace says, her eyes firmly planted on the tablecloth.

"Why?" Mike asks. It's the simplest of questions, but Grace can't bring herself to answer him. "Why, Grace?"

"Because," she chokes back a sob, "I haven't decided what I want to do about it yet."

"Are you talking about an abortion?" Trina asks, her words breathy with shock.

"Oh, no!" Mearl throws down his napkin. "We don't have abortions in this family, young lady," he says, wagging his sausage-round finger. Incidentally, that's the exact same thing he told Grace's mom when she found herself pregnant with Grace.

"What is wrong wit chu?" Malikah asks, her brows furrowed with disappointment. "Have you lost your mind?"

"Really, Grace," Grandma Doria says. "We raised you better than that."

"Now let's just calm down," Lani counsels smoothly. "Nobody said anything about an abortion, right Honey?"

All eyes turn to Grace, who's still standing behind her chair. She bites her bottom lip and flicks away the tear trickling down her cheek. "I don't know," she says, shrugging slightly.

The table erupts into irate murmurs and horrified gasps.

Without a word, Mike gets up and walks out.

Grace follows. "I'm sorry," she says, double-stepping to keep pace with his long strides.

"For what?" he asks, turning to face her only after they've reached their bedroom. "Because from everything I heard in there, the only thing you're sorry about is the fact that you're pregnant."

"I'm not ready to be a mother," Grace says, her quivering voice thick with emotion. "I didn't mean for you to find out this way, but that doesn't change anything. I can't...," she sighs, swallowing hard. "I don't want this baby."

"Since when?" he asks. "We talked about this in counseling, remember? We said we both wanted children—to raise a family together."

"Right," Grace says. "Eventually, but not now."

"Who are you?" Mike asks, his eyes sloped sadly. "Do you even know?" He shakes his head and runs his big hand along his stubbled jaw. "This…," he says motioning at her, "You. You aren't the woman I married. You aren't my Gracie."

A fresh batch of tears spring to Grace's eyes. "I don't know what to say to that," she whispers.

He paces the length of the room, combing his fingers through his dreads. "Why didn't you trust me enough—respect me enough—to come to me when you first found out? Why would you tell Tamara, of all people?"

"I didn't tell her," Grace says. "She found my bag under the bathroom sink."

He stops short and looks up. "What bag?" But before Grace can explain, he's started to the bathroom.

"Mike don't," she begs, chasing after him.

He flips on the lights, throws open the cabinet door, and snatches the brown paper bag, knocking over toiletries and bottles of cleaning products in the process. Without hesitation, he holds the bag upside down and dumps everything onto the counter.

Grace watches his expression change from curiosity to confusion to hurt as he rummages through weeks' worth of hidden evidence and withheld information. Her breath catches as he picks up her Baby on Board folder, and the abortion pamphlets that Dr. Noguez gave her fall out.

"What is this?" he asks, the muscles in his jaw tightening. He holds up the appointment card for her abortion still scheduled to take place in several weeks.

"It's not what it looks like," she says, no longer bothering to wipe away her tears. "The obstetrician, he thought setting a 'D-Date' might help me make a decision."

Mike puts down the lid on the toilet and sits, bending over, his forehead resting on his knees.

Grace's body aches at the sight of him—so vulnerable—so obviously pained.

"This isn't happening," he says over and over again. "This can't be happening."

"Mike, please," Grace cries, kneeling down in front of him. "You have to give me a chance to explain. Please." She rubs his arms.

"Don't!" he shouts, snatching away. "Don't touch me." He gets up, backing his way out of the bathroom, sour repugnance seeping from every pore.

Grace stays frozen in her kneeled position, too shocked, for a few moments, to move. Numb, she returns to the bedroom to find Mike lying diagonally across the bed staring blankly up at the ceiling.

"Can we at least talk about it?" Grace asks, maintaining her distance and sinking into the suede couch in front of the window.

"How could you not want this child?" he asks after a few seconds of silence. He sits up and looks at her. "It's a part of us—a living, breathing person that we made together, that we conceived in love. Didn't we? I mean, you *do* love me, don't you?"

"Of course I do," Grace says, her head tilted. "With everything that's in me."

"Then why?"

"I don't feel like it's the right time. I'm not ready. You don't have a job, my dad's sick, my writing career's just starting to take off," she says, listing a few of their obstacles.

"We're two married adults," he says. "We've got a home, we've got a savings, we've got each other. People bring children into this world with far less."

"And half of them end up miserable," Grace says. "I don't want to be miserable, do you? Or worse, raise a miserable kid."

"That's not going to be us," Mike says. "Where is your faith?"

"Faith has nothing to do with it. 'Happily Ever After' is a crapshoot," Grace says. "Plain and simple. The odds are bad enough without throwing children into the equation. I don't want to be like my mother. She wasn't ready to become a parent. Look what happened. She left my father and put her career before everything—even me."

"She loved you very much," Mike says. "You know that."

"Yeah, because she finally told me in a letter I received after she was already gone. What good does that do me? I needed to know when I was growing up—when I was tucking myself into bed, when I was warming up dinners the maid cooked, when I was waiting for good-night phone calls from her that never came. My childhood was empty and lonely and dismal because of *her* mistakes. Because she let my father and my grandfather pressure her into doing something she wasn't ready to do."

"And I'm glad they did," Mike says. "I am, because if she'd had an abortion, you wouldn't be here. You wouldn't be mine."

Grace stares down into her hands. "I wish it was that simple."

"You don't know who that is," Mike says, pointing to her stomach. "You don't know whose soul mate, whose best friend, whose teacher, whose confidant, whose happiness you're carrying right now. All you can think about is yourself and the mistakes you're scared of repeating." He shakes his head, awestruck. "When did you get to be so selfish?"

Grace glares at him. "It is my body. It is my life. It is my choice," she says, her words slow and final. "And I'm telling you, I don't want it."

"It's *our* child," Mike says, his words just as slow, just as final. "And I'm telling you that this marriage won't survive an abortion."

Grace blinks, her hands turning to ice. "Are you giving me an ultimatum?"

"I'm giving you the truth," he says. "As simply as I know how."

"So if I don't keep the baby, you won't stay?" Grace asks, her voice puny and frightened.

He shakes his head, his expression one of regret, yet certainty. "I don't think I can."

They sit facing each other for what seems like ages, neither of them speaking, neither quite sure what to do next. "I gotta get outta here," Mike says after some time. "I need air. I need to think."

Grace doesn't want him to go. She's terrified that if he gets into that elevator, he may never come back. But she stays where she is, seated on the couch, her hands folded in her lap.

"I'm sorry," she says again.

He looks down at her, his lashes glistening with tears. "I wish I believed you."

35

"Knock, knock," someone says, cracking open Grace's bedroom door. "Can we come in?"

Grace peers up from her tear-stained pillow to see Trina enter, Malikah following closely behind. They stand at the foot of her bed and wait for her to speak.

"I think Mike might leave me," she whispers.

"Why would you think something like that?" Trina asks, slipping off her shoes and crawling under the covers next to her.

"Because he said he would."

"If you abort the baby?" Trina asks gently.

Grace's face scrunches as she nods, her sore, red eyes squeezing out even more tears.

"Don't cry," Trina says, scooting closer and resting Grace's head in her lap. Grace's shoulders heave, her forceful sobs shaking the entire bed. Trina strokes her hair and waits patiently for her cries to subside.

"You know I love you," Malikah says. "Baby, I'd even lay down my life for you—no second thoughts—but you wrong on this one, no two ways about it."

Grace groans her exasperation. The noise, though muffled by the comforter, is still loud enough to echo throughout the bedroom.

"You can stomp and holler all you want," Malikah says. "There ain't nothin' stoppin' you from havin' this baby or keepin' yo man but you. Come on, now, tell her," she says, snapping at Trina. "You always cryin' 'best friend' so be one. It can't always be huggin' and hand-holdin'. She needs to hear the truth."

"It's not the time," Trina says. "Look at her. She's in pieces."

"And?" Malikah asks, her arms crossed. "This ain't the place for political correctness. She can lay there and cry all night. What that gone do? Nothin'. The same problems will be waitin' for her tomorrow right where her wailing behind left 'em."

Trina sighs. "Gracie, she's right."

Grace lifts her puffy face and glares at the two of them. "Is this why you came in here? After years of fighting, you've finally joined forces and it's to criticize and chastise me?" She snorts. "Just go back to hating each other and leave me alone."

Neither woman flinches or budges.

"The way you're handling this thing is all wrong," Trina says softly. "And so is your attitude." She sweeps Grace's hair out of her eyes. "But the good news is, they can both be fixed."

Grace leans away, her brows furrowed, her lips pressed tightly together. Trina's words are clearly not what she wants to hear.

"A child is a gift," Malikah says.

"I don't care! I'm just not ready!" Grace exclaims, clinching a fistful of sheets. "Why is that so hard for everyone to accept?"

"Cause ain't nobody ever really ready for a baby," Malikah says. "But when it happens, you embrace it anyway."

"Why? So I can be like you?" Grace asks, her tone nasty. "You had two kids by the time you were eighteen and it ruined your life."

"Stop it," Trina says.

"Why?" Grace seethes. "She gave me some truth," she says looking at Malikah, "now let me return the favor. You could've been anything you wanted. With your grades, your natural talent, your beauty, the sky was the limit. But you went and got knocked up—twice! And what did those little *gifts* get you?" she asks. "A loser husband and his loser family, bills you can't pay, a raggedy house you can't afford to fix, and a back-breaking job you hate but won't ever leave. *That's* the truth."

"I love my sons," Malikah says. "And I wouldn't trade them for nothin'. Not a nicer house or an easier job—not even a better husband. But you ain't got no idea what that feels like cause the number one person on yo list is still you."

"You haven't thought this through," Trina says. "If you have this abortion, you will regret it for the rest of your life."

"You would know, wouldn't you?" Grace asks, her tone spiteful. "You are, after all, the only person in this room who can speak from experience."

"I wasn't saved then," Trina says. "I didn't know what I know now. I'm different."

"Except you aren't," Grace says. "You're exactly where you were ten years ago—still settling, still pretending, still rationalizing, still stuck to the same, no-good man."

"How is insulting me going to solve anything?" Trina asks. "I'm trying to help you."

"How can you possibly help me?" Grace asks. "Tell me, what can you teach me? You, who's shacking up with her boyfriend, who…how did your friend put it? 'Drinks like a fish and curses like a sailor.' What exactly is it you think you can do for me?"

Trina looks away, unable to respond, not because she's angry or hurt or even offended, but because everything Grace said was true.

Grace nods. "That's what I thought," she says in response to Trina's silence.

"Ah'ight fine," Malikah shrugs. "We messed up. We got some thangs wrong. That don't mean you gotta follow in our footsteps."

"Exactly," Trina says. "Don't use our wrong choices as an excuse to make wrong choices of your own; use them as an example of what *not* to do, of how *not* to be."

"Enough," Grace says, tossing back the covers and rolling out of bed. "I was hoping maybe for some sympathy, a little bit of understanding—at the very least, a listening ear and a shoulder to cry on. What I didn't want was a sermon. I don't need a preacher; I need a friend." She tugs on her boots and zips them up.

"Where are you going?" Trina asks.

"Away," Grace says, snatching her gloves off the dresser. "From this place and from the two of you."

"Away" ends up being the park across the street. It's where Grace used to walk every day when she first moved to Memphis. It's where she used to go to clear her head. The quaint tree-lined path, the still waters of the Mississippi River, the pastel, sun-kissed sky—they were once the tranquil backdrop to her many thoughts.

Somehow she fell out of the habit of treading the three-mile course. She'd met Mike and then her father, mourned her mother's death, got published and then married. Life, as it often does, just got in the way.

But as she sets off down the well-trodden path, she realizes that she misses this place and she misses her walks. She misses the solitude, the serenity.

Despite the rapidly dropping temperature and whipping wind, she strolls the entire park, not once, but twice—lost in her mind, in the "what ifs" of Mike's ultimatum and of what a baby would require of them individually and as a couple.

She ends up with more questions and uncertainties than she had when she started. The air nips at her flesh through her coat and gloves, but she can't bring herself to go back home. Not yet.

There's a chance they might all still be there, in her loft, waiting for her, waiting to express their disappointment, to shove their points of view down her throat. The thought turns her stomach almost as much as the realization that she'd single-handedly ruined her father's special Thanksgiving dinner.

She can still see his face, the confusion, the hurt of hearing her confession. The idea that, that incident may be one of the last memories she will ever have the chance to make with her dad is almost unbearable. She's too ashamed, too embarrassed, too upset to go back. So she continues to walk.

Long after the sun has set and her fingers and toes and nose have been prickled numb by the cold, Grace is still walking—through downtown, past all of the closed restaurants and stores, across Main Street's cobbled sidewalk, and around the massive high rises. She walks until her lower back begins to throb and her legs grow weary.

The lights are off by the time she summons up enough nerve to return to the loft. The kitchen has been cleaned, all the dishes washed, all the food put away. No one's there, including Mike.

Grateful, Grace fixes herself a cup of tea, her fingers stinging and tingling as they thaw, and heads to the bathroom for a hot shower.

She washes slowly, caressing her belly, which is just now starting to protrude noticeably. She leans into the spray, breathing in the steam. Her muscles relax involuntarily. If she could've, she would've stood there all night, but as usual, the hot water runs out on her.

Grace wraps one towel around her sopping hair and another around her dripping body and heads to the closet. She flips on the light and freezes. Her chest seizes at the sight of Mike's vacant cubbyholes and bare hangers. Save his suits and dress shirts, his entire side of the closet is empty.

She rushes into the bedroom on rubbery legs, frantically pulling open all of his dresser drawers—empty. Her breaths come in loud, panicked wheezes as she dashes back to the bathroom. How did she not notice? His toothbrush is gone, his razor, his deodorant, his shaving cream, his mouthwash...nothing's left.

The bathroom spins as Grace steps to the left, and then to the right, and then to the left again. She doesn't know where to go, what to do, who to call. She wrings her hands, stumbling tearfully through every room in the loft, searching for a note, for a clue, a sign—anything that will confirm what her heart can't bear to accept.

But when she flings open the doors to the front hall closet and eyes the empty space where Mike's luggage usually sits, she can only sink to the cold, marble floor and sob.

Her worst fear has actually come true.

Mike is gone.

He left and Grace has no idea where he is or, worst of all, if he's ever coming back.

part three

Peace, Be Still

36

Trina closes her eyes and rolls onto her side, turning her back to the bathroom door just as Darius opens it. Warm steam from his morning shower billows forth and dissipates over the bed, where she's pretending to sleep.

She lies motionless and listens as he goes through his routine. The distinct swiping of silk against starched cotton when he puts on his tie, the methodic scratching of bristles as he runs his brush across his waves, the brassy clink of his belt buckle as he fastens it, and the speedy zip of his laces as he ties his shoes. They're all familiar noises—sounds she's long since memorized and learned to identify without thought or reason.

Only after his heavy footsteps forge their way to the kitchen does Trina dare to open her eyes. She and Darius haven't spoken since they returned home separately last night from that disastrous Thanksgiving dinner. The sudden news of Grace's pregnancy may have overshadowed his conduct, but it certainly hadn't erased it. Trina could barely stand to look at him and was relieved when he readily agreed to head back to his condo solo while she lingered around to tidy up and wait for Grace.

He was the first to give up hope on salvaging the dinner, but he wasn't the last. Malikah, who was lodging just three floors below in Grace's old loft, was next. She didn't want to leave. She wanted to stay behind with Trina, but after an eventful afternoon of wrestling with each other, the tired boys, whose stomachs were full of turkey and stuffing, were cranky and quarrelsome from exhaustion. "Call me as soon as you know something," she'd instructed Trina as she ushered her yawning, red-eyed sons into the elevator.

Trina promised she would.

Shortly after, Grandpa Mearl and Grandma Doria also decided to call it a night. But not until Trina assured Doria, multiple times, that she didn't mind clearing the table, storing the food, washing the dishes, and wiping down the kitchen. "You're a good friend," she'd said, patting Trina's cheek. "Try to talk some sense into her, would you?" she asked, referring to Grace's attitude toward her unborn child.

"And if that doesn't work, try knocking some into her," Mearl had grumbled, shuffling down the long, marble vestibule.

Lani and Grace's dad were the next to leave. By then, it had been nearly four hours since Mike and Grace had abandoned their own dinner. "If you see her," Anthony had said, wheezing loudly as Ron helped him into his coat, "have her call me. Be sure you let her know that I'm not mad," he'd quickly added. "Just worried."

Trina nodded. "Of course I will."

"Same goes with me and Mike," Lani said, hooking her arm through Anthony's and leading him slowly into the elevator.

"Thanks again for taking him home," Trina said.

"That's what family's for," Lani responded with a wink, just as the doors closed between them.

The last two standing were Ron and Tamara.

"I've got it covered," Trina said, walking into the kitchen where they were silently transferring the food from serving dishes to Tupperware containers. "You guys should probably head out. It's getting late."

"We're almost finished," Tamara said, snapping shut the lid on a bowl of collard greens. "Besides, I still need to load the dirty dishes into the dishwasher."

"Don't worry. I'll take care of it," Trina said.

"She's right," Ron said, rinsing off and drying his hands. "We should go. Come on, I'll take you home."

"But this is my job," Tamara argued, her eyes desperate and pleading. It's the same distressed expression she'd borne since sparking the hostile repartee that had, however indirectly, unearthed Grace's big secret. She'd spent the rest of the evening in penance, catering to everyone's slightest needs.

"Like Grace said, it's a holiday. You're not on the clock." Trina folded her arms, her chin tilted upward, and gazed down her nose at Tamara. "And, as it is, I think you've done more than enough."

Tamara backed away from the counter, her jaw set, miffed, not just by Trina's implication, but by her mere presence. Still, she had sense enough not to respond. She whisked by both Trina and Ron, sweeping her long bangs from her eyes with a stubborn flick of her neck.

"Have a good night," Ron said, gently squeezing Trina's arm. "Call if you need anything."

Trina nodded, knowing she wouldn't, and set to work where Tamara left off, packing up the food and arranging it neatly in Grace and Mike's refrigerator. At one point, she didn't think it would all fit, but with some clever shifting and stacking, she got everything in there and then turned her attention to the dishes.

They were piled high on both sides of the sink and along the counter to the left and to the right. She sighed, slipped on a pair of rubber gloves she'd fished from one of the cabinets, and began scrubbing away at the grease and hardened residue on the silverware and cooking pans before cramming them into the dishwasher.

With the food stored and the sink and counter free of dirty dishes, she turned her attention to the sticky kitchen floor. After a few minutes of searching for and gathering the right cleaning supplies, she wrestled a bucket and a mop from the storage closet next to the pantry, threw her hair up, and began the exhaustive task of mopping the sizeable kitchen.

She was so embroiled in the job that she didn't hear the elevator ding or the door open, nor any approaching footsteps. "Still at it?" Ron asked, his voice jolting Trina, who lurched and dropped the mop handle. "Sorry. I didn't mean to scare you."

"What're you doing here?"

He shrugged, and jammed his fists into his pockets. "Thought you might be able to use some help, but from the looks of it," he said, his eyes sweeping the almost pristine kitchen, "you've got everything under control."

Trina wasn't sure, but she could've sworn she'd heard a ring of disappointment in his voice. "Actually," she said, "my back's killing me, and I haven't even touched the dining room or the living room."

"You want me to finish this up?" he asked, pointing to the mop.

Trina looked down at the half-clean floor. *Yes!* Her throbbing arms seemed to scream. Her mouth, however, went for a less desperate approach. "You sure you don't mind?"

He slipped out of his sports coat and kicked off his shoes before tiptoeing over several wet patches to meet Trina. "I'm sure," he said, taking the handle. Their hands grazed and their gazes lingered just a bit longer than necessary.

Trina was the first to look away. "I'll start the vacuuming," she said, squeezing between him and the island. But just as she made it past, she felt his arm cup her waist and spin her back around.

Before she had time to react, time to think, he lowered his face to hers and kissed her. It was a gentle peck at first, a reacquainting of their lips, of each other's touch. Too stunned to respond, Trina just stood there, at a complete loss. What had suddenly changed?

After all this time chattering her teeth at the icy breeze off Ron's cold shoulder, she'd given up all dreams of reconciling with him. Yet, there she was, in his arms, snugly pressed against his chest. It's a place she'd yearned to be, long after he'd broken up with her and moved on with his life.

Misreading her surprise as rejection, Ron began to pull away. "Sorry," he whispered. "I—"

But before he could continue, Trina leaned in, hooking her hands around his neck and running her fingers affectionately through his soft hair at its base. That time, the kiss was less innocent, less tentative. He tightened his grip around her as she stood on the tips of her toes, stretching to get closer, to be nearer. Their slow kisses grew more intense—not lustful or greedy, but sweetly passionate; a token of their tacit gratefulness to have each other despite the long detour they took to arrive at that simple realization.

"What does this mean?" Trina asked, breathless, once they finally broke apart. "What're we doing?"

Ron closed his eyes and pressed his forehead to hers. "I don't know," he confessed, still gripping her closely. "But this feels right. This is where I'm supposed to be. It just took me a while to get here."

"Where is here?" Trina asked, leaning away so she could study his face.

Slowly, he lifted his lowered gaze to meet hers. "I want to be with you."

As exhilarated as Trina always thought she would be at hearing those words, she was surprised to find herself confused, her emotions conflicted. "It's too late for that," she said, shaking her head and stepping back. "We're both attached to other people."

"I'm not," he said, reaching for her hand. "Not anymore anyway. Tammy and I are over. I ended things tonight when I dropped her off."

"Because of what happened at dinner?"

Ron shrugged. "She just wasn't right for me," he said, clutching Trina even closer. "She's not you."

Trina smiled, despite her acute awareness of being wrapped in the arms of a man who was not her current boyfriend. "And what about Darius?" she asked.

"Same thing; you two aren't right for each other."

"Why, because he's not you?" she teased.

Ron didn't smile. "Yeah," he said with a serious nod. "And because he doesn't love you the way that I do or treat you the way you deserve to be treated. Because he's rude and selfish and manipulative. He's everything you don't need."

"How would you know what I need?" Trina asked, shaking her head and squirming loose from his embrace. "This is the most you've said to me since we broke up."

"I know," he said, the regret in his tone genuine. "I was angry—I still am—and I let it get the best of me."

"What reason could you possibly have to still be angry with me?" she asked. "What happened between me, Grace, and Mike was ages ago, and, truthfully, it never concerned you to begin with."

"This has nothing to do with Mike and Grace," Ron said. "I'm angry with you because I see the path you're headed down and I know you know better."

Trina rolled her eyes and sighed. Like Grace, she wasn't in the mood to hear how far off course she'd allowed herself to veer.

"Don't," Ron said, moving closer. "Don't do that. If I didn't love you, I'd sit back and watch you ruin yourself, but I can't. It's not okay. *You're* not okay. Once upon a time, you were a woman who was on fire for God. Now you're lukewarm. It's in your appearance, the way you dress and carry yourself, the way you speak. You're making a slow descent down a slippery slope, and if you don't resolve to stop, I'm afraid you won't be able to climb out of the pit you find yourself in when you finally wake up.

"I know the way things ended between us was abrupt and painful and that Grace's marriage was hard for you to handle, but that doesn't mean you fold your arms and abandon your relationship with God. You have to stop letting your circumstances dictate your happiness. Decide to trust God, decide to love Him, decide to honor Him, no matter what unexpected blows come your way.

"Each second you stay here, bound by your anger and your stubbornness, is a second wasted separated from Him and His goodness. Doesn't that make you sad?"

"Of course it does," Trina whispered, too ashamed to look up.

"Then tell Him you're sorry, turn around and start walking in the opposite direction." He shrugs. "That's all it takes. Make the decision to reside in His will again and do it."

"It's not that cut and dry," Trina argued, her voice delicate, her eyes brimming with tears.

"But it is," Ron said, softly wiping her cheek with his thumb. "The devil's got you coming and going. He's whispered lies to lead you down a dead-end road and he's whispered more lies to keep you there. But what you have to remember is that the only power he has over you is the power you give him. Just like you chose wrongly to get where you are, you can choose rightly to get back."

Trina didn't reply; she couldn't. She turned her face and licked away the salty tears that had dripped down her lips.

"I know it hurts," Ron said. "The truth does that sometimes, but I need you to get it together—we all do. There's so much you risk losing for good if you don't."

"Including you?" she'd somehow found the nerve to ask.

Ron's only response, before he stepped around her and began wielding the mop across the floor, had been a tender kiss on her forehead, followed by another on her temple.

The high-pitched whistle of the kettle in the kitchen, where Darius is fixing himself breakfast, jerks Trina from her thoughts. She rolls onto her back and touches her mouth. She can still feel the pillowy sensation of Ron's lips pressed lightly against hers.

She'd tossed and turned through the night considering his words. He hadn't said anything she didn't already know, nothing she hadn't tried to tell herself a million times before, but hearing it out loud—simple truth, simply spoken—was like the jolt of electricity she needed to jump-start her idle conscience.

For hours last night, as she listened to Darius snore softly beside her, she assessed her life, truly assessed it, with no excuses or rationalizations. The results were mortifying and startling, but more than anything, they were deeply disappointing. *How did I get here?* She wondered to herself. It was a question she couldn't answer. She still can't. The best she can figure is that the journey was a slow drifting, like falling asleep on a raft and floating ever-so-gradually away from shore. By the time she woke up, there was no land in sight. She was lost, alone, in open waters.

Ron wasn't the first person who tried to call her back.

Grace had tried too, on several occasions, but by then, Trina had allowed the waves to carry her so far out that she couldn't hear her. She sees now that they were both right. All this time she was convinced that she was moving forward when really, nothing's changed. She's still stuck in the same old patterns and routines, still clinging to the same destructive relationship—dusting it off and recycling it every so often and trying to pass it off as newly improved.

Then there's Kendra, Joss, and Tai—the sharks one is destined to bump into once adrift. When she thinks back to some of the places they've been together, the schemes they've planned, the nasty, unprovoked things they've said to one another and about others, her face burns with remorse.

Instantly, she's knocked down by the same persistent thought that plagues her each time she considers just how terrible a person she's become. *God won't forgive me. Why should He, after everything I've done?*

But this time, something unprecedented happens. Ron's voice speaks to her as clear as day. *The only power the devil has over you is the power you give him. Just like you chose wrongly to get where you are, you can choose rightly to get back.*

Trina hears the clank of Darius's dishes hit the sink, followed briefly by the sound of the faucet running. Then, his slow, steady steps travel down the hall toward the bedroom.

She quickly rolls onto her side, her back facing the door, and paces her breathing.

"Trina?" he whispers once he reaches the foot of the bed.

She keeps her eyes closed.

"Hey," he says, jostling her leg. "I know you're not sleeping."

She remains absolutely still.

"Fine," he sighs. "But you can't stay mad at me forever." He walks around to the side of the bed and kneels down.

Trina turns onto her other side, just as she feels the heat of his breath on her cheek when he leans in, like he does every morning, to give her a kiss.

Darius doesn't press the matter further. "Okay. I have to head into the office for a few hours to put the finishing touches on a presentation for Monday. I'll give you a call a little later," he says, standing.

Trina doesn't care, nor does she believe him. It's the day after Thanksgiving. His office, like everyone else's, is closed. Who puts on a suit and tie to sit behind a computer, alone, in a deserted office? She wants to ask—to challenge him, once and for all, on the countless aspects of his life that don't add up. Instead, she listens to him collect his cell phone and wallet from the top of the dresser.

She remains motionless, her eyes pressed shut, until she hears the front door open and close and his key lock it behind him.

Then, she sits up, propping her pillow against the lacquer headboard behind her, switches on the pole lamp beside her bed, and for the first time in nearly a year, reaches for the Bible resting on her nightstand.

37

The shrill ring of the telephone rips Grace from her sleep. She fumbles over the arm of the couch and dives for the cordless on the coffee table. "Mike?" she calls, holding her breath, every part of her hoping that the next thing she will hear is the sound of her husband's voice on the other end.

"No, it's Tammy."

"Oh." Grace's shoulders slump. She lowers her face into her hands and sighs. "Hi."

"How are you?"

"I've been better," Grace says, propping her back against the base of the couch. "Did you need something?"

"No, but I thought *you* might," Tamara says. "Do you want me to come in today? I could swing by Einstein's on my way in and grab you breakfast—a bagel and a carton of chocolate milk?"

"Thanks, but no," Grace says. "Why don't you just take the day off like we discussed?"

"Because I feel horrible and I want to help," Tamara confesses. "Please, Grace, let me do something—anything. I can't tell you how sorry I am. I know you must be livid with me. Who could blame you? But, I can fix this," she says. "I swear, just give me a chance."

"I'm not mad at you," Grace says tiredly. "I wish I could blame you, but I can't. Yesterday was my fault. If I had been up front with Mike from the very beginning, none of this would've ever happened."

"What *did* happen?" Tamara asks, her voice small, her tone curious.

"He left," Grace says, taking a deep breath. "He packed his things and he left."

"Oh, Grace," she gasps. "I'm so sorry."

Something about Tamara's aghast surprise strikes Grace as disingenuous, but she's too frazzled to care.

"I'm sure it's only temporary," Tamara soothes.

"Let's hope," Grace says. She looks down at the wrinkled shirt covering her body and behind her at the equally wrinkled comforter draped over the couch. She'd yanked it off of their mattress last night and dragged it all the way down the hall.

Lying in their room, on the same bed they'd slept together in—held each other in—was unbearable. When Mike was with *Life Sketch* and he used to go on extended business trips, his scent, which always seems to be embedded in the sheets and pillowcases, was a comforting reminder of him. She would burrow deep beneath the covers, hold his pillow close, and take solace in knowing he'd be back soon.

Last night, she couldn't do that. She kept wondering what would happen, if with this one betrayal, she had pushed him too far, had disregarded him and his feelings in a way he could not forgive or overlook? What if this time, he wasn't coming back? What would she do when his scent faded, when everything that represented him and their union was gone? How would she go on?

Those thoughts inevitably set off a steady stream of tears that flowed into the early morning hours without ceasing. Finally, exhausted, but still unable to break free from the haunting barrage of unsettling worst-case scenarios surrounding her marriage, she had abandoned their bedroom for the couch, where she curled up with the phone.

That's when she noticed the blinking light on the handset.

With twitching fingers, Grace dialed voice mail to discover Mike's message waiting for her:

"I want you to know that I love you," were his first words. "That's just about the only thing I'm sure of. The question for me is: when does that stop mattering? Before today, I would've said never. But before today, I didn't know I was a father. I can't make you keep the baby any more than I can make myself stay if you don't. It's not an ultimatum, Grace. It's not a condition of my love. It's just… There are limits to what I can take. We all have them and this is it for me.

"I know we promised to always come back home, no matter how major the fight. I'm hoping, with everything in me, to hold true to that pact. But for right now, I need to be away from you. Pray for us." The request came out as a whisper. "I'll call you soon."

She must've played his message a dozen times, dissecting every sentence, in search of a hidden meaning—anything more positive, more definitive than what he'd left her to ponder.

"Where did he go?" Tamara asks, pulling Grace from her thoughts.

Grace shakes her head, switching the phone from her left ear to her right. "I don't know, probably a hotel—somewhere quiet where he can be by himself."

"Are you sure you don't want me to come in today?" Tamara asks. "Some company might do you good."

"I'm sure," Grace says. "I'll be fine."

Tamara sighs. "Well, you know the number if you change your mind."

"Yeah," Grace says. "I do. Thanks."

She hangs up, climbs back onto the couch, and pulls the comforter to her chin. Closing her heavy eyelids, she tries to still her mind enough to fall back asleep, but she can't. It's truly a wonder that she'd ever drifted off in the first place.

She stares around the sun-drenched living room. Mike's art stares back at her from every wall. The familiar lump of panic and loss clogs her throat. She looks down at the phone cradled in her hands and wills it to ring. Shockingly it does.

Grace sits up, her adrenaline soaring and her emotions running high just as they had minutes earlier when Tamara called. She fights to maintain her composure as she presses the *Talk* button. "Hello."

"It's me," her dad's voice filters through the receiver. "I'm glad I caught you."

Grace's chin tremors, her hopes dashed. "Where else would I be?" she asks.

"Hiding out," he says.

Grace smiles, despite the painful tightness that seems to have taken up permanent residence in her chest and stomach. "Could you blame me?" she asks.

"You're stronger than that," he says. "You're a solver, not a runner."

"Couldn't tell it from last night," she says.

He chuckles. "That was a Thanksgiving for the books, huh?"

"I'm sorry, Dad," she says, her voice thick. "Everyone went through so much trouble to make that dinner special, and I ruined it."

"Just being with all of you together again was special," he says. "Dinners will come and go. I'm more concerned about you and Mike. How are you two doing?"

"I'm not sure," she says softly. "Turns out, this time, Mike was more of a runner than a solver."

"You know he'll be back," her dad says, his voice gentle, his words possessing a certainty she's been searching for since she'd discovered Mike's things missing.

"I just wish he'd call, you know? I just want to talk to him."

"What would you say?"

"I'd tell him I'm sorry," she answers tearfully. "That I love him and I need him."

"What else?"

"What else matters?" Grace asks.

"The baby, Honey," he says softly. "The baby is what matters most."

"Not to me," she says. "Not right now."

"Then you aren't really ready to talk to him."

Grace sighs, frustrated by her father's words, even though deep down she knows they're true. He remains silent and allows her time to process her thoughts.

"You were kind of quiet yesterday when all of this was unfolding," she finally says. "I know everyone's opinion except yours."

"Are you asking because you really want to know or because you're hoping to find someone on your side?"

"A little bit of both, I think."

He sighs. "Then you're going to be disappointed in what I have to say."

Grace shrugs. "I'm still listening."

"I can't imagine my life without you," he says. "That's the long and the short of it. Your mother and I weren't the world's most qualified parents—far from it. We made plenty of mistakes, but you weren't one of them. I look at you now and I'm so proud to call you mine. You are the one thing I got right—my only worthwhile contribution.

"I've adored you since the very first second of your life and I'll keep on adoring you until the very last second of mine. There's no other joy, no other fulfillment, quite like being a parent. Is it terrifying? Yes. Will you screw up? Tons. But it's worth it. *You* were worth it and so is your child."

"But Dad, what if I'm not strong enough? What if this baby needs more than what I'm capable of giving?"

"The Lord is your strength," he says. "And I guarantee you that He's got an abundant supply of everything you lack."

Grace smiles. "What I wouldn't give for a couple of extra helpings of your faith."

"It only takes a mustard seed's worth to move mountains," he says, his smile audible. "We're only asking you to give birth."

Grace laughs. It's the lightest she's felt since yesterday. "I want to want this baby," she says, the confession hushed, but real.

"Good," he says. "As long as you're willing to want what's right, the Lord is willing and able to make it happen."

38

"Have you seen it?"

"Seen what?" Trina asks, turning down the praise music she's been blaring throughout the condo for most of the morning.

"Today's paper," Kendra says. Her words are quick and choppy. If Trina didn't know Kendra as a woman immune to panic, she'd be alarmed at the fact that Kendra sounds dangerously close to hyperventilating.

"I'm still in my PJs," Trina says, astride one of the kitchen stools. "Why, what's going on? Neiman Marcus having a huge Day After Thanksgiving sale?" she teases.

"Rebecca Schmidt is missing," Kendra says.

It's Trina's turn to hyperventilate. "What do you mean 'missing'?" she asks, holding on to the counter to keep from tipping over.

"Gone, disappeared, vanished," Kendra says. "The housekeeper claims she dropped her off at school on Wednesday. Nobody has seen Rebecca or heard from her since."

"You think she ran away?" Trina asks, caught off guard by the whirling room and sudden lack of air.

"She's six!" Kendra hisses. "What do you think she did, packed up her Barbie and flagged a taxi to the airport?"

"You don't think…" Trina gulps at the unspeakable notion. "You don't think Councilman Schmidt hurt her, do you?"

"That's exactly what I think," Kendra says. "And from the swarm of squad cars parked on the lawn outside of his mansion, so do the police."

"How do you know all of this?" Trina asks.

"Unlike you, I don't live in a bubble," she says. "Turn on your television and join us in the real world."

Trina dashes to the living room and snatches the remote control from the coffee table.

"Channel 5," Kendra says.

Kendra isn't lying. There are, literally, a half dozen police cars stationed haphazardly on the councilman's precisely manicured lawn. There are also just as many news trucks with microphone-toting reporters sporting press passes around their necks and cameramen waiting on tenterhooks to shoot the first moving thing that emerges from the house's tightly guarded front doors.

The Channel 5 reporter, a diminutive brunette with slight shoulders and a somber expression, is standing at the end of the taped-off driveway, the sprawling estate's four-car garage several yards behind her.

In a monotone newscaster's voice, she informs the public that while no arrests have been made, the councilman has become the lead suspect in the disappearance of his six-year-old daughter.

She runs down a brief history of the councilman's spotted past and his long list of current legal woes, including his condemned day care centers and embezzlement charges. She only briefly makes mention of Becky, who she sterilely refers to as, "the child," and her record of emergency room visits (which is far less extensive, thanks to Trina's tampering), as well as her stint in foster care and the possibly criminal circumstances surrounding her release.

It isn't until Home Sweet Home is mentioned specifically and the screen cuts to a shot of Quinn behind a podium in front of flashing cameras and shouting reporters jockeying to ask the next question that Trina's heart nearly stops.

"I am unable to answer that at this time," is Quinn's pat response, her cool-as-a-cucumber façade perfectly intact. "But I assure you we are working hand-in-hand with the Memphis police and we will get to the bottom of this."

The screen returns to the diminutive reporter. "It's been nearly forty-eight hours since anyone has seen the little girl," she says. "But police, who have promised to leave no stone unturned, are hopeful that she is still alive."

"What have we done?" Trina asks, sinking into the couch, her body numb.

"Don't uncork the melodrama yet," Kendra squeaks, her attempt at stoic pragmatism a failed one. "Nobody knows for sure what happened. It's all speculation right now. She could be fine."

"Kendra, she's a child," Trina snaps. "A small one, and she's been missing for two days. She is *not* fine. What if she's dead?" Trina asks, shaking her head at the ceiling. "What if he killed her? We're the ones who sent her back."

"Okay, you have to stop," Kendra says, her voice forceful. "What did I tell you from the very beginning? We didn't do anything, but our jobs."

"We could go to jail for this," Trina says, too lost in a paralyzing malaise of consternation and remorse to listen to Kendra's words much less give them credence. "We deserve to go to jail."

"No, we don't," she says. "Whoever harmed her, if she's even harmed, deserves to go to jail."

"Don't you get it?" Trina shouts. "If someone harmed her, it's because we made it possible. We had a responsibility to protect her and, instead, we traded her for new cars and corner offices—just swapped her like a baseball card."

"I don't like what I'm hearing from you," Kendra says, her tone abruptly keen and alert—suspicious.

"I'm past caring what you like and don't like," Trina says.

"We were faced with an opportunity and we took it. We made the decision together, we followed through on it together, and we can weather this storm, but only if we stick together."

"A child is missing. She may very well be dead," Trina says. "Why is it so hard for you to understand that this isn't about us anymore?"

"Because it *is* about us," Kendra says. "We are knee-deep in a pile of you-know-what, and if you don't stop crying over your shoes and pick up a shovel, we *just might* end up sharing a cell with Councilman Schmidt."

Trina groans and closes her eyes. "I think I'm going to be sick."

"Just take some deep breaths," Kendra says. "We're going to be fine."

"You don't know that."

"Yes, I do. We didn't turn Becky loose off the cuff, remember? We were smart about it—organized and planned. Her master file is destroyed, and her case file is clean. There's nothing linking us to any of this. Like Quinn said, as far as the public is concerned, the councilman is the bad guy here, not us."

"Wait, you talked to Quinn? When?"

"This morning. She's confident this will blow over within a matter of weeks. In the meantime, we just have to stay calm, lay low, and maintain a united front."

"And how, exactly, are we supposed to do that?" Trina asks.

"Well, that's why I called," Kendra says. "Quinn wants us to meet her tonight at Houston's."

"For what?"

"So we can talk strategy," Kendra says. "Make sure our stories match and that they're airtight. You know, for police questioning."

"Why would the police question us if they don't suspect us?"

"Quinn says they plan to question all of the directors. It's just procedure."

"Dear God," Trina moans, doubling over, her mouth harboring the faint taste of bile. "We're going to prison and, after that, straight to hell."

"From what I hear, there's not that much of a difference," Kendra says. "Which is why you're going to be at Houston's tonight at seven o'clock sharp. Clear?"

The last time Trina answered, "Clear," to Kendra and Quinn was that day in Quinn's office when she first got enlisted into this whole debacle with Rebecca and William Schmidt. What she should have said was, "No! Never! Fire me, if you want. I don't care!" But she didn't.

Out of cowardice, she made the wrong decision. And to her everlasting shame, she does it again.

"Clear."

39

"Tammy," Mike says, swinging open the door to his hotel room. "What're you doing here?"

"Checking up on you. I thought, after everything that happened yesterday, you might be able to use a friend."

His brows furrow. "How did you find me?" he asks.

She smiles. "Where there's a will, there's a way."

Mike crosses his arms, his head tipped curiously to the side, and narrows his gaze.

Tamara shrugs. "Okay, I confess. I spent all morning thumbing through the phone book, calling every hotel within a fifty-mile radius, and asking if they had a guest by the name of Michael Cambridge. Let me tell you, it wasn't easy." She peeks up at him from beneath her long lashes. "But it was worth it."

"Look, I appreciate the effort and your concern, but I came here because I needed to get away and think—alone."

"Wow," she says, her eyes sprung wide, her mouth turned down into an impressed frown. "Grace had you pegged."

Mike uncrosses his arms and clears his throat. "You spoke to Grace?" he asks, shoving his hands into his back pockets.

Tamara nods. "First thing this morning."

"Well, how…you know, how is she?"

"Great," Tamara says. "She actually sounded relieved—said she was kind of grateful for the breathing room. May I?" she asks, stepping around Mike and into the room before he has the chance to object.

"What do you mean, 'relieved'?" Mike asks, following Tamara into the sunny sitting area.

"She's happy that the big secret's finally out. I mean, don't get me wrong, she feels terrible that you left, but on the other hand, now she can stop living a lie."

"She said that?" Mike asks, his forehead puckered with hurt disbelief.

Tamara shrugs. "Give or take a few words. So...," she sighs and lowers herself slowly onto the couch, "how are you holding up?" She crosses her legs and the split in her coat falls open, revealing a generous view of her bare upper thigh. She makes no move to cover herself.

"Okay, I guess," Mike murmurs, too sidetracked by news of Grace's cavalier attitude to bother looking down at Tamara's exposed skin.

"You don't seem okay," Tamara says, her voice the perfect pitch of sympathy and perceptive insightfulness.

"I don't know what I am," Mike admits. "Part of me pities her. First she lost her mom and now she's losing her dad. It's no wonder she's terrified of becoming a parent and starting a family. That part of me wants to rush home, pull her close, and promise her that whatever it takes, we're going to work it out—together. But then there's the other part of me—an equally big part— that is just enraged." He shakes his head. "How selfish can she be? I always knew Grace tended to be a little more self-involved than the average person, but this takes the cake.

"I've given her everything," he says, pacing the small space of the front room. "When there's an argument, I'm the one who concedes; when there's a fight, I'm the one who apologizes even when I haven't done anything wrong. If I quibbled or dug my heels in half as much as she does, our marriage would've been over before it began—and now this?" he asks, his volume rising as his timbre grows heated.

"How am I supposed to react? I have a right to be upset. Don't I? Where does she get off hiding something like this from me? Deciding to have an abortion; this is our kid, for crying out loud!"

Tamara nods, her face cloaked with an expression of compassion and mutual outrage. "You're right," she says. "One hundred percent right."

Mike's sigh is long and tired. "I'm sorry. I shouldn't be talking about this with you."

"Why not?" Tamara asks. "We're friends, aren't we?"

Mike smiles appreciatively, but shakes his head. "You're my best friend's girlfriend and my wife's assistant."

"Correction," Tamara says, standing and gliding gracefully over to Mike. "I'm your wife's assistant and your best friend's ex-girlfriend."

"What?" Mike asks, both disappointed and surprised. "Since when?"

"Last night," Tamara says.

"Tammy, I'm really sorry. For what it's worth, I thought you guys were great together."

"We weren't," she says, unbuckling her coat's matching belt and working her fingers down its long row of buttons. "Sometimes opposites are a little bit too opposite to attract. Kind of like you and Grace."

"Me and Grace?" Mike smirks. "If anything, we're too much alike."

"Tomatoes, to-*mah*-toes," Tamara sings. "The point is, you can do better. We both can." In one swift motion, she opens her coat and lets it slide to the floor. She's left posing in a miniature lace negligee barely long enough to cover her essentials.

"What do you think you're doing?" Mike asks, his gaze involuntarily falling to her cleavage. He blinks, flabbergasted, at the sight of her near-nakedness, before closing his eyes and looking away.

"Everything happens for a reason, Mike," Tamara says. "Me and Ron; you and Grace—ending things on the exact same night. It's not a coincidence. It's fate."

"Tammy," Mike says, his eyes still closed. "I want you to get out." Stumbling away from the sound of her voice, he trips over the coffee table and plunges onto the sofa. "Now."

"It's okay," she whispers, inching closer. "I know you're shy and principled. Those are the things I've grown to love about you."

"Whoa—love?" Mike scoffs. "Tamara, I'm married."

"To a woman who will never appreciate you. You said it yourself. Grace is selfish. She can't help it. So why fret over someone you can't change when you've got someone else, who's better for you, ready to take her place?"

"Could you just…" Mike combs his fingers through his dreads, his face still turned away. "Could you just put your coat back on? Please."

"Why? Don't you like what you see?"

"Tamara, I'm serious. You want to talk, we can talk, but not until you put some clothes on." He's relieved to hear the jangle of her belt buckle as she slips back into her coat and fastens it.

"All clear," she says.

Mike reluctantly pries one eye open. "Thank you," he pants. "Now, get out."

"You said we could talk," Tamara argues.

"Talk about what?" Mike exclaims.

"About us."

"There *is* no us," he says.

"But there should be," Tamara bleats, her tone sincere. "You'd realize that if you'd only be honest with yourself and accept that you married the wrong woman. It's nothing to be ashamed of. Grace is great in her own way, but she doesn't fit you the way I do."

Mike clasps his hands behind the back of his head and presses his eyes shut, as if pretending she's gone will make her disappear.

"It's new and unpredictable and scary," Tamara says. "But it's real and I know you feel it too."

"Tammy, the only thing scaring me right now is you."

"I see the way you look at me, Mike; the way you smile and admire; the way you laugh and tease."

"It's called being nice," Mike says.

"You honestly expect me to believe that you aren't attracted to me—that you aren't even the least bit curious about where you and I could lead."

"Yes!" Mike says. "That's exactly what I expect you to believe because that's exactly what I'm telling you. I love my wife. I fell in love with her from the instant I laid eyes on her. She was a complete stranger then, but I still knew she was The One. And there hasn't been a day—an hour—that has gone by since, that I haven't thought about her, smiled just envisioning her face.

"Grace may be neurotic. God knows she can be stubborn and selfish and vindictive and snide. Some days, she's downright mean, but she's my heart."

"I don't doubt any of that," Tamara says. "I'm just offering you the opportunity to be with someone who feels the same way about you."

"Grace feels the same way, trust me."

Tamara rolls her eyes. "Not from what I heard this morning."

"Like I would believe anything you had to say now," Mike says, his tone dry, his expression doubtful. "You want to talk about someone being selfish, you should take a look at yourself. Grace has nothing on you."

"What could be worse than the fiasco she created?" Tamara asks.

Mike folds his arms. "Taking advantage of the fiasco she created."

Tamara opens her mouth to retort, but quickly closes it.

"We invited you into our home and into our lives without question. We trusted you, relied on you, believed in you, and this whole time you had an ulterior motive."

"I didn't ha—"

"And then," Mike cuts her off, "when both of us are confused and suffering, you had the gall to hunt me down behind Grace's back, come over here like a cheap hooker in your underwear, and try to seduce me."

Tamara's jaw drops, her eyelids blinking rapidly, nervous and baffled by how quickly her seemingly clever plan is deteriorating right before her.

"Do I strike you as the kind of man who messes with cheap hookers?" he asks frostily.

"Obviously, I misread the signals." Her quiet words are accompanied by a weak shrug.

"No," Mike says. "You imagined them."

"I thought…" She bites the inside of her cheek and looks away. "I don't know what I thought."

"Remember how I mentioned that Grace can be a little vindictive—a little mean? That's not good for you," he says. "If she or Trina or Malikah ever found out about this, the outcome wouldn't be pleasant."

Tamara swallows hard and sets her chin, determined not to appear intimidated.

"That's why," Mike says, his nod slow, "I'm going to do you a favor and pretend this never happened. Now," he points to the door, "you have one more chance to leave this hotel room with no harm done, and I strongly suggest you take it."

Tamara runs her hands along the front of her coat and smoothes out the nonexistent wrinkles. She turns for the door and takes a few steps forward before turning around again and facing Mike.

Her mouth opens, but no sound comes out. She casts her teary eyes to the ceiling, licks her lips, and then tries again, but still, words escape her.

"Just get out," Mike orders.

And to his great relief and satisfaction, she does.

40

Houston's is crowded considering it's the day after Thanksgiving and most people Trina knows are holed up in their houses gorging on leftover mac-and-cheese and cold turkey sandwiches.

The hostess, a spry redhead with large, white teeth that set off a glow bright enough to direct airplane traffic, leads Trina to a booth in a secluded area of the restaurant where Quinn is already through her first bottle of Pellegrino.

"Trina!" she cries, throwing her head back, a warm, showy smile gracing her lips. "Glad you could make it."

As if I had a choice, Trina thinks, returning Quinn's stiff hug. "Where's Kendra?" she asks. "She said seven sharp. It's not like her to be late."

"She'll be here," Quinn says. "I asked her to give you and me a few extra minutes to ourselves."

"Oh?" Trina asks, swallowing nervously, her flight reflex kicking into hyper-drive.

"Can I get you something to drink while you wait for the rest of your party to arrive?" the hostess asks.

Trina shakes her head. "No," she answers distractedly.

"She'll have a Pellegrino," Quinn says with a wink. She taps the green bottle in front of her. "And I'll have another also."

The hostess nods and bows into the shadows.

"Extra time to ourselves," Trina says, forcing a laugh. "I don't know whether to be scared or flattered."

"Neither," Quinn says. She studies Trina's face for a brief yet nerve-wracking moment before continuing. "Kendra seems to think you're cracking under the pressure of this investigation into Rebecca Schmidt's disappearance."

Trina scoffs, a semi-smooth attempt to discredit the allegation. In her mind she's imagining how wonderful Kendra's neck would feel between her hands right now. "What pressure?" she asks. "I just found out about it this morning."

"She says you were hysterical, that you kept going on and on about being sent to prison."

"I—um, I don't think those were, you know... I didn't—those weren't my exact words," Trina stutters. She shrugs. "It was a knee-jerk reaction, if anything."

"You're not a very good liar," Quinn says, leaning against the high, buttoned back of the leather booth. "Before this predicament I found that quality amusing—maybe even a little endearing—but now, it's dangerous."

"Dangerous," Trina echoes.

Quinn nods. "And when you're a danger to yourself, you're a danger to me."

Trina blinks, at a loss. Bottom line, she's being threatened and she doesn't like it. "What do you want me to do?"

"Monday morning, Detective Fontaine is going to come by your office and ask you a few simple questions: Have you ever had any personal contact with Rebecca Schmidt? Have you ever met Councilman William Schmidt? Where were you on Wednesday between 11 a.m. and 3 p.m.? How long have you been a director at Home Sweet Home? When were you promoted from case manager? Do you have any idea how Rebecca's master file disappeared or where it could be? Things along those lines.

"We're going to make sure you have logical, believable explanations to all of those questions, and anything he asks you that we haven't rehearsed, you're going to simply answer: 'I don't know.'"

Trina exhales slowly, siphoning strength from her incredibly depleted reserve of courage. "Don't you think this has all gone too far?" she asks.

Quinn's arched brow and clamped jaw are not good signs. "Sorry?"

"It's just, ultimately, the reason why we returned Rebecca to her father was to help him get re-elected so that Home Sweet Home could continue to benefit from his support. But that's never going to happen now. She's missing and he's the prime suspect." She shrugs. "It's over. Shouldn't we do everything we can to help the police find Rebecca? That way, at least, someone has a happy ending."

"Happy endings are for fairy tales," Quinn says, her lofty demeanor shooting a chill down Trina's spine. "The simple truth is that a happy ending for Rebecca Schmidt means a very bad ending for the rest of us." She leans forward, folding her hands on top of the lacquered wood tabletop. "And I'm just not willing to make that kind of trade. Are you?"

"No," Trina mumbles, looking away.

Quinn gives a curt, satisfied nod. "I didn't think so."

"Am I interrupting?" Kendra asks, strolling slowly up to the dimly lit booth.

Quinn flashes her infamous plastic smile. "Not at all," she says, standing and engaging Kendra in a round of air kisses. "In fact, you're just in time. Trina and I chatted and we're all on the same page."

"Great," Kendra says, removing her leather gloves and carefully slipping out of her tiered Burberry coat. The $1600 herringbone tweed trench is one of many extravagant gifts she's awarded herself since their promotion.

She hands it to the hostess, who takes her order for a Sangria and assures Quinn that the Pellegrinos will be out shortly.

"So I did some digging," Kendra says, leaning forward, her voice hushed conspiratorially. "Police found a blood-splattered tennis shoe thrown behind an old generator in the councilman's garage during their search this morning. They're expected to issue a warrant for his arrest any hour now."

Quinn gazes off into the distance, considering this new piece of information. "Where are they on Rebecca?" she asks after a few moments of thought.

Kendra shakes her head and shrugs simultaneously. "Completely stumped. Last thing I heard, they were digging up his backyard."

"You mean…" Trina grips her chest. "Looking for a body?"

Neither one of them answers her.

"How did the interrogation with Detective Fontaine go?" Quinn asks Kendra.

Kendra smiles. "Smooth as ice. He only asked a few questions—the exact same ones you said he would. Then he gave me his card and left."

"So no glitches?" Quinn double-checks. "Not tension? No suspicious looks? No suspect behavior?"

Kendra shakes her head. "He was actually really nice." She smirks. "And kind of cute, in that unshaven, rugged, wannabe-superhero kind of way. Under different circumstances, I might've asked him out."

Quinn chuckles. "Keep that card then. You never know. After this is over, he just might need someone to help him release all of that pent-up police frustration."

Trina sits frozen, not wanting to believe what her ears are hearing. The police are no longer looking for Becky; they're looking for her body. That means not even Memphis's finest believe she's alive. And Quinn and Kendra are cracking sex jokes about the lead detective.

"Here we go," their waiter intones, sidling to their table, tray in hand. "Two Pellegrinos and a Sangria. I'll give you ladies a few more minutes to look over your menus," he says.

They fall silent as they sip their drinks; Quinn and Kendra scanning the specials, Trina incapacitated by dread, fear, and guilt.

The rest of the evening is a blur to her. She nibbled on her steak to be polite and to deflect Quinn's probing gazes. She laughed and nodded when it was apropos. She pretended to listen intently to their coaching, even parroting them when she was told.

She ordered dessert, stirred her coffee, and waited with them for valet to bring their cars.

And when she got home, she walked straight to the bathroom and threw up.

41

"Is this seat taken?" Trina asks.

Grace looks up, an instant smile spreading across her face. "Only if you hate me," she says.

"Well, in that case..." Trina grins and sits down.

"I'm sorry," they both blurt.

Grace laughs, gripping Trina's hand and pulling it into her lap. "What're you sorry for? I'm the one who said those horrible things."

"You're right. They were horrible." Trina nods. "But they were also true."

"Not everything," Grace says.

"No, every word was pretty much right on. But I'm glad you said them— even if you were being evil," she teases with a nudge of her elbow. "It was a wake-up call."

"You're the only one who feels that way," she says. "Malikah's not talking to me."

"Did you try to apologize?"

"I couldn't," she says. "By the time I went downstairs this morning, she'd already packed up the boys and left."

"She just needs time to simmer down. She's a hothead, but we both know she loves you almost as much as I do."

Grace exhales loudly and slouches in her seat. "I really screwed up," she says, gazing at the intricate woodwork of the church's cathedral ceiling and the massive, majestic chandeliers hanging overhead.

"There's a lot of that happening lately," Trina says.

Grace's eyes travel from the ceiling to Trina, her brows slanted inquisitively. "Spill."

Trina shakes her head. "It's nothing," she says with an unconvincing shrug. "I just got myself into a situation at work and...," she sighs, "it's spiraling out of control."

"What're you going to do?" Grace asks.

"I think I might quit," Trina confesses, her eyes glued to her lap. "The only thing is, even if I leave, the damage is already done. There are just some things you don't get second chances on."

"Sad, isn't it?" Grace asks.

They sit in reflective silence for several minutes. "Remember in junior high, we went through that phase where we were obsessed with jumping rope?"

Trina laughs. "We bugged your mom until she finally broke down and bought us a matching pair of Razzle Dazzle ones—with the pink handles."

"We'd spend hours out back, counting skips and seeing who could go the longest or make up the trickiest routine, and whenever one of us would mess up we'd shout. 'Do over! Do over!'"

Trina nods. "I remember."

"I'd give anything for a 'do over,'" Grace says wistfully.

"Me too," Trina says, entwining her fingers with Grace's.

"You think they exist in real life—for grown-ups with real problems?"

Trina shrugs. "I don't know. But we've come to the right place to ask."

The pianist pounds the first few chords to "I'm Glad to Be in the Service," and the congregation rises as the choir processes to the beat down the side aisles like they do every Sunday morning.

Grace and Trina clap side by side. It's been almost a year since they've stood next to each other in church and raised their voices together. The occasion would've been joyous were both their hearts not burdened with such immense heaviness.

Trina cannot erase the image she'd seen late last night on the news. Earlier that afternoon, police had gotten a tip that Rebecca's body had been dismembered and dumped in a certain stretch of the Mississippi River. The search immediately gravitated from the councilman's backyard to Mud Island, just blocks away from Grace and Mike's loft.

Dozens of police led by trained canines combed the brush and debris lining the river's edge with flashlights while rescue boats with search divers scoured the muddy waters.

Trina's chest contracted and her breathing became labored each time she stopped to consider what horrible circumstances must've surrounded Rebecca's murder. Had the councilman beaten her to death? From her hospital records, that seemed to be his M.O. Had he strangled her? Drowned her? Shot her and then tried to cover up the evidence by disposing of it at the bottom of the Mississippi?

At six years old, Becky had no way of fighting, of protecting herself against the violent temper of a fully grown man. Had anyone heard her cries—her screams for help?

Trina had. She'd heard Becky through her drawings, through her hospital records and her case file. She'd heard her pleas, perhaps, the loudest of all and she'd done nothing.

The reality of it made Trina sick. If her regret could be measured—if it could be contained—it would spill from every window, every door, every vent of every building and house in every neighborhood on every street in every city. It would continue to pour from her long after it covered every inch of the earth and it overtook the globe. But what good does that do Rebecca?

The only thing truer than the extremity of Trina's regret is the uselessness of it. And that irreversible fact vexes her without abatement.

Meanwhile, Grace is lost in thoughts of Mike. He still hasn't called. She'd assumed that was because he'd planned on seeing her at church. She barely slept last night, tossing and turning alone in a bed meant for two.

The church parking lot was nearly empty when she pulled through the gates nearly an hour and a half before the first service was scheduled to begin. Mike never missed church. He lived for Sunday morning worship and he wouldn't let a tiff with her, no matter how angering, keep him away.

She sat in an aisle seat near the back and watched the choir rehearse and the white-gloved ushers prepare. She wanted to be able to spot him when he entered, to rush over to him, fling her arms around his neck no matter how hard he resisted, and apologize profusely and shamelessly.

But as the crowd filed in and the seats around her began to fill up, a sinking sensation settled in her stomach. He wasn't coming, which told her a lot of things, but mostly it told her that the situation was far worse than she'd realized or wanted to believe.

Grace and Trina cruise through the first part of the service's program on auto-pilot, mindlessly reciting the Statement of Faith, half-heartedly clapping through the choir's praise selections, and mechanically dropping their tithes into the basket when it passes down their row.

The soloist, who'd serenaded the collection with a beautiful rendition of "His Eye Is on the Sparrow," smiles graciously at the audience's applause and bows before exiting stage left.

Knowingly, Grace and Trina retrieve their Bibles from underneath their chairs and wait for the bishop to take his place before them.

"My message this morning will be brief," the bishop begins, gripping both sides of the podium and leaning in to the microphone attached to its base. "It's taken from two passages in Luke."

The wispy symphony of hundreds of turning Bible pages echoes throughout the mega-sanctuary.

He gives them the specific chapters and verses and then waits patiently for the ruffling to cease before he proceeds.

"'No servant can serve two masters,'" his authoritative voice booms. "'For either he will hate the one and love the other, or else he will be loyal to the one and despise the other. You *cannot*...,'" he pauses and sweeps the attentive congregation with his piercing gaze. "'Serve both God and mammon.'

"Now, flip with me to the second passage, if you will," he says.

They all do.

"'Do not worry about your life, what you will eat; nor about the body, what you will put on. Consider the ravens…God feeds them. Of how much more value are you than the birds? Your Father knows you need these things. Seek first the Kingdom of God, and they shall be added to you.

"'Provide yourselves money bags which do not grow old, a treasure in the heavens that does not fail, where no thief approaches and no moth destroys. For where your treasure is, there your heart will be also.'" He looks up. "This is the Word of the Lord."

"Amen," the congregation responds in unison.

"The title of my message is, 'God or Mammon: Where Is Your Treasure?'"

His poignant topic is punctuated by several rapt grunts from random members in the crowd.

Trina's palms leak sweat and Grace's heart thumps loudly, the theme of the message hitting close to home for both of them. They sit motionless and listen to his words, knowing that he's delivering his sermon to the hundreds of people present, but feeling as though he's only speaking to them.

He begins by explaining how mammon represents more than just money. "It's that new car you've wanted for some time now. It's that promotion you've been gunning for, the career you've been coveting, the lifestyle you've always had to have. The definition of mammon differs from individual to individual," he says. "For one person, it's a three-story house, and for another, it's the number of zeros tacked on to the end of his paycheck. Mammon can be any physical possession or earthly want.

"Does that mean we're not to have desires? That we're not to have goals and ambitions? No!" his strong voice resonates throughout the large, open space. "Of course not, but there can be only one God of our lives. The instant," the word comes out as a hiss, "that physical possessions or earthly desire begins to challenge or compete with your relationship with Christ," he throws up his hands, "you're trying to serve God and mammon, my friend."

Trina shifts uncomfortably in her chair, crossing her legs and then her arms, too convicted to even follow along when the bishop rereads the passage.

"The Bible tells us that we are not equipped to serve two masters. We are incapable—unable. It is utterly impossible. Why? Because we will, literally, start to despise, hate, detest one master and love the other. We will eventually have to choose to whom we will be loyal, to whom we will devote our service entirely."

Trina instantly thinks of her promotion. She stares ahead, her burdened mind wandering from the sermon as she ponders the complete accuracy of what the bishop has already said.

All of the perks—the salary hike, the secretary, the car, the office—they all seemed so lovely at first, so shiny and new and exciting. But she really does hate them now, knowing how they were acquired—at what cost and at whose sacrifice.

She could hardly bear to climb into her Audi this morning as it sat waiting in front of Darius's building, beaming up at her in all of its brilliance. The new-car scent she'd gushed over mere weeks earlier made her stomach flip. If she hadn't been absolutely desperate to spend time in the Lord's house today, she would've left the car where it was parked.

"The wonderful thing about the true Master," the bishop continues, "is that He promises to supply all of our needs and desires according to His will. Don't fret over your next meal, He says. Don't think about where your next change of clothes is coming from—as a matter of fact, don't worry about your life. I've got it covered."

The bishop paces the length of the stage, his hands clasped behind his back. "Do you know what kind of stupid choices we make—what boneheaded predicaments we get ourselves into—when we operate in a faithless spirit of worry?" He shakes his head. "If we'd only learn to be still and know that He is God."

"Tell the truth, Bishop!" someone down front shouts.

It's Grace's turn to squirm. She too shifts uneasily in her seat, feeling awkward and exposed. The bishop continues, the bulk and thrust of his message lying in his following points and sub-points, which he backs up powerfully with even more Scripture, but Grace only half listens. She can't bring herself to move forward from his preliminary avowals.

To say that the situation she's in with Mike—her pregnancy and the abortion—is a boneheaded predicament created from her faithless spirit of worry would be an understatement.

Money, financial stability, a comfortable lifestyle—ease and convenience, her budding writing career—those were her mammon, and she was determined to procure them, even at the cost of her marriage and her child. What she had failed to realize was that without them, mammon would cease to matter.

She shakes her head and swallows hard against the briny truth.

The bishop continues, "God loves and cares for every last one of His creations—even the birds. How much more important are we—His sons and daughters, fashioned in His image—than them?

"The Lord's love is a passionate, unchanging adoration too profound, too perfect, too pure, for our finite minds to even begin to comprehend. But what you must always remember is that He is your Father, and like any father it is His good pleasure to provide for the needs of His children. He doesn't do it because He has to or because you need Him to, He does it because He *wants* to. Feeding you, clothing you, blessing you, anointing you, and watching you thrive brings Him great joy. So let Him."

Grace blinks rapidly, but the tears trickle from her eyes regardless.

"What He can give you," the bishop continues, "is far more than anything you can earn, acquire, gain, or give yourself. Don't let the devil fool you into chasing earthly riches—into thinking that genuine happiness is something you can manufacture in this fallen world. Money is paper and metal. Power is an illusion. Houses are brick and mortar. They are mammon. Sooner than later, they will lose their worth," he warns.

"From dust we were all formed, and to dust we shall all return. Instead of hoarding what you cannot take with you into eternity, invest the mammon God gives you in others. Use it to achieve great works for the Kingdom. The return will be permanent and incalculable. Build for yourselves fortunes that do not fail and riches that cannot be stolen or destroyed. Place your treasures in Heaven. For where your treasure is, there your heart will also be."

He nods, signaling the end of his sermon, and bows his head. "Let us pray. Heavenly Father, here we are, Your sheep, coming humbly before You with praise and thanksgiving. What an honor it is, Lord, to belong to You, to be made by Your perfect hands in Your perfect image—to know Your matchless love, Your daily forgiveness, and Your bountiful provision. All we can say is, 'Thank You,' Father."

"Yes," murmur several people scattered throughout the sanctuary. "Thank You."

"You say that the harvest is plenty, but the workers are few. Here we are, Lord! Show us how, when, and where to invest our mammon. The enemy wants us to believe that the real treasure is in mammon itself. He would love nothing more than to see us forfeit our royal inheritances for a few earthly trinkets. And despite Your many blessings and assurances, we entertain his lies.

"Forgive us for our faithlessness—for succumbing to the worries of the world when we are told to be anxious for nothing. We repent, Lord. Fix what, in our carelessness, we have broken. Make our wrongs right, and restore us as only You can. In Your precious and holy name we pray, amen."

"Amen," Trina whispers.

Grace nods her head and wipes the tears from her cheeks. "Amen."

42

Mike's idea of "calling soon" is Sunday evening.

Grace doesn't know how to respond as her mind registers his flashing cell phone number on the Caller ID. She abandons the half-sorted laundry and carries the cordless into the living room. Though she's been aching for this moment, every moment, for two days, she's not nearly as nervous as she'd thought she'd be. "Hi," she answers softly.

"Hey," Mike's equally soft voice replies.

"Where are you?"

"Near," he says.

"Are you still angry with me?"

"Yeah," he admits, following a few silent seconds. "But not as much as I should be."

"I missed you at church today."

"Ron and I visited another church out in Frasier."

"Oh," Grace says, slightly wounded, though she knows she doesn't have the right to be. "How was it?"

"Good," Mike says. "You know me. I love church no matter where I go."

Grace nods, but says nothing.

"So, how are you?" Mike asks.

Grace sighs and nibbles her bottom lip to keep it from trembling. "Miserable," she says. "I don't want us to be this way. It feels awful—*I* feel awful. I feel…," she searches for the word. "Lost."

"Yeah," Mike gently says. "I know what you mean."

"So come back," Grace pleads. "We'll work it out like we always do."

"This is different, Grace. I can't just come back."

"Why?" she asks, the word escaping her lips in a whine. "I made a mistake—okay, several, huge mistakes. I realize that, but I don't want mammon anymore. I want you and I want the baby."

"What?"

"You heard me. I want the baby—I do. All this time I was trying to serve God and mammon, only I didn't know that's what I was doing. But the bishop reminded me today that God is our Provider and that as His children we aren't supposed to worry about anything. So it doesn't matter that your gallery isn't off the ground yet or that my own career is just taking flight. It doesn't even matter that my father is sick because the Lord is sovereign and He will make a way out of no way."

"Grace," Mike begins, but pauses momentarily to consider his response. "Baby, I am so glad to hear you say that and to know that you've had a change of heart."

Suffocating dread takes hold of Grace. She senses a definitive "but" coming. Sure enough...

"But," Mike says, "I think we should separate for a while."

"No!" Grace chokes, her body instantly convulsing with wails. "Mike, no!"

"Hey," he calls quietly. "Listen. Shhhh," he tries to calm her pained cries. "Gracie, listen to me."

"Don't leave me," she begs, dropping to the ground, her tears forming miniature puddles on the sealed hardwood floors.

"Baby, I'm not leaving you," Mike says. "Please don't cry." His tender, emotional pleas have no effect.

"Why can't you come back?" she asks between distressed hiccups.

"Because I don't trust you," Mike answers.

The blow of his words sends Grace into another series of gagging weeps and piercing caterwauls. "I said I was sorry," she bawls.

"I know you did," Mike says softly. "I know and I appreciate that, but it's just not enough."

"What more can I do?" she snivels helplessly. "Tell me and I'll do it."

"Gracie," Mike beckons soothingly. "Sweetheart, calm down and listen to me."

Grace does her best to arrest her tears, gulping air greedily to slow her knocking heart.

"I've spent this whole weekend torn between staying where I am and coming back home. There's nothing I want more than to be with you—to go back to life as usual."

"Me too," Grace sniffs. "So then let's do that. Let's go back to life as usual. There's nothing stopping us."

"Yes, there is," Mike says. "What you did was indefensible. It was dishonest, and it was cruel and selfish. But in the end, *what* you did is not the problem—it's why you did it."

"I already know," Grace says. "Remember? I told you, I was chasing mammon."

Mike sighs. "Yeah, but it's deeper than that. Do you ever notice that when we pray together, I'm the only one who prays? Or when we read the Word together, I'm the only one who reads. I'm the only one who has regular morning quiet times. I'm the only one who goes to Bible study. You're not even in town half the time to go to church. You've all but cut God out of your life. I know it may not feel that way, but you have. It shows in your fruit."

"I have a lot on my plate, Mike."

"And I don't?" he asks. "When you're overwhelmed, you streamline, you prioritize, you shift and rethink, but your relationship with God should always remain the center of everything. When it doesn't, you wind up operating in your own power and making foolish decisions."

Grace nods. "I agree with everything you're saying, and we'll work on it."

"*We* can't work on it, Grace. My walk with God can't substitute your personal walk with Him. And that's exactly what's happening. You depend on me to make the decisions, to carry both of us spiritually, which I've been doing because I love you. But that only lasts so long. Eventually, a crisis that I know nothing about, and can't fix, will present itself—like your pregnancy. Then what?

"You can apologize a thousand times and really mean it," he says. "But before I can trust you again, I need to know that you're strong enough in the Lord to make right choices for yourself—that you can sustain your half of this marriage. I need to see you grow. I need to see you change."

Grace blows her nose and dabs at her sore, stinging eyes. "How long of a separation?" she whispers.

"I don't know."

"Well, how are you going to know that I've changed if you aren't around to watch me do it?"

"We'll talk," he says. "We'll move forward, slowly—one step at a time. I don't have any answers, Grace. I'm figuring it out as I go."

She exhales loudly, her face hot and sticky. "Is this really necessary?" she asks, her raspy voice quaking.

"I wouldn't put us through it otherwise."

"But I don't want to," she whimpers, fierce agony wracking every inch of her body. "I can't."

"Yes, you can."

"Mike, please."

"I'm gonna hang up now, okay?"

"Don't," she begs.

"I love you, and I'll call you soon. I promise."

Crushed, Grace doesn't fight. She simply bows her head and braces herself for the sound of the soft click on the other end of the line.

43

Thoughts swirl in Trina's head; lines of rehearsed dialogue, cultivated statements, suggestions, prompts, and requests; polite threats and insidious demands. They buzz around her rotting conscience like angry flies.

Quinn and Kendra's instructions have been playing loudly in her ear all morning, and their voices only seem to get louder as her meeting with Detective Fontaine grows nearer.

She glances down at her watch continuously, the steady tick of the second hand sending her further and further into a silent anxious frenzy. She'd long stopped pretending to work and ditched the mounds of folders on her desk for the much more serene view out of her office's floor-to-ceiling windows.

This is a crossroads if she's ever encountered one. She knows the right way to turn—the moral way—but she fears she's already traveled down too many wrong roads for the moral road to lead her anywhere good.

She could confess, lay her cards on the table, and let the chips fall where they may, but what will that change? The evidence still points to Councilman Schmidt—it still points to Becky's death. She won't be able to tell the detective anything he doesn't already know other than that she, Quinn, and Kendra were accessories to murder. And as responsible as she is for this debacle—as much as she deserves to be punished—she doesn't want to go to jail.

The only other alternative is to remain tightlipped, to speak when she's spoken to, to recite what she's told to say, to blend into the shadows and wait for the storm to pass. Except something tells her that no matter what the outcome of this situation, the storm inside of her will continue to rage. It will thrash and slam her mercilessly until she redeems herself and brings into the light what was done in the dark.

"Ms. Calloway?" Trina's secretary's pleasantly professional voice calls through the intercom on her phone. "Detective Fontaine is here to see you."

"Send him in," she says, standing and patting down her already sleek French twist. She straightens her collar, throwing her shoulders back, and folds her arms confidently across her chest.

Moments later, the detective appears in her doorway. Trina understands what Kendra meant when she'd called him ruggedly handsome.

He's statuesque with strong, prominent features that disclose a quiet yet sturdy confidence. His sharp jaw and heart-shaped chin are blanketed with dark stubble. Judging from his plain getup of loose-fitting jeans and untucked button-down shirt, the facial fuzz is more likely the result of sleepless nights in pursuit of Becky than a fashion statement, but it still looks good, adding that extra oomph to his sexily unkempt appearance.

His striking hazel eyes contrast sharply with his olive skin. Trina can't decide if he's black, white, Latino, or an aesthetically pleasing combination of the three.

"Ms. Calloway," he says, stepping toward her, his hand out. He smiles as Trina shakes it, revealing a sizeable gap between his two front teeth.

"Please, call me Trina," she says.

He nods. "Thank you for your time. I appreciate it."

"Of course; whatever I can do to help." Trina motions to the chairs opposite her. "Have a seat. Can my secretary bring you anything? Coffee, water, juice?"

"No." He shakes his head. "Thank you. I'll only take a few minutes of your time."

Trina unbuttons her blazer before sitting down and lacing her fingers on top of her desk. *Measure your reactions,* Quinn had instructed. *Don't cower, but don't overcompensate. The only way to keep the interrogation under control is to keep yourself under control.*

Trina doesn't know if she's passing for calm and collected on the outside, but inside, her lungs feel punctured and the lack of air is making her woozy. "Fire away," she says.

He does, regurgitating the same questions Quinn had prepped her on—some verbatim. Her fourth answer flows more naturally than the third and her sixth more naturally than the fifth, until even *she* starts to believe her artless responses.

Detective Fontaine sporadically jots down information in his palm-sized spiral notebook, nodding and prodding her on with interested grunts.

"And how long have you been a director with Home Sweet Home?"

"About a month,"Trina says.

"That was some jump," he says, referring to his notes. "From case manager to director in just over two years."

"Well, I was initially hired as a director, but ended up accepting a lower position when my department was dismantled last year. I stuck around hoping to make my way back up the ranks." Trina gives what she hopes is a light, casual laugh. "Guess good things really do come to those who wait," she says. "A director's position opened up in the Case Management department, they were looking to promote from within, and I happened to catch the right person's attention."

Detective Fontaine flashes his gap-toothed smile. "Right place at the right time," he says.

Trina shrugs. "Guess so."

"Do you have any idea where Rebecca's master file could be?" he asks.

Trina knows what she's supposed to say—a modified version of what Kendra had said: *I have no idea. Directors and case managers rarely ever have direct contact with master files.* And then for good measure, she's supposed to lean in and say: *Between you and me, I think it's lost somewhere in the Records Room. There are tens of thousands of files down there. The likelihood of one being misplaced is very high. The system is good, but it isn't perfect.*

Instead, her gaze gravitates across the room to her four-tier file cabinet. It's the only piece of furniture that made the transition from her old, downtown office. She could end this right now, just get up, unlock the small compartment above the first drawer, hand him everything she knows, and surrender peacefully.

He stares at her across the desk and waits for her answer.

"No clue," she says, after taking several moments to feign deep thought.

Detective Fontaine sighs and flips his notebook shut. "That about does it," he says.

"Really?" Trina's surprise is the first genuine reaction she's had since he stepped into her office. "That's it?"

He grins and stands. "Told you I'd be brief."

"I don't feel like I was much help," she says.

"I wasn't expecting you to be," he confesses. "I'm just making the rounds, hoping to stumble on a new lead."

"And yet, you don't sound very hopeful," Trina says, walking around to the front of her desk and perching on its edge.

The detective runs his knuckles along his stubble. "That's the hard part about jobs like yours and mine," he says. "We want to solve every case. We want to change the world. But somewhere down the line, we have to face that that's never going to happen. There are some people who don't get saved."

Trina nods her understanding.

"I hate it when they're kids, though, you know? They're so innocent— seems like it should never be too late for them."

"So you think it's too late for Rebecca?" Trina asks. "I mean," she looks away before forcing herself to utter the words, "you think she's dead?"

"I'd be really surprised by a different outcome," he says softly.

They stand silently, both lost in the somber mood of the conversation. "Well," Detective Fontaine stretches out his hand, "I'll let you get back to work."

Trina smiles sadly. "It was nice meeting you," she says.

"Likewise. And hey," he fishes in his back pocket and produces a black leather wallet, "call me if you think of anything new or hear anything that might be helpful." He passes her his business card. They shake hands one last time, and then he's gone.

Trina flops down in her chair and releases a long, noisy pant. It's not a breath of relief, however; it's a despondent sigh. She'd heard it from the horse's mouth; Rebecca Schmidt is dead.

Detective Fontaine's sincere compassion and his real appreciation for the tragedy of Becky's untimely demise was a welcome change from Quinn and Kendra's hard, look-out-for-number-one attitudes. But it also brought another chilling thought to Trina's attention.

If the saying is true, and evil really does prevail because good men fail to act, then those, so-called "good men" are as evil as the deeds they condone through inaction. In truth, they're even more evil because they know better— they've been taught a better way and choose, regardless, not to enlighten the ignorant.

That means that Trina is, by far, the most culpable person in all of this— more so than Quinn and Kendra, more so than Councilman Schmidt.

This whole time she's been comparing herself to everyone else involved—watching in awe at how easily they adjust to their corrupt circumstances. It's a startling evolution, like sprouting webbed feet or growing water-resistant fur. No matter how high the waters rise, no matter how strong the current, they adapt with seamless ease. But as a Christian, even a backslidden one, Trina can't follow suit. She refuses.

She gets up and closes her door, locking it behind her, and lowers the bone-ivory shades. Only after she's sufficiently closed herself off from the busy hustle taking place in the halls outside of her office does she retrieve her keys from her purse and unlock the compartment in her file cabinet where Becky's master file is hidden. She carries it back to her desk and flips through it again—for the last time. It belongs with Detective Fontaine and that, she decides, is where she's going to take it, whatever the repercussions.

She skims through Becky's hospital records, through the paperwork and receipts from far too many emergency room visits. She fingers the little girl's sad drawings and scans concerned reports from one psychologist after the next.

The master file falls open to Georgia Kenny's letter just as it had that night in her office. Trina picks it up and reads it again. Georgia's words haven't lost their poignancy or their passion.

"I will fight for her," Kenny wrote. *"I will do whatever it takes to make sure she survives."*

Trina's breath catches at the jolt in her ribs. She reads the statement again and then again. "Dear God," she whispers. She slams the file closed and crams it into her briefcase.

"Send all my calls to voice mail," she says, dashing past her secretary, keys in hand, her purse dangling from her shoulder. "I won't be back."

44

Doo, doo, doo. The three-toned chime rings in Grace's ear. "The area code or telephone number, as dialed, is not valid. Please check the area code and telephone number and dial again," an automated female voice says. She repeats the statement, her tone paced and mechanical, but just pleasant enough not to seem impersonal.

Grace hangs up and tries Tamara's cell phone number. She gets a slightly varied version of the same message.

It's the fourth time she's called both numbers. She knows by now that the disconnect messages are not some bizarre phone company glitch, but she'd tried again anyway, for reasons she can't quite put her finger on.

Grace's initial reaction when she'd discovered, early this morning, that Tamara had bolted without so much as a "Good-bye" or an "I quit" was indignation—a sour mix of offense and irritation that gradually simmered to bewilderment.

Ducking quietly into the night seemed out of character for someone with Tamara's moxie. If she was upset with Grace or discontent with the job, Tamara would have said something—made a stink, a final farewell production; if not to make sure her position was known, then to bask in the limelight one last time.

But hours later, mid-afternoon, with nothing to do but think to the steady hum of the heater, Grace believes she understands.

Tamara's sudden disappearance has nothing to do with Grace and everything to do with the humiliation of Ron's rejection. Yesterday, after church, Trina had recapped what happened Thanksgiving night in the kitchen after Grace had stormed off and everyone else had dispersed.

"He left her," Trina said with a snap. "Just like that." And then she smiled, her dancing eyes jubilant. "Because he wants me."

"What does this mean?" Grace asked, forcing herself to stay neutral because she was too ashamed to admit to herself that she was far more envious of Trina than she was happy for her. Here her marriage is falling apart and Trina's dream guy denounces his supermodel prototype girlfriend and proclaims his undying love to Trina with a knee-knocking kiss.

"I gotta get it together," Trina says, her brows slanted, her mouth turned down into a disturbed frown. It was clear she knew what needed to be done, but no idea how to do it.

"You could start by cutting ties with Darius, once and for all," Grace suggested.

"I know," she said, her tone nowhere near as certain as her words.

"If you don't let go of the past," Grace counseled, "you will never be able to grasp your future. Just take the plunge," she said. "Ron did it for you."

Little did Grace know, at the time, that Ron and Trina's fledgling re-romance would grow at the cost of her personal assistant. But it makes sense. What could Tamara possibly gain from sticking around? There's not much worth the agony of having to be in the company of an ex, especially one who dumped you suddenly and seemingly without cause.

As hard as Tamara worked to ingratiate herself, she probably recognized that Ron is a permanent, irreplaceable fixture in Grace and Mike's lives, Grace reasons. So, under the circumstances, walking away almost seems noble.

Grace will miss her though, not necessarily her incessant doting or her tiresome need for perfection, not even her cleaning or her office wrangling. She'll simply miss Tamara's company.

With Mike gone and Trina wrapped up in Ron and her current work crisis, Grace's life echoes with loneliness. At times like this, she usually immerses herself in work, booking signings or agreeing to speaking engagements that she doesn't really want to attend. Tiring herself to the point of not caring has always been her response to trouble, but it's also that exact behavior that drove Mike away.

The knot in her throat tightens at the thought of him. They haven't talked since last night. She hadn't expected them to. Mike is very laid-back. He works on a different timetable than most. That's why his first call to her came two days after he left. He probably won't call until mid-week. The call will be random—out of the blue, like 4:24 on Wednesday evening. By then, she will have succumbed to her depression, roaming aimlessly around the loft in her bathrobe, numb and detached.

His voice will seem surreal like a patch of lush vegetation in a dry and sandy desert. He'll be cordial and tender. The conversation will hover somewhere between small talk and awkward banter. Then he'll say he's got to go, promising, of course, to call her again soon, and that will be it. He'll be gone for a few more agonizing days and she'll be left to wait.

She sighs and picks up the phone, dialing his cell phone number by rote. It'll be off, she knows. His voice mail will kick over, and she'll leave him a message telling him…telling him…she's not sure what she'll tell him. She just wants to feel connected to him, to hear his voice, even if it's telling her that he's unavailable. It rings twice.

"Gracie?"

She sits stunned, too paralyzed to speak.

"Hello?" Mike calls again.

"Yeah," Grace whispers.

"Are you okay?" Mike asks, alarmed by her quietness. "Is the baby okay?"

Grace smiles at the protective tinge in his voice. "Yeah," she says, instinctively resting her free hand on her stomach. "As far as I know, we're both fine."

"What's wrong?" he asks.

"Nothing, I just…," she hesitates, but decides that now is not the time to be censored by her pride. "I miss you," she confesses quietly. "And I wanted to hear your voice."

"I miss you too," he says without missing a beat.

"No, you don't."

"I do," he says. His sincerity is palpable, and she doesn't know how, but she can tell that he's smiling. "I miss you whenever I'm not with you."

Several people laugh boisterously in the background. Grace stiffens, figuring that he's holding, what she assumed was an intimate conversation, in front of mutual friends as a cruel joke. The thought is irrational and paranoid, but that doesn't stop her heart from sinking. "Who's that?" she asks.

"The people behind me in the checkout line," he says. "I'm buying groceries."

"Oh," Grace says. It's better than her cruel joke theory, but not by much. The fact that he's buying groceries means that his leave isn't going to be a short one. Mike knows what she's thinking.

"I'm in the express lane," he says. "I got a loaf of bread, a jar of peanut butter, some bananas, and a gallon of milk. Not exactly gourmet, but I gotta eat something, right?"

"You should get a box of those frozen French toast sticks you like so much," she says, making an effort, through tears, to be supportive, positive. "Otherwise, you'll never eat breakfast. And get a few frozen dinners. Peanut butter and banana sandwiches aren't going to hold you for long."

"That's a good idea," his tone is hushed, sad. "Thanks."

"I'll let you go," Grace says, unable to bear his distance, but more pained by the closeness of his voice. "I just called to say hi. I honestly didn't even think you'd answer."

"Why wouldn't I answer?" he asks.

"I don't know," Grace says. She really *doesn't* know, she just assumed.

"Hey, I love you. You know that, right?"

Grace sighs. "I know. I just can't figure out why."

"That's the best kind of love," he says. "The kind that needs no reason."

Grace smiles, her clouds of gloom parting.

"There aren't any rules," he says. "This isn't a punishment. When you want to talk to me, call me. My phone will be on twenty-four hours a day."

"Okay," Grace says.

"Okay," Mike repeats, his okay cementing hers. "So, I'll call you soon—unless you call me first," he adds.

Grace nods. "Sounds good."

"You know I can't let you go until you say it back." His voice is playful.

Grace laughs. She knows exactly what he wants. "I love you too," she says.

They hang up. Strangely, Grace feels lighter and emptier at the same time. This separation is not the worst-case scenario she'd imagined. He loves her and he misses her and he won't hesitate to tell her as much. Those are all comforting thoughts. But the somber reality is that he's still living somewhere else, stocking up on food that they already have at home, because he won't come home—he can't. And while she respects his decision, Grace can't stay in this loft pining over him, sinking into his absence, and obsessing over the things she could've and should've done differently to prevent the situation from ever taking place.

"What should we do?" Grace asks, caressing her belly. It's the first time she's directly addressed her unborn child. She feels silly at first, hokey and ridiculous. But immediately after the pang of embarrassment comes fuzzy comfort.

"You hungry?" she asks. This time there's no embarrassment, only the sense that a precious and delicate bond is being made. "Me too."

Grace rifles through her purse for the yellow box of Swedish fish she'd purchased yesterday on her way home from church. She'd never been a big fan of the chewy red candy. She'd never been a big fan of chewy candy, period—not even as a child. She didn't like the way it stuck to her back teeth. But she's had a hankering for them ever since she'd accepted a few of Beth's in Dr. Noguez's waiting room.

She chews pensively and pulls out her wallet, sorting through bank receipts and gum wrappers until she finds Beth's card. Had she given it to Grace just to be nice? Because they'd bonded over baby talk? Was benignly suggesting that they get together just a civilized way to end the discussion? Or could she, like Grace, use a friend in a similar boat?

Grace shrugs and dials the number. It rings and rings and rings. She's about to hang up when she hears Beth's voice: "Sorry I missed you. Leave it at the beep."

It's a concise message, to the point, no nonsense, but still upbeat in Beth's inclusive, there-are-no-strangers demeanor.

"Hey, Beth. This is Grace. Grace Cambridge. We met a few weeks ago at Dr. Noguez's office. Hope your Thanksgiving went well—better than mine at least," she laughs nervously, instantly regretting the slip. "Anyway, I ran across your card and thought you might want to hang out. I understand if you're too busy, just thought I'd give it a shot." Grace leaves her number along with an invitation to call anytime and hangs up, hoping she didn't sound as needy or desperate for someone's company as she knows she really is.

She stands and heads to the kitchen to eat lunch solo when the phone rings.

"I'd love to!" Beth says, the instant Grace answers. "Are you hungry? Of course you are; you're pregnant. Let's eat and then go baby shopping. Ooooh, you know what I could go for right now? Pancakes and bacon—with syrup, lots and lots of syrup!"

Grace laughs at her childlike zest. "But it's almost two," she says.

"So? Pancakes and bacon can be eaten anytime. Why do you think Denny's serves breakfast all day?" The question is rhetorical. "Because anytime is a good time for pancakes."

"Okay," Grace says, already feeling lighter. "Pancakes it is."

They make plans to meet at Denny's on Union in 15 minutes because, according to Beth, her baby has a grown man's appetite and if he doesn't get food soon, she is certain he'll break out the salt and pepper shakers and start feasting on her liver.

Grace rolls her eyes and shakes her head, but deep down, she can't wait to get to know her own child just as well.

45

Georgia Kenny's house is a three-story Tudor with pale-yellow paneling and hunter-green shutters. Unlike her drab neighbors who've stuck to neatly trimmed shrubs, Georgia has lined her home with rows upon rows of flowers in impossibly bright shades of pink, fuchsia, and orange. They're an eye-catching assortment even now as they droop and brown, slowly losing the battle against winter's nip.

Cement turtles and coral bunnies flank the steps to her porch and dot her emerald-green lawn. A tire swing hangs from a thigh-thick branch on a massive, leafless tree to the right of her detached garage.

Windmills and chimes and homemade wooden signs with cute aphorisms painted on them give her place a touch of whimsical enchantment and wonder. To the casual passerby, the abode might seem tacky or flamboyant, but to Trina it is more than fitting for a kindergarten teacher.

She unlatches the white picket fence surrounding the property and heads up the cracked walkway to the screened front porch. She pulls back the door slowly, wincing at the noisy squeak of its hinges and the loud creak of the floorboards under her heels as she sidles past several potted plants and a quaint set of wicker rocking chairs.

The porch was unlocked, but Trina feels like an intruder nonetheless. The nervousness she'd anticipated hits with sudden and full force as she finds herself, at long last, standing inches away from Georgia Kenny's front door.

She'd compiled her arguments on the ride over, practicing and refining what she would say, how she would introduce herself, the suggestions she would make, what proof she would divulge, and what facts she would withhold. But those words escape her now; now that it's time to cross over the threshold of planning into action.

Trina knocks before common sense gets the better of her. There's no stir-ring inside, but she knows, despite the empty driveway and closed blinds, that Georgia is home. She knocks again, this time using the brass knocker. "Hello?" she calls.

Slow, cautious footsteps are followed by the scrape of the metal peephole cover as it's slid aside and then dropped. "Yes?" a woman's muffled voice finally answers.

"Georgia Kenny?" Trina asks.

Hesitation is followed by another tentative, "Yes."

"My name is Katrina Calloway. I'm a director at Home Sweet Home. I was hoping to talk to you for a few minutes."

"What about?" Georgia's muffled voice asks.

Trina clears her throat and steadies her voice to sound professional and non-threatening. It's not an easy balance to achieve. "Rebecca Schmidt," she says.

"I'm sorry. I can't help you." Even through the door Trina can hear Geor-gia's apprehension.

"I know you can't," Trina says, her tone infinitely patient. "But I thought that, together, we might be able to help Becky."

"I don't know what you mean."

"Georgia, please." Trina rests her hand on the door. "I know she's in there. I don't blame you; you had every reason to take her, but this isn't the solution. Think about what's best for Rebecca long term. You can't hide her forever."

Trina braces for a barrage of ironclad denials, maybe an onslaught of unpleasant threats sprinkled with a few curse words, and a finale of, "Get off my property before I call the cops!" After all, she's accusing a woman she's never met of kidnapping.

No matter what, though, Trina plans to stand her ground. Unbridled boldness, she's fast learning, is one of the only benefits of being a woman with nothing to lose.

But the grand standoff Trina had played out in her mind remains tucked safely in her imagination. Georgia unlocks the door and steps away.

Trina waits several seconds before pushing the door open and entering. The house is dim; its sole source of light coming from a small lamp in the living room. Her eyes adjust to see Georgia standing in the archway by the staircase, her arms crossed.

She's older than Trina thought she would be. Her sand-colored hair, which is pulled back and up with a jeweled barrette, is streaked with gray. And her rimless bifocals rest primly on the edge of her nose. She looks like someone's grandma in her ankle-length, blue jean dress and long-sleeved cardigan—harmless and docile. Trina would've even ventured to say friendly, if only she wasn't scowling.

"What would you have me do, Ms. Calloway?" Georgia asks. "Hand her over to Home Sweet Home so you people can give her back to her pig of a father? Is that your idea of looking out for Becky's long-term interests?"

"No," Trina says. "We need to go to the police."

Georgia gives a derisive snort. "Because they've been so much help in the past," she says acerbically.

"I understand you're angry," Trina says, pressing her hand to her chest as if to pledge her sincerity. "You have every right to be, but I'm on your side."

"My father doesn't beat me black and blue," Georgia says. "I'm not the one who needs support; Becky is."

"And she's got it." Trina holds up her briefcase. "I promise you, she's got it. I just need you to hear me out."

Georgia sighs, the hardness in her features softening at Trina's earnest request. "We were just about to have snack time," she says, nodding to her left. "Would you mind talking over milk and cookies?"

Trina smiles. "Not at all." She follows Georgia past the staircase, down the hall lined with shoes, and into the kitchen.

Becky's seated at the table, her miniature bare feet dangling freely, her chubby right hand wrapped around a fat purple crayon. She looks up from her coloring book, her sharp, dark-brown eyes locking on Trina with an alert awareness that no child should possess.

Her face is round and ripe, her skin dewy and flawless with a natural flush that would mark her innocence were it not for her expression. Her brows slant accusingly, revealing a level of mistrust that usually takes a lifetime's accumulation of hardships to achieve. And her bow lips curve downward disapprovingly like those of a jaded middle-aged woman. She's timeless; beautiful, yet guarded, beyond her years.

Trina freezes, much like a person freezes in the presence of an unfamiliar animal. Is it friendly or rabid? Will it bite or lick, nuzzle or attack? The only way to know for sure is to wait for it to approach first.

"Can you say hi to Ms. Katrina?" Georgia asks, her poised, sing-songy teacher's voice kicking in.

Becky swats her coal-colored hair out of her face and continues to stare silently, sizing Trina up—determining her intentions and deciding whether to categorize her as friend or foe. "Hi," Becky whispers after a few more moments of careful consideration.

"Hi," Trina says, her timbre high and sweet, the way people speak to blinking newborns or frisky puppies. She takes a few, cautious steps toward her. "What're you coloring?"

"Bob," Becky says, without looking up. She trades her purple crayon for a brown one.

"Sponge Bob?" Trina asks.

Becky shakes her head. "Bob the Builder," she says in a tone that screams, Where have *you* been? Hiding under a rock?

"Oh," Trina nods, her eyes wide, her expression cartoonish. "I don't think I know him." She pulls out the chair next to Becky, easing into it and glances over at Georgia who's arranging Oreos on a plate. She doesn't look up, pretending to busy herself with preparing Becky's snack, but Trina knows better. Georgia is scrutinizing her every move.

"Can I see?" Trina asks, reaching to angle the coloring book in her direction.

"No!" Becky slams both of her hands down on top of the book and slides it back to her side of the table. "It's not finished yet."

"Come on now, Becks," Georgia admonishes kindly. "Remember what we said about sharing?"

Becky sighs, bunching her little pink lips together, while wracking her brain for an equitable solution. "Here." She hands Trina a scrap of construction paper, rolls her one crayon, and goes back to coloring.

Georgia continues to bang around the kitchen, putting on the kettle, fetching tea cups, napkins, spoons, sugar, and slicing lemon wedges.

The tranquility Georgia has cultivated—the safe place she's managed to manufacture—is a feat to be marveled at, Trina thinks as she doodles senseless designs and snatches peeps at Becky.

It's as if today's a day like any other day for them, never mind the teams of police officers searching for Becky's lifeless body, never mind the extensive news coverage, the dozens and dozens of organized volunteers who've set up hot-lines and posted fliers, the heated speculation or finger-pointing.

The city is up in arms over a little girl who's sitting across from Trina, humming, without a care in the world.

"Cartoons are on," Georgia announces. "Let's take your cookies to the other room so Ms. Trina and I can talk."

Obediently, Becky packs up her crayons, including the one she lent to Trina, collects her assorted papers and coloring books, and relocates to the living room.

Trina listens as Georgia sets Becky up with her milk and Oreos in front of the television. They talk quietly, Georgia's measured voice answering and responding to every one of Becky's questions and insights, as they flip slowly through the stations, until Becky finally settles on *Dora the Explorer*.

Georgia emerges several minutes later. She places a pot of Earl Gray tea and a tray of shortbread cookies on the table and sits down across from Trina. "So how did you figure it out?" Georgia asks, passing her the saucer of sliced lemons.

"I managed to get my hand on Rebecca's master file," Trina says, dumping several sugar cubes into her cup. "I know what you did, taking her to Arkansas, and I read your letter. It moved me."

Georgia shrugs and sips her tea. "Too bad you were the only one."

"I wasn't," Trina says. "Your actions were commendable. They made a difference."

"Is that why last week Becky came to class with welts on her legs, bruises on her shoulders and back? Is that why she cries and wrenches in her sleep at naptime? Why she wets herself in response to any loud noise?"

"She was removed from her father's custody after you took her to Little Rock," Trina says.

"For a year," Georgia says. "One measly year."

Trina nods understandingly at the unsatisfied tint in Georgia's voice. "It should've been much longer."

"No." Georgia shakes her head. "It should've been permanent. She was improving. I watched her last year in pre-K. I watched her deteriorate by the week. That's why I took her to Arkansas. She was slipping away, and nobody would do anything about it. For a while, I thought my stunt did the trick.

"When she showed up this fall for kindergarten, she was different—rambunctious, curious, energetic—everything a six-year-old should be. Until a couple of weeks ago when she wouldn't take off her coat. I knew that instant, before she stopped talking, before she refused to participate, before the bruises started to show, that she'd been sent back. And I knew, then, what I had to do."

Trina slides her tea to the side and folds her hands on the table. "What if I told you," she begins slowly, picking each word with care, "that Rebecca was never supposed to go back home? That strings were pulled and drastic measures were taken to return her to her father."

"I'd ask if you could prove it," Georgia says, also pushing her tea to the side.

Trina nods. "I can."

"How?"

This is the part of the conversation Trina knew would be the hardest. She's not sure if it's fear or shame lodging the words in the back of her throat, but they're stuck nonetheless. She swallows and exhales heavily, determined, after months of compromising and cowering, to do the right thing. "My boss, Quinn Dawson, she's the Executive Director at Home Sweet Home and a close, personal friend of Councilman Schmidt. She had Becky's master file destroyed and her case file cleaned." Trina bows her head. "And I'm one of the case managers she got to do it."

"I'm not sure I understand," Georgia says, her reaction even.

Trina relays the story in its entirety. She breaks it down plainly, starting with the initial meeting she and Kendra had in Quinn's office, the promise of a promotion and the explicit instructions that followed. She recounts her experience in the Records Room, what she'd learned through Becky's master file, and how she couldn't bring herself to destroy it. She pulls the folder from her briefcase, sliding it across the table to Georgia, and confesses the changes she'd made to Becky's case file, how she'd tweaked it and buffed it enough to justify the little girl's return home. She continues to talk, one sentence spilling into the next, until it's all finally out—the new car, the meeting at Houston's, even Detective Fontaine's interrogation. By the time Trina's lips stop moving, Georgia knows the whole truth.

"And that's why I'm here," Trina says. "Between that master file and your testimony, we can make someone listen. We can make sure that, this time, Becky's escape is permanent."

Georgia flips silently through Rebecca's file, skimming the sheaves of reports, records, charts, statements, evaluations, and drawings.

Trina doesn't stop her; she doesn't speak or narrate. She just sits and sips her tea and gives Georgia the time she needs to digest everything she's heard and read.

Eventually, Georgia looks up, her eyes narrowed dubiously. She crosses her legs and drums her fingers against the table. "How can I trust you?" she asks with a shrug.

"You can't," Trina says. "Or at least you shouldn't, but I'm asking you to anyway."

"So I'm just supposed to let you have her on your word? Because you made *one* right decision in the course of many wrong ones? How do I know that you won't take her to this Quinn person? That the next time the police search the bottom of the Mississippi, Becky won't actually be there?"

"I don't want to take her," Trina says. "I wouldn't ask you to give her to me. I don't have the right."

"Then why are you here, Ms. Calloway?" Georgia closes the folder and pushes it back in Trina's direction. "What do you want from me?"

"When the time comes," Trina says, "I want you to give Rebecca up without a fight."

Georgia lowers her gaze and shakes her head. "I can't. If I don't fight for her, who will?"

"I know someone," Trina says. "He can make it right, but you've got to trust me."

Georgia doesn't say anything, but continues to shake her head.

Trina reaches across the table and squeezes her hand. "You're a good woman," she says. "With a good heart. But the reality of this situation is that you've stolen a child. People are looking for her, good people, who want to see her make it just as much as you do."

Georgia looks at Trina's hand on top of hers. She doesn't move it.

"How long do you plan to keep her here?" Trina asks. "Until she's ten, fifteen, twenty? And what about your job? Whatever excuse you've given for your absence is only going to buy you so much time. Then what? This has got to end sometime. Let's do it while we've got the power of the public behind us."

That catches Georgia's attention. "The public?"

Trina nods. "Up to this point, everything that's been done concerning Becky has taken place privately—in the dark, behind closed doors. A signature here, a blind eye there, but now the media is involved. You'd be hard pressed to find a news station that's not covering that little girl's disappearance," Trina says, pointing to the flickering television lights in the living room. "Let's use that to her advantage. The only way to stop this cycle, once and for all, is to take down the people behind it. And right now we have the ammo and the coverage to do just that."

Georgia's nod is slight, her forehead wrinkled, as she chews intently on everything Trina's just said. "We'll force their hand. They won't have a choice, but to do what's right," she murmurs, mostly to herself.

Trina grins. "That's the idea."

Georgia looks up, her fortitude giving way to concern. "Are you sure you're prepared for the outcome?" she asks. "I'm not afraid. I knew what I was risking when I took Rebecca the first time around just like I knew what I was risking by taking her this time. But what about you? Have you thought this through? Weighed the possible consequences? Those people are looking for a scapegoat, not a hero."

"I know," Trina says. She sits up straight and meets Georgia's questioning stare. "But I'm tired of making everything about me. This is the right thing to do. And that's enough." She smiles, grateful to finally believe what she's known all along to be true. "That's enough."

46

"You do know that the term, 'eating for two,' is just a figure of speech, right?" Grace asks, scanning the plates of waffles, bacon, pancakes, eggs, hash browns, sausage, and toast, cluttering the table.

Beth rolls her eyes. "This is the fun part of being pregnant," she says, dragging her sausage link through the moat of syrup around her buttered pancakes and chomping half of it away in one bite. "We get to stuff ourselves, for nine straight months, without shame. You better enjoy it while you can."

Grace laughs and stabs at her western omelet.

"So, I'm guessing the secret's out," Beth says, holding a ketchup bottle over her hash browns and pounding its bottom.

"Yeah," Grace nods. "He knows."

"And…" Beth prompts. "How did he take it?"

Grace nibbles on a green pepper. "He left."

"When?" Beth asks, screwing the cap back onto the bottle and licking a stray dollop of ketchup from her pinky.

"Thanksgiving night."

Grace recaps the catastrophic dinner in detail.

Beth nods, moaning and grunting, as Grace mimics the reactions and comments made by the motley bunch of characters in her tale. "No!" she exclaims, around a mouthful of eggs and pancakes, her eyes bucked, when Grace recounts Trina and Tamara's covert catfight. And, "you gotta be kidding me," is her response to the way the news was finally revealed for the first time in front of everyone.

"So what happened?" she asks, leaning forward, completely engrossed, a crisp strip of bacon hovering in front of her gaping mouth.

Grace relays the other half of the story in equally rich detail; Malikah and Trina, her cold, long walk in the park, followed by the gruesome discovery of Mike's missing belongings.

Beth swigs her milk. "Has he called?" she asks, wiping away the resulting white mustache with the back of her hand.

Grace nods. "We've talked a couple of times. He's being pretty great about it, all things considered."

"He'll be back," Beth says, devouring her second sausage link.

"How do you know?"

Beth shrugs. "The ones that leave for good don't call," she says. "When they go, they never look back."

Grace sips her cranberry juice. "Like Mark?" she asks, referring to Beth's fair-weather husband.

Beth stares down at her half-eaten pancakes. "I'll tell you a little secret my mother taught me when my father died," she says, looking up and tilting her head. "Birth and death are the only true beginnings and endings in life. Everything in between, both the good and the bad, is just a continuation of what already is." She shrugs. "Different chapters—same book. What happened at your Thanksgiving dinner was unfortunate, not conclusive. Same thing with my marriage," she says. "It's not over. It's just a story for another day."

Grace smiles, gazing admiringly across the table. "You're gonna be a great mom, you know that?"

Beth dips her head from side to side. "I'm gonna try," she says, taking a bite of her jelly-slathered wheat toast.

Grace chuckles. "Well, if nothing else you'll be well fed."

"Don't hate." Beth smirks and slides her untouched plate of waffles toward Grace. "Participate."

Grace throws her head back in laughter. "I think I will," she says, reaching for the flagon of maple syrup.

"Atta girl!" Beth hoots. "Now you're gettin' in the spirit!"

Grace must admit the warm buttery waffles are much more satisfying than her rubbery, tasteless omelet. She inhales them in a matter of minutes.

"Hey, Mikey. I think she likes it," Beth teases.

Grace rolls her eyes, but doesn't object when Beth orders another plate of pancakes and a side order of bacon for them to share.

"Do you still want to go baby shopping?" Grace asks after the waitress has cleared away their first set of dishes.

Beth smirks. "Did Jesus wear sandals?"

"I'll take that as a yes," Grace laughs. "Where do you want to go?"

"Who knows?" Beth shrugs, her smile adventurous. "The world is our oyster."

After sufficiently gorging themselves on greasy breakfast food, Grace and Beth end up in Collierville at The Land of Nod, a charming children's furniture store that Beth's sister was kind enough to tip them off to.

They roam through dozens of model playrooms, nurseries, and studies, each with its own unique ambiance and décor.

Beth chats away, voicing her likes and dislikes and giving every room a rating before they move onto the next. "A solid five," she says about the nursery they're currently in. "Would have been a six, but I just can't get with the pea green."

Grace laughs and tilts her head, giving the room a second look. She kind of likes it. This one, unlike the others, is unisex. Contrary to Beth's opinion, she finds the pale, mint-green walls serene. And they're an ideal backdrop for the tastefully situated collection of white, distressed furniture. The crib, changing station, padded rocking chair, and checkered window treatments make the space look like something out of a high-end catalogue.

They continue to roam, arm-in-arm, pointing and cooing at select items, claiming how *that* would be darling for a boy or how *this* is what every baby girl needs. Grace's chest swells with the excitement. She'd been so consumed with concealing the pregnancy that she never stopped to consider what an enjoyable experience it could be.

"Whoa," Beth says, stopping abruptly, her wide eyes blinking. "Now this is a ten."

Grace rounds the corner and halts also, her mouth dropping involuntarily in response to the room before them. It's a nursery unlike any other she's ever seen before—an ideal blend of sophistication and merriment.

It's painted a deep aquamarine blue. A meticulous underwater mural, replete with wildly colorful fish, frolicking seahorses, and wading turtles, takes up the entire left wall. In the center of the room, resting on a nude chenille rug, is an exquisite crib constructed of dark espresso wood. Its lines are straight and simple, pure and minimalist, and it's adorned with dark tan sheets and a matching quilt and bumper.

In the corner behind it is an oversized chair and ottoman; their umber upholstering coordinates with the lush bedding and pillows. The chair is slanted outward to make room for a delicate, paper accordion lamp, which is standing beside a tall bookcase that is stocked with an assortment of toys, games, and children's books.

In the opposite corner is a matching espresso armoire. For presentation's sake, both of its doors are open, revealing five shelves and two drawers, tidily stacked with every conceivable baby supply. Next to it is a waist-high changer, also espresso. A mobile of miniature chenille teddy bears spins and sways above it.

Grace's gaze sweeps the room from left to right and then again from right to left. "This is it," she says. "This is the one."

Like clockwork, a saleswoman appears from out of nowhere, a clipboard in hand, a hopeful glint in her eye. "I see you ladies have stumbled onto our Cape Cod collection," she says with an approving wink. "This line of furniture is truly superb."

Grace nods, her stare fixed on the espresso crib. "It's gorgeous."

"And it probably costs an arm and a leg," Beth says.

The saleswoman grins. "This collection *is* for the more...," she gazes upward and hugs her clipboard against her blazer. "Discriminating buyer," she says.

Grace doesn't necessarily consider herself all that discriminating when it comes to furniture, but she knows what she likes and she likes this. "I want it," she says.

"What, the crib?" Beth asks.

Grace shakes her head. "Everything," she says. "The whole room."

The saleswoman smiles broadly, no doubt the sound of cha-chinging cash registers going off in her head as she tallies her commission.

"Are you sure?" Beth asks.

Grace nods. "I think so."

"Okay, wait." Beth holds up her hand. "Let's talk it out first—pros and cons," she says.

"Pros," Grace says. "It's beautiful, it's the perfect size for the second bedroom, and it fits my loft's atmosphere."

"It comes with a five-year guarantee," the saleswoman adds. "And the armchair can be purchased as a sleeper sofa. It pulls out into a twin bed so your little one's nursery can also function as a spare bedroom."

"See?" Grace smiles smugly at Beth.

"And...," the saleswoman walks over to the ottoman and pulls on a hidden tab. It opens, revealing a deep cedar-lined trunk. "Extra storage," she says.

"Okay, good," Beth says. "Now cons." She starts. "This furniture is very masculine, and you don't know if you're having a boy or a girl."

"A ribbon or two here, a few floral throw pillows there, some pink paint, and voila," the saleswoman throws up her free hand. "A room fit for a princess."

Grace shrugs, satisfied with that solution, and waits for Beth's next counter. "This is the first store you've been to. You have months to shop around and to decide what you really like. There's no rush. This set will be here."

"Actually," the saleswoman pipes in, her finger raised, "they've discontinued this line. It'll probably only be a matter of weeks before the warehouse sells out. And then it's gone for good."

Grace looks nervously at Beth. She doesn't want to dawdle and miss out, but Beth is not moved.

She purses her lips and glares at the pushy saleswoman. "Which is exactly why she *shouldn't* get it." Beth turns to Grace. "Baby rooms should be individual and unique. God only knows how many mothers across America have this exact same set. Take your time. Mix and match pieces, create your own vision; don't just rip off someone else's. That," she points to the aquamarine bedroom, "is commercial glitz. You want sentiment. You want heart."

"Well, if you *do* decide on the entire collection," the saleswoman says, inching closer to Grace. "I'll give you thirty percent off—a little customer appreciation discount."

Beth grabs Grace's elbow. "Will you give us a minute?" she asks, leading Grace a few nurseries over to a salesperson-free zone.

"I know, I know," Grace says. "You think I should wait, that I might find something I like better, but I don't think I will. Why not get it now, while it's still in stock and I can get thirty percent off?"

"Because, for starters, you haven't discussed it with Mike," she says.

Grace's smile fades. In all the excitement, she hadn't considered that. "You don't think he'll like it?"

Beth shrugs. "How would I know? I've never even met him. I just think that every dad would like to be part of this process, you know? Picking out the stroller, assembling the crib—those are things you guys should do together." She squeezes Grace's arm. "Call and ask him. If he gives you the green light, go for it. But at least you will have included him somehow. He'll know he has a place in this—that his opinion matters."

"Okay," Grace says. "You've got a point. We'll let him decide." She fishes her cell phone out of her purse and calls Mike.

"Hi, Baby," answers his muffled voice.

"Hey."

"Everything okay?"

"Yeah, I just... Do you have a minute?"

"For you? Always." He swallows and his voice becomes clear. "Why, what's up?"

"Well, I'm out in Collierville with a friend, shopping for nursery furniture, and we came across the most adorable suite, but I don't want to get it unless it's okay with you."

"Adorable, huh? Describe it to me."

"I've never seen anything like it before," Grace begins. She paints a verbal picture, dusting off her most descriptive vocabulary to express just how nonpareil she feels the set is.

Mike listens, throwing in an occasional, "nice," or "wow," between bites.

"What d'you think?" she asks, throwing in the saleswoman's offer to knock off 30 percent.

"Sounds unbelievable."

She smiles, giddy. "So, should I get it?"

He sighs. "Yeah, I guess. If you want."

"You don't sound too enthusiastic," she says, her forehead bunching at his tone. "If you hate it, tell me."

"No, it's not that," he says. "You love it and I'm sure I will too. I just—I don't know—I thought shopping for the baby is something we'd do together, a little further down the road."

Beth had hit the nail on the head. "Mike," Grace says softly, regret washing over her. "Sweetie, I'm so sorry. I just don't think sometimes."

"You don't have to apologize," he says, trying unsuccessfully to mask his disappointment. "You're excited and that's good. If that's the set you want, get it."

Grace frowns. "Actually, I think I'll wait. We've got plenty of time and now that I look at it, it's not *that* great of a set. It's kind of commercial, no personality or sentiment." She glances at Beth, who's flipping slowly through a giant storybook while swaying back and forth in a plaid rocker-glider.

Beth grins slightly, but keeps her face turned toward the book, too diplomatic to acknowledge that she'd overheard the conversation and too sweet to ever gloat about being right.

"You sure?" Mike asks.

Grace nods. "Positive. I'm glad I called."

"Yeah," Mike says. "Me too. Thanks for that."

They exchange I love you's and hang up. Grace makes her way over to Beth and plops down in the identical plaid rocker-glider next to hers.

"So what'd he say?" she asks, feigning oblivious.

"He said if I want it, I should get it."

"Are you going to?"

Grace shakes her head. "You were right. It's not fair to deny him the joy of this part of the experience."

"Your friend over there is going to be mighty disappointed," Beth says, jutting her thumb at the pushy saleswoman, who's lurking like a vulture nearby.

"Yeah." Grace grins. "But my husband's proud of me and that's all that matters." They rock in silence for a while. "I think I've had enough baby shopping for one day. What d'ya say we blow this popsicle stand?"

"As you wish," Beth says, flinging herself out of the chair. She offers Grace her hand and tugs her up. "Where are we off to now?"

"I dunno," Grace says, hooking her arm through Beth's and leading them out of the front door and into the crisp winter air. She gazes up at the fluorescent sky and smiles. "Anywhere our hearts desire."

47

The downtown police precinct bears the unpleasant scent of stale cigarette smoke and day-old lunches, mixed with the faintest whiff of B.O. Trina's
passed by the building a hundred times on her daily travels to and fro, but
she's never been inside it before now.

The tiled lobby is swarming with an array of people: delivery guys wheel-
ing loaded dollies; a handcuffed prostitute, dressed in a hot-pink, pleather
mini and ripped fishnet stockings. There's a belligerent old man with vomit
down the front of his sweatshirt and a nasty gash on his forehead. He's mum-
bling obscenities to the female security guard as she firmly tells him to calm
down.

Trailing in and out are dozens of police officers clad in their blue and
black uniforms, badges clipped to their shirt pockets, holsters fastened to
their hips. There are several worn-looking women clinging to fidgeting children, all dressed in their Sunday best, no doubt waiting to visit an incarcer-
ated loved one. Dotted throughout the bustling throng are also a few
briefcase-toting lawyers. They're impossible to miss with their confident
strides and their impeccably tailored suits.

Trina locates the precinct directory hanging on the wall just beyond the
metal detectors. She scans the long list of departments and sub-departments,
squinting at the small print, until she locates Detective Fontaine's floor.

She steps quickly, past the prostitute and around a small group of chatting
officers, to the elevators across the hall from the vending machines. Her
clammy hands cling to her belongings as she stabs the button. Anxiousness
makes her breathing shallow, but her mind remains focused solely on what
needs to be done.

The ride up to the detective's fifth floor office is crowded and takes a considerable amount of time, the elevator stopping at every floor in between to
let current passengers off and new ones on.

Trina stands in the corner, her back pressed to the wall, and watches the numbers climb. She's thought herself out, analyzed the situation, the people in it—considered their actions, their motives, and every possible solution. This definitely isn't the only way. But it's the *right* way, and after all she's been through, the incredibly bumpy journey marked by wrong turn after wrong turn, doing this the right way is the only way to get both her life as well as Becky's back on track.

"This is me," Trina says upon the fifth ding. "Excuse me," she bogarts her way through the other passengers, who are packed like sardines in the small space, and into the office commons.

The fifth floor of the police department has the same busy buzz and smell as its lobby. Only in place of brown tile floors and an unmanned Information Desk, there's dingy indoor-outdoor carpet and cubicles stacked on top of cubicles. People are shouting over the padded partitions, smacking on gum and sipping black coffee while speaking sternly into their telephones. It's a scene straight out of *NYPD Blue.*

Trina's not sure where to find Detective Fontaine among the commotion or who to ask. Everyone looks so busy—rushed and impervious to the chaos reigning around them.

"Excuse me, hi," Trina says, trying to get the attention of a passing woman. She blows by Trina, not even attempting to stop or slow down.

"Hi," Trina tries again with a fair-skinned guy, plowing his way in the other direction. "Do you know where..." He, too, continues on as if she's vapor.

She abandons trying to address moving foot traffic and sets her sights on a mousy-looking woman typing at her desk. "Hi. Do you know where I can find Detective Fontaine?"

The woman tosses her thumb over her shoulder without looking up and continues to type.

Trina heads in that direction, scanning the cubicles to her left and right, hoping to spot the detective's familiar face. She asks several more people where she can find him. Their responses are the same: a bothered shrug and a tossed thumb over the shoulder.

She wades through the sea of cubicles and into the surrounding glass offices overlooking them. "I need to speak with Detective Fontaine," Trina says to the platinum-blond receptionist. She's wearing large, gold hoop earrings and purple eye shadow that coordinates with her purple sweater and the specs of violet in her glittering nail art.

"Do you have an appointment?" she asks.

"No," Trina says. "But it's extremely important."

The woman arches her brow dubiously. "Well, I'm sorry," she says, sounding anything but. "He's in a meeting."

"Can I wait?" Trina asks, knowing that what she's got to do cannot be put off for another day.

The receptionist shrugs, her eyelids listless. "Suit yourself."

Trina takes a seat in one of the gray vinyl chairs lined against the wall beneath a string of tasteless office art and she waits. She waits for one hour and then for a second and then for a third. She waits until the receptionist and most of the cubicle occupants pack up and head home.

The fifth floor is deserted, save a few stragglers, by the time the detective rounds the corner with two other men. They're laughing. One chews on a toothpick while the other looks down at his Palm Pilot. They each have matching leather MPD duffel bags hanging from their shoulders.

Detective Fontaine slows at the sight of Trina sitting in the hall. "Ms. Calloway?" he says with a look of concern and confusion.

Trina stands. This is it—the point of no return. "I need to talk to you," she says. Her eyes dart to his two cohorts. "Alone, if that's okay."

He nods. "Of course. I'll catch you guys later," he says, dismissing his friends. He leads Trina a few paces to his office, where he turns on the lights, lowers the blinds, and shuts the door.

"What's going on?" he asks, pointing for her to sit down. He takes off his jacket and sits in his chair across from her. "You look like you've seen a ghost."

Trina tries to smile, but she can't, the onus of what lies before her weighing too heavily on her spirit. "I don't know exactly how to say this." She runs her hands through her hair and glances nervously around the room. "So I'm just gonna say it."

The detective leans forward. "Okay," he nods.

"Today, you asked me if I had any idea where Rebecca Schmidt's master file could be and I said no." She tucks a strand of hair behind her ear and licks her parched lips. "That was a lie."

"Okay," he says again, still nodding slowly. "I'm listening."

"I have it." She opens her briefcase, pulls out the file, and places it on his desk. "I was told to shred it and I couldn't, so I've been hiding it in my office ever since."

He opens the folder and thumbs through the first few pages. The muscles in his jaw tighten as he digests the information.

"I made a mistake," she says. "One that could have cost Becky her life."

He looks up. "Could have?"

Trina nods. "She's safe. I can take you to her."

"I don't understand," he says, his brows furrowed. "You kidnapped her?"

"No," Trina says, her head lowered, her voice hushed. "But I could've stopped it from happening."

"What're you saying to me?" Detective Fontaine shakes his head at a loss.

"I'm saying, I'm sorry." She steadies her voice, meeting his gaze for the first time since she entered his office. "I'm so, so sorry—for everything. And I'm here to turn myself in."

48

"Go home and get some sleep."

Those were Detective Fontaine's instructions to Trina. She'd expected to be handcuffed, read her Miranda rights, and escorted to a stark interrogation room with a table, a chair, a tape recorder, and a surly cop looking to play hardball. But Detective Fontaine's demeanor remained moderate, his tone level and surprisingly benevolent.

He asked her to start from the beginning—to tell him everything she knew. He needed to know what happened in detail, he said. No omissions or lies.

Trina obeyed. Confessing to the detective didn't come as easily as it had when she'd divulged everything to Georgia Kenny. Maybe because Georgia, though acting out of what she felt was necessity, did not have clean hands either. Maybe knowing that Georgia was also a woman who'd made a few questionable decisions in regards to Becky had bonded them in a way she hadn't realized.

Detective Fontaine, however, was the law. He was someone, Trina could tell, with a steady moral compass. He thrived on social order and he put tremendous faith in the legal system that governed them. So confessing all the ways that she, Quinn, Kendra, and Councilman Schmidt had bucked that same system was no small feat.

Trina stuttered and stammered, swallowed and stalled, sighed and cried, but by the end of it, the story, in its shameful entirety, was out. Detective Fontaine encouraged her forward with reassuring nods during the hard parts, like when she had to describe her spell in the Records Room and the specific changes she'd made to Becky's case file. He took notes and reacted through expressions, but he never once interrupted.

"If I could go back, I'd do everything differently," she'd concluded tearfully.

Detective Fontaine nodded. "Your being here speaks volumes."

"How much trouble am I in?" she'd asked.

He shrugged. "I'm not sure. Try not to worry about that. You should go home and get some sleep."

Trina blinked, nonplussed. "I'm not under arrest?"

He grinned. "You did a brave thing coming down to the station," he said. "I'm not going to punish you for that."

"But what about Becky? Don't you want me to take you to her?"

"I've got the address." He tapped his black, ballpoint pen against his handy spiral notebook. "We'll get her."

"But——" she'd tried to protest.

He held up his hand. "Trina," he said softly, calling her by her first name instead of referring to her as Ms. Calloway as he'd done up to this point. "Trust me to do my job. I promise you, I'll get her and I'll make sure she's safe. The only thing you can do right now is go home and get some rest."

Trina acquiesced. "Okay." She gathered her things and started for the door. "Do you…" She turned around and forced herself to look at him. "Am I going to go to jail?"

He smiled and shook his head. "No. Not if I can help it."

The drive back to Darius's place is slow and quiet.

Trina had intended to follow the detective's instructions implicitly. Until it dawned on her, while she was stopped at a trolley crossing, that the direction she was headed in was not home.

There's one more barrier she has to knock down on her road to redemption. She can't continue to live with Darius. As physically and emotionally exhausted as she is, she has to leave and she has to leave immediately. Spending even one more night with him will jeopardize her clean slate and she's gone through too much and come too far to ruin this fresh start.

That's the only thought running through her head as she unlocks the front door.

He's sitting in the living room. He's in his boxers, shirtless, munching on dry cereal straight from the box and cackling at a sitcom. "You worked late," he says without taking his eyes off the television.

"It was a long day," she says, leaving her briefcase and purse in the hall.

"Anything interesting happen?"

"Yeah." She sighs and sinks tiredly into the love seat opposite him. "We need to talk."

He looks up, his chewing slows. "That doesn't sound good."

Trina reaches for the remote control on the coffee table between them and turns off the television. "I'm moving out," she says.

"Here we go again," Darius groans and rolls his eyes. "What's wrong now?"

"This arrangement is wrong. It's dirty and suffocating and I don't want to live this way anymore. I can't just play house with you. You're not my husband and I'm not your wife." She shrugs. "And that's that."

Darius's mouth tightens, his expression stern. He sets the box of cereal on the floor at his bare feet. "I'm not going to be pressured into getting married," he said. "I've told you that."

Trina laughs, not because his words are funny, but because his frame of mind is so detached from hers that it's absurd. "I don't want to marry you," she says.

"Then what is this about? Things between us are perfect right now. Why are you trying to ruin this?"

"I'm not ruining anything that wasn't already ruined from the start," she says. "We've always been doomed; we just got really good at pretending we weren't. But I'm tired of pretending like I don't know the truth."

"And what truth is that?" he asks, his voice coarse, his tone antagonistic.

"I can do better." She shrugs. "I deserve better."

"See, that's your problem," he says, pointing at her. He sneers derisively. "You're self-righteous. Nobody *deserves* anything. You make your own luck. You create your own fortune. And, I'm telling you, if you walk out of here, you're going to be sorry."

"I guess that's a lesson I'll have to learn the hard way," she says, standing. "Because I'm still leaving."

"No, you're not," he says, glaring up at her.

She nods. "Yes, I am."

"No," he snatches the box of cereal and chucks it across the room. Frosted mini squares skid and bounce across the floor. "You're not!"

Trina flinches. She recognizes the violent ember in his eyes. She knows it well from their many fights that have escalated beyond words. Her gut instinct tells her to backpedal, to apologize, claim temporary insanity until the morning, and then when he leaves for work, she can sneak out, unscathed. It's what she would've done in the past.

The problem is, she's not that woman anymore. Her pulse is racing, her hands are shaking, tingling with fear, but she cannot be bullied. She refuses. A whole new world, a better world, is hers to claim and she won't wait until tomorrow to get it. *Please, Lord,* she prays silently. *Help me.*

"What're you going to do?" she asks. "Beat me up?"

He smirks daringly. "It won't be the first time I've had to knock some sense into you," he says.

She steps around the sofa and walks toward the bedroom, moving with a certainty and confidence she doesn't feel, hoping that he'll let her pass, but knowing from previous experience that he won't.

He snatches the back of her neck and spins her around by her hair. "I've done everything for you," he seethes, his hot breath scraping her face. "I took you in and I put up with you when no one else would. I pay your bills, remember? Or have you forgotten which side your bread is buttered on?"

Trina stares into his vacant eyes, petrified. "'The Lord is my light and my salvation,'" she whispers. "'Whom shall I fear?'"

Darius's nostrils flare. "What?" he snaps.

She doesn't know where it came from. The Psalm popped into her head and the words just came spilling out of her mouth. "'The Lord is the strong-hold of my life,'" she continues. "'Of whom shall I be afraid?'"

"Me," Darius hisses.

She closes her eyes and continues to recite, from memory, a Psalm that she never memorized. "'When evil men advance against me to devour my flesh, when my enemies and my foes attack me, they shall stumble and fall.'"

"Where was your God when Grace kicked you out, huh?" he shouts. "Where was your God when you were about to be homeless?" he spits. "How do you think you got this comfortable lifestyle? Me!" He yanks her head back and forth by her hair.

"'Though an army besiege me, my heart will not fear.'"

"We've been 'doomed' from the start," Darius says nastily, scoffing at Trina's earlier statement. "I didn't hear you complaining when I took you on that shopping spree. I didn't hear anything about us being doomed when I gave you this." He rips the chain and locket from around Trina's neck and throws it.

She feels the sting of the gold chain slice against her skin and she hears it when it hits the wall behind them, but she keeps her eyes closed. "'Though war break out against me, even then will I be confident.'" She feels his grip on her hair loosen.

"You know what?" he says, his breathing hard and furious. "Just get out."

She opens her eyes. Tears that she did not know had accumulated trickle down her cheeks.

"You can do better and so can I," he says, shoving her aside. He storms to the bedroom and locks the door.

Trina stands motionless, unable to catch her breath, unable to cry, unable to move. She listens numbly to the crashing, banging, and shattering taking place down the hall. Several minutes later, Darius comes stomping back into the living room. He's dressed in jeans and a sweater.

"You've got an hour," he says, turning for the front door. "If you're still here when I get back, you're gonna learn what it really means to be 'doomed.'"

Trina waits for him to slam the door behind him. Then she grabs her suitcase from the front closet and rolls it to the bedroom to assess the damage. It's considerable.

Her Bible is lying on the floor; several of the pages have been torn out and strewn across the bed. Every dresser drawer that contained her belongings is pulled out and empty. Her clothes—underwear, socks, shirts, nightgowns, jeans, sweaters—have been thrown everywhere; some are even slashed. She picks up her favorite cashmere cardigan. It's ruined; the wire hanger he used to rip it is still dangling from the delicate fabric.

She unzips her suitcase, throws back the flap, tosses everything inside and heads to the closet where she finds more of the same. One heel, from every pair of high-heel shoes she owns, has been snapped clean off. She runs her finger across the multicolored dent on the frame of the door, where he must've hooked the shoes to break them.

Her suits and blouses are lying in a pile on the floor. They're drenched in a champagne-colored liquid. Trina lifts one of the sleeves to her nose and sniffs. It's perfume.

She groans and leaves the closet for the bathroom. Sure enough, every last one of her perfume bottles is topless, empty, and lying in the sink. He's also tossed her makeup, toothbrush, contact case, prescription allergy medication, deodorant, and face cream into the toilet.

SO LONG! is scrawled across the mirror in red lipstick.

Trina's blood boils, but she will not be deterred. She fishes what she can out of the toilet, collects her broken shoes and drenched suits off the closet floor, and dumps them, by the armload, into her waiting suitcase.

Her flesh prods her to return Darius's favor, to drop a few of his belongings into the toilet, to take a wire hanger to a couple of his Armani suits. But she ignores the impulses and keeps moving.

Fifteen minutes later, she's packed, and no sorrier for leaving than she was before Darius destroyed everything she owned.

Material possessions are a small price to pay for freedom.

And it's that single thought that has her smiling as she rolls out of Darius's condo, as well as his life, for the very last time.

49

"Yeah?" Grace calls into the intercom. Suppressing a yawn, she rubs her eyes and presses the *Listen* button to find out who has the nerve to buzz her at one in the morning.

"It's me," Trina's voice calls back. "Can I come up?"

"Sure," Grace says, her sleep-dulled senses becoming immediately alert.

Minutes later, Trina steps out of the elevator, her heels clacking against the percussive marble floor of Grace's vestibule. Her hair is sticking every which way, her mascara has dried down her cheeks like mini skid marks, and her stockings are streaked with runs.

"What's all this?" Grace asks, taking in Trina's disheveled appearance and sizeable black suitcase.

"I didn't know where else to go. I quit my job," she says, looking down at her feet as though she expects to be scorned. "And I left Darius."

Grace smiles, closing the gap between them by pulling Trina into a long, tight hug. "Good for you," she says.

"Oooo," Trina winces, reeling back and pressing her hand to the side of her neck. "Careful."

Grace spreads Trina's collar open to discover a string of dried blood where Trina's necklace had scraped and broken her skin when it was snatched off. "What happened?"

Trina offers a subdued smile and shrugs. "You know Darius was never one to give up without a fight."

"Did he hit you?" she asks, brushing a wiry patch of hair off Trina's forehead and examining her face. "Are you hurt anywhere?"

"I'm okay," Trina says, nodding down at her suitcase. "Unfortunately, I can't say the same thing about my clothes."

"Come on," Grace says, taking Trina's hand. "Leave that. Let me put some peroxide on that cut."

"It's not a big deal," Trina protests, but allows Grace to tug her to the kitchen.

"Sit," Grace orders, pointing to one of the stools lined against the island. She disappears into the pantry and returns seconds later with a basket of gauzes, rubber gloves, Band-Aids, Neosporin, hydrogen peroxide, Q-tips, and cotton.

Trina laughs. "You look like you're getting ready to remove a bullet," she teases, secretly relishing Grace's love and attention.

"Just hold your hair up," she says, taking the stool behind Trina's and uncapping the bottle of peroxide. They sit without speaking, while Grace gingerly dabs away the blood and cleans the cut. "So I watched the ten o'clock news," she says, squeezing a dollop of Neosporin onto one of the Q-tips.

"Uh-huh," Trina murmurs.

Grace unwraps a Band-Aid. "Have you been following what's been going on with that missing girl?"

"Um, yeah," Trina says. "A little, I guess. Why?"

"They found her," Grace says, unwrapping another Band-Aid. "News says police got an anonymous tip."

"Wow," Trina says, her amazement clearly artificial. "That's great."

"Yeah," Grace says, her glove coming off with a rubbery snap. "All done."

Trina lets down her hair and turns around. "Thanks."

"So..." Grace busies herself with screwing the cap back onto the Neosporin and collecting the paper wrappers and soiled cotton balls. "Your current state of unemployment wouldn't have anything to do with what I saw tonight on the news, would it?"

"Do you really want to know?"

Grace studies Trina's small tired frame. She has no idea what happened, but whatever Trina got herself into, she obviously had a fight getting herself out of it. At this juncture, the important thing is not how she got caught in the predicament, but that she found the strength to make it through to the other side. "No."

Trina's face lights with relief, her eyes slope with gratitude.

"But," Grace says, heading to the trash compactor, "since you're jobless and homeless, I have a proposition for you."

Trina grins. "I'm scared to ask."

Grace tosses the handful of used medical supplies into the can and turns around, resting her back against the counter. "Work for me," she says.

Trina's too stunned to react. She blinks, staring at Grace like she just morphed into another life form.

"What?" Grace shrugs, wide-eyed, her arched brows, sprung high. "You need a job. I need an assistant. It's a simple case of supply and demand."

"What happened to Tamara?" Trina asks.

"Gone—couldn't hack it after Ron dumped her. She changed her numbers and rode off into the sunset, which means," Grace says, flashing two rows of retainer-corrected white teeth, "her job is yours for the taking."

"You really think that's such a good idea?" Trina asks, looking skeptical.

"No, I think it's a brilliant idea," Grace says, returning to the stool beside Trina. "I mean, come on. The salary's decent, the hours are flexible, and, if I do say myself," she preens dramatically, "I am a fantastic boss."

Trina laughs. "There's no arguing with that."

"And," Grace says, "as a signing bonus, I'll rent you the loft downstairs at a dirt-cheap rate."

"How dirt-cheap?" Trina asks.

Grace wrinkles her chin and looks up at the ceiling in good-humored consideration. "Free," she says. "For now—until you get back on your feet."

Trina tilts her head and bites the inside of her cheek. "You're a good friend," she says, her voice thick.

"You'd do the same for me," Grace says. "Plus my offer's not entirely altruistic." She shrugs. "With Mike gone, the world's been pretty lonely. Having you near will make it better."

"In that case," Trina says, sticking out her hand, "I guess you got yourself a new personal assistant."

Grace takes her hand, but instead of shaking it, pulls Trina in for a hug.

"How long do you think we'll make it before we're at each other's throats?" Trina asks, once they've separated.

Grace shrugs. "Couple of weeks. Three tops."

"We'd better make them count then," Trina says through laughter.

Grace smiles, the unmistakable pinch of adoration in her eyes. "Every day I've known you has counted."

It's in that moment that Grace understands with spectacular clarity what Beth was telling her about beginnings and endings. After all of the fights and fallouts, the disses and betrayals, the disappointments and mistakes that seemed, many times throughout the years, to signal the end of her sisterhood with Trina, they're still here, still them; kooky and complex and unorthodox in every way. They're still Trina and Gracie—different chapter, same wonderful book.

"I'm so thankful to have you as my best friend," Trina says.

Grace nods, but doesn't say anything else. She doesn't have to. They both know she feels the same way.

50

"Gracie, telephone!" Charlene calls.

Grace groans just at the thought of having to get up.

"Jen, help her," Trina says, pointing at the woman sitting next to Grace on the couch.

Jen shoots Trina a mock glare, "Isn't that what you get paid to do?"

Trina smiles smugly. "You're closer," she says, tightening the throw wrapped around her shoulders. "And besides, it's eight. I'm off the clock."

"Scandalous, isn't she?" Grace asks.

The ladies from Grace and Trina's women's Bible study laugh and nod their agreement. Dana chucks a pillow at Trina and buoyantly chides her for being a terrible best friend. Grace sighs contentedly at the noisy chatter and floating laughter filling her living room. Bible study ends at seven, but several weeks ago a select few, including Beth, started hanging around afterward to talk and relax and to help clean up. It's a tradition with which Grace has quickly fallen in love.

"Come on, Willy," Jen says, referring to Grace. It's a nickname the ladies gave her after the whale in the *Free Willy* movies. "I'll help you up."

Grace thinks the moniker is too amusing to be offensive. Six and a half months into her pregnancy and her bump has taken on a life of its own. It protrudes dramatically, entering and leaving rooms long before the rest of her. It's all Grace sees when she looks down. In fact, she's completely forgotten what her feet look like.

Most days, she credits her burgeoning belly to a big, strong, healthy baby. But she can't discount her nonstop eating thanks to Beth, her pregnant partner in crime, whose own bump, though two weeks ahead of Grace's, is not as large. When the two of them get together, which is often, Ben & Jerry's, pret-zels, cookie dough, and frozen pepperoni pizza are almost always involved.

Jen stands in front of Grace and holds out both of her hands, steadying herself and leaning back as Grace uses her support to hoist herself off the couch and onto her feet.

"Quack! Quack!" They all shout after her as she waddles by them.

"Y'all leave Big Willy alone!" Beth shouts.

Grace rolls her eyes, dismissing their teasing with a wave of her hand, and shuffles down the hall to her bedroom where she can take the phone call in private.

She picks up the cordless only after she's sunk comfortably into the suede couch and propped up her shoeless swollen feet. "Hello?"

"Is it a bad time?" Mike asks.

Grace smiles. "It's never a bad time for you to call. You know that."

"Sounds like you still have company."

"Yeah well," Grace sighs. "You know how sistas like to overstay their wel-come," she jokes.

Mike's laughter lulls, and the line goes quiet. Lately, many of their daily conversations are marked by long stretches of silence. They're not uncomfort-able or awkward; they're just gaps that words aren't sufficient to fill.

December turned into January and January into February, February to March and March to April, still Mike refused to come back home, opting instead to board at Ron's. The first month he was gone was the hardest. Grace tried to remind herself that her marriage wasn't over, that there were no "ends" in life, just continuations, as Beth had contended. But when Mike announced that he would not even return home for Christmas, she quickly and tearfully lost all hope for a reconciliation.

He thought it would be best if he spent the holiday with his mom in Nashville and Grace spent it in Memphis with her dad.

"This has gone on long enough," Grace had screamed into the phone. "It's been a month! Enough already!"

But Mike wouldn't budge.

How could he force them to spend her first pregnant Christmas and their first married Christmas apart? She'd asked. It was unfair and spiteful, she'd claimed, accusing him of getting back at her under the guise of rebuilding the trust in their relationship.

"If you'd just stop shouting long enough to listen," Mike had said, his words pervaded with an untouchable calm, "you'd see that I'm right."

Grace hung up on him, tired of, what she perceived as, his lack of emotion. She wanted him to shout back or argue, to exhibit any feeling toward her, good or bad. At least then she'd know that he was still vested in what they'd built together in the short time they'd been married. But to her dismay, his responses bordered more and more on indifference and that frightened her.

Her imagination quickly ran away with her on the heels of that conversation. She refused to answer his calls for the next few days, screening her Caller IDs vigorously. Grace was convinced that he'd met someone else, someone who possessed everything she didn't, and that he was simply waiting for the right time to let her down. He said he'd be in Nashville with his mom, but he was probably going to visit his mistress. Grace envisioned the two of them huddled in front of a crackling fireplace, sipping eggnog, and kissing passionately.

The thought kept her up at night. By the time her Wednesday women's Bible study rolled around, she had Mike married with kids and a dog, living a double life in a cookie-cutter house in a suburban utopia.

The twelve women crowded into her living room took one look at her tormented state, sat her down in the middle of them, and laid hands on her, binding the spirits of fear and jealousy, of anger and unforgiveness, of bitterness and speculation. They interceded with such fervency and urgency that by the time they'd each taken a turn, many of them were sweating, some were even crying, including Grace, who herself had repented and prayed for forgiveness.

Of course, as soon as they'd dispersed, leaving her alone with her thoughts, Grace realized that Mike was right. Their marriage, though bound by love, was undeniably strained. They had a lot to work out, more than Grace had initially realized before Mike left, and she didn't want to bring those tensions into the holiday, especially when she considered her father's illness.

Christmas was very likely her last shot to make and collect memories with him. But as much as she loved her father, Grace would've been more focused on reconciling her marriage, if Mike had come back, than on making the most of the dwindling time she had left with her dad. Mike knew that. He also knew that if Christmas turned out like Thanksgiving, Grace would resent him for it, and resentment was one thing that was already abundant in their relationship.

She called him and apologized, confessing to a change of heart. Too ashamed to go into detail about the silly and elaborate daydream she'd concocted, all she could say was, "I'm sorry." Mike, being Mike, forgave her without hesitation and without need of any explanation.

They spent Christmas apart. Grace had expected to feel gaping loneliness with Mike in Nashville and Trina in Detroit, but she didn't. She stayed with her dad from Christmas Eve through New Year's Day and she cherished every minute of their time together. From setting up and decorating her father's artificial tree to holding hands while watching the ball drop in Times Square on TV, the week was filled with enough love to last a lifetime. And the experience would not have been as special—as memorable—if they'd had to share it with someone else.

Mike shipped his gifts a week before Christmas, numbering them in the order in which she should open them. Three of the five boxes were massive, carried in by two beefy delivery guys.

Unable to wait until Christmas like a mature adult, Grace summoned Trina and Beth, who rushed over to discover, with her, what was inside. Together, using steak knives to cut away the many layers of thick tape, they opened each box.

In the first one was the oversized chair Grace had gushed over in The Land of Nod. In the second one was its matching ottoman. The third box held the beautiful espresso crib she'd so desperately desired, and the fourth box cradled an original canvas painting by Mike of pudgy black cherubs with wings spread against a wistfully blue sky. It was lighthearted and serene, timeless and yet innovative—a new flare on an old image, and absolutely perfect for a baby's nursery.

The fifth and final box contained a professionally framed and matted collage of personal memorabilia. Forever preserved was one of their wedding invitations, several dried and pressed petals from Grace's bouquet, love letters she'd sent to Mike when he was out of town on business for long stretches of time, a poem he'd written her one Valentine's Day, pictures of them together and with friends, and countless other reminders of their love and their loved ones. But the most touching part of the collage, the piece that sprung tears to Grace's eyes, was the letter she'd received from her mother after her mother had died. The heart of the entire piece, it was prominently mounted in the center.

The card that accompanied his gifts read:

A little bit of commercial mixed with a touch of sentiment.
Merry Christmas!

Beth, who was the first to label the Cape Cod set commercial, knew exactly what Mike meant.

Even though she adored it, Grace had claimed she didn't want the espresso baby furniture because it had no sentiment. Picking a couple of pieces and accenting them with his original art and the framed collage was Mike's creative and unique way of compromising.

Grace sent him his presents, via Ron: a copy of their baby's first ultrasound and his father's antique watch, which had sat in a box in his closet for as long as Grace had known him. She'd had it fixed, cleaned, and engraved with Mike's initials. Granted, her gifts were nowhere near as nice as Mike's, but he didn't seem to notice. He called her Christmas morning and thanked her profusely, assuring her that the watch and the ultrasound were the most thoughtful gifts he'd ever received.

Things fell into a natural sync after that.

They talk every morning and every evening and several times in between. Sometimes they pray together, often they catch each other up, share little anecdotes, or ask for advice. Mostly, they phone just to hear each other's voices and to say, "I love you."

Mike found the perfect studio space in Cooper Square, a funky, affluent area in the heart of the city that is fast filling with what his real estate agent disdainfully refers to as, "Yankee Yuppies." With Grace's blessing, Mike bought the unfinished 3,000-square-foot commercial loft and has fully dedicated his days to getting it ready for his gallery's grand opening, which will be some-time after the baby is born.

Grace has also found ways, some more productive than others, to occupy her time. She continues to host her women's Bible study and she joined Sun-day school class with Trina. On Saturday's she and Beth go to a water aerobics class for expectant mothers, where they laugh and splash around more than they exercise. And during the week, Grace throws herself into her almost completed second novel. She's made a few local appearances, but for the most part she's content staying home, with her feet up, hanging out with Beth or Trina or both and enjoying the joys of pregnancy and motherhood.

There are times when she's lonely, like at night when she tries to imagine how Mike's arms would feel around her, how his hand would fit over her belly if only he were there to spoon her. She also finds herself growing melancholy when she's around Trina and Ron, who, in recent months, have picked up where they left off during their first go around as a couple.

They're incapable of being in a room together without touching: holding hands, rubbing backs, playful whispers, adoring gazes.

Grace is happy for them. Trina and Ron are a match made in Heaven. She'd rather see them with each other than with any of the other people they've dated, but witnessing their budding romance blossom, intensifies Grace's desire for her own marriage to bloom into something new and beautiful as well.

"You still there?" Mike asks.

"I'm here."

"I have a confession to make," he says.

Grace grins. "Uh-oh. Sounds serious."

"I saw you today," he says. "In the park with Trina. I was driving by."

Grace thinks back to her afternoon walk. She heads to the park across the street every day like clockwork, and he knows it. It's not the first time he's just happened to drive by and spot her. "Spying again?" Grace tisks.

"I can't get over it. You're huge!"

Grace laughs. "Careful!" she warns.

"No, I mean…," he sighs, "you looked beautiful and happy. You couldn't stop laughing."

"Yeah, well, you know, when she wants to, Trina can be quite the comedian."

"I miss your laugh." His tone is serious.

"It's right here waiting for you," Grace says.

Mike doesn't respond.

"Come home," she says, the petition hushed but heartfelt.

"It's not time yet," Mike says. "It doesn't feel right."

They have this conversation every week; Grace asking Mike to come back home, Mike politely declining.

Grace sighs. "Well, what about my prenatal appointment on Friday?" she asks. "You haven't been to one yet. Will you come to this one?"

"I don't know," he says, audibly hesitant.

"Mike." His name comes out as a groan. "We've got to start moving forward at some point. I'm spiritually grounded, which is what you initially said you needed to see. I don't know what more I can do to prove how much I love you or how dedicated I am to this marriage. I made a mistake, albeit a huge one, but I've done everything in my power to make it right."

"I know," he says softly.

"Do you?" Grace asks. "Because I feel like you're waiting for me to morph into your notion of a perfect wife—an ideal mate—which, I can tell you, I'll never be. I'm just me and you're you. The best we can hope for, the best any couple can hope for, is to grow together. You have to let that be good enough."

He stays quiet. Grace can hear his soft breathing on the other end. She knows he's considering her words.

"You've missed so much," she continues. "Too much. Like when the baby kicked for the first time, you weren't here to feel it. And you've never heard its heartbeat. We haven't talked about names or painted the nursery. We haven't signed up for Lamaze classes. You've never even met Dr. Noguez. I just—I feel like our lives are on hold right now and I hate it."

"Me too," comes his regretful reply.

"So then let's do something about it; small steps in the right direction. We don't have to rush. If you don't feel like it's time to come home, fine. But at least come to the appointment," she pleads. "It'll be a start."

"Can I think about it?" he asks.

"Of course," Grace says. "That's all I'm asking." She gives him the time and the location. "Pray about it."

He chuckles. "That's usually my line."

"Promise me."

"I promise," he says. "I'll pray about it."

"'Kay. Good," she says, satisfied. Mike, if nothing else, is a man of his word. "I should probably get back," she says, referring to the women cackling down the hall.

"I love you," he says.

"Love you back."

"Let me say good night to the munchkin."

Grace laughs and holds the phone to her stomach. She hears Mike's muffled voice, but can't make out what he's saying.

She waits for the line to go quiet before raising the phone back to her ear. "I'll talk to you in the morning."

"Till then," he says.

Grace returns the phone to its base. "What d'ya think, Sweetness?" she asks, affectionately rubbing her bump. "Is Daddy going to show up?" She feels a dull thump against her hand. The baby kicked.

Grace laughs. "Yeah," she says. "Me too."

51

"Care for a refill?"

Trina looks up from her notes at the young waiter standing next to her, his coffee pot hovering over her half-empty mug.

"Yeah, thanks," she says, glancing at her watch. She'd told Grace that she was going out to pick up a toner cartridge and a couple of reams of computer paper, and then go to the post office to mail a few packages. Really, she's supposed to be meeting with Beth to finish planning Grace's baby shower. But Beth is late—20 minutes late, and Trina only has another half an hour or so to get back before Grace gets suspicious.

Trina digs her cell phone out of her purse and dials Beth again. "Where are you?"

Beth laughs. "How many times are you going to ask me that? I told you I'm stuck in traffic."

"You're always late," Trina says. "And it's never a fashionable five or ten minutes with you." She's irritated, but not angry. Beth's too likeable to get mad at.

"Stop whining," Beth says. "I'm almost there."

"You said that ten minutes ago."

"Just order me a vanilla shake."

"You do know I actually have to run the errands I said I was going to run. Grace is no amateur. She makes it her mission to sniff out surprise parties. If I don't come back with toner and paper, the jig is up."

"Oh, and a piece of lemon pound cake," Beth says, ignoring Trina's nervous ranting.

Trina can't help but smile. "Is food the only thing you think about?"

"Of course not," she says. "I also think about eating."

Trina shakes her head and laughs.

"Vanilla shake and lemon pound cake," Beth repeats her order. "I'll see you in five."

Trina flips her phone shut and surveys the restaurant in search of her waiter. She spots Joss and Tai instead.

Her reaction is curiously mild, considering that their company, for a short while, was the closest thing she had to friendship. She hasn't seen or spoken to them in months. Severing ties with that part of her past came naturally.

Kendra, Joss, and Tai were a package deal. Once Trina turned herself in, dragging Kendra and Quinn down with her, parting ways with Joss and Tai seemed logical. Trina doesn't miss them and she rarely thinks about them. She assumed they felt the same way because they never tried to call her, never emailed or stopped by. But the hopeful sparks in their eyes as they watch her watching them across the small café tells another story.

Trina returns their cautious smiles.

"Can we come over?" Joss mouths, pointing to Trina's table.

Trina nods, waving them on.

The reunion is tentative. The three of them stand uneasily, unsure how to greet one another. Tai is the first to make a move. She throws her arms around Trina's neck and hugs her warmly. "How've you been?" she asks, smiling brightly.

"Really good," Trina says.

"You look it," Joss says, taking Tai's lead and spreading her arms for a hug.

Trina's surprised. Tai, she would expect a hug from. Tai's loveable, tac- tilely affectionate, with a big thumping heart that she wears right on her sleeve. Joss, however, was always more like Kendra: chilled with sophistica- tion, prone more to meaningless air kisses than to genuine embraces. "You guys look good too," Trina says, returning her hug. "Do you want to sit?" she asks, pointing to the two empty chairs across from her.

They do.

"So how're things?" Trina asks, purposefully keeping the question general. "What's new?"

"Well, for starters, we're roomies, now," Tai says, nudging Joss.

"Really? What happened to Alan and Eli?"

"It was time for a change," Joss says.

Trina nods. If anyone understands the need for change, she does. "Change is good," she says. "I've done a lot of it myself over the past few months."

"We had hoped you'd call," Joss says.

Tai nods. "But we understand why you didn't."

"It's nothing personal," Trina says.

"Have you heard from Kendra?" Joss asks, gazing out of the window at the passing downtown traffic.

"Once," Trina says. She thinks back to the heated message Kendra left on her voice mail. She'd accused Trina of being spineless, called her a traitor and a few other names that weren't so PG. She'd vowed her revenge, promised Trina that if they ever met up in a dark alley, she would take great pleasure in ripping her limb from limb.

"You didn't prove anything," Kendra had said. "This little stunt you pulled is just a minor setback. You don't think Quinn and Councilman Schmidt have connections in the Memphis PD?" In her anger, she rattled off a few names. "They'll have this cleared up in no time. If I were you, I'd watch my back, Calloway. Your name is on the top of everyone's hit list," she spat nastily. "This is far from over."

Trina had agonized over the voice mail for about 30 seconds. Then she promptly drove to Detective Fontaine's office and let him have a listen.

The following week, a breaking news report interrupted the evening television show Trina and Grace were watching. Three more arrests had been made in the scandal surrounding Rebecca Schmidt, the stoic newscaster informed them. Three mug shots flashed onto the screen. They were all high-ranking police officers; all behind bars thanks to Kendra's big mouth.

Trina hasn't heard from Kendra since.

Detective Fontaine later told Trina that he'd offered Quinn's and Kendra's lawyers a deal. If they confessed to their parts and testified against Rebecca's father, he'd let them off with two years probation each.

The police were more concerned with convicting Councilman Schmidt than sticking it to a couple of Home Sweet Home employees. Becky was safe and happy in her new foster home and, after some debate, they'd let Georgia Kenny go without punishment. They were willing to show Quinn and Kendra the same sort of leniency.

But Quinn and Kendra had refused his offer, claiming that if they accepted his plea bargain, they'd be admitting guilt, which they simply wouldn't do because they'd done nothing wrong. They'd rather go to trial and prove their innocence.

With all the evidence the police had gathered on them, Detective Fontaine warned, it would behoove them to take the deal. If they went to trial, a conviction and jail time were imminent.

Still, bound by pride, both Quinn and Kendra refused.

The last Trina heard, Kendra's position at Home Sweet Home had been eliminated and Quinn had resigned as the company's Executive Director.

"We don't speak to her that much either," Tai says.

Joss scoots her chair closer to the table. "We want you to know," she says, leaning in, her voice hushed. "That we know what you did and we respect you for it."

Tai nods. "It was the right decision."

Trina forces a smile. Though they mean well and their words are kind, she doesn't feel comfortable discussing the matter with them.

Luckily, she doesn't have to. Beth, for once, is right on time. "Where's my shake and cake," she asks, waddling breathlessly up to the table.

"I was just about to order them when I ran into a couple of old friends," Trina says apologetically. She introduces Beth to Joss and Tai. "You remember my friend Grace from Heckles?" Trina asks.

They nod.

"She's pregnant too. Beth and I are planning her shower."

"You should come," Beth says. "I'm sure Grace would love for you to be there."

"They don't know each other that way," Trina says, smiling politely in Joss and Tai's direction. "They've only met once." She hopes Beth will take the hint, but in addition to being likeable and chronically late, Beth is also, at times, blissfully dense.

"So?" she shrugs. "You throw a baby shower for the gifts, not the guests. More people mean more presents," she says. "Remember that when you and Grace plan my shower."

"Where are you going?" Trina asks Beth as she plods back to the front of the café.

"My shake and cake aren't going to order themselves," Beth calls over her shoulder.

Trina laughs, shrugging as she turns back to Joss and Tai. "She can be a trip sometimes."

"I'd love to go to Grace's baby shower," Tai says.

Joss nods. "Sounds like fun."

Trina takes a few moments to gather her thoughts and to weigh her words. "I don't know if that's such a good idea," she finally says. "You and Grace are opposites." She smiles. "You and I are opposites now too. I'm differ-ent—happy—and I don't want to go back to the way things used to be. I can't."

"We don't want to go back either," Tai says.

Joss tucks her hair behind her ears. "Did it ever occur to you that we just want to be happy, too?"

Trina laughs. "Hanging out with me isn't going to make you happy," she says, both flattered and amused. "Not the kind of happy I'm talking about."

"Then what will?" Joss asks.

"Jesus," Trina says. The answer is simple and automatic, no thought required. "If you're searching for answers, He's got them. That's all I know to tell you." She waits for Joss and Tai to scoff or poke fun, to say something snide or ignorantly arrogant the way they used to whenever the topics of God and religion came up. Instead, they sit quietly; Joss with her hands folded on the table, Tai hugging her purse to her chest.

"Is that what you did?" Tai asks.

Trina nods. "That's what I did."

"Can you show us how?" Joss asks, looking shy and vulnerable.

Trina smiles, flummoxed yet ecstatic at this unexpected opportunity to share her faith. "Why don't you guys come to church with me this Sunday," she says. "And, if you want, to Bible study at Grace's on Wednesday."

Joss and Tai accept her invitation with enthusiasm. They chat a while longer until Beth returns with her vanilla milkshake and a slice of lemon cake (plus a triple chocolate brownie and a Rice Krispies treat for later).

Trina promises to call them, they leave, and she and Beth set to work coordinating the last minute details of Grace's shower.

And while Trina enjoys discussing confetti and party favors and watching Beth suck down every last drop of her shake, her mind and her heart cling even more joyously to one simple truth: God really can use for good what the devil intends for evil.

52

"We're ready for you, Grace," Kim says.

Over the past five months, Grace has gotten to know most of Dr. Noguez's staff on a first-name basis. They quickly became like a second family, calling her at home every week to make sure she's doing and feeling well.

As much as she appreciates their uncanny over-and-above approach to patient care, Grace finds herself dreading her monthly prenatal appointments. That's because they consist of more waiting than anything else. Dr. Noguez's office runs behind schedule without fail, often by hours, and waiting patiently has never been one of Grace's virtues. This afternoon, though, she was grateful for the 45-minute delay, hoping with every borrowed second that the next person to walk through the office door would be her husband. But it's clear to her that Mike's a no-show.

Grace looks up from her magazine and smiles at Kim through the knots of disappointment in her stomach.

She'd barely slept, overwhelmed by the thought of seeing Mike for the first time in months—of touching him, smelling him, kissing him, holding him. What would they say to each other, she wondered? Would their reactions be reflexively affectionate? Clumsy and forced? Would he take one look at her and finally realize what she's known for a while now, that it's time for him to come back home? That it's time to start putting to practice all that they've learned from their mistakes?

Determined to leave nothing to chance, Grace had woken up bright and early, beating her alarm clock to the punch, and gave up breakfast in order to allow herself more primping time.

Once she'd hit her fifth month of pregnancy, style went permanently out the window. Comfort became her top priority, which meant, apart from her church attire, her maternity wardrobe was limited to baggy sweats, roomy shirts, and sensible flats. But for her reunion with Mike, Grace dusted off the good stuff. After an hour of modeling possible outfits in front of Trina, she had settled on her dark-wash, boot-cut jeans (with the cotton stretch waist) and her wine-colored wrap sweater. Its plummeting V-neck revealed just the right amount of her newly acquired cleavage, and its clingy fabric hugged her body, accentuating her bump and flaunting her pregnancy in all of its glory.

Trina, ever the dutiful best friend, had lent her helping hand in every part of the process, even shaving Grace's legs for her, since bending over in Grace's condition is a near impossibility. She curled Grace's hair, applied her makeup, and even ran downstairs to grab one of her own purses and a pair of her earrings to further accent Grace's look.

"His jaw is going to hit the floor," Trina had predicted as Grace boarded the elevator.

Grace nodded and held up her crossed fingers, too flustered by nervous excitement to say anything back.

But this morning's preparation turned out to be a waste of both their time and effort.

She tries to remember, as she weighs in, answers the standard checkup questions, and follows Kim down the long hall to her examining room, that Mike hadn't made her any promises. He had said he would pray about it. And maybe, for reasons that are not hers to understand, God said no. The idea that Mike's absence is a result of obedience and not personal preference is a small consolation. Still, she can't help but feel hurt and not just a little bit angry.

"You got a hot date after this?" Kim asks, eyeing Grace's outfit and shrugging her eyebrows. She hasn't seen Grace sport anything other than her velour sweat suits since Grace started coming to Dr. Noguez.

"I wish," Grace says, staggered by how painful it is to try to laugh.

"All dolled up with nowhere to go," Kim says with a dramatic shake of head. "Such a travesty." She tosses Grace a folded gown. "You know the drill."

"Change into this trendy little number," Grace says, fanning out the flimsy frock. "And the doc will be in to see me shortly."

"You got it," Kim smiles, setting Grace's chart on the sink by the disinfectant hand soap before leaving.

Grace peels off her carefully selected clothes, places them in a neat pile on the chair next to Dr. Noguez's rolling stool, and climbs onto the examining table. The sterile paper covering crackles beneath the weight of her bottom as she lies down.

What if he doesn't come back? The thought had occurred to Grace more than a few times over the course of her separation with Mike. But now, lying alone for the fifth consecutive time in her obstetrician's office, the possibility seems more plausible than ever.

What would it mean to raise their child alone, to have to live with the knowledge that her marriage failed before it ever really began? Would she and Mike be civil and work out a visitation schedule or would a nasty custody battle turn their relationship sour? She can't imagine him being hostile or dragging her through a bitter divorce, but then again she never would've imagined that he'd force them to spend five months apart. And she never, ever thought she'd make a mistake that he couldn't forgive.

Without effort, she loses herself in the terrible what-ifs, cooking up scenarios, each more tragic than the one before it. She closes her eyes, determined not to cry. "Your will be done," she whispers to the Lord.

Dr. Noguez raps on the door. "You decent in there?" he calls.

Grace sniffles and quickly fans her face. "Yep." She sits up slightly, leaning on her elbows for support.

"Good." He opens the door and enters, decked out in his white lab coat replete with pocket protector and a stethoscope draped over his neck. "I think this belongs to you," he says, nodding behind him.

Mike steps in looking adorably sheepish and out of place.

Grace leaps up, moving far faster than any pregnant woman her size would seem capable of moving, and flings herself into Mike's arms nearly bowling him over.

"Whoa," he says gently, catching her with ease.

"You're here," she says, clinging to him painfully tight. "You came."

"Yeah," he says, pulling her as close as her belly will allow.

"I missed you," she says, her tears soaking into the wool of his ribbed turtleneck.

Mike strokes her hair and back, planting a kiss on the top of her head. "I missed you too," he says. "Let me get a good look at you." He tries to pull away, but Grace tightens her fierce grip and shakes her head, her cheek rubbing against the coarse fabric of his sweater.

She can't let go, not just yet. This sensation feels too good; elation beyond her wildest dreams or expectations.

Mike lets her cry against his chest, whispering in her ear the sweet nothings she's longed for months to hear in person. He waits for Grace to pull away, at which point he wipes her cheeks dry with his thumbs and the back of his hand. "You okay?" he asks.

She nods and leans into his tender kiss on her forehead. "Sorry," she says, facing Dr. Noguez, who's been waiting patiently in the corner on his stool, flipping through the chart Kim left.

He tilts his head and winks. "I wish I got that kind of greeting from *my* wife," he jokes.

Grace puts her hands on her hips and stares sternly up at Mike. "Why are you so late?" she asks.

Dr. Noguez points his pen at Grace's scowl. "That's more the kind of reaction I'm used to."

Mike laughs. "I got into little fender bender."

Grace's hands drop and her expression softens. "Are you okay?"

"I'm fine," he says, twirling one of her curls around his finger. "As long as I didn't miss anything."

"Nope," Dr. Noguez says, standing. "We're just getting started."

Mike helps Grace back onto the examining table, handling her like she's delicate china. "Can I?" he asks, reaching to touch her stomach for the very first time.

Grace smiles. "Of course, Baby."

Mike's grin spreads from one ear to the other as he rests his hand on Grace's bump. He bends over and gently kisses it.

"Now that's a proud papa if I've ever seen one," Dr. Noguez says, beaming at the sight of the two of them. "Would you like to see your child?" he asks. "Hear its heartbeat?"

Mike nods, and Dr. Noguez wastes no time setting up the ultrasound machine and lathering Grace's stretch-mark streaked belly with cool KY jelly. Mike holds her hand, his eyes wide, his expression one of fascination as he follows the doctor's every move.

Dr. Noguez glides the transducer over Grace's stomach until a white, grainy image pops up on the monitor facing them. "There it is," Dr. Noguez says. "Your baby." He points out the head, the tiny arms and legs, the tightly curled fists.

Grace has seen it before. She watches Mike's amazed expression, the miracle of the life growing in her moving him visibly.

"Would you like to know the sex?" Dr. Noguez asks.

Mike squeezes Grace's hand. "You don't already know?" he asks, his voice swelled with excitement.

Grace shakes her head. "I wanted us to find out together," she says, smiling.

Mike looks at Dr. Noguez, then again at Grace for approval, then back at Dr. Noguez. He nods. "What is it?"

Dr. Noguez smiles. "A girl." He prints out the ultrasound scan and hands it to Mike, who stares down adoringly at it while Dr. Noguez attaches the Doppler, placing it in like manner on Grace's gel-smeared abdomen. The room instantly fills with the rapid, *swish, swish, swish* of their baby girl's heartbeat.

Mike laughs, overwhelmed, and plants a series of kisses on Grace's cheeks, jaw, and neck.

After explaining how both machines work, Dr. Noguez wipes the jelly from Grace's stomach and proceeds with the rest of his examination. He patiently catches Mike up, as he works, answering all of his questions and quashing every last one of his concerns.

"Why don't you get changed," Dr. Noguez says to Grace, lowering the stirrups and snapping off his rubber gloves. "Then we'll talk."

He leaves, and Mike slowly helps Grace out of the office gown and into her wine-colored wrap sweater and her dark-wash, boot-cut jeans. Though their reunion didn't happen like she'd envisioned, her outfit still causes her desired effect.

"Look at you," Mike says, shaking his head in disbelief as he draws nearer. "Are pregnant women supposed to be this sexy?"

"I'm so glad you came," she says, but before he has a chance to respond, Dr. Noguez returns. Mike gives Grace the chair and stands behind her, affectionately massaging her shoulders.

Dr. Noguez sits on his stool and crosses his legs. "Your blood pressure is still up," he says. "That concerns me. Your high numbers are probably due to your pregnancy weight gain, which, as I've already explained, is a bit excessive."

Grace nods guiltily remembering the tub of mint double-fudge ice cream that she, Beth, and Trina had annihilated the day before yesterday.

"I'm ordering some blood work and a urine sample to test for protein, just to be on the safe side," he says. "In the meantime, try to cut back on high sodium foods and limit your fat and sugar intake. Okay?"

"Okay," Grace says, meaning it like she does every month, until she gets home and her relentless cravings compel her to do otherwise.

"Everything else looks good," Dr. Noguez says, closing her chart. "So sit tight, and Eliza will be right in to draw your blood. Mr. Cambridge," he says, standing and shaking Mike's hand, "it was a pleasure. I hope to see again."

"You will," Mike promises.

Dr. Noguez leaves, and Mike takes his seat, rolling close to Grace, situating her bent legs between his.

"I don't think I've ever been happier," Grace says, running her hands through his hair. "Come here," she says softly, pulling his face to her. She kisses his forehead, his temples, his nose, his closed eyelids, his cheeks, his chin, and lastly his lips.

Mike's hand cups her jaw as he returns her kiss with a passionate one of his own. "I love you," he says, pulling back just slightly, his eyes still closed, his forehead still pressed to hers. "So much."

"Does that mean you'll come back?" Grace asks, her tone breathless and eager.

"Yes." He nods and seals his answer with another kiss.

53

"A little more to the right," Grace instructs.

Beth shakes her head. "No, your other right," she says, licking the peanut butter from her celery stick.

"I think that's it," Grace says, her smile broad.

Beth tilts her head, squinting her eyes. "Nope," she says, reapplying a thick glob of Jiffy to her celery. "Still off center."

"She's right," Grace says. "Move it just a smidge to the left."

"No!" she and Beth squawk simultaneously. "Your other left."

"Hernia," Ron huffs, shuffling two inches forward and two inches back with his end of the antique armoire that Grace and Mike stumbled into a couple of weeks ago at a Mississippi flea market.

"Yeah," Trina snaps, her tired arms shaking as she struggles to keep the other end lifted, while Mike covers the front. "Make up your minds."

"There is good," Grace says, sipping her lemon water.

The three of them ease down the solid oak monstrosity, murmuring their relief. Mike bends over, his hands resting on his knees, and catches his breath. "How's it look?"

Grace nods, pleased. "I like it."

"Ohmigosh!" Beth says, waving her now peanut-butter-less celery stick above her head. "I just had the greatest epiphany."

"What?" Grace asks, sitting up, her curiosity peaked by Beth's over-the-top enthusiasm.

"You're gonna love me," Beth squeals. She turns to the still panting trio in the corner. Her smile tapers. "You three, not so much."

They groan as Beth points out how if they flipped the room around, moving the changing station and dresser to the opposite wall, angle the armoire, push the chair and ottoman under the window, and roll the crib closer to the bookcase, they'd create enough wall space to hang all of the art that Grace and Mike had selected to inspire their forthcoming new addition. "Plus," she shrugs. "It'll just look better."

Mike folds his arms and studies the room, envisioning Beth's changes. "She's got a point," he says to Ron and Trina, his tone apologetic.

Beth smiles smugly. "Don't I always?" she says, applying more peanut butter to her celery stick.

"You do realize the celery is edible," Trina says.

Beth snorts. Three days from her official due date and she's more determined than ever to eat what she wants, when she wants, until her heart's content. "That's entirely a matter of opinion."

"Then why bother with the sticks," Trina asks. "You might as well get a spoon and scoop the Jiffy straight from the jar."

Beth shrugs. "Dr. N said I need to add more fruits and veggies to my diet."

Grace, Trina, Ron, and Mike crow robustly. "I'm sure celery residue from your peanut butter lollipops is not what he had in mind," Trina says between chuckles.

Beth casts a devious grin. "Well, then he should've been more specific, shouldn't he? Besides, Grace has been eating healthily enough for the both of us."

It's true. As much as she enjoyed stuffing her face with abandon, Grace had developed proteinuria during her seventh month of pregnancy. That coupled with her already high blood pressure made her a dead ringer for preeclampsia.

"You have to start monitoring what you eat," Dr. Noguez had warned. "If not for your health, then for the sake of your daughter's." The only cure for preeclampsia is to have the baby, he'd explained. "The closer we can get you to your due date, the better. We should do everything we can to prevent a premature birth."

Which meant Grace had to start doing her part.

From that moment on, her chocolate chip cookie dough binging days were history. Grapefruit halves and grilled chicken breasts didn't offer quite the same kick as caramel sundaes and ketchup-slathered onion rings, but she's adjusted. And now, eight and a half months into her pregnancy, she's all but out of the danger zone.

Grace smiles. "I *have* been pretty good, if I do say so myself."

"Yes, you have," Mike says, making his way toward her across the small, cluttered nursery in progress, his deep voice teeming with syrupy pride. "Hasn't she?" he asks, addressing her taut drum of a belly. He smothers it with loud, ardent kisses.

"There he goes again," Beth says, rolling her eyes, but her admiring smirk betrays her approval.

"What about me?" Grace asks, twirling one of his dreadlocks around her index finger.

"Just saving the best for last," Mike says, obligingly transferring his kisses from Grace's stomach to Grace's lips.

"Now, there *they* go," Trina says.

"What's wrong with showing a little affection to the one you love?" Ron asks, pulling Trina to him and snaking his arm around her waist.

She smiles up at him, puckering knowingly as his mouth inches toward hers.

Grace glances over at Beth, worried that this double whammy of PDA might make her feel like a fifth wheel. But her attention is focused solely on scraping the last remnants of peanut butter from the bottom of the jar.

This is how it should be, Grace thinks to herself, sighing contentedly as Mike strokes her bump and tells their baby girl, for the millionth time in the two months he's been back home, that he can't wait to meet her.

Late last year, Grace would never have imagined she'd be where she is— this completely satisfied or profoundly joyful. She couldn't have fathomed that

Kodak moments like this one would ever be hers to store in her photo album of life.

To say that her transition into wifedom and motherhood was a turbulent one would be a gross understatement. But the storm clouds have finally parted, leaving behind golden rays of promise; and the raging waves of life that, mere months ago, she was certain would subjugate her, have given way to placid and peaceful waters.

"Okay, enough with the canoodling already," Beth says. "Get to work."

Grace smiles sympathetically down at Mike kneeling before her, and wipes the sweat from his forehead. "If you guys hurry, you might be able to finish before the food gets here."

"Right," Ron says, surveying the room. "So how should we attack this?"

"Let's get the hard part over with," Trina says, patting the side of the armoire.

"No, the chair first," Beth says.

"Yeah," Grace agrees. "And then the changing table and the crib." She points where each piece should end up.

"If she had a crown and a scepter, we'd be calling her, Your Majesty," Mike kids.

Ron nods. "Not a bad gig," he says, his smile good-natured. "Relaxing with a chilled glass of water while you boss the rest of us around."

"Hey," Grace shrugs. "Doctor's orders. I'm supposed to stay off my feet."

"What's your excuse?" Trina asks, pointing to Beth.

Beth blinks down at her own bursting bump, peeking from beneath her maternity blouse and then back up at Trina. "You didn't just ask that," she says, tossing the bare celery stick into the empty Jiffy jar and screwing on the top.

For the next half an hour, Mike, Ron, and Trina push, shift, shove, lift, scoot, drag, pull, and roll the room's contents, arranging the furniture to Grace and Beth's exact specifications.

"That's it," Beth says, sweeping the finished product with a starry-eyed gaze.

"It better be," Trina wheezes, flopping down on the floor next to Grace.

Grace smiles. *It is.*

Her daughter's nursery is stunning—pure perfection beyond anything she could've imagined, much less copied out of a catalogue or borrowed off of a showroom floor.

The walls are pale yellow, the backdrop to Mike's meticulous and detailed enchanted forest mural complete with weeping willows housing curious squirrels, fluttering butterflies, rosy-cheeked fairies, hopping bunnies, inching snails, fastidious toads perched on hunter-green lily pads, bubbling brooks, and wide-winged birds with colorful beaks and feathers. It's far more intimate and apropos for a baby girl than the azure fish mural she'd so coveted in The Land of Nod display.

The furniture is also meaningful with sentiment. The only new items are the crib, the chair, and the ottoman. Everything else, she and Mike had bought secondhand, like the weathered armoire, or had accepted from friends and family, like the leaning bookcase, which was Lani's contribution, and the teddy bear mobile, a hand-me-down from Malikah, who finally gave in and forgave Grace for her reprehensible behavior.

It's those small yet personal touches that authenticate the room, breathing verve and warmth and experience into it. The nursery feels lived in, homey and familiar, like it's been there all along in spirit.

"I love it!" Grace says, gripping her chest. "The only thing left to do is hang the art," she says, raring to see the finished result.

The front buzzer stridently beckons from down the hall.

"Saved by the bell," Ron says.

"We'll finish it after we eat," Mike promises, kissing Grace's hand. "Where did you leave the money?"

"Coffee table," Grace says.

"I gotta wash some of this gunk off," Ron says, following behind Mike.

"Bathroom break for me," Trina says.

"Oooo," Beth claps her hands and holds out her arms for Trina's help. "It's about that time for me too. I swear, this kid is using my bladder as a whoopee cushion."

Trina tugs Beth up, helping her to the door, and just like that, Grace is left alone to admire their handiwork. She tries to arrange the art on the walls, mentally hanging one painting next to the pole lamp or above the armoire, then taking it down and replacing it with another. All of the pieces, most of which were painted in love by Mike, would go nicely anywhere in the room. She's certain of one thing, though. She wants the elegantly framed collage that Mike gave her for Christmas to hang prominently above the bookcase.

Grace hoists herself out of the chair, actually making it to a standing position on her fourth attempt, and shuffles the few feet to the ladder, both hands supporting her sore lower back.

She drags it across the area rug and locks it in front of the loaded bookcase. Then, she picks up the heavy collage, framed in glass and wood, and ascends the ladder, one tentative step at a time.

The climb, though short, is enough to leave her breathless. She rests the collage on the ladder's top ledge and gives herself a moment to rest and to eye the set of anchors and screws that Mike has already drilled into the wall.

"We can do it," she says, patting her stomach. Her pelvis aches from the pressure of the baby's weight. She climbs two more steps, ignoring the discomfort. The problem, she realizes as she takes yet another step up, is that the bookcase's leaning structure prohibits her from getting close to the wall. If she wants to hang the collage, she's going to have to reach for it.

She turns sideways, balancing her hip against the top step (since her stomach hinders her from stretching into the ladder like she's supposed to) and leans forward, reaching up with the collage simultaneously, hoping her arms are long enough to hook it onto the waiting screws.

A quick, sharp lightning bolt rips through her abdomen. Grace gasps, teetering from the unfamiliar pain. She blinks, dizzy, and grips the top of the ladder with one hand while clinging to the collage with the other.

Another bolt, exponentially worse than the first, tears through her. This time, the razor-sharp pain is followed by a tightening so excruciating that her body folds in half. Her mouth gapes open in a silent cry as she grabs her stomach.

The framed collage slips from her fingers, smashing loudly against the floor, and breaks into shards of glass and chunks of wood, its invaluable keepsakes strewing every which way.

"What was that?" she hears Beth ask.

Grace's moan is deep, guttural, as a third bolt, worse yet, pierces her, throwing her from the ladder.

Trina appears in the doorway just in time to see Grace fall, her stomach, chin, and forehead slamming into the first shelf of the bookcase, the second and then the third. "No!" rings her ear-splitting cry. She rushes to block the heavy books and knickknacks raining down on Grace's writhing body. "Mike!" The stentorian scream is wracked with terror. "Mike!" she screams again, pressing her shirt to Grace's bleeding face.

Grace coughs and spasms unable to breath against the searing pain. She feels Mike scoop her into his lap.

"Call 911!" he shouts. "Grace, Baby, look at me," he says. "Look at me."

Grace turns her head, trying to follow the sound of his voice. A fourth bolt—hot febrile electricity, ravaging and mangling her from the inside out— it shoots from her chest all the way down to her knees and back in pulsating waves.

She routs, seizing Mike's hand, as her eyes roll back giving way to blinding white nothingness.

"No," Mike says, angling her face toward his. "Baby, stay with me," he orders. He says it again, only this time it's a fraught plea.

Grace feels herself slipping, the world around her growing distant, the people smaller, as a fifth bolt surges through her. Her limbs turn numb, then limp. An odd warmth builds between her legs.

"Oh God," Beth gasps. "I think she's hemorrhaging."

"Help is coming," Mike says, rocking Grace's flaccid body in his sturdy arms. "Help is coming, just stay with me. Please," he kisses her temple. "Stay with me."

Grace's body convulses violently, white flashes of glaring light blend together until they blind her—until the brightness envelops her. Her eyelids flutter, growing heavier and more uncooperative by the second.

Mike summons her to stay.

She can't. Against her will, his presence fades.

"Don't leave me," he whispers.

They are the last words she hears as his echoing voice ushers her into static darkness.

54

Tumbling weightlessly—head over feet, head over feet. Grace free-falls through a thick, pillowy haze of fuzzy voices and even fuzzier thoughts.

Scenes from her life flicker around her, a built-in projection screen of the subconscious mind, unearthing misplaced snippets of time, bittersweet reminders of dreams and people already lost.

What's your name? someone demands, his distorted request serenaded by the shrill blare of sirens. *Can you tell me your name?*

Look at me, the voice is no longer distorted, but irritated and rushed. It belongs to her mother. *Do you know where you are? Open your eyes!*

She does, only to find herself spinning in her mother's office chair, the way she'd done countless times as a little girl. The office was off limits. That was the only law in their house without rules.

But the office is where her mother could be found most hours of the day. To say, "Don't come in here," was to say, "Don't come near me." And Grace had felt an unshakable need to be near her always, to see her and to been seen by her.

The brief, forbidden ride was worth the spankings and the threats, the angry glares and the disapproving scowls. No cost was too high for the rare jewel of her mother's attention.

This is not a playroom. My chair is not a toy, barks her mother's stern reminder. Stop it!

On her command, the chair halts abruptly, throwing Grace to the floor with jerking force. Her abdomen contracts, seizing her organs. One bolt, two bolts, three bolts of agony in rapid succession followed by the sound of her sobs.

Her mother hurries, cradling Grace protectively, her cool hands caressing Grace's cheek. *Don't cry,* she says, her lips move, but the voice that comes out belongs to Mike.

Sir, please. Back up and give us room!

No, don't go. Stay near. Grace forms the thought, but can't communicate it. Suddenly, a mask covers her nose and mouth. Air flows from it—magic air that seems to untwist her lungs.

She takes a deep breath, inhaling her mother's lovely scent—her forgotten, lovely scent—and feeling sheltered and tired, closes her eyes to sleep.

Stay with us, Grace! We're almost there. Stay with us.

Go away, she wants to say. I'm sleeping.

Wake up. Look at me. Can you look at me?

When Grace opens her eyes, she's lying on a blanket in the grass. Cackling children toss balls and run around her. Smoking barbecue pits and lawn chairs, ice cream sandwiches and roller skates, just like their summer trips to Kensington Park. The mood is festive, laughter floats above her.

Gracie, over here.

Grace turns her head to see Trina waving at her. She's wearing a bikini top and the shorts she'd cropped to daisy dukes against her aunt's wishes when they were in the eleventh grade.

Where's my mom? Grace asks, wanting only to be back in her arms.

Right there, Trina points to a blurred figure in the distance. *Don't worry; I'll take you to her. Follow me.*

Grace chases after Trina who sprints ahead, her legs pumping and her hair blowing behind her as she picks up speed and then takes flight. Wait! Grace calls, slowing as her panting becomes more labored. She drops to her knees. Come back.

Hang in there. You can do it. Just a little bit farther.

No, I can't. Grace shakes her head and claws at her chest. *I can't breath.*

Lie still, we've got you. One, two, three—lift!

She floats through the air—out of the shadows and into the blazing sun. Its warm light blankets her cold, shivering body. She hadn't realized she was so cold.

"What've we got?"

"Female…thirty…pregnant…thirty-four weeks…fall…ladder…hemorrhaging."

Voices, voices—too many, indecipherable voices, Grace thinks as they hover over her, rolling her out of the safe brightness of day and into a chilly corridor.

Concerned faces peer down at her, checking stats, snipping away her clothes. "Grace, squeeze my hand if you can hear me."

"Mom," Grace whispers, calling for her own.

"Yes, you're going to be a mom," says someone—a nurse, Grace thinks.

"Sleep," Grace mumbles, closing her eyes—only this time, instead of a vociferous demand for her to wake up, someone leans close and whispers gently, her breath brushing Grace's ear like a healing, balmy breeze. "That's right," she soothes. "Just rest."

"Your wife's body has sustained significant trauma as a result of the fall," the doctor begins. Mike didn't bother to catch his name.

He's young—too young, Mike thinks, to be able to understand, much less accurately convey, what's happening to his wife. "In addition to a fractured ankle, she has what's known as placenta abruptio."

"I don't know what that means," Mike says. "What does that mean?"

The young doctor nods slowly, patiently, his demeanor calm and understanding while at the same time professionally unattached. "Her placenta separated from her uterus," he clarifies. "She's lost a lot of blood."

"She's going to be okay, isn't she?" Trina asks.

The doctor blinks, looking somber, and lowers his chin. "It's too soon to tell."

"What about the baby?" Beth asks.

The doctor shakes his head. "Again, we won't know until she's out of surgery."

"Well, what *do* you know?" Mike barks, consumed with frustration and fear.

Ron grips his shoulder and pulls him back against the plastic orange chair.

The doctor studies the four anxious faces in front of him and sighs, uncrossing his legs and leaning forward, ready to reason. "The placenta is the lifeline between mother and fetus. It's how the unborn child receives nutrients, including oxygen, which your daughter was deprived of—for how long, we don't know.

"This was a severe placental separation, exacerbated even further by your wife's high blood pressure," he says. "She's undergoing a cesarean section as we speak, after which they're going to try to repair the tear in her uterus, though, I should warn you, there's a strong possibility that they'll have to remove it altogether."

Trina doubles over, dizzy and sick from his assessment, and rests her head against her thighs. None of his scenarios garner much hope. If Grace makes it and the baby doesn't, the doctor, in his roundabout way, has just told them she'll probably never be able to have another one.

"As soon as we know something," the doctor says, looking at Mike, "you'll know."

He goes on about a family waiting room with reclining chairs, blankets, and pillows. "You might be more comfortable there," he says. There are televisions with individual headsets, phones, and a private cafeteria.

"Chapel," Mike says. It comes out softly, raspy—almost inaudible. He clears his throat. "Do you have a chapel?"

"Second floor. West Wing."

The young doctor shakes their hands, promising each of them that absolutely everything humanly possible is being done to save Grace and her baby. "The only thing we can do now is wait," are his parting words.

Trina, Ron, and Beth sit quietly, looking at Mike, waiting for his cue.

He stares blankly ahead, his torso rocking, his hands gripping his knees. "Can you call everyone?" he asks, not addressing any one particular person.

"Don't worry," Trina says. "I'll take care of it."

Mike stands suddenly, jamming his hands in his pockets. "You know where to find me," he says.

"Yeah," Ron nods. "We'll get you the minute the doctor comes back."

"Where is he going?" Beth asks, as soon as the door closes behind him.

Trina and Ron glance at each other, knowing there's only one place Mike goes in the midst of a crisis.

"To pray."

The chapel is tiny, comprised of four pews bolted to gray speckled linoleum and a narrow pulpit behind which there is a life-size image of Jesus, hanging from the cross, a crown of thorns resting on His head. He gazes out among the empty, dimly lit chapel, His face tilted with empathy—a mysterious juxtaposition of misery and hope. The solemn atmosphere is appropriate.

Mike sits down at the end of the first pew, too stunned at first to speak or move—too shocked to cry. He looks down at his T-shirt. Grace's blood is smeared across it. He can make out her handprints at the bottom, where she'd reached for him repeatedly.

The vision of her sprawled amongst books and glass, choking as her body wretched with pain, is enough to shake him from his daze. He closes his eyes just as the tears spill forth, streaming uncontrollably from beneath his shut lids.

"How will I make it?" he asks, coughing out a question that has just one answer. "I can't." His words are smothered in sorrow. "She's everything. Everything," he cries.

His shoulders heave, his groans growing more despairing, as he considers what it would mean to go on living without Grace, what it would mean to have to wake up every morning knowing she will never be back, that her smile and her laughter and her touch would forever evade him.

If, God forbid, their daughter doesn't survive, like any parent who's lost a child, Mike would grieve, and his pain would be considerable and normal and he would never quite be the same again. But if he loses his wife, Mike knows that the world will cease to exist for him. Words would no longer possess meaning; food would no longer have taste. His life would switch from color to black and white—vibrant images to dead pixels.

"Take me," his deep, scratchy voice beseeches as he falls prostrate at the altar, his quaking body stretched across its three shallow steps. He looks up at the image of Jesus hanging overhead. Surely He, the Sacrificial Lamb, would take pity on such a selfless, humble request. "Take me instead."

He keeps his head down, his tears forming small puddles on the floor, and offers himself instead of his daughter—instead of Grace. The hours blend one into the next, but Mike remains where he is.

His fervent prayers, to anyone else, might sound like the ramblings of a madman. But he knows the Lord hears him and as long as he has strength enough to move his lips, he will continue to intercede, to murmur, implore, beg, and entreat on behalf of the loves of his life.

Mike travails through the night, the neck and arm pits of his shirt stained and damp with sweat. He battles, uttering the same simple request, long after his river of words has run dry and consciousness has ebbed into delirious exhaustion. "Take me. Take me," he chants without ceasing, meaning it more each time he says it than all the other times before.

He continues like this, languishing—investing every ounce of thought and concentration, every pound of reason—until he hears Trina's broken voice behind him.

"Mike," she says, sniffling, her eyes swollen and red, her cheeks streaked with tears. "The surgeon is waiting to speak with you."

55

"She's in a coma," a familiar gruff voice insists.

"Ain't nobody in a coma," Malikah says, sounding tired and exasperated.

"Yeah," Trina says. "Stop saying that."

"Well, look at her," Grandpa Mearl says. "She hasn't moved in two days. Nothing's changed."

"I think she's got a bit more color today," Lani says.

"She's black," Mearl barks. "We've all got color."

"Mearl!" Grandma Doria snaps, aghast along with everyone else present. They murmur apologies and encourage Lani to ignore him.

"Ssshhhh, keep it down." Grace recognizes her father's steady voice.

"I meant more color in her lips," Lani clarifies, her tone hushed and not the least bit offended. "They're not as pale."

Grace lies motionless, listening to the floating banter. Where is it coming from? Is this another dream? She's not sure. Should she open her eyes and find out? Can she?

She remembers falling—tumbling into inexplicable pain. And then her mother. Her mother's certain grip, her unduplicated scent. When she opens her eyes, will she be back in her mom's arms, safe against her breast? Grace wonders. Because if not, she'd rather not wake up. She doesn't see the point—the purpose.

"When she's ready," Mike's quiet, sure voice says. "She'll come back." Grace feels the warmth of his breath on her forehead and then the pressing sensation of his soft lips. A kiss so sweet, so simple. She groans and turns her face toward his delicious scent. Like her mother's, it's also an unduplicated redolence, personal and intimate—swathing her in a sense of security that cannot be breached, reminding her why she should stay—why she must stay.

"Did you see that?" Ron asks.

The world outside of Grace's still darkness falls silent, apart from the shuffling of multiple footsteps crowding near.

"Say something else," Trina orders.

"Gracie," Mike whispers. Grace feels his hand envelope hers, his rough thumb rubbing across her knuckles. "I'm right here."

Grace turns her hand, palm up, and slides her fingers through his. He squeezes. She squeezes back.

"Don't stop," her father says. "Keep talking."

"What do you want me to say?" Mike asks.

"Tell her to wake up," replies Grandpa Mearl's rough voice.

Grace's eyelids flutter and then blink before opening. Her eyes roam, up and down, side to side, struggling to register her bright surroundings. Gradually they focus to discover eight faces forming a semicircle around her hospital bed.

"There she is," Lani sings sweetly.

"I'll go get the doctor," Ron says, breaking from formation and rushing out of the room.

"Thank God," Mike says, kissing her hand and pressing it to his cheek.

Grace takes in the beeping, chugging machines flanking her, the hanging IV bag leading to the needle in her free hand, and her hospital bracelet…the flowers, stuffed animals and cards lining the window seal. There's a cast on her right foot. It doesn't bother her as much as the fact that she can see her right foot. She can see it because her belly is gone, deflated like a balloon.

She looks at Mike, the adrenaline of panic slowly but steadily replacing her foggy confusion. "Where's the baby?"

"I hear someone decided to wake up," a boisterous voice says, just as Mike opens his mouth. The semicircle parts to reveal a young man in a white coat, his small stature and fine hair adding even more to his youthful appearance. "Hello, Grace. I'm Dr. Barnett," he says. "You had quite a fall."

"Baby," Grace says. Her throat is parched, grainy like sandpaper. She reaches for her stomach. "Where is my baby?"

Dr. Barnett smiles. "She's just fine," he says. "Healthy and strong. As soon as I finish examining you, I'll have a nurse bring her in. Folks," he turns to her roomful of visitors, "I'm going to have to ask you to step out for a while."

They comply, but not before taking time, one by one, to say good-bye.

"Don't you ever scare me like that again," Trina says, hugging her gently.

"Welcome back," Ron says, giving her a peck on the cheek.

Her father pinches her chin with tears in his eyes. "I'll be back later," he promises.

"Me too," Lani says, patting her leg.

Down the line they go, Grandpa Mearl and Grandma Doria and then Malikah, until Dr. Barnett, Mike, and Grace are the only ones left in the room.

"You too, Dad," Dr. Barnett says. "I'll only be a few minutes."

Mike nods, clearly reluctant to leave. "I'll be right outside," he says, gazing down at Grace.

Grace grins sleepily. "I'll be right here," she says, her first attempt at humor in the aftermath of her brush with death.

Mike leaves, and Dr. Barnett, assisted by a nurse, sits her bed up. It's then that Grace realizes just how much pain she's in. As he works, poking and prodding, flashing lights into her eyes, listening to her chest, changing bandages, checking the machines and marking down his observations, Dr. Barnett explains what happened to her from a medical standpoint: her mild concussion and broken ankle, her premature abruption, her C-section and her torn uterus. "Which your surgeon was able to repair successfully," he adds.

Grace listens politely because she has to—because the sooner he finishes his tiresome exam, the sooner he'll stop talking about everything but the one thing she wants to hear about.

"Everything is healing nicely," he says, smiling. "You should be out of here in a few days."

"Can I see her now?" Grace asks.

"Sure," Dr. Barnett nods. "I'll send your husband in," he says, turning with the nurse to leave.

The beeping on her heart rate monitor quickens when Mike enters. Without a word, Grace scoots over as far as the guardrail will allow, creating a space for him on the narrow twin bed.

Mike slides in next to her, turning on his side to face her. "Hi," he whispers.

"Hi." Grace smiles. "How're you?"

"Good." He sweeps her hair over her shoulder. "How about you? How're you feeling?"

"Beat up," Grace says, pouting. "Like I lost a fight."

"You did," Mike smirks. "With gravity."

Grace laughs and grips her stomach. "Oooo," she winces, sucking in her breath sharply. "Don't," she says, biting down her smile to subdue her chuckles. "It hurts to laugh."

"I love you," Mike says, his eyes twinkling. He drapes his arm gingerly across her stomach.

Grace leans closer, her face tilted up for a kiss. "I love you, too," she says after they pull apart.

"So guess who also became a mommy this weekend?" he asks.

Grace smiles. "Beth," she says, recalling in that instant that Beth was the only one missing when she opened her eyes.

"With all the commotion going on around him, I guess Mark Jr. decided it was as good a time as any to make his grand entrance—all nine pounds, eight ounces of him."

"That big?" Grace asks with a smirk.

Mike nods with a smirk of his own. "Huge," he says.

"No wonder she ate so much."

"Look who's here!" chirps a nurse, different than the one who had assisted Dr. Barnett. This one is wearing brightly colored scrubs that are spotted, both top and bottom, with an array of jolly cartoons. She enters, her excited smile stretched wide, pushing what looks like a miniaturized, shallow librarian's cart.

Stuck to the side of it is a label that reads, CAMBRIDGE, in big block letters.

Grace sits up, clutching Mike's hand, as the nurse rolls the baby to the side of her bed.

The vision of her daughter sleeping, wrapped in a pink blanket, sporting a matching pink cap, her tiny fists curled up at either ear, her chest rising and falling in a quick, methodic rhythm, brings tears to Grace's eyes.

"Gorgeous, isn't she?" Mike asks.

Grace nods, barely able to sit still as the nurse scoops the baby up and gently places her into Grace's waiting arms.

Grace stares down at her, studying her button nose and her pink tongue peeking out between her bow lips, her smooth butterscotch skin and chubby cheeks. She seems weightless to Grace; yummy and angelic—a small bundle of Heaven on earth.

"So this is what it feels like," Grace whispers, kissing her daughter's fingers.

"What's that?" Mike asks.

She smiles. "Love at first sight."

"What's her name?" the nurse asks.

They'd talked about naming her Cheri after Grace's mother, but holding her now, gazing down at her sweet, precious face, Grace knows exactly what to call her. "Faith," she says, the name spilling automatically from her mouth. She glances up at Mike.

"Faith," he says, nodding in agreement.

They talk to her while she fidgets in her sleep, telling her about the members of her family—about Auntie Trina and Grandma Lani, cousin Malikah and Uncle Ron—all of the people dying to meet her, to kiss her and cuddle her, to love her unconditionally, always and forever.

"And if Daddy has anything to say about it, soon you'll have a little brother or sister to keep you company," Mike says.

Grace smiles. "Don't make promises to our daughter that you can't keep," she says.

"What?" He shrugs innocently. "You can't honestly tell me that you don't want at least a couple more of these." He cups the crown of Faith's head in the palm of his hand.

"Yes," Grace nods. "I can honestly say I don't. Not anytime soon, anyway. I don't know if you noticed, but this delivery wasn't exactly a walk in the park."

"Well, yeah," Mike smirks. "But now that we've established that you can't fly, you've got nothing to worry about."

Grace socks him.

"Did you see that?" he asks Faith. Her eyes flutter open. She blinks up at them, sighs contentedly, kicking her legs beneath her blanket and falls back to sleep.

"We've got plenty of time," Grace whispers.

"So in other words," Mike says, pulling them both closer, "be grateful for our happy ending."

"It's not an ending," Grace says with a smile. She raises Faith to her chest and nuzzles her silk-soft skin.

"What is it then?" Mike asks, kissing Grace's temple. "A beginning?"

Grace moans peacefully, resting against the sureness of his support, and closes her eyes. "No," she says. "Just a story for another day."

CONTACT INFO

RyanMPhillips@excite.com

SAVING GRACE

As the only daughter of a successful businesswoman, Grace grew up with nothing but the best. Sheltered by her single mother and educated in an exclusive private school in Detroit, Grace was not ready for the harsh realities of an unforgiving world.

Grace's naivete coupled with her desire to experience life on her own terms leads her down a path of emotional devastation and physical abuse. Through a chance encounter Grace meets Mike, a successful design artist who introduces her to a relationship very different from her usual one-night-stands and affairs with married men.

Things take a turn for the worst, however, when Grace's roommate walks in on her and her married personal trainer in their apartment. This betrayal tears apart Mike and Grace's romance and shatters the trust and friendship between Grace and Trina.

In the midst of torn relationships, Grace's mother dies in a tragic plane crash leaving Grace with no one to turn to except the God she thought had long since abandoned her.

ISBN 0-7684-2204-3

Available at your local Christian bookstore.

AFTER THE FALL

Abigail Walker and Jarvis Daniels are longtime sweethearts headed in opposite directions. Abby, an aspiring cellist, wants out of her humble Detroit surroundings and is willing to shed blood, sweat, and tears to make it happen. Jarvis, on the other hand, is perfectly content with life. For him there's plenty of time to become a "responsible adult." For now, he's got everything he could want: a roof over his head, a PlayStation, and the love of a good woman.

When Abby's music career takes off and she moves to Chicago, Jarvis gets the boot—sort of. Abby still loves him, but his penchant for faded sweaters and meatball subs just doesn't fit into her new, sophisticated world of designer gowns and concert halls. They're in different leagues and Abby makes no qualms of reminding him of it whenever she deigns to visit him.

When the couple is involved in a near-fatal car crash, they are broken, stripped, and broken again both stumbling through a journey of healing and self-discovery as they struggle to accept the merciful hand of the only One who can help them up after a fall.

ISBN 0-7684-2204-3

Additional copies of this book and other
book titles from DESTINY IMAGE are
available at your local bookstore.

Call toll-free: 1-800-722-6774.

Send a request for a catalog to:

Destiny Image® Publishers, Inc.

P.O. Box 310
Shippensburg, PA 17257-0310

*"Speaking to the Purposes of God for this
Generation and for the Generations to Come."*

For a complete list of our titles,
visit us at www.destinyimage.com